I0563419

A Time to Reap

William Cobb

SixFinger

Copyright © William Cobb, 2013.

The right of William Cobb as the Author of the Work has been
asserted by him in accordance with the Copyright, Designs and
Patents Act, 1988.

First Published in 2013
by SixFinger Publishing
an imprint of Great War Literature Publishing LLP

Apart from any use permitted under UK copyright law, this
publication may only be reproduced, stored or transmitted, in
any form, or by any means, with prior permission in writing of
the publishers or, in the case of reprographic production, in
accordance with the terms of licences issued by the Copyright
Licensing Agency.

All characters in this publication, with the exception of any
obvious historical characters, are fictitious and any resemblance
to real persons, either living or dead, is purely coincidental.

ISBN 978-1905378326 (1905378327) Paperback Edition

SixFinger Publishing US Office
PO Box 1042
Sarasota
Florida 34230
USA
www.sixfingerpublishing.com

Born in Demopolis, Alabama, William Cobb was educated at Livingston State College before attending Vanderbilt University. He taught at the University of Montevallo, serving as writer in residence of twelve years. His novels and short stories have reached a wide audience and he has won many awards, including Story Magazine's Story of the Year in 1965, the Alabama Library Association's Fiction Book of the Year (2000) and the Harper Lee Award (2007). In addition, he was nominated for the Pulitzer Prize in Fiction in 1992 for his novel A Walk through Fire. He has also written a memoir (Captain Billy's Troopers), and non-fiction.

William is married to the short story writer, Loretta Cobb. They have one daughter and two grandchildren and continue to live in Montevallo.

PUBLISHER'S DISCLAIMER

Due to the historical nature and setting of this novel, some of the language employed could be deemed offensive. Whilst the publisher recognizes the sensitive nature of the language, it is deemed that this is acceptable within the context of the period in which the narrative is set.

ALSO BY WILLIAM COBB

Coming of Age at the Y

The Hermit King

A Walk Through Fire

Harry Reunited

Somewhere In All This Green

A Spring of Souls

Wings of Morning

The Last Queen of the Gypsies

For Jayne Cobb Brasfield

The blood-dimmed tide is loosed, and everywhere
The ceremony of innocence is drowned...

W. B. Yeats, "The Second Coming"

CONTENTS

Prologue

Bay Springs, Louisiana
October, 1965
OLGA FOUNIER

I KEPT ASKING myself, why am I doing this? It was an insane thing to do. Deirdre, my fourteen year old daughter, told me it was a totally insane thing to do. She is probably close to correct. The official reason for me jumping out of an airplane and parachuting into the football stadium was to draw attention to my band and the football season, to get people excited. But the real reason was I wanted to do something outrageous, something daring, something shocking. I have this idea – I know it's crazy, but I have it–that something I do, some act, something I've never done before in my life and that I wouldn't ordinarily do, that when I do it, it'll jump-stop the way my life is going, will jar it into a reversal, will somehow take me back to before I got diagnosed, to before I lost my breast, to before my husband ran off, louse that he is. I ought to see a psychiatrist, I guess. Since I rationally know anything I do is really unlikely to do that. But I also wanted to make this daffy jump because it was me and it was not something you would expect a woman to do. And, too, it was a flip-off to those people in town who gossiped about me and my husband Patrick.

I was crouching there in the open door of Boyd's little Cessna, no real sense of motion except for the rushing air. He was practically gliding, but the racket from the engine made it impossible to talk. My parachute seemed too light on my back, too weightless to be something that would hold me up, a feeling I had every time I jumped. I looked over at him and he nodded and I could read his lips. He said, "Now!" We had practiced for what seemed like a thousand times, but was really only seven or eight, on a mowed strip out near the little West Feliciana Parish Airport. I had time to change my mind. That would please Deirdre; I didn't know about Max and Willie. The boys acted – maybe pretended – as though they were excited; they were both hard to read. But the jump had been in the weekly paper and people had been buzzing about it. Boyd had given me two stout shots of Vodka. I was nervous, yeah, but falling to my death didn't take on the same terror it would have before my surgery. I took a deep breath and pushed myself out the door.

The quick cool air attacked my face, like plunging into a swimming pool, and I felt the familiar sense of exhilaration, the momentary sensation of being suspended in the air, no sense of dropping, but I knew I was. I counted four seconds, then pulled my rip cord; I could hear the whisper and rustle as my parachute opened behind me. I braced, then felt the jolt as it opened; I felt it in my shoulders and my hips. I began to drift.

It was dusk, still plenty of light to see the earth spread out under me. I could see the lights of the stadium below (my "landing zone," or my LZ, as Boyd called it), the street lamps and scattered windows of the town, the wide river moving away to the south, toward New Orleans, the reds and yellows of the trees picking up what was left of the sun. The air – wind that I was creating – whistled in my ears. I could see that the stadium was full. Deirdre and Max and Willie would be there – not so Patrick, over there in Vietnam – they would see me coming down, see me land, hopefully not see me crash into the goal post or lose my balance and break my legs or something worse. I could see my band, lined up precisely at the end of the field. My band.

I continued to float down toward the field, twisting my body and pulling on the steering cords just as Boyd had taught me. Now I could clearly see the lines on the field. One moment I seemed to be drifting aimlessly, the next descending rapidly. I could feel my pulse surging in my veins, feel the ripple of adrenalin sluicing through my entire body, and I laughed out loud.

I watched the earth rise up to me. I was thinking of my family. My fractured and broken family. My children. My eyes scanned the crowded stands, but they were still a blur, still just a mass of faces and bodies. All unrecognizable.

The streaking wind was cool and soothing on my face, tinged with the lingering traces of burning leaves and the sharp, tantalizing scent of charcoal from the hamburger stand below. Every time I jumped I was astonished anew at how huge the world seemed, and how small, rising up so rapidly to meet me. I seemed to pick up speed as I got closer to the ground, the field a blinding green, the sounds of my band playing *"The Washington Post March"* penetrating the whistle in my ears, and the last few seconds of the jump went by so fast, it was surprising when my feet hit the ground and I felt the jolt to my body, running, just as I'd practiced, knowing in a flash that I'd kept my balance, that I'd done it, feeling the drag of the parachute, hearing the roar of the crowd and the blaring of my band, the best marching band in Louisiana. I exhaled and relaxed.

The game went by in a blur. I didn't see Deirdre and Willie. I saw Max down along the sidelines a couple of times; he had been on the football team but had gotten suspended for getting caught drinking beer. Like they say: like father, like son. I was feeling pretty satisfied, pretty proud of myself, for jumping, and people – students and townspeople – kept coming up to me to congratulate me. It had been exciting, but it was over, and I was back to reality. Back on the ground so to speak.

I think, really, the main thing the jump made me feel is that I was alive, fully – if just for a brief moment – that tempting death that way (if that's what I was doing; Boyd kept telling me there was 'no way') and then dodging it – maybe bypassing it – for maybe only the briefest time was my way of flipping off my mortality, too, because I'd been forced to face it and I didn't like it.

I was tired, and my hip hurt, but I had to stay after the game because the band boosters were serving hot dogs and hamburgers in the gym for both bands. All I wanted to do was go home and get myself a Scotch. I was the only teacher there, except for the Parish High School band director, a little man who seemed extremely uncomfortable around me. I could tell he thought I was nuts. I couldn't much blame him.

One of the band members, an eighth grade trumpet player named Helen Nelson, came over to where I was sitting. "Mrs. Founier," she said. "Somethin's goin' on outside."

"What?" I asked wearily.

"The police and an ambulance are there," she said.

Oh shit, I thought. When you're a mother, especially if you're practically a single mother, the first thing you think of is that it's your kids. The Parish High band director overheard the news and looked disturbed and nervous. He and only a couple of band mothers were responsible for all his kids.

I went outside and over to where the ambulance and a police cruiser were sitting at the curb. Only then did I recall hearing the sirens and wondering what was happening. The policeman was a city cop.

"Hey," I said. "What's goin' on?"

He glanced at me, irritated, until he saw who I was. "Rape," he said tightly.

I could see someone on a stretcher, two paramedics preparing to put her in the ambulance. It was dim; there was still one stanchion of lights on over at the stadium. "Who is it?" I asked. He didn't answer me but he didn't have to, because I was close enough now to see that it wasn't Deirdre, which made me feel immediately guilty at the sense of relief that swept over me. Then I recognized the girl. She was a majorette in my band, an eleventh grader. She still had on her majorette costume, ripped and torn. Jane McKissick. What was she doing out here? She was supposed to be in the gym.

"It happened over there," the policeman said, nodding his head at a patch of woods behind the school near an old abandoned house. "Some man. She didn't get a good look at him."

"It was so dark and I couldn't see his face," she was saying. The policeman was writing in a little pocket notebook. "He called me a harlot, or something," she said. She sniffled. When she saw me she began to cry harder.

"A harlot?" the policeman asked.

"That's what he said," Jane replied. "A harlot. He kept gruntin' at me that God wanted to punish me."

"What..." I started to say. I was going to say 'what were you doing out here', or 'why did you leave the gym', but she interrupted me.

She started to cry harder. "He hit me. He hit me," she said. Sobs shook her body. I could see blood on her face. Her eyes were clenched shut, her battered cheeks chapped and red. My heart went out to her. Seeing her there, her size, her blonde hair so like Deirdre's, rocked me to my core. I was stunned. My majorette, too much like my daughter. I was responsible for her. I tried to maintain my cool, to appear calm and in control, but inside I was trembling.

A crowd had gathered, curious band members. The two paramedics began to shove the stretcher into the ambulance. When the police car and the ambulance drove off the students immediately began to shout questions at me. I was shook up. I didn't know what to tell them, so I just told them all to go home. They muttered in protest, but then they broke up and began to drift away.

I stood there for a while, wishing I had a cigarette and a drink. The night air had a soft chill, the prelude of winter.

Chapter One

Near Chen Thien, South Vietnam
October, 1965

PATRICK FOUNIER'S squad was on recon patrol. With his eyes narrowed, he watched across a creek bed for movement. It was sticky smothering hot; the sweat ran down his face in droplets and he had to keep wiping it with his sleeve. He thought he saw something way downstream and he knelt, peering through a stand of ferns. The high sun danced on the water in the creek. The only sound was the trickling of the water: no birds, no insects. He could smell the deep rich decay of the jungle floor and the thick springing of new growth, pungent with life.

Mac, their Sergeant, kept reminding them the Viet Cong were out there, more and more of them, and they'd heard the PAVN were moving down The Ho Chi Minh Trail from North Vietnam. The scuttlebutt was they were massing for an assault. Everyone said it would be the first major battle of the war. Rumors flew around the compound at Chen Thien. They were hard to believe, since everything at the base camp was so slow and dull. Maybe the brass knew much more than they were telling the men. They told them very little.

Patrick's squad was told that on the patrol they were to observe and cover their own asses. Patrick suspected that half the time the brass didn't know what the hell they were doing. Nobody seemed to know what was going on.

"What are we lookin' for, Sarge?" Patrick had asked earlier.

"Don't call me sarge," McMillan had said. "Call me Mac."

"Well, what are we looking for, Mac?"

"What do you think, Cajun? We're lookin' for Charlie."

"I mean..."

"I know what you mean. You mean what's different from yesterday, and the day before, correct?"

"Well..."

"You're a dumb fuck, Cajun," Mac said. Then he grinned. He was a big man. He seemed to like Patrick, but he didn't smile very much. "Here's the deal, motherfucker," he said. "You see one of them gooks, you write it down, take his picture, and then you shoot him. Clear?"

"Go fuck yourself, Mac."

"Well, why're you askin' me? Shit. Like I know what the fuck's goin' on."

They had moved through chest-high elephant grass, being careful against the cuts. It was so sharp it would cut through canvas. They had come out on the bank of the creek they'd been looking for. The bank across the stream was thick with fan palms and banana trees. There was a row of taller trees a hundred yards on the other side. The Sergeant pointed toward the trees. Something was clearly moving over there, but they couldn't see what. And Patrick was sure he'd seen something downstream. He knew that at that moment there was a Viet Cong sniper rifle aimed squarely at his forehead. He slid his helmet forward.

His jungle boots were drenched and soggy and the crack of his ass burned and itched. He was thirsty. The straps of his field pack irritated his shoulders. Just as he'd anticipated there was the pop of a rifle. The round hit the water right in front of him. They all hit the dirt.

"Motherfucker," he heard his buddy Henry Haskins say. Henry, along with another guy in the platoon, Warren Seelbach, had been in the country only about a month. Haskins was a boot from Valdosta, Georgia. He was the first black friend Patrick had ever had.

There was a burst of fire from his right, Seelbach's M-16. Then everything was quiet again.

"Stay down," Mac said. He crawled up behind Patrick. "See anything?" he asked.

"Some movement downstream," Patrick said. Sweat leaked down and stung his eye. He squinted. Something was definitely moving on the opposite bank. The thick bushes shook. If it was a Viet Cong he was an idiot. He trained his own M-14 on whatever it was. The undergrowth parted and a water buffalo emerged, looking around.

"Jesus fuckin' Christ," Seelbach said. He was from a small town in Pennsylvania, big and muscular, with a strong jutting chin, blonde with blue eyes. His head, squeezed inside his helmet, seemed too big for his body. The other grunts had taken to calling him "Nazi."

"Shout it louder, why don'tcha?" Mac said.

"Sorry," Seelbach muttered.

"You will be, asshole," Mac said.

"Let's kill that thing and barbecue it," Haskins said.

"Quiet!"

"Ain't nothin' but a fuckin' water buffalo, Sarge," Seelbach said.

"I never saw such a sorry goddam collection of goldbricks in my life as you guys," Mac said. "Stop the fuckin' talkin'. Charlie might be right over there, for all you know."

"Bring it on, motherfuckers," Haskins said.

"Goddam! Muffle it," Mac said.

They were quiet then. The only sound was the faint rustling from the water buffalo at the edge of the stream, the stirring of its hooves in the water. After a while they moved upstream and the ridge got higher, giving them a better view of the flooded rice paddies behind the growth along the creek. They took positions at the highest point and Mac trained his binoculars on the treeline across the field. "Jesus," he muttered.

And then Patrick could see them, too. A long line of Viet Cong moving along the edge of the rice field. They were moving silently and steadily south. Toward Chen Thien. Mac was counting under his breath. "Fifty one slopes," he whispered.

The last of the Viet Cong disappeared into the undergrowth below the field, and Mac motioned for them to move back. They crept back through the thick elephant grass, away from the stream.

The only sounds were their breathing and the dry slapping of the blades. They regrouped about three hundred yards from the stream. Mac sat back against a tree, his radio at his ear. Patrick found a flat place to sit and lit a cigarette.

Being in the army and being in Vietnam was not quite the adventure Patrick had thought it was going to be. He had joined up impetuously, maybe because he had fucked up royally and was looking for a way to set it right, to get back on Olga's good side. He wanted to regain some of the respect and love he was afraid he'd lost with his dumb fooling around. But he didn't know how to do that. Sometimes he felt like a complete dunce for joining up. For one thing, he was scared he would run when the going got rough. He didn't have a very good track record in that regard. He didn't want the other men to find out what a fucking coward he was, because for the first time in his life he felt a part of something, felt accepted.

He missed the hell out of Olga and his kids. He loved them. He knew that now: sometimes, in the night, when he couldn't sleep, couldn't rest, he marveled that he'd had to come all the way over here to this hell hole to finally realize that he loved them.

"That's the most of them fuckers I ever saw at one time," Haskins said.

"Shit, wasn't but about fifty of 'em. They get close to the compound we can take 'em easy," Seelbach said.

McMillan had finished his report. He looked at the men. "You dumb fucks," he said.

Chapter Two

Bay Springs, Louisiana
October, 1965
WILLIE

I GOT THE IDEA when my sister Deirdre and I were walking to the football game, when we passed the gym and saw the big bass drum of the Parish High School band sitting on the back of a pickup truck. They had this humongous bass drum, so big they had to have a pickup truck to haul the thing around in. It was just sitting there, tied down with cords. Their band was famous for the oversized drum, so big it had to ride on a little cart with the guy playing it walking behind it. They had another band member who didn't do anything but walk in front and pull it. They were the Eagles, and the drum had this gargantuan green eagle painted on it with its wings outstretched. As Deirdre and I walked by, I noticed that the eagle was cross-eyed looking, a real amateurish paint job. That's when a little 'ding' went off in my head. Suppose I was to steal the drum after the game and hold it captive and do something with it? I had been trying to think of something to do to impress this girl, Amy Newhouser, that I was in love with. I figured that would do it.

My mom had told me the band boosters were having hot dogs and hamburgers for both bands in the gym after the game. They'd all be inside. I figured they'd have to do something with the drum;

I mean, they weren't going to carry it into the gym with them. So they'd probably put it back on the truck, and there it would be.

I would have much preferred to be walking to the game with Amy and Donly, her twin brother, but my mom made me go with Deirdre. I had to sit with her, too. I was under strict orders from my mom to sit with Deirdre and not run around with Donly during the game. Deirdre wasn't too happy about that. But to tell you the truth, I was sort of relieved. Donly and a bunch of other guys our age ran all over the stadium, up and down the aisles, and they played tackle football behind the stands, which I wasn't very keen on. I didn't care to have the crap knocked out of me and slide around in the mud. They were loud, and their antics pissed my mom off. She said I had to stay with Deirdre, and under no circumstances was I to run around with those boys, which I was secretly glad of. I hated playing freaking football.

My dad was over in Vietnam. Fighting the gooks, he wrote me in this letter right after he got over there. If he was home, I'd have someone to hang out with and joke around with and talk to. Deirdre was always asking me didn't I miss him terribly, and I would lie and tell her no. I missed him but I was pissed off at him because one day he just up and left home without saying a word to us and we didn't know where he was. Then my mom found out he had joined the army and then got sent over to Vietnam.

My mother was the band director at Bay Springs High. She was always pulling off some stunt to attract attention to the band. That's why Deirdre and I were walking to the game a little early. My mom had been practicing this parachute jump down into the stadium just at twilight. It really made me nervous as hell. I wouldn't even consider jumping out of any airplane. Deirdre, who is two years older than me, was just mortified by it. She said it was embarrassing. She said my mom was too old to be doing it, and she was not in the best of health. I assumed she meant my mom's cancer and surgery and all. Everybody had been all relieved and happy when they said the doctors got it all, but people's faces told me they weren't completely relieved. I was mostly in the dark about it. Nobody told me much, and I didn't want to ask too many questions. Maybe because I didn't want to hear the answers.

When my mom went to the hospital, she wrote each one of us a note for us to read after she was gone; I don't know what she wrote in theirs – probably pretty much the same thing she said to me. She said that I should believe as hard as I could that things were going to be all right, that we were all going to come through this better and stronger, and it was an opportunity for me to grow and become a man. She said she loved me and that no matter whatever happened I should never forget that. I'm not one to hang onto stuff like that, but I kept that note folded and tucked away in my sock drawer, and I plan to keep it for the rest of my life.

I was remembering this one afternoon when I'd come home during the time she'd been having the chemo treatments, and her hair had fallen out and she had this wig she got somewhere, and I walked in. She'd been drinking. She was lying on the couch, asleep, passed out I guess, and her wig had fallen off, and there was her bald head shining in the lamplight, as startling as if I'd walked in on her naked. And after I got over the shock, I was overcome with love for her. With how much I wanted to do things for her, to make her well, but I couldn't.

So Deirdre and I found our seats. We went almost to the top; Deirdre liked to sit up that high so she could look at all the other people – read "boys" – at the game. The stands were full. Every redneck in West Feliciana Parish had come to see my mom jump out of an airplane. I was just hoping her parachute would open. She had trained with this barnstorming Korean War pilot named Boyd Floyd who came through town and gave a demonstration out at the municipal airport. My mother met him, and she got this idea of jumping out of his airplane into the stadium.

The band was formed down on the field. They were playing *"The Washington Post March"*. It was dusk, but still light. And here she came. She looked like she was coming down very fast. The crowd was buzzing, louder and louder. She had a bright orange parachute. I closed my eyes. I couldn't watch. But I couldn't keep them closed. I opened them just as she touched down and sort of galloped down the field, her parachute dragging behind her like a balloon that's lost all its air. Everybody was cheering their heads off.

"Holy shit," my sister said. The band kept playing. I didn't say anything. When I had closed my eyes I was thinking 'Oh no, not my mom, too'. Again. Her cancer had scared the hell out of me, still did. Because somewhere inside me I just knew that my dad wasn't going to come home from Vietnam alive and I would be without both of them. I mean, I was glad she was on the ground and all, but I still had this puffed up feeling in my chest, like things were still not right.

The band started marching down the field, *'The Marching Troubadours'*. I don't know why that's what they were called; the team was the 'Bulldogs'. Each band member this year was wearing a wide brimmed straw hat with a large white feather sticking out the side. Even the majorettes. The bass drum had a picture of a straw hat and feather painted on it.

I was looking all around the stadium to see if I saw Amy or Donly. They're twins, did I say that? They don't look alike, thank goodness, because they are of course fraternal twins, being a boy and a girl, and I was glad as hell Amy didn't look like Donly. I didn't see either one of them anywhere.

The band was blasting away on the Sousa. They were really quite loud. My mother's band was much larger than the bands of other schools we played football with, so everybody always said we 'won' the halftime if we didn't win the game. I sometimes felt sorry for the scraggly bands from other schools.

I was wishing the game would hurry up and be over before it ever even got started good. Until I had come up with my plan to steal the drum, I was going to go straight home and read. When I was a little kid, in the third grade, I had rheumatic fever and missed half a year of school, which didn't matter because I was so far ahead of everybody else. I had to stay in the bed for five months, so I started to read, and I read everything I could find. I really liked The Wizard of Oz books. There must be about a hundred of them, and I read every one of them at least twice. The Swiss Family Robinson. Stuff like that. Ever since then I'd really liked reading.

Deirdre was all smiles now that Lester Underwood had come and sat down with her. I had to scrunch over to give him room. Lester was a junior and he wore a coat and tie to the games.

He sometimes got to drive his grandmother's big blue Buick around. I could smell the whiskey on his breath when he pushed by me. It was a big deal to drink at the games. I saw him pour some out of his bottle into Deirdre's coke. She caught me looking.

"You want some, little kid?" she said.

"No thanks," I said.

She would tell my mother in a second if I ran around at the game, but would I tell on her for drinking? No. I'm a better man than that.

I was wondering how I was going to get through the last half of this game and get with Amy and Donly. We were losing about ninety to nothing. We had a shrimpy little quarterback, Teddy Means, whose father, Rayford Means, was the preacher at Dogwood Baptist Church. Reverend Means was a real weirdo. He had gotten the last coach fired for cussing. What Rayford Means didn't know was that Teddy Means was the foulest mouthed kid in the school. Every other word was fuck. And every other time he touched the ball he fumbled. The way Rayford Means strutted on the sidelines you'd think he hadn't even noticed that we hadn't won a game and his son was constantly stinking up the joint. Deirdre went to his church one time with a friend; it was a summer revival, and she said Brother Means hugged all the girls real tight so he could feel their boobs. She said he creeped her out, the way he looked at her.

Deirdre did go off with Lester Underwood when the game was over and left me to walk home by myself. I was pushing through the crowd when I saw Donly and Amy up ahead. They had already reached the corner and I could tell they were walking home, too. Their parents were probably going out to dinner or something after the game. I had to sprint to catch them.

"Wait up," I yelled. They heard me and stopped. I knew my mother wouldn't be home for a couple of hours. We had plenty of time. They were standing there waiting for me, and I swear I started to get a boner just seeing her up there ahead. I stole a quick look at her ass in her slacks when I walked up. Heaven on earth. This has got to be the time she'll really notice me, I thought.

"What's goin' on, Willie boy?" Donly said.

"I've got a project," I said. I was just about out of breath.

14

"What?"

I looked at Amy. She wasn't even looking at me.

"Let's swipe that hideous eagle drum," I said. That got her attention. I knew it would.

"That's crazy, Willie," she said. But her eyes were sparkling in the street lamp. I could tell she thought it was a pretty neat idea.

"Hey, all right," Donly said. "What's the plan?"

I looked at Amy. After a minute she said, "Okay, Willie, what's the plan?" I started to speak.

I outlined it for them. I said chances were whoever was driving the truck was in the gym eating, too. So we headed back toward the high school and the gym. We kept to the shadows when we got to the campus and went around to the gym. One of the light stanchions at the stadium was still on, but the truck was on the other side of the gym and was in shadow. We couldn't see in the high windows of the gym, except that the lights were on. We could hear the party going on inside. Sure enough the drum was sitting right there on the back of the truck. There didn't seem to be anybody around.

"What are we gonna do with it?" Amy asked.

"We don't know," I said.

The knots were no problem at all, but the drum weighed a freaking ton. It took all three of us to lift it off the truck and lower it to the ground. We were careful to sit it down softly.

Then we just started walking, rolling the drum along beside us. When it would hit the cracks in the sidewalk it would make this little wheezy kind of sound. We went slowly so as not to make a lot of noise.

"Where are we goin' with it?" Amy asked.

"To the park," I said. I knew what I wanted to do with it. She was going to love it. We went through the park and came out on the next corner. "There," I said. I was pointing to the statue. The Confederate soldier. Standing on his tall concrete pillar, or maybe it was marble. Holding out his rifle. The inscription on the statue, which we couldn't see in the slicing shadows from the street light, read: "IN LOVING MEMORY OF OUR CONFEDERATE DEAD. Their glory be not forgotten as long as fame her record keeps". We'd had to memorize the words in elementary school.

"Up there," I said. "We'll tie it to his rifle. It'll look like he's poundin' the damn thing. I'm gonna run home and get some twine." We lived only a couple of blocks south of the square. I sprinted home and went around back to the porch. I knew my mom kept a ball of white cotton cord on a shelf back there. I found it without any trouble. I noticed, sitting there on the shelf, a small can of red paint and a brush. There was even a church key to open it with. I grabbed all of it. When I got back, we all three stood looking up at the statue.

"Shoot," Amy said. "I ain't climbin' up that thing."

"Why not?" I asked. I had already thought about her climbing up.

"Cause I don't want you lookin' at my ass," she said. What is it about girls?

"What's that for?" Donly asked, pointing to the paint.

"His hat," I said. "It's red paint."

"Good idea," Amy said.

Amy and I were already rolling the drum up the side of the statue. I could hear her breathing heavily through her nose. I could smell her, girl sweat and deodorant. I felt dizzy, like I might faint. Donly and I supported the drum while Amy scooted up the side of the statue. I looked at her ass, took a good long look, and it was glorious. Her slacks were tight and I could see the outline of her panties.

Donly and I pushed the drum up to her, rolling it up the base. We struggled with it. We almost dropped it. Finally I tied the cord to the drum and tossed the ball up to Amy. I scooted up close to her. "Loop it around the barrel of the rifle," I said. I wanted to be able to pull the drum up like a winch.

The drum bumped and rolled on up the side of the statue. When it would bump against the concrete it would make this tinkly, hollow boom that I was afraid could be heard from the park. Once it sort of swung out and we could see the green eagle looking crookedly at us in the light from the street lamp.

"That is one ugly eagle," Amy said.

We got the drum securely tied to the soldier's rifle. It did look like he was holding it out in front of him, ready to march with it. This huge harvest moon had risen in the sky. I could see everything in the moonlight, wide Main Street stretching away north and south and Capital Street going east and west, like spokes of a wheel with us and the statue as the hub. The park spread out in the square, elm and live oak trees, the fountain with a statue of some Greek goddess standing in the center of the goldfish pond. It seemed chillier up there with the soldier, as if autumn was slowly settling down from above. I breathed the fresh cool air. There I was, with the girl of my dreams, just the two of us up there with the statue, right in the center of the universe, with our world spread out beneath us.

All of a sudden we heard this siren coming up Main Street, wide open, getting closer and closer. Then I saw the lights flashing, red and blue, a police cruiser.

"Oh, shit," Amy said.

We froze. There was no time to do anything. The police cruiser went flying around the statue and continued on up Main with its siren wailing. When it went by, I could see the little red dot of the policeman's cigarette between his fingers on the wheel.

I was relieved they hadn't been coming after us. I thought it was probably something out near the high school, a fight or something. We heard another siren, and in a minute or two the rescue ambulance from the fire station went by. The tires squealed as it veered around the statue and raced on after the police car.

"Must be somethin' goin' on," I said.

"Yeah," Amy said, using her sarcastic voice. "You'd think so, wouldn't you?"

I had carried the little paint can up in one back pocket of my corduroy pants and the brush in the other. Amy and I struggled to get the paint can open. We could use only one hand apiece. Amy held it and I pried on it with the church key. It popped open and red paint, like movie blood, splashed down the side of the statue. "Shit," Amy muttered under her breath. She pulled herself upwards. I put a hand on her thigh and shoved, helping her. Her leg felt hot under the cloth of her slacks. "Hands, boy," she said.

"I'm just tryin' to help," I said.

"Yeah," she said. "Right." She began to slap the paint onto the soldier's wide brimmed hat. The red was so bright it seemed to glow as it picked up the moonlight. She finished with a flourish and slung the brush off into the street. We shimmied down the statue. We could hear faint voices in the street in the block beyond the park. We could still hear both sirens, much fainter now.

We shoved the empty can and leftover twine down a drain in the gutter. We went to the other side of the intersection, away from the square, and stood behind a privet hedge. It seemed to take a long time before any cars came along. Then, several cars eased down the street, one by one, and none of them even slowed down very much except to veer out around the statue.

I recognized my mother's car coming along Main toward us. It was an old black Cadillac that my father'd bought years ago, when I was a little kid. I could see somebody in the passenger seat, and I recognized the silhouette of the head. It was Boyd Floyd, the barnstorming pilot who'd taken my mother up to jump.

They saw the drum. The car pulled over to the curb and my mother got out. She stood with her hands on her hips, looking up at the statue. The cross-eyed eagle looked back at her.

"What the hell is it?" we heard Boyd Floyd ask.

"A bass drum," my mother said. She got back into the car and they drove off.

We watched ten or twelve other cars come by. Some stopped, others made a U turn and came back and sat in the street while the people inside looked at the statue with the drum. We could hear laughter.

Pretty soon there were no more cars, and we started out around the privet to the street.

"Wait!" Donly said, squatting down, squinting through the hedge. "Somebody's comin'."

I could see the figure coming through the park. It was a man, walking fast, on the other side of the street. I could see he was in a hurry, his collar pulled up around his face. He was breathing heavy, like he'd been running. He kept to the edge of the sidewalk, out of the direct light from the streetlamp, and I couldn't see his face. There was something furtive about him, something eerie. He kept glancing backward over his shoulder. He walked briskly on up the sidewalk, out of the light and into the shadows, disappearing in the darkness.

We came out and walked on to their house. We sat out in their back yard and smoked a couple of cigarettes that Amy had swiped from her dad's pack. The tree frogs were making a racket back in the bushes. I could feel Amy's thigh, warm and soft against my leg. She smelled like sweetened spice. We were side by side and I couldn't see her face, but I didn't have to. I knew how blue her eyes were. I looked at them all the time at school.

She pressed her leg against mine. I just sat there. My leg felt like it was on fire. It was throbbing; I was afraid she could feel it pulsing, and I didn't know if that was a good thing or a bad thing.

She sighed. "Good job, Willie boy," she said. And my heart literally jumped up and rolled over.

She kept her leg pressed against mine. I could have sat there like that forever.

Amy leaned toward me, smiling. "Night, night, sweet Willie," she said, and she kissed me, sort of brushed my mouth with her lips, and I felt her tongue dart out for just a split second.

"Good night," I sputtered. I watched them walk across the lawn to their back door and slip inside. I just sat there for a little while longer, not in any hurry to leave. I was still glowing from that tongue. I was a happy man.

But as I was walking home, I kept imagining that I heard footsteps behind me, and I would turn around and there would be nothing but shadows. It was very dark. The streetlights in Bay Springs are at the corners, and they aren't all that powerful, so along the blocks, under the trees, it was sort of spooky. When I got near Miss Madeline Key's house I walked in the middle of the street, like I always did, because her mangy old collie would run out at whoever was walking by and bark and growl at you. He wouldn't bite, just scare the shit out of you. I walked in the middle of the street, really fast, until I got home.

Chapter Three

Chen Thein Base Camp, South Vietnam
October, 1965

PATRICK PULLED on a Lucky, letting the smoke caress his lungs. He was hot, and his field jacket stank on his body. He was sitting with his friend Henry, leaning back against a sandbag. He could hear the pop, pop of sniper fire in the near distance, tiny quick explosions like firecrackers on holidays back home. He could smell the muck of the damp ground, see the little stream at the edge of the perimeter where it drifted into the bamboo and banana trees, sparkling in the muted afternoon sunlight.

"Us niggers got to have somebody to look down on," Henry Haskins was saying. "That's why the Lord sent us cajun motherfuckers like you." He giggled. He was smoking one of his wilted looking joints. Patrick could smell the pot, sweet and heavy in the humidity. He liked Henry. He was fifteen years younger than Patrick was, but it seemed like even more. He seemed younger than Max, Patrick's older boy, who was seventeen.

"Cajuns feed dark meat to the fuckin' alligators," Patrick said.

Henry laughed.

There was a sudden burst of gunfire much nearer, and a round ripped into a sandbag across from them. They scrunched down, slapping their helmets on and shoving them down firmly onto their heads. Maybe today, finally, they would get into some real action, something more than the desultory, directionless eruptions of sniper fire that were so erratic they seemed unplanned. They rarely saw anybody to shoot back at.

"Goddam, this is some mean shit," Henry said. "You can't even see these little motherfuckers."

"Yeah," Patrick said. They crouched there waiting, but there was no more gunfire. Patrick leaned back against a sandbag, his rifle draped across his lap. In the long interludes of quiet, when nothing – not a damn thing – was happening, he had time – maybe too much time – to think about home, about his family. About Olga.

He and Olga had been so young when they'd hooked up he hadn't really known what he was doing. He only knew that they were passionately attracted to each other and their relationship was intensely physical and satisfying from the start. He fell hard for her; she was so damn beautiful and sexy.

And he was a father before he was anywhere near ready for it and as a result he'd been distant with and confused by the children when they were little and as they grew into adolescents. But he knew he loved them, especially Willie, with whom he had a special bond.

He loved Olga, but he resented the holds she had over him. She had a college degree and he didn't, and she never let him forget it. Sometimes he felt like everything she did – like becoming a fucking band director! – was calculated to make him feel more inadequate. She wasn't content to be a little loyal wife, which was what he wanted. But he had wanted her, too, with all her fire. She made him feel like a real man in the bed but like shit the rest of the time. That black hair and olive green eyes. Man! Up until the time she got sick and had to be cut on. He didn't understand why that had confused him so; he had been shocked to realize he'd lost his desire for her. Sometimes he thought she'd brought it on herself with all the tension she created in the family. He couldn't stand to see her naked chest, where her beautiful breast had been; he had to turn his eyes away. The first time that had happened he'd seen that she was watching him, had seen his revulsion. But he couldn't help it.

They had told Patrick when he was recruited – and again in boot camp – that serving in the army in Vietnam would be "character building", and he hoped that was true. But he was scared of dying. He thought about that all the time. You just had to try to forget it, put it out of your head. Some of the time your mind did that for you. It displaced what you saw with what you wanted to see. There was no way a man could really live with this shit. Dead children blown in half. People singed with napalm. It was too fucking awful, as though somehow some grotesque, horrible nightmare that smelled like burning garbage had taken shape and he found himself in it, and he couldn't wake up. When things got to him, he tried to conjure up pleasant images from his youth, like the way the sunlight lingered on the water hyacinths in the swamps – his old man was always complaining that the plants were choking out the bayous, worse than kudzu – the thick growth like carpets of emeralds dotted with pink flowers floating on the still, dark water. It was like a painting he carried with him that he could get out and look at whenever he needed to.

They had been at this place for a couple of months, he was not sure exactly how long. He and Henry were relaxing, leaning back languidly against the sandbags. That was about all they did, except for some grunt work now and then. There'd been no sniper fire for three days. Henry was eating a Vietnamese candy bar, or what passed for a candy bar. It looked like chocolate, wrapped in cellophane, but it was dry and crumbly. It was not even sweet. Patrick had thought they looked good, but they weren't; he had no idea what was in it, but it wasn't chocolate. Henry didn't seem to mind. He munched contentedly.

A guy named Bob Odum, a corporal, came by in a jeep. He stopped and looked at the two of them, his face hanging loose in an indolent grin. He was high.

"Look what I got," he said.

"Where'd you get it, Odum?" Patrick asked.

"I borrowed it," he said. "Come on!"

"Where we goin'?" Haskins asked.

"Joy ridin', get your asses in."

They piled in, Haskins in the jump seat and Patrick in the passenger seat. Odum eased the jeep down the rutted road. The compound was shaped like a large triangle, and there were narrow, muddy roads inside. There was nowhere much for them to go.

"Where the hell we goin'?" Patrick asked. He felt light headed and free, as if they really were going on some trip or something.

"I'm gonna drive this mother to fuckin' Hanoi, Pappy!" Odum said. They had taken to calling Patrick 'Pappy' because he was so much older than everybody else, except the higher officers. Odum bounced the Jeep through a mud puddle.

"You can't drive worth shit," Henry said, from the back seat.

"I can drive circles around you, boy."

"Who you fuckin' callin' 'boy'?"

"Put a sock in it, Haskins," Odum said.

"What kinda goddam college boy talk is that? Put a sock in it. Shit. You don't know shit."

"I'll have you court marshaled, son," Odum said, in a deep voice that sounded exactly like Captain Emerson's. They all laughed. It was the funniest thing they'd heard in weeks. There was a high sky, pale blue with a few cottony clouds. The jungle was so green it hurt your eyes to look at it; the sunlight exploded off the leaves of fan-palm trees like shattering glass.

They were all thinking the same thing, because Henry said, "Where my fuckin' shades?"

"Ain't it the truth," Odum said.

"We ought to go to the beach," Henry said. "There's got to be a beach around here, with all these fuckin' palm trees."

They rode around and around inside the compound. There were storage sheds. A mess tent with a wooden floor that was so muddy it might as well not have even been there. A couple of makeshift latrines. Some shacks and bamboo huts; it had been a Vietnam village inside an old triangular French fort. They called the place Las Vegas. Someone had made a sign: WELCOME TO LAS VEGAS, DROP YOUR DRAWERS. They passed it.

"Hoowee, what I wouldn't give for fifteen minutes in the real Las Vegas," Henry said. "How long since you two white boys had any pussy?"

"Been awhile," Odum said. "I ain't been to Saigon in over five months."

They passed two old Vietnamese women sitting next to a shack. "They all looks the same," Henry said. "All these gooks. I think I'm gonna fuck me one of these mama sans."

"They're all a hundred years old," Patrick said.

"They 'bout as old as you are, but they still got cunts, ain't they? You still got a dick, ain't you, Pappy?"

They stopped in the shade of a huge mahogany tree that dominated the center of the compound. They sat there for a while, listening to the Jeep's engine cooling. Nobody said anything for a long while; they were all lost in their own thoughts. Finally, Henry broke the silence when he said:

"I seen a rainbow this mornin'." There was no response from the others. "They say where there's a rainbow, you can find a pot of gold." The fulsome quiet crowded around them. Their minds and memories were drifting randomly.

"Shit," Odum said suddenly. "Fat chance."

Sudden sniper fire rang out and Odum shoved the Jeep in gear and ground away through the mud, getting them back to their stations. Their company commander, Captain Emerson, had made a speech. They had to hold this outpost at all cost. Just why was not clear to the men. There was nothing here but the men in Alpha Company, an ammo dump and a few old Vietnamese who sat in the shade and smoked weed all day. Patrick, beyond that, did not know where he was, only that they were somewhere southwest of Saigon, north of the Mekong Delta. They had come out in troop helicopters and then by foot; there was no road to where they were. The only way in or out was by helicopter.

The Jeep fish-tailed its way back around the compound. They could hear more fire, several more rounds, but distant now. That's the way it always happened, sudden sporadic firing from unseen enemy. Patrick imagined that lone Viet Cong just took it into their heads to go out and shoot at them, almost like target practice. It was difficult to tell where the fire was coming from, usually from way up in trees, and sometimes someone would get lucky and shoot one of the snipers out. They would tumble down like dead raccoons.

When they got back, several men from Patrick's platoon were sitting around eating rice and beans. Others were smoking and talking.

"It's true. There's a big push," Warren Seelbach said. "The Charlies are comin' down, directly from Hanoi. The whole fuckin' shebang of 'em."

"How the fuck you know that?" Sylvester McChesney asked. He was a Morman from somewhere in Tennessee. "Why the fuck would they want to come here?"

Chen Thein was in the middle of a jungle and on a sea of black, sticky mud. The mosquitoes and the rats were terrible. They had insect repellent, but there was no way to get rid of the rats. Some grunts used them for target practice with their Colts. But they were as persistent as the snipers.

"Fellow that had been at HQ told me," Seelbach said. "Said he heard it on the radio."

"Fuck the radio," McChesney said. He was angry. His face was reddened and he was shaking.

"What's got into you?" Seelbach asked.

"Tellin' them rumors! Gossip. Like a goddamned old woman. Don't do anybody any good." He talked fast, not looking at Seelbach.

"I just said I heard it, that's all."

"Well, keep it to yourself," McChesney said.

"Fuck you," Seelbach said.

"This fuckin' rice ain't anything to write home about," Whitfield said.

Patrick leaned back and lit up a Lucky. He tuned the men's voices out. Olga hadn't written him in six weeks, not that he blamed her. Not after the shitass he'd been. Sometimes when he wrote her he wrote some lovey dovey stuff that he had to force because he wasn't good at it, but she never responded to it. He wanted to make up, but she wasn't having any of it. He still felt vaguely guilty about how he'd acted when she'd had her surgery. He hadn't even wanted to go to the hospital. He still didn't understand it.

In the last few years they'd spent more time arguing and fighting than they did loving each other. He was not sure she still loved him at all. He had done plenty to drive her away. But there wasn't much he could do about it right then. He was a long way away, not even in the same world with all of them anymore. He was afraid they thought he had just up and deserted them without any thought, and the idea of that cut him to the quick.

But they demanded too much. They thought he existed just for them; he was supposed to just be a daddy or a husband. He wasn't supposed to have any kind of life in his own right. He got fed up with that. He had begun to think that he was missing out on life. There were things he wanted to do, places he wanted to go. He had been angry and drunk when he left, and he'd thought he was embarking on a whole new adventure, but when he dried out he realized he'd done just another dumb fucking thing. He had no job, no money, nothing to do. He couldn't remember all the things he'd been so sure he was going to do.

The last letter he'd gotten from his family, a week ago, had been from Deirdre. She was a sweet child. She'd asked him if he was coming home for Thanksgiving. If not then, maybe Christmas. In fact, she'd written the letter as though he really were coming home. As if she expected him to. He wondered why Olga didn't straighten her out. He wasn't surprised at that. Olga was too busy being a fabulous band director to take care of their daughter. He should have put his foot down back when she'd first floated the idea of going back to college and completing her music degree.

"What you thinkin' about, Cajun, crawfish pie?" Cosper asked, startling him out of his reverie, and everybody laughed.

"Don't knock it till you've tried it," Patrick said.

"I've tried it. One time in New Orleans. Got me some good Cajun pussy, too."

"You wouldn't know what to do with Cajun pussy, Cosper."

He heard sniper fire abruptly start up on the other side of the compound. He didn't even look in that direction.

Chapter Four

Bay Springs, Louisiana

October, 1965

OLGA

AFTER THE policeman and the ambulance left I stuck around long enough to see the Parish High band and all my band members off. Some were being picked up, others were walking home, which made me nervous, but there was no way I could call all their parents. I did call Jane McKissick's parents, though, but there was no answer. The police had called them and I guess they had already left the house.

When I got to my own car I almost jumped out of my skin, because there was a man sitting on the passenger side. But I quickly saw it was Boyd Floyd. I'd forgotten I'd told him I'd give him a ride back to the motel where he'd been staying after the game. I was antsy. I thought I knew Boyd pretty well, after all the practice sessions, but I still took a good long look at him. I was thinking I might be sitting in the car with a rapist. No. I was getting giddy because of the shock of it all.

When I dropped him off at the Moonwinx Motel, he asked me to come in for a drink. To "celebrate the jump." I could have used a drink; I was still shook up. And I was tired; ever since my "bout with cancer," as they say, and my surgery, I get tired easily, and marching band season always wore me out, so I said no. I guess Patrick would have deserved it if I'd had an affair, but I wasn't attracted to Boyd Floyd. I wasn't attracted to anybody. The idea of any new man seeing my body now made me too tired to even think about it.

I was the first one home. The kids were still out. I made myself a Scotch on the rocks and kicked my shoes off. That's the way it is, I was thinking, something like that happens and every parent in town is panicked out of their mind and the kids are still out galavanting, clueless.

I started worrying more as it got later, all these awful scenes popping into my head, especially about Deirdre. She was so trusting she was foolhardy. You have to worry, even if it does no good. I did it every time they were late coming in, but that night I had a reason. I think it was worse being a single mother, which was what I'd practically been for a little over a year, in reality a lot longer than that, to tell you the truth. I worried about my kids all the time anyway; I knew how much my and Patrick's drinking, and the fights they had to witness – or at least be aware of – had damaged them. And my surgery – my being in the hospital for the first time in their lives, and the fear and shock that their mother had cancer – had further traumatized them. I had my mastectomy eight months before Patrick left, and three months of chemo, and the doctors said I was cancer free. Whoopee! I was tired, still afraid, and I had just one tit. I had to struggle not to let it all defeat me, beat me down. If it hadn't been for my children, I think I would've just let go and sunk under. But I loved them more than anything. I was all they had, unless Patrick could somehow come home a changed man, a miracle which I was not really counting on. I had to somehow keep their lives together. At that point, all I wanted to do was survive, but to survive with a little dignity, goddamit.

And I was very lonely. I had no really close friends. I mean, I had my teacher friends, but I didn't have much in common with them other than being teachers. That's the thing about alcoholic families, especially if both of you are rummies. You make no good friends, because you don't want them, you don't need them. They'll interfere with your misery, the pain that's the only thing that assures you you're alive.

Willie's jacket was slung over the chair in the hallway. I had told him he had to wear it to the game, and either he hadn't worn it or he'd come home and gone back out. Sometimes you just have to let them go. It's not worth quibbling about the little things. The doctors said he was completely over the rheumatic fever, except for a small heart murmur that we needn't be concerned about, but I still worried about it. I went into the kitchen and poured me another glass of Scotch. I sat down at the table and sipped.

They were three beautiful kids, three good kids, especially under the circumstances. Ever since that spring Willie was sick, he has been pretty much a loner, and he brooded a lot. I couldn't get him interested in an instrument, and the other two? Deirdre seemed to hate my guts, and I just couldn't figure out what to do about it. My friends have told me that all fourteen year old daughters hated their mother's guts, but that didn't make me feel much better. And Max drove too fast. Ever since he'd gotten his car – which he'd bought with money he made working in the summers and on Saturdays out at Miller Lumber Company – he'd stayed out later and later.

For a long time before Patrick left, things were pretty bad. I guess he was what you'd call emotionally abusive ever since we were married. Hell, since we were dating, but I didn't have any better sense. For one thing he's a real looker. And we had a very satisfying relationship, in a physical way. But he got more and more controlling. The arguments got steadily more heated and more frequent. The excessive drinking didn't help, but it seemed to be getting worse. I was beginning to realize that there I was, with three kids and a gorgeous, no-good husband, so I decided I needed to get a little more independent just in case. It's really funny, but I think ironically it was my decision to go back to school and finish up my music education degree that really made things finally fall apart. That and the sudden appearance of the big C. Patrick couldn't stand it, but there was an opening coming up at the high school for band director, and I knew I could get it if I got that teaching certificate. I had taken lots of hours of music in college, so I didn't have too much I had to take to qualify. I got the job. That gave me an income that was actually a little more than Patrick was making, and that didn't sit too well with him either.

I think not very long after I started at the high school, Patrick got his first girlfriend. He didn't know I knew about it. I didn't know what to think, to tell you the truth. I didn't confront him then, even though it hurt me, especially after I found out that other people around town knew about it. My reaction? I've thought a lot about it; I think I just sort of filed it away, like okay you son-of-a-bitch, that's one black mark in the books for you. I let it stew, but I knew I wasn't going to live out the rest of my life putting up with that shit. Then there were other women, hairdressers. Maybe they weren't all hairdressers, but hairdresser types, you know? So I confronted him, and we started fighting about it. There was always an argument du jour.

One day in the shower I discovered a small hard lump in my breast and the doctors quickly confirmed my worst fears. I had the surgery and Patrick went on a drunk while I was in the hospital. I think my illness, my vulnerability, hurt and frightened Patrick more than it did me. He couldn't handle it. He ran from it. He was drinking so much during my chemo, and away from home God knew where, that Max had to drive me into New Orleans almost every time.

And then, about the time my chemo ended and I got pronounced "cancer-free" (it was all very tentative, my doctors cautioned me; I would never be completely away from it. I was a "cancer survivor," I always had that word attached to me) he met Joy. She was a little whore, nineteen years old. I have to admit she was beautiful. But dumb as a turtle shell. It had gotten so that I could abide Patrick's little dalliances, they got him out of the house and out of my hair, away from my children. But Joy was different, because he fell in love with her, or at least he claimed he did. I would say he was obsessed with her. It wouldn't take a psychologist to figure out why. She had big tits, two of them. He was dumb that way. Whatever, I was tired of it.

And then one night he got very drunk (if I'm going to be honest I should say we got very drunk) and he stormed out of the house and didn't come back. I don't even remember whatever the hell it was, specifically, we were fighting about, but it had to be something about Joy. He didn't come home. He disappeared and I had no idea where he was. But, in a way, I was relieved he was gone. If it hadn't been for the kids, that would have been a simple enough solution.

I knew we had been terrible parents, with our drinking and all, especially after things got so bad over the other women. Like I said, I felt really bad about it, but I don't think Patrick had a clue. I knew my children's lives had been shattered by everything they'd had to abide, and I vowed to be a better parent, which meant, I guess, fighting for them and standing by them. But I don't know if they'll ever get over what we've done to them.

I got up and made myself another stiff drink. That's another thing. I'm going to eventually have to stop drinking again, and I dread it. Boyd had given me a couple of shots of vodka in the plane to shore me up for the dive, and one more on the ride home. I wondered how Patrick was making out with that. In the army, I imagined, not so good. We'd always – since we'd been together – been bad to drink; we'd even sometimes gone to AA meetings together. We'd go for a few months dry, and then we always went right back to boozing.

The house was so quiet I could hear the ticking of the clock on the wall. The idea of an empty Saturday ahead was as relaxing as the whiskey. I heard the front door open and close. I could tell by the footsteps it was Deirdre, and I felt an immense sense of relief; she walked into the kitchen.

"Have a good time?" I asked.

"What's that supposed to mean?" she said. She was rummaging around in the refrigerator. I wondered if she'd even heard about the rape. Maybe not. Probably not. She would have already mentioned it if she had.

"Just what it says," I said. I sighed. She was an innocent. No matter how sassy she got she was still my little girl.

"It's not every night you get to see your mother jump out of an airplane," she said.

Her head was inside the refrigerator and her words had a weird, frosty echo. She had on a tweed skirt. Her blouse was untucked at the side, over her hip. It had the look of hasty repair. I wondered what she'd been up to, but I knew better than to ask her where she'd been. The important thing was she was home.

She sat down at the table with a fist full of chocolate chip cookies. She had flawless skin and high sharp cheekbones, like Patrick. All the children looked like him in their own ways. If you have children with a man you can never be completely away from him.

I took a soothing drink of the Scotch. I could feel it churning in my blood. Deirdre loved Patrick intensely. Her constant finding fault with me was largely about him, I knew. "Where'd you go after the game?" I asked. It just popped out. I held my breath.

"Around," she said. She shrugged. She looked away, munching on a cookie. There were crumbs on her lower lip. I wondered again where she'd been. "The parachute down was pretty cool," she said, offering an olive branch.

"Thanks," I said. "It was fun. An experience."

"I bet," she said. She shrugged again. "Whatever floats your boat."

"I'm glad I get your approval."

"Don't patronize me, Mom," she said.

"I wasn't..." I said. I stopped. I was too tired and it was too late to be baited. I finished my drink. I got up to pour another. "What are you doin' tomorrow?" I asked. I sat back down with my fresh drink.

"I don't know," she said, shrugging. "Sleep in."

"Sounds good," I said. "Me, too."

"Why do you ask?"

"No reason. Just making conversation."

"Oh."

Hearing the front door opening I wondered whether it was Willie or Max. Max walked into the kitchen. "Mom, I need ten bucks," he said. He had the same cheekbones, Patrick's blond hair. Willie and me, we were the dark ones. "I need to drive Martha Louise home to Plantersville."

"Martha Louise who?" I asked.

"Parker," he said.

"What happened to her ride?" I asked. Deirdre laughed. Why does a mom ask such useless, stupid questions? I'd never heard of anyone named Martha Louise Parker before. "Who is she?"

"She's a Parish High cheerleader," Deirdre said.

"Does she play the bass drum?" I asked.

"You saw that, too?" Max asked.

"What are y'all talkin' about?" Deirdre asked.

"She stayed over and we went out to the Cherokee," Max said. "I need some gas."

"Like you don't have enough already," Deirdre said.

"Can it, princess," he said. "Hey, did y'all hear..."

I interrupted him. "Okay, you can go," I said. I shook my head at him, as imperceptibly as I could. I pulled my purse up from the floor. "Let me smell your breath."

"Ewwww," Deirdre said.

He opened his mouth wide in front of my face. I sniffed for Sen Sen. Nothing but coffee. "Come right back," I said, handing him a ten. I looked at my watch. Eleven ten. It was an hour over to Plantersville, an hour back. On Louisiana Highway 41, that everybody called Blood Alley. And there was a rapist on the loose. I probably wouldn't get much sleep tonight. "And drive slow, Max," I said. "I mean it. Another ticket and the car goes into the garage."

"It's my car," he said.

"But I'm the boss."

He was gone. I don't know if he even heard me. The front door slammed.

"He thinks he's Mario Andretti," Deirdre said.

"Mario Andretti doesn't drive a 1957 Chevy," I said.

"Heard what?" she asked.

"Huh?"

"Have we heard what?"

"I don't know, Dee. He didn't finish."

She was looking at me with her eyebrows arched. I started to tell her. Keeping it from her wouldn't protect her from it. But I didn't have to tell her then. I'd tell her in the morning. My glass was empty again. As the years have gone by, I have acquired quite a capacity. "Be a doll," I said, holding the glass out to her, rattling the shreds of ice. I wanted to change the subject. She pretended to pout, but she took the glass, put ice in it and poured Scotch. She set the glass on the table in front of me.

"What's to eat?" she asked.

"You'll get fat," I said. The whiskey was loosening my tongue. She frowned. I had said it lightly, as a joke between girls. I must have been getting a little too high.

"What's that about a bass drum?" she asked.

"Didn't you see it? Somebody put the Parish High School bass drum up on the statue in the park."

"No shit?" she said. "I think I'll go see."

"No," I said. "You don't want to be going back out this time of night."

"Why are you always telling me what I want to do and what I don't want to do?"

"Because you're fourteen years old," I said.

"Who do you think did it?" she asked. For a moment I thought she was asking me about the rape; then I realized she meant the bass drum. It was a rhetorical question. She wasn't really asking me.

"I don't know," I said anyway. "And the soldier's hat is red now."

She giggled. "Red?"

"Yeah."

"Red, like in painted?"

"Yep. Tomato red."

"Damn, I've got to see that," she said.

"You can walk over there in the morning," I said.

"They might have it all cleaned up by in the morning."

"I doubt it."

She was chewing on her lower lip. It was a gesture of Patrick's. His "tick", as he called it. Like sucking your thumb. "Don't chew on your lip," I said.

She frowned and looked away. I wanted to be able to see inside her mind, but I knew that as long as I lived I would never be able to do that. I wanted to know her secrets. I wanted to share her life with her. You can't share someone's life, not even your own daughter's.

"I got a letter from Daddy," she said after a minute. I knew she had; I'd seen it in the mailbox. I didn't know if she'd mention it or not.

"How is he?"

"Like you care," she said. "He's okay."

"Good," I said.

"He thinks he might be able to come home for Thanksgiving," she said.

I sighed. "Deirdre, they don't let guys in Vietnam just 'come home for Thanksgiving'."

"They have furloughs and R and R and stuff," she said. I could see she was about to cry. Her face was flushed.

"But we would know already, if he was coming home."

"You just don't want him to come home," she said.

"Honey," I said. "Honey. Okay." She sniffled a little. She wouldn't look at me. "Anyway, it's a long time till Thanksgiving. You don't need to be worrying about it now."

"I'm not worryin' about it, Mom," she said. She sat there staring at the floor. I wanted to fold her up and pull her close to me, but I knew this was not the time. Things were so off kilter with us in that moment that I knew any gesture might easily infuriate her. I longed to make her a little girl again. A senseless, hopeless wish. She had long ago left that child state behind. And there was nothing I could do about it. "I'm goin' to bed. Good night," she said. I heard her clomping up the stairs. I couldn't take away her sadness. That was one of the most difficult things about being a parent for me. I would gladly absorb all her sorrow into myself, but I couldn't. I knew that I'd probably pass the genetic tendency of the cancer on to her, and the thought was almost too much for me to bear. She was so unsuspecting, so deeply concerned with stuff that would pale in significance next to breast cancer. But there it was, ticking. Waiting.

Knowing I probably shouldn't, I made myself another drink. I didn't want to have too bad a hangover tomorrow. But I wanted to sleep, to blur the images in my mind of Max hurtling down the highway and smashing into a tree or encountering some pervert. And the images of Patrick being blown to bits in Vietnam. No matter how angry and disgusted I was with him, I couldn't bear to think about that. In spite of everything he'd done, I still loved the bastard.

I heard Willie coming in the front door. "Lock it!" I called out. Half the time he forgot to lock it behind him. I heard him coming down the hall.

"Were you waitin' up for me?" he asked suspiciously from the doorway. His face was scrunched into a frown.

"Just having a nightcap," I said. "Where you been?"

"Out," he said.

"With Donly?"

"Yeah." Then he broke into a big grin. What was so funny about Donly? I didn't want to ask. I was weary of Donly.

"Crappy game, wasn't it?" I said.

"Yeah."

He just stood there looking around the kitchen, with that smile. It occurred to me to say something about his jacket, but I didn't. He was home now. There was no point in hassling over his jacket until the next time he was going out at night. Unlike Deirdre, Willie never mentioned his father. But he was the one I worried about the most. He was so quiet, such a loner. He needed his father. Max, on the other hand, didn't have much patience with Patrick.

"What did you think of the jump?" I asked.

"Cool," he said.

"That's all you can say?"

"What do you want me to say?"

"Good night, Willie," I said.

"What was all the excitement tonight?" he asked.

"Excitement?" I didn't want to get into it, right here before bedtime.

"The sirens and all," he said.

"Oh, I don't know," I said. "Probably a fire."

"They weren't fire sirens, Mom," he said.

"Well," I said, "I don't know, then."

He mumbled a good night and went on down the hall. I heard him on the stairs. I felt limp. The Scotch had totally worked its magic. I listened to the water in the pipes, dying away after Willie flushed the toilet. I knew he was climbing into bed with his clothes on. He slept that way most nights.

Chapter Five

Saigon, South Vietnam
Late October, 1965

PATRICK WAS sitting in the rooftop bar at the Rex Hotel drinking a double Chivas Regal on the rocks. It was early evening and he had been watching the smoke on the horizon from the distant battles. Now he could see the tracers against the dimming sky. He had three days of In-Country R & R, the first he'd had since he'd been in Nam. He was glad he was not out there under the smoke. He wanted to pretend it wasn't there, wouldn't be waiting for him after two more days, but he couldn't. The idea of going back lingered constantly in his mind, and each time it came to the forefront of his thoughts his scrotum would contract with a vague anxiety. What had at first been terror was now only a constant restlessness, but the fighting, as long as you were in country, was never very far away.

The dusty street in front of the hotel was crowded with bicycles and pedestrians and only an occasional old car or ox cart. While he sat there sipping his drink, an American tank came down the street, rumbling and grinding. A few people cheered as they got out of the way and watched it go by; others threw clots of mud at it. These fucking people: we are here to save them and they throw rocks at us.

He was excited to be in Saigon, but he was wary. It was the first time he'd ever been in a foreign city, and everything was unfamiliar, even bizarre. The streets were teeming with beggars, old people and young Vietnamese men missing legs and arms. There were outdoor cooking kitchens all along the streets, with molded plastic chairs and tables; some of the people were sitting eating in the middle of the street. The spicy sharp smells of the cooking were enticing, and slants all along the way were calling out to him to come and eat. ("Don't eat that shit," Bob Odum had said to him, "it's roasted dog meat. Dirty. You're gonna get dog brains in the cafés anyway, but at least it'll be cleaner in there. Maybe.")

Patrick wasn't hungry. Not for food, anyway. As he walked, all along the street he saw Vietnamese girls; some of them looked at him shyly and looked away; others looked boldly into his eyes. All of the girls wore brightly colored, figured silk tops over loose fitting trousers. And they were all beautiful. Patrick had never seen so many alluring women in his life. He had been told about them, but he hadn't believed it. ("They're gonna all look hot, cause you're so horny, but hey, okay, if they look hot, they are hot," Odum had said.) Patrick had the itch, all right, but what he really needed and wanted was to touch somebody, to hold someone warm and soft. He wanted to connect with someone. Maybe he didn't know how to do that. Maybe that was his problem. He'd done all right with women before he had met Olga; he had boasted to his buddies that his philosophy was "love em and leave em." But Olga had confused him, turned everything upside down. He hadn't known how to deal with her.

Patrick ordered another drink. There was music playing: The Righteous Brothers, "You've got that lovin' feeling." That's exactly what I've got, Patrick thought. Loving on my mind. And the latest American music, right here in the middle of Saigon. Was that gut twisting conflict really going on only twenty miles away? No, fuck it, he wouldn't think about it. Every now and then he thought he heard artillery, but then he decided it was only wooden carts rumbling in the street. The streets were full of oxen shit, and stank like an outdoor privy. Up on the rooftop, the air was fresh and cool. He thought he got occasional whiffs of napalm, but he chose to ignore it.

He had never tasted whiskey as good. There was not enough ice for his taste, but what the hell. He had already asked for more and was brought a tiny saucer with two cubes melting in it. The bar girl waiting on him was a little hefty. He wasn't going to take the first thing that came along.

Sitting there, smoking, blowing the smoke skyward, he wondered what his family was doing right at that moment. Probably sleeping; what time was it there? He could never get it straight. Olga. That body, stretched out on the bed, inviting him. He felt a stirring in his gonads. She was gorgeous, a stunning woman. Dark haired and sexy. Long slim legs, perfect breasts. One perfect breast, he remembered abruptly. He had tried to understand why that had made such a difference to him. He knew he had no right to be repulsed by her ruined, spoiled, lop-sided chest. But he was.

She was also a hell of a woman. Strong willed and crazy as hell. He had finally admitted to himself that she was smarter than he was; he sure as hell wouldn't say that to anybody else. She claimed she'd never slept around, but he knew better. Any woman that looked like her.

After dark, Patrick went down to the street and around the corner to a dim bar called The Poodle. Maybe that's what they serve to eat, he thought. He sat at the bar and ordered a Scotch. All they had was some bar brand that Patrick had never heard of, but he'd already had three doubles so he didn't mind. He was feeling freed up and loose, a little drunk. He looked around the bar. It was deep and narrow and poorly lit and smelled of beer and cigarette smoke. There were a few grunts–he didn't recognize any of them–and a couple of Marines. Several slants drinking beer or rice whiskey. And some girls.

He sat there drinking. He lit up a Lucky. Someone sat on the stool next to him and he smelled her before he turned and looked at her. She smelled heavenly, like a hot house full of fresh roses. She was doused in perfume. She was looking at him when he turned toward her. She smiled. His confidence fluttered. He wasn't sure he could even speak to her.

"Hey, cowboy," she said. She was astonishingly beautiful. Classy. Her eyes were radiant and black, her hair raven, straight and shoulder length. She had on a light blue silky blouse over loose white pants. The top clung to her body, but she was flat chested. She looked to be a couple of inches over five feet. She continued to smile at him, her eyes incandescent and alert.

"Hey," he said.

"You buy me drink," she said, not really a question, with a slight nod of her head.

"Hey, yeah," he said. "What you drinkin'?"

"Whiskey water," she said. Saigon Tea. He'd heard some of the men talking about that; it was incredibly expensive, they said. He ordered her one.

"You like Red Sox?" she asked. Her eyes danced and glittered in the light from the neon sign behind the bar. The bartender, an older mama-san with a green rag tied around her head, put a glass with light brown liquid in front of her. The mama-san held her hand out; Patrick peeled off several bills and gave them to her. She continued to stand there with her hand outstretched. He looked at the girl, who was looking around the bar. He started slapping American dollars into her hand, not even counting, until she turned and walked back down behind the bar.

"Yeah, I like the Red Sox," he lied. He cared nothing about baseball.

Her makeup, her size, and the egg-shell tone of her skin made her look like a doll.

"You American grunt," she said, again without the question mark.

"Yeah, I'm American grunt," he said. "What's your name?"

"Kim Ly," she said.

"Patrick Founier," he said. "Glad to meetcha." Smooth, boy. "Smoke?" he asked, holding out his pack toward her.

"No smoke lots," she said. Okay, not even a little.

She had a luminous smile. Her teeth were even and white, her lips thin with just a touch of color. Her breasts were small swells. He could see the nipples through the thin cloth. He guessed she was eighteen or nineteen. But it was hard to tell with these people; she could have been anywhere from fifteen to thirty. He hoped she wasn't fifteen, considering that he had a fourteen year old daughter.

"You lookin' for good time?" she asked.

"Yeah, I'm lookin' for a good time," Patrick said.

She sipped her Saigon Tea, looking at him over the glass. Patrick wondered what was in it, if there was any liquor in it at all. Her eyes were so black they reflected light like marbles. She set the glass back down and smiled at him. She licked her lips, her tongue like a kitten's.

"Fifty dollar," she said. "Sixty dollar if you want mary-juana."

"Yeah, I want 'mary-juana'," he said, pronouncing it like she had. She sipped her drink again. She made no move toward leaving.

"You mind if I have another drink first?" he asked.

She looked at him as though she didn't understand him. He held up his glass. "Another one?" he said.

"Okay," she said. "Okay." She nodded. He picked up her glass and held it up. "No, no," she said. She took it and put it back down on the bar.

Patrick got his fresh drink. He told himself he'd better slow down. He was getting bombed. He looked around the bar. Almost all the Americans had hooked up with a woman. It looked like prom night. He laughed out loud. She looked at him inquisitively. "You're beautiful," he told her.

"You beautiful, too," she said. She giggled. Patrick liked her. He felt an almost overpowering attraction to her.

"Where have you been all my life?" he asked.

Her thin eyebrows arched up. She looked puzzled. She had no idea what he meant.

"Never mind, baby," he said. He drank down his drink in one gulp. "What the hell we waitin' for?"

"Okay. Okay," she said.

He followed her down the crowded street. He couldn't take his eyes off her tight little ass. His nostrils were assaulted with the cooking smells and dung, his ears jolted with the twisted chatter of the people. He was jostled several times and each time he patted his pocket to check his wallet. She turned down what seemed to be an alley. They came to a wooden and bamboo house. She, smiling, pulled him through the door and then closed it, smothering the street sounds to just a murmur. It was one big room with a mattress on the floor. There looked to be other rooms opening from it.

She kissed him, darting her tongue against his lips. He grabbed her buttocks with both hands and pulled her roughly against him. She laughed and leaned back. "You wait, Patrick Fooon-yay," she said.

She disappeared into another room. She came back with a cloth bag and an old brier pipe like some that Patrick had seen given away free with cans of Prince Albert. She began to pack the pipe from the cloth bag. She reached up and pushed him down onto the mattress by his shoulders. He watched her light the pipe. She got it going with several long, sucking drags that she held in her lungs before spewing them out. She grinned, handing him the pipe. "You smoke, Patrick Fooon-yay," she said.

He leaned back on his elbows and puffed the pipe. He watched her start to disrobe. He was in heaven. The weed staggered his brain immediately, then smoothed him out. It was good shit. His body felt bathed in warm syrup and his asshole tingled. Her nipples were dark, the size of quarters. She tugged the pajama-like pants down, no panties. Her ass was so taut and trim she almost looked like a boy, and when she turned around he almost expected to see a dick. Her black bush was thick and seemed too big for her thin body. He was afraid he would come just looking at her. She looked as delicate and fragile as a child.

She came over and pulled his pants and briefs down around his ankles and began to suck his cock. The smoke was swirling around his head. He could have sworn he was on a boat or a waterbed because he was rocking, rocking. Her mouth was steaming hot. She held his balls and he watched her head bob up and down. His pulse was racing; he could hear her heavy, rhythmical breathing. He could see himself being sucked down inside her, his whole body, everything, his brain boiling.

"Patrick Fooon-yay taste good," she said, climbing up on the bed beside him. She giggled. She helped him with the rest of his clothes. She climbed on top of him. He felt himself slipping inside her. Soft, slick heat. She was panting, moving almost frantically. Jesus Christ! She made a sound like meee, meee or maybe it was coming from somewhere outside on the street. When he started to come he thought it was going to last forever; he arched his back and moaned while she screwed her body down as tightly as she could. She cried out, loud, next to his ear, and he knew the other sound had not been her, but the thought was a fleeting one that was gone the second he had it. He flopped back on the mattress, his head swirling, his heart drumming.

"Jesus!" he said. She snuggled against him.

When he had his next conscious thought he knew he'd been conked for a while, out of it, his mind inactive; he didn't know for how long. He was disoriented. He didn't know where he was. Until he felt her light body pressed against his. He could hear her breathing. He looked around the unaccustomed room, its unadorned walls made of something woven and fabric-like. He felt strange and alienated. It was impossible that at that moment things were still the same back home, still the same sky, the same river. The world was altered forever. He was going to die here, with the smell of yellow smoke on his tongue, and he didn't care.

He slept. He awoke with Kim Ly running her tongue around his mouth. She had the pipe lit and put it between his teeth. He let her set the pace and they made love again, and then once more before he settled into a deep sleep.

He woke up, aware that the light in the room was the light of day. He looked at his watch. It was eight o'clock. He was alone on the mattress. He could hear voices, faint street sounds. He grabbed his pants and quickly checked his wallet. All his money was there. He sat up and put on his shirt. He had to piss really bad, so he went over and looked in a narrow door and there was what he assumed was a toilet and a sink. Neither looked like anything he'd ever seen before. When he was finished, he went back and continued dressing.

He heard someone coming in. He held his pants over his lap. Kim Ly walked in, still naked. She was carrying a bundle that he knew immediately was a baby. He could smell it, and it took him back immediately to the times when his own kids were babies. Little babies smelled the same all over the world. She had even used some kind of lotion that was familiar to him, and it jolted him, unhinged him. The quiet presence of the baby – so close to the chaotic war, in the arms of its mother who was a whore – discomposed him. The ordinariness of seeing the child seemed somehow even more intimate than their lovemaking. She smiled and showed him the child, a shock of straight black hair, eyes slits as it slept, wrapped in a dark blue blanket. She looked like a naked little girl with a doll. He felt his cock begin to get hard, unsettling him further.

She held the baby out to show him. "Hao Duc Binh," she said.

"Hey, there Hao Duc Binh, how you doin', man?" Patrick said.

The baby was sleeping peacefully. It looked like every baby he'd ever seen. Even a gook baby was beautiful. But then, it was probably only half gook. For reasons that he could not fathom he felt his eyes begin to water. He was afraid he might sob.

Quickly, he pulled his pants aside and showed her his erection. She laughed and wagged her finger at him. She came over and, still holding the baby in one arm, gave him a peck on the lips and pulled his cock a couple of times. She laughed again. "Patrick Fooon-yay want some more pussy," she said. It was easy to know where she'd learned most of her English. He pulled her to him. He cupped her little buttocks. The baby whimpered and then gurgled. "I got go now," she said.

He had a bleary, hazy memory that she had told him during the night that she worked at a noodle shop on Ly Chinh Thang Street. "Can I see you again tonight?" he asked.

"You come Poodle," she said.

He had breakfast at the Rex Hotel. They served what they called an 'American' breakfast. There was a pile of cold scrambled eggs and a scoop of rice. The meat was a thin slice of something that looked like Spam that had been fried. Two hard rolls and a cup of sweet custard-like stuff. They had pretty good coffee, though, thick and rich. And he drank about five glasses of ice water and two Budweisers.

When he finished he sat smoking a cigarette. He had already decided he was going to find the noodle shop and see her. Have lunch there. Maybe he was in love with her. Maybe he could marry her and start a whole new life, forget all the turmoil at home. Maybe his marriage didn't even count over here and it was legal to marry again, he didn't know. He knew she wasn't married, not whoring around like that. He figured the kid was some grunt's who'd gone back stateside. His loss was Patrick's gain. He'd get her to quit whoring. It would get him out of that tangled mess he'd left. Olga was going to divorce him, anyway. Just because he wanted to get out and do something, like everybody else.

He walked around the streets near the hotel. You had to watch carefully for the bicycles or you'd get run over. In one tiny shop he found a pair of little tongs that were probably meant for a woman's makeup kit, but would make perfect tongs for Willie's hobby. He bought them and got a fistful of piasters in change. He gave most of them to two dirty little boys that he saw sitting in a doorway. Back at the hotel, he took a nap.

Then he took a taxi to the noodle shop. He went in and found a table. There were lots of girls who looked like Kim Ly working there, but he didn't see her. He had a cup of green tea. The girl who waited on him was Kim Ly's size and coloring, but she was not as perfect. She was pretty, but there was something off-balance in her face, something asymmetrical in her eyes. He had a bowl of soup. It was pale yellow broth with pieces of meat floating in it. The meat looked like it came from internal organs. It was chewy and tough, so he just sipped the broth.

He sat there, waiting, looking around expectantly. He didn't know how long he sat there before it became clear to him that she was not there. She had lied to him. He wanted to be angry. Hey, she's a whore, he told himself, what'd you expect? But he felt betrayed. He had felt something with her, and he'd been sure that she felt it, too. They had connected, hadn't they? An old too recognizable sense of estrangement crept over him. He began to feel even more out of place in this unaccustomed land, as though he were all alone in the world.

That evening he went back to the Poodle Bar. He had been drinking vodka all day, and by the time he was into his third drink at the bar his head was reeling and he was seething. He went to the bathroom; it was cramped, dark and damp, and smelled so strong he couldn't breathe. There was only a hole in the middle of a concrete floor, and somebody had taken a shit right next to the hole and left it there. "Motherfucker," Patrick muttered.

When he came out of the bathroom, his handkerchief over his nose and mouth, he saw her at the bar. She was sitting with another guy. From his haircut Patrick guessed he was a marine. He went back to the bar and ordered another drink. Goddamit. When his drink came he carried it down the bar and sat on the stool on the other side of her. She was wearing the same blue top. She turned and looked at him. She broke into a big smile.

"Hey Patrick Foon-yay," she said.

"How's the kid?" he asked. Her eyebrows went up; her face was blank. "The baby, the fuckin' baby." Their baby. She must have seen that he was drunk, heard something ugly in his tone because a shadow flitted across her eyes.

"He good," she said. "He good fuckin' baby." She grinned and licked her lips. She was drinking another glass of Saigon Tea.

"Where were you?" he asked her. She gave him the same vacuous look. "Today? The Noodle Shop?"

She shook her head and looked away. He grabbed her upper arm.

"What the fuck's your problem, buddy?" the marine said. "Take your hand off her."

"Fuck you."

"What'd you say to me?"

"This is between me and her," Patrick said.

"Why don't you shove off, buddy?" the marine said.

"I ain't your buddy, jarhead."

"Goddam, you're lookin' to get your ass beat, ain't you?"

"Come on, Kim Ly," he said, tugging on her arm. She just sat there, staring at her hand on the bar.

The marine stood up. He came around Kim Ly and stood beside Patrick. "I said get lost, you fuckin' boonierat."

Patrick swung at him, a wild right. He connected a glancing blow on the marine's chin and the marine jabbed him in the stomach and then drove his fist into Patrick's mouth and nose. His eyes flashed bits of hazel light. He tasted blood in his mouth, felt it on his face. His knees buckled. He went face down and lay there, his cheek on the sticky floor, among the cigarette butts and beer bottle caps. The shadowy, close room swirled around his head. He felt sick. He caught a whiff of the nasty bathroom and thought he might throw up. But he couldn't do that, not in front of Kim Ly. He was so drunk he couldn't lift his head.

He must have blacked out because the next thing he knew he was sitting outside the bar in the street, his back against the wall of the building. His head felt like a balloon and his mouth was sticky dry. His clothes were filthy; they smelled rancid, a vinegary sourishness. He had never felt so isolated, so disjointed, in his life. He wanted to be away from this hell hole, he wanted to be home or anywhere but here. He started to cry, and he was ashamed because he was afraid Kim Ly would see him. But she was nowhere around. He was alone in the grimy street. He loved her. He felt forsaken, abandoned. He loved her, but in his drunken bedeviled self he was not even sure who she was.

Chapter Six

Bay Springs, Louisiana
October, 1965
DEIRDRE

W HEN I LEFT the house last Saturday morning, I went straight to the park to see the statue. My mom had told me about this rape at breakfast. Jane McKissick! She probably raped him! I had thought my mom wasn't even going to let me go out, but she did. They had already taken the drum down but the soldier's hat was bright red. I waited on a park bench for Lydia. I love the fall. It was almost noon but it was still morning cool. After the summer it felt good. I had enjoyed wearing my new tweed skirt to the football game the night before, and I'd be able to start wearing sweaters soon. I wanted Lester to see my boobs in a tight sweater. And pretty soon it'd be Thanksgiving and Daddy'd be home. I know he's coming home. My mom says no, but I know better. I can't wait. I worry about him so much. I think I'm the only one in the world who understands him.

I sat there, wondering where Lydia was. I know it was silly, but I was worried that what I had done the previous night would cause something bad to happen to my dad, like him getting hurt or worse, which I can't even put into words. At least I think it was silly. I got a little bit tipsy off Lester's liquor and we did some powerful heavy necking in his grandmother's car down near the marina, and I let him touch my boob. Maybe that was a sin, and they say you have to pay for your sins, and I hoped my punishment would not be that my dad would get hurt or worse. I hoped it wouldn't be that Lester wouldn't want to be with me again. But that kind of thinking is probably totally silly. If you did get shot down for doing bad things, my mom would be dead about ten times over.

"Where's the drum?" Lydia asked when she walked up.

"I don't know," I said. She sat down with me and we looked at the hat and laughed.

"I bet it was senior boys," Lydia said.

"Probably."

It felt Saturday good. That there was no school again until Monday felt as comfortable as a soft pillow. We had all that day and Sunday to chill out. Lydia had on dark gray corduroy slacks and a long sleeved, blue T-shirt. She was really pretty. She had her black hair cut really short. I liked it. Everybody did. And that's another thing. I knew even then that Lydia liked Lester, too. She would have denied it, but she totally did. I could just tell. My mom would call it woman's intuition. A thought occurred to me then: maybe my punishment would be Lydia stealing Lester right away from me, just as we're getting started. She was a whole lot prettier than me.

"Did you hear about Jane Mckissick?" she asked.

"Yeah," I said. "I can't believe any boy would have to rape her."

Lydia laughed. "What you want to do today?" she asked.

"I don't know," I said. I stretched my legs out. I could feel my legs tingling as the blood ran faster.

"Where'd you go last night?"

"To the game," I said.

She looked at me smiling. "I saw you with Lester Underwood."

"Yeah," I said. "It was fabulous."

"Come on," she said. "Moment by moment. I want to know all of it."

"There's nothing to know."

"What was 'fabulous' then? Did he kiss you?"

"Yeah," I said.

"Dee Dee, you prick-tease," she said. "I bet you did more than that."

"He wanted to."

"And you didn't want to. Ho ho ho."

"I let him go under my blouse. Outside my bra, though."

"Shit! No kiddin'?" Lydia was all poised to hear more. I was watching her real carefully to see how she would react to all this.

"He got really horny and hot," I said.

"Did you feel it?"

"When we were kissin'. Not with my hand!"

"Why'd you make him stop?"

"Lydia, I'm not going all the way with Lester Underwood!"

"What's wrong with him?"

"You're crazy. Shut the fuck up."

"O ho, don't want to talk about it, huh?"

"You're nuts."

We sat there for awhile, like we were glued to the bench. A few cars went slowly past us. They were all old people and I didn't recognize any of them. It was like Lydia was reading my mind because she said, "All the cute boys are still asleep."

"Yeah," I said.

We walked through the park and down Washington Street to Bailey's Drug Store. We went in and each ordered a grilled cheese and a milkshake, chocolate for me and strawberry for her. We were the only two people at the tables in the back. Mrs. Tolbert brought our sandwiches back to us; I don't know why it was called Bailey's, since it was owned and run by Mr. and Mrs. Tolbert. He was the pharmacist.

Lydia twirled a rack of greeting cards around and around. "Sissy said she and Margaret got drunk last night," she said.

"When did you talk to her?"

"This mornin'."

"Where did they go to get drunk?"

"Margaret's folks' basement."

"Wine?" I asked.

"No, she said they had some whiskey."

"I had a couple of drinks last night," I said.

"No shit? Lester?"

"Yeah. He had a bottle at the game. We parked down by the marina afterwards."

"Yeah, baby!" she said, chewing on her grilled cheese. "You get drunk?"

"Not so loud," I said. "No, I didn't."

Sissy and Margaret came in. They got cherry cokes at the fountain and came back and sat down with us. "I feel like crap," Margaret said.

"You don't look hungover to me," I said. I was actually pissed, because I thought for a minute that Margaret was competing with me, until I realized that she couldn't know what I'd done last night.

"And how does that look, Miss Founier?" she said. She was tall and skinny and had an over-bite. Margaret was taller than Lester, and skinny as a rail. Sissy was so bland and uninteresting she disappeared into the wallpaper. I never had to worry about her.

"Dee Dee got drunk, too," Lydia said.

"I did not," I said. "I never said that."

"Parish High School sucks," Sissy said.

"Seems like to me it was us that sucked last night," Lydia said.

"Yeah," Sissy said. "I bet it was one of those Parish High boys that attacked Jane."

"You think?" Lydia said.

"You mean that Jane attacked!" Margaret said. We all laughed. After a minute, Margaret said, "Seriously, you think she was really raped?"

"Yeah," Sissy said. "She wouldn't make somethin' like that up. And she was beat up, I heard."

"You girls want a sandwich?" Mrs. Tolbert asked, coming around the card rack, looking at Sissy and Margaret. She was kind of hovering. I figured she was trying to eavesdrop. She probably picked up the words drunk and rape.

"No mam," Sissy said. Mrs. Tolbert looked at me then.

"Deirdre, isn't your father stationed overseas?" she asked.

"Yes mam," I said. "He's comin' home Thanksgiving, though."

Mrs. Tolbert went on back up front.

"Your dad's coming home?" Lydia asked. She was looking at me with her eyes squinted. I didn't answer her.

"Nosy old bitch," Margaret said.

"Why did your dad join the army?" Sissy asked.

"Speakin' of nosey," Lydia said.

"He wanted to defend our country," I said.

"That's not what my dad says," Sissy said.

"And what does your dad say?"

"He said Patrick Founier probably got drunk and was in there before he knew what was happenin'. He said your dad was a hell-raiser."

"Well, your dad is mistaken," I said. "And your dad's an asshole."

Sissy looked shocked when I said that, but she didn't say anything.

"Where are all the guys?" Margaret asked.

"Still in bed, probably," I said. "Max sleeps till late in the afternoon on Saturday."

"All older boys do," Lydia said.

"What about Willie?" Sissie asked.

"You interested in Willie?" I asked.

"Sissie's interested in Willie," Lydia said laughing.

"No, no, just," Sissie said, "He's your brother, too. I was just askin'."

"Yeah, you're interested. Cradle robber." I poked her on the arm with my finger. "Cradle robber!" I sort of sung it in this squeaky voice.

"Up yours," Sissie said. Her face was red. She looked like she was getting angry.

I was finishing my milkshake, and we all sat there listening to the farting sound of the straw in the bottom of the glass.

Mrs. Tolbert came walking by from back in the pharmacy toward the fountain up front. She cut her eyes at us when she passed.

"Y'all keep your voices down," I said when she was gone.

"She doesn't give a shit," Margaret said.

"She knows my mom," I said.

"She knows everybody's mom," Lydia said.

"Speakin' of your mom, Dee. Wow," Margaret said.

"Why'd she do that, Dee Dee?" Sissie asked. "I mean, why?" She was all friendly again.

I shrugged. I could be asking the question. I was asking the question. But it was more like why did it have to be my mom? "She wanted to make the homecoming game interesting, I guess," I said. That's what she had told me. "It's not that big a deal." I hated it. I couldn't stand to think about it. It was that big a deal.

"I would have been mortified if it'd been my mom," Margaret said.

"How'd she keep from breaking her neck?" Sissie asked.

"She knew how to do it. The guy taught her. The stunt pilot."

"She didn't break her neck. Or even her anything, that's the important thing," Lydia said.

"I thought it was great," Sissie said. She was trying to get back on my good side. I just sort of sneered at her and looked away.

"It was okay," I said. But it was not okay. My mom was like an embarrassing nightmare I kept on having, over and over again. I would never get away from it until I could leave home, if even then. And it was a long time until I graduated. I couldn't imagine what it would be like to be a senior, when I could start to think seriously about going somewhere and finding some place where me and my father could live when he got out of the army. That was my plan. A simple little apartment with sliding glass doors, maybe a complex with a pool. I dreamed about that sometimes. Of us just being together. That's all I wanted.

"Here comes Granny Creeps," Lydia whispered.

Mrs. Tolbert came by headed back to the pharmacy. "You girls need anything?" she said.

"No mam."

"She's probably going back to remind him to bring some rubbers home," Margaret said.

"Ugh," Lydia said. "Don't make me hurl."

"I wish I had a Bloody Mary right now," Margaret said.

"Jesus," I said. She just wanted everyone to know she knew what a Bloody Mary was.

"Don't use the Lord's name in vain," Sissie said.

"How do you know it's in vain?" I asked.

"Huh?" she asked. She looked confused. Blank.

"You are one dumb cluck, Sissie," Lydia said.

And it was the very next week that my "best friend forever" Lydia moved in on my boyfriend. She kissed Lester one day behind the gym. Margaret wasted no time coming to me to tell me about it. I was totally hacked. I figured they were probably going together then, not going out because neither of our moms will allow us to date for real. And maybe he wasn't officially my boyfriend, but of course Lydia knew I liked him. I told my mom about it. She said I should be pissed at him before Lydia. "You're learning about men, Dee," she said. "Most of them are shits."

"Lester's not a man, he's a boy," I said.

"He's got one dangling between his legs, hasn't he?" she said.

"Mom!" I said. It was like something Lydia or I would have said to each other, but it shocked me to hear my mom say it.

I was so depressed. I didn't think things would ever get any better. And I was worried about my dad. There were times when I thought I'd just imagined that my father'd written he was coming home. Actually, he didn't come right out and say "I am coming home Thanksgiving definitely period." He more or less implied it, though. I'd gotten the letter out and re-read it about one thousand times. What he said was "I'll see you soon." In my letter I had asked him to please come home, and he'd said "I'll see you soon." Which sounded pretty clear to me. Except then I'd wake up and it wouldn't sound very clear at all. And everybody was talking about my mom, which was mortifying to me. Lydia's mom said that some woman had told her that she'd heard that my mom was drunk at school one day. I don't think that was true, but sometimes I couldn't tell if my mom was drunk or not. So I couldn't have sworn on a Bible that she didn't do that. She was drunk plenty, I know that.

I was leaving the campus after school one afternoon when I saw Lester. He was with a bunch of other guys, and I stuck my nose in the air and kept walking. I heard him shout, "Dee!" and I kept walking. "Hey, Dee!" he called out. I heard his sneakers on the pavement. He came up next to me and fell in stride. I could smell his boy smell, sweat and cinnamon life savers that he sucked on to mask the cigarettes.

"Where you goin'?" he asked.

"Home, if it's any of your business," I said.

"Awww, don't be like that," he said. He tried to pull my book bag off my shoulder. I shrugged and jerked away. "Come on."

"Go carry Lydia's book bag," I said.

He just kept walking beside me. I could hear his breathing. I could feel him next to me, in his blue windbreaker. It was a gray, overcast autumn day. It had been threatening to rain all day, and the streets were damp, as if they'd absorbed moisture out of the air. I walked a little faster and he kept up with me.

After about a block I said, "Where do you think you're goin'?"

"Home with you," he said.

"No way, Jose," I said. I stopped and he stopped. A carload of older kids went by and I saw one of the girls looking at us and laughing. "Who are you lookin' at?" I yelled. I shot her a bird.

"Huh?" Lester said. "What was that all about?"

"I wasn't talkin' to you. I'm not speakin' to you."

"Why?" he asked.

"You know very well why," I said. I was really pissed.

I still hadn't looked at him. I didn't want to look at him. I was afraid I couldn't keep my composure.

"No, I don't," he said.

"You do."

"I don't. Tell me why."

I looked at him then. He looked a little flustered. He seemed to really be confused. It was a good act. He was a smoothie.

"Because you were kissing on Lydia and probably feelin' her up, too," I said.

He looked like I'd thrown some cold water in his face. "I was not!" he said.

"Margaret saw you, and she told me, so don't try to deny it."

"That bitch," he said. He seemed to be angry all of a sudden.

He had me addled then. I wasn't quite as surefooted as I'd been a few minutes earlier. I wasn't clear on exactly what he was saying. He was confusing me on purpose. I started walking again.

"Where you goin'?" he asked. I just kept moving.

I could hear him walking behind me. "Wait a minute, Dee," he said.

"No," I said. I headed down Walnut Street toward Main. I was still fuming. He followed me. We walked in step for a few blocks, stride for stride. His sneakers slapped the pavement. He was mocking my stride, but I didn't turn around. Boys are totally dumb. I had on my gray tweed skirt and I knew he was looking at my ass. I knew it looked good in that skirt. I didn't mind him checking it out, even if I was mad.

We got to the edge of downtown and crossed the railroad tracks. "You want to go to Bailey's?" he asked behind me.

"No," I said.

"Come on, Dee!" he said.

I turned up Washington Street. That was when I saw that old crazy preacher Rayford Means coming out of Maude's. Means stopped on the sidewalk and watched us walking up. He gave me the creeps. He stared at me. I stopped and Lester ran into me from behind.

"Hello, Brother Means," Lester said.

Mr. Means just looked at me, like he was fixing to say something, but he didn't.

"What make you wear your pants so tight?" I asked him. It was what Lydia and I always said to each other when we'd see him around town. He always looked cinched up, holding his stomach in. Lester burst out laughing. Mr. Means' eyes narrowed to slits.

"Say what?" he asked, and the smell of liquor on his breath like to knocked me down.

"Never mind," I said.

"Have respect for your elders, young lady," he said.

"Yes sir," I said, and tried to go around him.

"Young people have no respect any more," he said. He was blocking my passage.

"Excuse us, sir," Lester said, stepping around him on the other side.

Mr. Means looked at him like he was seeing him for the first time. "And what is your name?" Mr. Means asked.

"Robert E. Lee Prewitt," Lester said. He was a character in this novel that the eleventh grade boys had been passing around.

"Well, Robert, you're very polite," the preacher said. Lester had a tight grin on his face. He was holding in a laugh.

"Thank you, sir," he said. Then he did laugh, a couple of muffled cackles that escaped him like bubbles.

"And happy, too," the preacher said. His look told us that he knew very well that we were being smart asses. He was not amused by us. He looked like he hadn't been amused by anything in twenty years. For the first time I realized how much Melissa Means, his daughter who was in the grade behind me, looked like her father. Then he shocked the hell out of me when he said, "You are the drunken harlot's daughter."

"I...what?" I wasn't sure what he'd said.

He repeated it. "You are the drunken harlot's daughter."

Then he grabbed my arm, at my wrist. He pulled me toward him. He gripped me so tight he hurt my arm. He stared at me, his frosty eyes glistening. "What...what..." I stammered.

"Come with me," he said. "You need to come see Jesus."

He scared the hell out of me. I was looking around frantically. There was nobody else on the street but us. Lester looked frightened, too. Mr. Means kept pulling my arm, and I kept resisting. "Let me alone!" I said. Pretty loud.

"Come on, we'll get in my truck and go see Jesus," he said.

He kept glaring at me, gritting his teeth. My arm was starting to get numb, but he kept pulling. His old pickup truck was parked at the curb. I could smell the coffee he'd been drinking in Maud's all mixed up with the whiskey on his breath. I was just about to scream.

"What's goin' on, Brother Means?" Lester said, stepping between me and the preacher. "What's your problem?" His voice was high and thin, with a tremor, and I could tell that he was scared, too. He was almost as tall as the preacher, but the old man was solid and chunky, like a block of granite.

And all of a sudden I liked Lester again. I loved him. The preacher still held my arm, still pulled on me.

"Goin' on?" Mr. Means said. "What do you mean?" He was grunting, like he was out of breath.

"You have no right to say somethin' like that to my girlfriend," Lester said. "And take your hands off her!" He was almost shrieking. Mr. Means looked all around to see if anybody had heard him.

"I'm just tryin' to take her to Jesus," Mr. Means said.

"Well, she doesn't want to go to Jesus," Lester said. We all three just stood there for a few moments. Then Lester said, "Do you know who my father is?"

"No, I don't," said Mr. Means.

"Dexter Underwood, the lawyer," Lester said.

"I thought you said your name was Prewitt."

"I was just shittin' you," Lester said.

"Don't curse at me, boy," he said.

"Yes sir. But get your hands off my girlfriend."

Mr. Means released me then and moved aside and let us pass. I could feel him standing there watching us walk on down the sidewalk. I was rubbing my arm where he'd gripped me. It was still stinging. I could feel his old eyes like freezing drops of rain on my back. It really gave me the creeps. When we got to the end of the block and turned the corner I looked back and he was still standing there, looking after us.

"What a fuckin' asshole," Lester said. "That old man was drunk as hell. And him a preacher."

"Thanks," I said. He had called me his girlfriend! "For getting us out of that."

He looked proud of himself. "That's okay," he said. "That's what boyfriends are for."

"Really," I said. I don't know why, but I tried to make it sound sarcastic and flirty, but it came out kind of flat and neutral. I was grateful to him for protecting me. Mr. Means scared me. He was like the devil or something. Lester made me feel safe. And he said he was my boyfriend. As we were walking, I decided not to tell my mom about what Mr. Means did, because she'd never let me out of the house at all if I did. It would freak her out more than she already was. And I was planning on seeing as much of Lester as I could.

When we got to my house he walked with me up to the front porch. I could tell he wasn't going anywhere. I just stood there. I knew nobody was home. Mom was at band practice and Max and Willie never came home until supper time.

"Aren't we going to go in?" he asked.

"I forgot my key," I said. Which was a lie. I had my key in my book bag. My mom made us lock the door now when we left, even when we were home. I just had this feeling that if we went in I'd do something I might regret, something that made me feel warm and sweet in my belly just to think about. I had done a total flip. Just the idea of being alone with him made me feel good all over. Like I was starving and there was a big bowl of caramel ice cream right there in front of me, and just the anticipation of the sensation of that cold nectar on my tongue made me shiver. This older girl, Emily Simmons, told me and Lydia that that's what you felt like when you were horny.

"We can go around and sit on the back porch," I said. So we went around back and walked up the steps. There were little streaks of sunlight coming through the heavy clouds, but it was already starting to get dark, specially under the live-oak trees in the back yard.

Lester sat down on the sofa glider. I sat on a folding chair facing him. I was already wishing I hadn't lied about the key, because I wanted a glass of tea. I wondered if being so thirsty was part of being horny. I wondered if Lester was horny. He didn't look like it especially, but of course he was, boys are always horny. I was thinking of when I let him feel my boob. I was wondering what he and Lydia said to each other when they were together. And just thinking of them together jerked me up like I'd been jabbed with a pin. I wanted that image to go away.

"Are you really my boyfriend?" I asked. It made me feel like a stupid little girl to say that. I wanted to take it back.

"Yeah," he said. I waited, but apparently that was all he was going to say. Like I said, boys are totally dumb. But I felt better.

After a minute, he said, "What an asshole that guy is. I'll get my dad to do somethin' about him."

"No, I wouldn't do that," I said real quick.

"Why not? He hurt you. No tellin' what he'd do if he got you in his truck."

"He's not gonna get me in his truck. Listen, my mom would croak." He just kept looking at me with this curious look on his face. "She'd keep me locked up in the house, okay?"

"Okay," he said, after a minute. "If you say so."

I got up then and went over and sat on the sofa glider beside him. It squealed and rocked back and forth. It had thick, soft cushions. He put his arm on the back and I snuggled inside it, against him. He kissed me then, with his cinnamon tongue. My insides felt oily and smooth, everything drifting downward. We kissed like that for awhile, then he kissed my boob on the outside of my blouse, and a bolt of something sharp and tingly shot through me. It was a surge of power. It sat me up straight again. He felt my boobs. He had my blouse unbuttoned all the way down and his hand inside fumbling at my bra when Willie walked through the back gate.

We both jerked upright and tried to act as if nothing was happening. I pulled my blouse to and held it. Willie stopped and stood there looking at us.

"Hey, Willie, what's happenin, man?" Lester said, trying to be casual, normal.

Willie didn't say anything. He walked up the back steps and toward the back door. When he passed by us he said, without even looking at us,

"Why don't y'all get a hotel room?"

Then he went on through the back door and into the house. If Lester noticed that Willie didn't use a key, he didn't say anything. I knew Willie had been home already and had gone back out and left the door unlocked. My mom would go nuts if she knew.

Chapter Seven

Chen Thien, South Vietnam
Late October, 1965

PATRICK AND Warren Seelbach were watching planes go over, dropping supplies. The parachutes drifted down. The platoon was waiting to go out and haul the crates of ammo and provisions into the compound. It was hot, grunty work. That's why they call us grunts, Patrick thought. The closest encounter they'd had with the Viet Cong was seeing them from a distance that day. Every day there were a couple of random sniper shots, but no real action. That's just about all the fuck we do, Patrick was thinking, grunt work. They kept hearing rumors that the North Vietnamese Army was coming into the Ia Drang Valley, up in the Central Highlands near Pleiku, gearing up for a big push to the south. The valley was a pretty good distance from where they were, but you never knew. And there was always the Viet Cong.

"I'm gonna get me one a them Chicom machine guns," Seelbach said.

"No way you'll ever get it home," Patrick said.

"I'll figure out a way. Don't you worry about it."

"All right, I won't."

Seelbach didn't seem to mind that some of the men had started calling him "Nazi." He carried himself very erect; he had been in an

ROTC program in a small college in Pennsylvania but had dropped out and been drafted. "I'm a stupid fuck," he said. "I was 2-S, and now look at me! Shit."

"Yeah, I'm lookin at you," Alvin Cosper said. "You make a good, big target for the gooks to shoot at."

"They better not fuck with me," Seelbach said and everybody laughed.

Mac came walking up. He was naked above the waist and had on a droopy fatigue hat. His upper arms bulged and his solid, imposing chest, with its thick patch of black hair, looked like something out of a movie. He stood looking out over the rice field where the parachutes were landing. "Is that fucker flooded" he asked.

"Naw, it's dry," Patrick said.

"Get busy, then," Mac said.

They spent the afternoon carrying the crates inside the compound and storing the supplies. At sundown they were sitting smoking when Bob Odum appeared. He had a big grin on his face, which was a sign he'd been into the weed.

"You guys'll be happy to learn that we got three crates of beans and motherfuckers," he said. It was what they called cans of beans and ham.

"Puke," Cosper said.

"Plenty of farts in three cases," McChesney said.

"Be glad for what you got," Seelbach said. "There's guys up in the highlands eatin' bugs and green bananas."

"How the hell you know that?" Morrison said.

"That's where our asses are going," Odum said.

"I told you, didn't I?" Seelbach said. "When?"

Odum ignored him. He bummed a Lucky from Patrick. Patrick was kind of glad something was about to happen. He had been expecting an attack on the compound by the Viet Cong they'd spotted that day, but it hadn't come.

"The bastards are out there," Odum said. "You can count on that."

"Why the hell don't they come out and fight?" Patrick asked. He was anxious to kill somebody. He wanted to kill somebody. The first

Viet Cong whose face he blasted off he was going to imagine was that marine in Saigon who'd stolen his girl. Kim Ly. It had been long enough now that he allowed himself to think about her. He was in love with her. She reminded him more of Joy than she did Olga. When he thought of Kim Ly his nose stung and moisture welled up in his eyes. He had told Haskins about her.

"What you mean, you love her?" Haskins had asked skeptically.

"I mean I'm in love with her."

"Ain't you married?"

Patrick had glared at him. "What's that got to do with it?" he spat.

"You don't fall in love with no gook whore, man," Haskins said.

"Don't call her a whore."

"You paid her didn't you? Don't that make her a whore?"

"She's not a whore. She's a prostitute."

"Same difference. Hoowee, white folks ain't got shit for brains."

"Don't you tell anybody else about this," Patrick said.

"Who I'm gonna tell? I don't tell these crackers nothin'."

Chapter Eight

Bay Springs, Louisiana
October, 1965
WILLIE

I WENT TO the library instead of staying in home room for study period. It was quieter there and I could read. The librarian was an elderly lady named Mrs. Probst, who was my friend. Not many students came to the library to study, which was fine with me. I think it was fine with Mrs. Probst, too. She sat at her desk reading books. One day I was the only one in there and I asked her what she was reading. She motioned for me to come over to the desk and she showed me. It was a novel called *The Catcher In The Rye*.

"It's wonderful, Willie," she said. "I'm going to pass it on to you when I finish it."

And she did, and she was right, it was wonderful. I loved it. I didn't know there were books like that. I'd never read a novel that seemed to be about people I knew. I really liked Holden's little sister Phoebe; I could just see her when Holden said she was "roller-skate skinny." I really was crazy about the book and read it twice. I gave it to Amy and she liked it, too. Donly wouldn't read it. "I'm not readin' any book that's not assigned," he said. He reminded me of my brother Max. Mrs. Probst also gave me this terrific novel, *From Here To Eternity*. She told me it probably wasn't "age appropriate," but I loved it.

It was always hot and stuffy in the library; it was in a little separate wing off the back of the school, and even though Mrs. Probst kept the windows propped open there was hardly ever any breeze. And it smelled like books in there, a kind of closed-in musty attic smell. There were only a couple of other kids in the library and they were studying. I was reading this novel called *Mutiny on the Bounty*, that Mrs. Probst told me she thought I would like. I didn't much. It wasn't nearly as good as *The Catcher In The Rye* or *From Here To Eternity*. It was sort of boring, to tell you the truth. I guess she thought I would enjoy it because it was about adventure on the high seas, but I'm just not too interested in adventure on the high seas.

Maybe one reason *Mutiny on The Bounty* was so boring was that I couldn't keep my mind from jumping to my family and all we were going through, my mother's drinking and my dad running off and all that. I love my mom so much I just can't stand to think about her having cancer; her doctors said she was over it, but I don't know. I sure as hell wasn't over it. I knew it wasn't good to dwell on stuff like that. There was nothing I could do about it, but it was heavy on my mind all the time except when I was working with my butterfly collection, which I didn't do too much any more, or when I was thinking about Amy, which I did all the time, or when I was reading a really good book, the kind Holden said when you finished it you wanted to call up the author. I knew exactly what he meant. I wouldn't want to call up the guys – it took two to write it – who wrote *Mutiny on the Bounty*, even if they weren't dead. I think they'd be about as boring as their book. But I would sure like to call up the writer of From Here To Eternity and have a talk with him. There was a lot I could ask him, about being in the army and all. And other things I needed to know.

Maybe, when my dad came home from Vietnam, I could ask him all those questions, but I doubted I'd get much of an answer. My dad and I had never had a single really serious conversation about anything but maybe butterflies. I asked him once to tell me about God, and he gave me this real vacant look and asked me what I wanted to know about him. I didn't know what I wanted to know about God; if I did, I wouldn't have had to ask him. He told me to ask Mom. But what I was really wanting to know was what he thought about God. I think he knew that, and that's why he wouldn't answer me.

Another reason I couldn't concentrate on *Mutiny on the Bounty* was that I kept looking up every few seconds to see if Amy was coming in the door. I hadn't talked to her since that night that I now thought of as "The Night of the Kiss." Not the "Night of the Bass Drum" or the "Night of the Statue with the Red Hat," or anything like that. I couldn't get the feel of that tongue darting on my lips out of my mind. I worried that I hadn't known what was coming and had my lips closed, when I was supposed to have them open or something. I didn't even know how to kiss. Which was sort of embarrassing. Maybe if my lips had been open Amy's tongue would have gone in my mouth where it was supposed to go, and I was so stupid and inexperienced I had maybe missed my chance forever. That's a terrible feeling. So the memory of "The Kiss" was not only thrilling, it was also an "ouch" moment at the same time. Things were so mixed up in my head I thought I was going batty.

And that's when things started to get really weird. I was just sitting there, pretending to read but thinking about Amy, when this guy, Jerry Broadhead, came slouching in and sat down over near the card catalogue. He was frowning. He had the look of someone who'd been sent to the library for talking or chewing gum or something. He was an eighth grader that I didn't know very well. Jerry Broadhead came over to my table and sat down. "Your old man's in Vietnam," he said, not a question.

"Keep your voice down, Jerry," Mrs. Probst said.

"So your old man's in Vietnam," he whispered.

"Yeah," I whispered back. Jerry had a real short buzz cut. His hair looked sun-bleached.

"He a marine?"

"He's in the army."

"Then he ain't a marine." Jerry looked almost disgusted or angry that my dad wasn't in the marines.

"No, he's not," I whispered.

"He kill any japs?"

I looked at Jerry, to see if he was joking me or something. "You're thinking of World War Two," I said. "We're fighting the Vietnamese now."

"Same difference," he said.

I wasn't going to argue with him. "He doesn't say," I said.

"Doesn't say what?"

"Whether he's killed anybody or not."

"Well, shit, then," he said.

I didn't know what to say to that.

"Maybe he's not even in the fightin'. Maybe he's not in them trenches with the marines," he said. He was peering at me, his eyes narrowed. His eyes were the color of watered down coca cola.

"Maybe not," I said. That seemed to satisfy him. He just sat there, looking off out the window.

I didn't like to be reminded that my dad was over there in the middle of all that. I didn't know if he was actually shooting at anybody or not, or being shot at, but I assumed he was, since that's what was going on. Deirdre and I watched stories about it on the TV news. Just thinking about it made me nervous. When I thought of him being hit by a bullet or a bomb, maybe right at that very second I was thinking it, it made me flinch and shudder. I tried to put my mind on something else, and what usually popped up there was Amy. I just plain loved the way her blonde hair curled around her face, and I tried to concentrate on that. And she was funny. We always seemed to be on the same wave-length; she always seemed to know what I was thinking and would say it first and we'd laugh. I liked just being with her. It was comfortable. Not much made me comfortable any more.

At least ten minutes went by with me reading the same paragraph over and over, trying to get into *Mutiny on the Bounty*, and Jerry Broadhead just sitting there, staring at me. Weird city. I figured he wasn't going to say anything more. But he was right there, crowding me. I read it in a book: he was "invading my space." I understood exactly what that meant. In spades. I didn't like it if people got too close to me, unless it was Amy, of course. Or some other girl I was maybe going to have sex with, if that ever happened. Maybe I would feel crowded by that, too, I didn't know. But I sure as hell wanted to find out. Jerry kept on eyeballing me with this kind of glare.

"What's your problem?" I said. I had heard Max say that to some guy who was annoying him.

"Huh?" he said.

"What's your problem?"

"I ain't got no problem, that I know of," he said.

"Then quit lookin' at me," I said.

"I can look at whoever I want to," Jerry said. "It's a free country, ain't it?"

I could see Mrs. Probst looking at us out of the corners of her eyes. Though we were still whispering, I could tell she was about to say something to us. I decided to pack up my book bag and head on back to home room. When I went by Mrs. Probst's desk she said, "Bye, Willie, stay out of trouble."

"Yes mam," I said. I knew that was a reference to Jerry Broadhead whispering with me. She probably thought we were trying to cook something up.

Last period of the day I had American History and Amy had Algebra One, so I looked for her in the crowd after school. We hardly ever walked home together any more. She was usually with a bunch of other girls. Some days she'd be talking with some high school boys, who shouldn't have been hanging around with a seventh grade girl, but I understood why they were there. She was such a knock-out. I hoped she wasn't accepting rides home from any of them. I also hoped I wouldn't see Max messing around with her. I knew what was on his mind.

So I walked home by myself. Every now and then Max would give me a ride home in his Chevy, but he usually had some girl with him. I decided not to go straight home, so I walked through town and on down to the river, near the marina. I wasn't in any hurry to get home; I would be the only one there until supper time, when everybody else would come bustling in late, Max and Dee in a hurry to leave again, my mom heading straight to get a drink, her first of the evening. They would all be hungry and irritable, getting in arguments – specially my mom and Dee – so I'd usually stay in my room until things settled down and got quiet.

I thought about stopping by the house and getting one of my butterfly nets, but I didn't. I hardly ever went out hunting for them anymore. I didn't enjoy working with my collection anymore. I don't know why. It made me restless. Maybe I was just bored with the whole business; maybe it was something only a little kid could get all involved in.

Down by the river the oddest thing happened: a visit from my second weirdo of the afternoon. I was sitting on a bench watching a boat pushing about twenty barges loaded with coal down the river toward New Orleans, when I happened to look up and saw that preacher, Teddy Means' dad, coming along the sidewalk. He stopped in front of this old homeless-looking man sitting on a bench near where the pedestrian bridge went over into Riverside Park. I had seen the old guy there several times before. I watched Mr. Means give him what looked like a little pamphlet. The old guy squinted at it. Mr. Means stopped and talked with an old couple. He gave them one, too, and they went on with their walk. He came on toward me. I saw him see me sitting there. He did a kind of left oblique and marched right to me. He just stood there, looking down at me with his arms folded across his chest. He had a stack of little pamphlets in his hand.

"Hi, Mr. Means," I said.

"You know who I am," he said. "Good morning."

"It's afternoon," I said. I knew that was cheeky, but I said it anyway. I didn't like him and I didn't know why. I didn't even know him.

"You are the F...F...Fooon-yay boy," he said. He had trouble pronouncing our name.

"I'm one of em, yes sir," I said. He sort of gave me the shivers the way he kept staring at me with these ice-blue eyes, almost the same way Jerry Vance had looked at me. He just kept staring. I wondered if I had a booger hanging out of my nose or something. I sort of swiped at my nose with the back of my finger. Mr. Means looked like he had his belt cinched up about two holes too much.

"I'm going to run for mayor," he said. "Somebody needs to clean this town up."

"Yes sir," I said. "I can't vote."

"I know you can't vote, you're just a little boy."

"Okay," I said. He just stood there looking at me. Boy, I had sure hooked up with some real conversationalists this afternoon! I didn't say anything else. Finally he picked one of the little pamphlets out of the stack and handed it to me.

"Here, read that, boy," he said.

"Yes sir," I said. I took it. He didn't move. His eyes were bolted to mine. "You want me to read it right now?" I asked.

"Might as well," he said. "You might have questions."

I looked at it. It was about the size of these little dirty comics that kids at the middle school passed around. We called them "fuck-books." But this one wasn't a fuck-book. The title on the front was "The Beast." Under the title was the number 666, in red ink. It looked like it might be fairly interesting. I opened it. It was a comic book about this family. I liked comic books pretty much, but this one was different. Every page had this quote from The Bible in letters so small I couldn't read them, especially in the late sunlight. I sort of flipped through it. He was watching me. He had moved closer to me, and that made me uneasy. The last page was one picture, with the family sitting around all sad, big tears coming out of their eyes, with one of them, a woman – I took her to be the mother – flying up toward heaven where Jesus was standing waiting for her. I looked up at Mr. Means. I didn't know what he wanted me to say.

"It's the rapture," he said.

"The what?" I asked. I knew vaguely what he was talking about, but I didn't particularly want to hear him explain it. I sort of slid down the bench, away from him, but he moved with me.

He pointed with his finger toward the picture. I noticed his fingernail was very long and needed cutting. It was shaking like it had the palsy. "She's saved. Jesus came, and she's flyin' up to heaven. The others ain't saved."

"She's just goin' off and leavin' her family?" I asked.

"They ain't saved," he repeated. "They're harlots and sinners, and that's God's judgement."

I thought that was a hell of a thing. A terrible thing. Of course I saw immediately the parallel with my own family, my dad leaving home and leaving us behind. And it brought back to me how scared I was when my mom had cancer. I wondered if that was why he was showing it to me. He was a preacher. Was he trying to comfort me? Or frighten me?

"You never know," he said.

"Huh?"

"When Jesus will come. Or the devil. You never know."

"Okay," I said. I didn't know what else to say. Whatever he was doing, he wasn't trying to comfort me. He was pale and unfeeling. Cold and distant. I realized that he really was crazy. I started to ask him what his problem was, but I knew that would be too cheeky, and I was getting pretty scared of him. I had slid down the bench as far as I could; half my ass was hanging off the end. Finally I said, in this quivery voice, "You're scaring me, Mr. Means."

"We all ought to be scared," he said. "We all ought to be. I want you to come over here with me."

"Where?" I asked.

He pointed to the park. "I'm fine right here," I said. I wasn't going anywhere with this guy.

"There," he said. I saw he was pointing toward this old concrete block restroom in the corner of the park. It was dingy and the roof was sagging.

"The restroom? What for?"

"To pray with me."

"It stinks in there, Mr. Means," I said. I tried to press myself more firmly on the bench.

"Come on, boy," he said. He was reaching for me when he saw where my eyes were looking. A police cruiser was coming slowly along River Road. We both watched it as it glided by and stopped in front of the old homeless-looking man. The policeman got out and went around his car and started talking with the old man. Mr. Means was staring over there. He stood there for a minute more, then turned and walked off down the sidewalk. He walked funny, stiffly, like he was all corseted or had a broomstick up his ass or something.

What a relief. I was so glad the cop had come along. I sat there a few minutes, watching the policeman and the old man chatting. I was breathing easy again. There was a nip of autumn cool in the air and the leaves on the big live oak trees in the park were starting to change. October, the month I was born in. It felt kind of odd and funny to think I was the same person as the little squawking baby that had come into the world twelve years ago. I'd had no idea back then that all these years later I'd be sitting here on this bench, with my family all torn apart and my dad in Vietnam maybe getting killed tomorrow for all I knew. It's quite uncanny and astonishing how life goes. A little dumb baby not knowing anything that was to come, and this day, in this October, I had no inkling at all of everything that would happen soon in my family. I just knew for certain that it wouldn't be anything like what happened in Mr. Means' little comic book.

Chapter Nine

Chen Thien Base Camp, South Vietnam
November, 1965

ONE NIGHT they were awakened by a mortar barrage on the compound. At the first whump everybody jumped up and scrambled for helmets and rifles. Then they hit the ground and huddled against the sandbag walls.

"Where'd those raggedy little bastards get mortars?" Seelbach asked, perplexed.

"Goddam, Seelbach, didn't you ever read the newspapers? Or look at the fuckin' Huntley Brinkley?" Cosper asked.

"Well, yeah," Seelbach said.

"They got em from the fuckin' North Vietnamese, dumb fuck, and the Chinese Commies. Where you think?"

"Hey, that's why they call them machine guns chicoms!"

"Jesus fuckin' Christ," Cosper said.

"You sure you ain't a marine, Seelbach?" McChesney said.

Whump, whump, whump. More mortar fire came in. They pulled their helmets tighter against their heads. They couldn't see where the rounds were landing, or even if they were all landing inside the compound. Whump, whump, whump. There was a burst of fire from a Thompson submachine gun. They were all holding their M-16s close. They had all heard plenty of stories of in-close fighting with the Viet Cong and their bayonets.

"We shoulda killed every goddam one of the bastards when we saw em the other day," Morrison said.

"They were too far away," Cosper said.

"I know they were too far away," Morrison said. "You callin' me an idiot?"

"Fuck off."

There was a cessation of firing from the mortars and they fanned out to fortified positions at the perimeter. Patrick was with Haskins. They peered over the wall of sandbags. They could see a few shadowy rubber trees in the near distance, beyond that blackness. There was prolonged fire from an M60 machine gun. Patrick could see the tracers ripping into the rubber trees.

They had their rifles propped on the sandbags. Whump, whump. Two more rounds of mortars. Suddenly there was a rapid popping from the woods that Patrick recognized as Cong AK47s. A round smacked into the sandbags in front of them.

"They gonna charge?" Haskins asked. In answer he pulled off three quick rounds.

"Goddam, Henry, now they know right where we are."

"They know right where we're at anyhow," Henry said.

"You ain't gonna hit anything out there," Patrick said. "You can't see shit."

"Shit is all I can see," he said, and fired three more times.

The machine gun fired again. They could see the tracers tearing through the trees and disappearing into the darkness. They heard a shrill voice cry out in pain. It was drowned out by continued fire from the machine gun.

"He hit one of those motherfuckers!" Haskins said.

Suddenly the machine gun stopped and everything was silent except for some sporadic firing from the other side of the compound. They waited a long time and there were no more mortars. Time went ticking by, and his head nodded. He closed his eyes. He thought of Kim Ly, pictured her naked and willing, imagined her sucking his cock and he realized he had a boner. He must have dozed, because when he opened his eyes it was dawn. Haskins was asleep, his helmet askew on his head, his cheek pressed against a sandbag. He was snoring softly. Patrick kicked his leg.

"Wake up," he said, and Haskins sat up, looking wildly around.

"What is it?" he said. "What is it?"

"Wake up, so you'll know it when they cut your balls off," Patrick said.

"Fuck you," Haskins said. He rinsed his mouth out from his canteen and spit in the dirt. Then he rummaged around in his pack and came out with another of the Vietnamese candy bars.

"I don't see how you eat that crap," Patrick said.

"Don't you worry none about it, white boy," he said.

Ropes of light fog hung in the air in the open area outside the perimeter, like streamers of decoration. Patrick heard movement behind him. It was Mac. With him was Gerald Abbott, one of the other black guys in the platoon. "See anything?" Mac asked.

"Naw," Patrick said. He nodded to Mac and Gerald. Haskins was focused on the wall of bamboo trees and fan palms. He was pretending he hadn't heard them come up. Haskins did not like Gerald Abbott; Abbott wore thick horn-rim glasses and was a college boy. He'd been drafted right out of a black college in Mississippi. He was from the little town of Batesville, and he claimed that his classification had been changed so they could draft him instead of a white boy. "Motherfuckers," Gerald Abbott had said. "It was the mayor's little boy!"

"They ain't no more done that than nothin'," Haskins had said.

"You a fuckin' uncle tom, Haskins. Fuck you," Abbott had said.

The jungle was quiet. There was no movement. Patrick checked his rifle. He had two hand grenades attached to his belt along with his Colt. It was loaded and ready. Patrick was silently pleading: Come on. Come on.

"Stay alert," Mac said, and he and Abbott moved on down the perimeter.

"What that ass kisser doin' with the sarge?" Haskins asked.

Patrick didn't answer him, because at that instant there came a sudden burst of fire from the jungle, close, the rounds thunking into the sandbags and whining over their heads. The firing became a steady, ear-splitting clatter. Patrick and Haskins both pulled off round after round. He heard the machine guns on both sides of him pumping away. He began to discern forms among the thick trees and he tried to aim at them. It reminded Patrick of those target games in carnivals. The open area was filling up with acrid gray smoke that mingled with what was left of the fog. He thought he saw one of the forms go down. Yes! he said to himself. The forms got closer and became men, some in tattered uniforms, others in loose pants and shirts with bandoliers crisscrossing their chests. Most of them wore battered pith helmets that reminded Patrick of the coolie hats he had seen the workers in the rice fields wearing. Gradually he could make out faces, and he aimed at them. One face became a bloody mass and the man went over backward like he'd been jerked by the neck.

"I got one," Patrick said. It was the marine who'd stolen Kim Ly. He sighed with satisfaction and kept firing.

The fire from the perimeter rattled on. They were giving the Viet Cong all they'd asked for. This was more like it. This was better than trooping through flooded rice fields and elephant grass hunting the little weasels like hunting squirrels or coons.

Gradually the firing from the jungle eased down. Their own machine guns became more intermittent and spotty. The greasy smoke began to lift. Patrick heard several cheers from down the line.

There was nothing across the clearing then but some crumpled bodies along the edge of the undergrowth. Well, what the fuck, Patrick thought. He'd survived his first battle. And there was really nothing to it. Of course, there was nowhere for him to run if he'd wanted to.

They were sitting around finishing up plates of cold beans and motherfuckers. Some were already smoking. "We crushed those shitheads," Cosper said. "I hope that makes the Huntley-Brinkley."

"It won't," Gerald Abbott said.

"Come on, Abbott, what do you know?"

"I know they ain't puttin' anything about us on any TV news. I know that."

"Shit, Abbott," Morrison said. "My wife wrote me she sees shit all the time on the TV."

"Yeah," Abbott said. "About those goddam marines at Da Nang."

"Well..." Cosper said.

"They don't care anything about a bunch of boonierats out here in this mosquito hole. We ain't even fightin' an army, just a bunch of gooks that got together and said let's go kill us some fuckin' American imperialists."

"Imperialists?" Marvin Whitfield said. "You stayed in college too long, Abbott."

"What do they call us?" Jason Morrison asked.

"Assholes," Patrick said.

"No doubt," Abbott said.

"They some dumb motherfuckers," Haskins said. "What'd they think they doin' this mornin'? We chopped 'em up."

"No so dumb," Odum said. He had taken off his shirt and lit up a joint.

"Give us the lowdown," Cosper said sarcastically.

"Fuck you, Cosper," Odum said. "They'e just keepin' us busy. Softenin' us up."

"I guess you know, huh?" Seelbach said.

"I ain't sayin' I know everthing, Warren. I just heard some shit, that's all."

They all fell silent and looked at him. Finally, Patrick said, "Well, what?"

"All I know is, there's some big plans for this unit," Odum said. He sucked in smoke and leaned back, holding it in. "I can tell you this, though," he said, when he exhaled. "Things are gonna be so fuckin' worse on down the road you ain't even gonna believe it."

Chapter Ten

Bay Springs, Louisiana
November, 1965
OLGA

SUNDAY MORNING, everybody asleep but me, so I made myself a Bloody Mary and opened the newspaper at the breakfast table. I had "everything bagels" in the pantry and chive and onion cream cheese in the fridge. I put out cereal for the boys. Deirdre would want a bagel. I'd be willing to bet that Knox Pitts will call this morning. He's a vice president at Robertson Bank, a widower, and he's called the last two Sundays to ask me to go with him to church. He's an Episcopalian. He says church will be a great comfort to me with Patrick overseas. I don't want to go to church with him. All I really want to do is stay home and drink Bloody Marys.

There were several men who had come on to me since Patrick left. I was lonely, and of course I was horny as hell. It had crossed my mind. I admit I was curious about what it would be like with a new man and my mangled breasts; not good, probably, judging from the way Patrick had come unglued about it. Men slobbered after women's bodies but they were frightened and repulsed by them at the same time. Men didn't know what the hell they wanted. I wasn't about to make such a move. I didn't need that; it was too messy. I had my kids to think about, and they'd been through plenty already.

My hip has ached since that Friday night jump. I wonder if I hurt something. It was foolish, but fun, worth it every bit to see people's faces. "You're a nut," my friend Wren told me on the phone yesterday. "One of these days, Olga!"

"Yeah," I said. "I'm gettin' too old."

"Bite your tongue, girl," she said.

Winston Larkin, the principal of the high school, had called me into his office to talk about what had happened that night after the football game. I felt bad about it. He said the girl's parents were upset that she had left the gym unsupervised, but he had told them they couldn't very well lock the doors and force the kids to stay inside. The girl was a junior; she had some responsibility, too, he said he'd told them. He had peered at me questioningly. "You weren't drinking that night, were you, Olga?" he'd said. "No, of course not," I'd said. I mean, I certainly wasn't drinking at the game or in the gym afterwards. And I was completely sober.

I was not reading the paper. There had been a couple of brief stories about the rape in the New Orleans paper, at first calling it an "alleged" rape and then a follow up story that a medical examination had revealed that she was raped. She had had contusions and bruises on her face. At practice, I couldn't stand up there and look at the band without surveying the boys, wondering if it was one of them. Which one?

I was just sitting there, sipping my Bloody Mary. 90 proof vodka. Good stuff. More good Autumn weather outside. I felt a prick of guilt knowing I wasn't going to get out in it. I wondered briefly what kind of weather Patrick was in. Over the years, when the weather was good, Patrick would always want to go on picnics; picnics were a pain for me, ants and heat and sitting on the damn ground. I was glad not to have him flopping around slobbering like a puppy with a leash, ready to go.

The phone rang.

"Come on, Olga, go with me this mornin'," Knox Pitts said. He was persistent, you had to hand that to him. I almost laughed at myself when I thought "could the rapist be him?" But, then, it could be, couldn't it? No, I didn't think so.

"No," I said. "Maybe next Sunday."

"Well, how about lunch, then?" I hesitated. Why not? "We can go to Sapfat's," he said. Sapfat's was a catfish place down at the marina.

"Okay," I said.

"Great! One o'clock?"

"Sure."

I was lonesome, but was I so forlorn and desolate I'd go to lunch with this man who was frankly something of a bore? Yes. So I would get out in the weather, at least enough to ride to the marina. I put on some coffee and made myself another Bloody Mary. I had thought I wouldn't even shower today, just grub out. Maybe stay in my pajamas all day long. Now I guessed I'd have to shave my legs, since I needed to wear hose to lunch on Sunday. Knox Pitts would still be in his church clothes, which would be a blue serge suit with a red bow tie. So I needed to wear a skirt. Why hadn't I just said no to the lunch?

The perking coffee filled the kitchen with its aroma, making me hungry. I got the bagels out; I needed to go on and eat if I was having a big lunch later.

Knox Pitts tooted his horn for me when he pulled up outside.

He looked like a chunk of porous rock behind the wheel. He was a little on the heavy side and balding in a very unattractive pattern, sort of from the back forward. At least he didn't do a comb over. But he was nice enough. It would be good to have someone to talk to.

When we were seated I ordered another Bloody Mary. I had had two earlier but it had been several hours. He had an annoying habit of pursing his lips daintily when he read a menu. And I wasn't especially fond of his bow tie. It left too broad an expanse of white across his chest and belly.

"Wonder Woman," Knox said. "Flyin' in from the sky!" He winked at me.

"Yeah. But I forgot my cape."

"Did Wonder Woman wear a cape?"

"I don't know," I said. "Okay, my big shiny belt."

He had a bourbon and water. "Seriously," he said. "That was quite something else."

"Well," I said. "Just part of the show."

"And what happened afterwards. Too terrible," he said. "I heard the police had some leads. An awful thing."

"Yeah," I said.

He sipped his drink. "You really would enjoy hearing Father John's sermons," he said.

"Yeah," I said. "I don't know. Probably."

"You would. Sometimes he talks about the war, about how unjust it is and how we shouldn't be there and all that."

"Oh, really?" I said.

"Yeah. It's a moral thing, he said."

I tried to take a swig of my drink. Sapfat's put a huge stalk of celery in their Bloody Marys, so I pulled it out and laid it on the table cloth. He was watching me. "Useless," I said. I didn't want to talk about the war.

"It's your stirrer," he said.

"Like I say, useless," I said. Sapfat's made their Bloody Marys strong, and peppery, too.

"This morning he talked about William Butler Yeats," he said.

"Really?"

"Yeah. You remember that poem about some rough beast, you know."

" 'The Second Coming'," I said. I remembered it from sophomore English.

"Yeah. That one."

"What did he say about it?"

"Well, you know, about how it related to Christianity and all."

"How did he say it related?"

"How it related to the Vietnam conflict and all. I remember one thing he kept repeating. 'The best lack all conviction'."

"Yeah, I remember that," I said. "Go on."

"What?"

"Tell me the rest."

"Well," he said. He paused. He took a drink of his bourbon. "I can't give you his whole homily, Olga."

"Okay."

"Hey, I'm sorry I brought it up," he said.

"No, that's okay. I just wondered, that's all," I said. He didn't have to be so touchy. After all, I was the one with a spouse in Vietnam.

We ordered the catfish and hush-puppies and coleslaw, too heavy a meal for the middle of the day, but the choices at Sapfat's were limited. I didn't want to order just a salad; I needed more than that. But I didn't have to eat a lot. Or if I did I could get a good long nap in the afternoon.

He cocked his eyebrow and looked at me. "You're in a weird mood today," he said.

"I'm sorry. Really?"

"Yeah," he said.

"Well..." I said. I looked down and saw that my drink was almost gone. He saw me look and waved for the waitress. She brought us two fresh drinks to the table. I took a sip. This one was hotter, spicier.

"I don't know, Knox," I started. Was I really going to talk to him about anything important? "I just..." I paused.

"It's not..." He paused. "It hasn't come back, has it?"

"No, no, it's not that." Only a man would blurt that out like that.

"Is it your husband?" he asked.

"No," I said quickly. "I don't want to talk about him, Knox." He reached out and put his hand on top of mine. I moved it hastily away. "It's not Patrick. I don't know. I just feel..."

"Lonely?" he asked. I thought it was a little too hopeful.

"No," I said.

"Oh, I forgot. You've got the airplane man."

"Boyd Floyd? Pssst." I made a raspberry. I realized I was getting pretty high.

"You're not havin' an affair with him?"

"I'm not havin' an affair with anybody, Knox. I don't have the time nor the inclination nor the energy to have an affair."

"Oh." That seemed to satisfy him. He was sipping his drink and looking around the room. He didn't say anything for a minute. "I thought maybe you might want to talk about it, whatever it is," he said. "I can't believe they haven't caught the guy."

"Huh?"

"You know, the guy or whoever raped your band member. They need to catch him. It's makin' this whole town jumpy."

"It's certainly hard on people who have daughters," I said.

"Or you, what about you? You're a beautiful woman."

"No, I'm old. Besides, men don't rape women because they're good looking," I said.

"Oh? Why do men rape women?"

"I don't know. Look, do we have to talk about this?"

"No, of course not," he said.

My second Bloody Mary was almost gone. That was four before lunch. I really had to cut back. I was sliding backwards, I knew, and before I knew it I'd be in another AA meeting listening to all that boring shit. I wanted to avoid that as long as I could.

"Another?" he asked.

"Why not?" I said.

"The Rotary Club is selling smoked pork butts for Thanksgiving, and I want to get y'all one," he said.

"What?"

"You know, smoked pork. I'm gettin' one for me, and I thought I'd order one for you and your family. You've got to reserve them ahead of time. Do somethin' nice for the family of a guy in Vietnam. After all, it's not his fault he's over there." No, I thought, not entirely. But it sure as hell was his fault that he just disappeared one day, and then joined up.

"Do you want one?" he said.

"One what?"

"A smoked pork butt."

"Well, sure, I guess," I said. "You're not having turkey?"

"Turkey, too, probably," he said, grinning, and for a moment I thought he was going to make a joke about how much he always ate at Thanksgiving. But he didn't.

"Okay," I said. Every little bit helped. I thought it was incredibly generous of him. I was grateful. The boys would be okay with barbeque, but Deirdre would probably whine about not having a turkey. The vodka was really getting to my head. I was getting drunk. I wanted to get drunk. I tried to eat more of the catfish. "Order some more hush-puppies, will you?" I asked. I was going to have a headache tomorrow. It wouldn't be the first time I'd gone to work with a hangover; those days were getting more frequent again. I would have to cut back. But not right now. Goddamit.

"The thing is, you have to pick them up the week before Thanksgiving. Out at Fosque Park."

"Okay," I said. "It's awful nice of you to do that, Knox. Maybe you could come over Thanksgiving and eat some barbecue with us." Now why the hell did I say that? Because I wanted to be nice back. And because I was getting drunk.

"Well, I just might do that," he said.

My stomach was hollow and queasy at the same time. The food was bland. I really missed the spicy Cajun food we used to have in Breaux Bridge and Lafayette.

"How long before your husband comes home?" Knox asked. I wondered if I'd said something out loud.

"Why?" I asked. "I don't know, when his tour's over. I can't keep up with it."

"I just wondered."

"That's okay," I said. I wasn't sure I had the thread of the conversation. I hoped I wasn't completely slurring my words. If I was, he didn't seem to notice it. He was on his second, maybe third, bourbon and water.

"I'm sorry. I didn't mean to say something I shouldn't have," he said.

What the hell had he said? "That's okay. Forget it."

"I don't want to forget it."

"Knox..." I said. I wasn't sure what I was going to say.

"It's just that you're a beautiful woman. You're alive and real..."

"Yeah, I'm real all right. Look, cut the beautiful shit, okay?" I surprised myself. If I hadn't been so drunk I wouldn't have burst out with that.

"Oh," he said. "All right." He looked befuddled. I noticed how glassy-eyed he was becoming.

While he was paying the bill I went to the restroom. I looked at myself in the mirror. I looked drunk. I realized I'd forgotten to put on my mascara. I didn't wear it very much. I looked like hell. I couldn't pretend to be surprised to be hit on. Around town I was probably available meat, a rummy with a husband halfway around the world.

I wasn't looking forward to going home. All three of the kids were probably there: Max in his room playing his stereo, Deirdre in hers listening to the radio. Willie watching television downstairs. Or Deirdre would be in the living room and give me grief for being drunk. She'd already been telling me I ought to go back to AA. A fate worse than death. Tedious. In the extreme.

He took the highway north, toward the river bridge. The weather was fantastic. A high, crystal blue sky; you read and heard about air pollution, but in this part of the world the air was clear. Nothing but swamp gas in the atmosphere. You could smell the swamp on the other side of the river, but it was a good smell, like a freshly turned garden. From the top of the bridge span you could see for miles. The leaves were turning. Looking out over the view, I felt a sense of release, of freedom, of abandon. I was really sloshed, and I was enjoying every minute of it.

He was just driving around. I knew he kept a bottle of bourbon under the seat if I decided I wanted another drink. Needed another drink. I definitely didn't need one, but something was propelling me. I couldn't even fight it. I didn't want to resist it. I knew I was telling myself that all the shit in my life gave me every right in the world to drink all I wanted to. I began to wonder how I could bring it up. His car smelled like Old Spice. It was a nice car, a new Buick. So much cleaner than my old Caddy.

"Have you thought about what the band will do next Friday night?" he asked.

"Knox, we do the same thing every Friday night. Just a couple of new wrinkles." I wondered how thick my tongue was. I couldn't really tell. I didn't care.

"Oh," he said. "Guess I haven't paid much attention. What's your stunt gonna be?"

"I'm not gonna do a stunt. That was a one time thing." I didn't want to talk about my job. I was tired; I was rehearsing for symphonic band during the school day and practicing the marching band every afternoon. It was a long grind.

"Okay," he said.

He pulled into the Dairy Queen. "Want some ice cream?"

"No, but I tell you what," I said. "If you've still got that bottle in the car, why don't you order me a cup of ice."

"Two cups of ice," he said. "Comin' right up."

He had a fifth of Old Crow. He poured us both a stiff one. He held his up. "Here's to those who wish us well, those who don't can go to hell," he said.

"Not very Christian," I said. I bumped my cup against his.

"Not meant to be," he said.

He had driven out to Langly Bluff. He stopped and made us another drink. We sat there for a little while, watching a river boat go by. "I never get tired of seeing that," he said.

I saw about three tugs on the river. I was bombed.

"You better take me home," I said.

I didn't remember much of the drive home. The kids were there but I managed to get in and get to my room without running into one of them. I piled into my bed. I was gone in seconds.

Chapter Eleven

Chen Thien, South Vietnam
November, 1965

"I'M NOT goin' out there," Ernest Davidson said. "I'm not." He was shaking. They were leaving on another recon.

"Come on Cue-ball, what the fuck?" Mac said. He pushed Davidson roughly on the shoulder.

"Leave me alone," Davidson said.

"We're goin' out, Davidson, get a move on."

"No, I'm not goin'."

"Whattaya mean, 'you're not goin'?' I'm not invitin' you to the prom."

"No."

"Move, goddamit!" Mac said.

The other men in the platoon stood around nervously, watching Davidson and Mac.

Patrick was fearful as to where this was going. He knew Cue-ball was scared shitless; he'd told Patrick he was the previous night. He'd even told Patrick that he wasn't going back out in the jungle. His eyes had been wild and spacey. "I'll never come back," he'd said. "They can't make me go back, they have no right to make me go back." He was losing it. "I'm gonna die, I know it, if I go back out there. I'm gonna die!"

"Hey, man," Patrick had said to him, "you better chill out. You're..." Patrick had felt an affinity with him; he'd had the same thoughts and feelings himself. It shocked him to see his own secret inadequacies displayed so openly in another. They all admitted to being scared, but Patrick had been covertly certain that he was more frightened than anybody else.

Davidson had been curled up in a tight ball on his ground cloth. Patrick had felt a guilty relief that it was Cue-ball and not him. "Fuck you," Cue-ball had said.

Now Patrick stood looking at the man. In the bright daylight. Davidson was trembling. His eyes were wide. He cringed back against the wall of a lean-to. His face had turned a ghostly white. "No," he said.

"It ain"t your choice," Mac said. He grabbed Davidson by the arm.

"What's goin' on here?" a voice said. It was Peter Lott, a First Lieutenant. He had just walked up. He had ferns stuck in the netting of his helmet. The other men shrank back, giving the officer room. None of them knew him very well. He hadn't been in country very long; he still had a spit and polish look. He looked pissed off.

"Soldier won't follow orders, sir," Mac said. Davidson fell to the ground and rolled up into a tight ball, just as he'd done last night when Patrick had tried to talk with him.

"Get up, Private," the lieutenant said. Davidson just lay on the ground trembling. "What's his name?" the lieutenant asked.

"Cue-ball," Mac said.

"Get the fuck up, Cue-ball, now,' Lott said. "Get up!" Lott looked at Mac. "Move your men out, Sergeant," he said.

Mac motioned and the men fell in step in a ragged formation, trying not to look at Davidson. The platoon moved silently and awkwardly away.

"Godddamit! Motherfuck! Shit!" they heard Cue-ball scream.

They stopped and turned. Davidson was sitting with his back against the hut, his Colt M19 pointed at the officer's chest. Even though the handgun was shaking wildly, Patrick noticed how tiny the muzzle looked. Davidson pulled the trigger and the explosion was so loud and unexpected that everybody recoiled away and the lieutenant bowled over backwards, his arms flailing, his rifle slinging, his helmet going flying as he skidded and came to rest on his back, his mouth open, his eyes focused on something unseen in the sky.

There was a stunned, split second of silence before the men fell on Davidson. Patrick was first to him, grabbing the pistol out of his hand and pinning him to the ground. Davidson bucked against him, muttering, crying. He was wet with sweat; Patrick could smell his fear. Patrick held him under his weight until he lay still. Nobody said anything. The only sound was Davidson's whimpering. Patrick could not look at him. He was afraid he would see his own face, his own strained eyes looking back at him.

The business with Davidson had happened so fast that Patrick was still in a state of shock as he waded through a flooded rice field, keeping off the ridges to avoid mines, stumbling along, his mind flipping and rolling over the images of the lieutenant, the way his body was flung back and lay quivering on the ground, the gaping, wet red hole in his chest, the astonished and frozen expression still on his face. Cue-ball had flipped out, gone crazy, which did not surprise Patrick at all after last night and because he thought he himself was existing on the edge of that same insanity. There were times when he thought that in the next second he was going exactly where Cue-ball had gone, and he would flinch and close his eyes. He didn't know how he kept going. He was like an automaton. At an order from the Sergeant his body moved on its own before he could think, and when he did think, his mind resisted what his body had already done.

They were dug in later that day on the side of a low, rocky hill. The sun was going down, the sky dimming. Haskins lay back in a shallow foxhole, smoking one of his wrinkled hand-rolled. There was a droopy flower tucked through the netting on his helmet next to his Marlboros.

"What you reckon got into Cue-ball?" Haskins asked.

"He's scared shitless," Patrick said.

"Hell, I am, too," Haskins said. "Anybody out here that ain't scared ain't been payin' attention."

Patrick was quiet for a minute. "I start thinkin' about the folks back home, my kids, and it makes me scareder. I'm afraid I won't ever see them again. I can't bear to think about that."

"Get stoned," Haskins said. "It helps."

Patrick didn't fully understand why he didn't like weed. He'd always been too busy drinking to try it much back home. When he had smoked it, like with Kim Ly, it had made him feel even more paranoid and off center than he already did. But there was little booze out here, except now and then, and then not very much. He hadn't had a drink of hard liquor since his in-country R & R in Saigon. He missed it. But then he didn't miss it. There was a sameness about being here, day to day, an endless stream of sunsets and sunrises, a dull routine that lulled him into a kind of trance, with fear and terror hovering always just over his head. Suspended from his reality, like a nightmare from which he can never wake up. He took a toke off Henry's joint. He tried to relax.

Chapter Twelve

Bay Sprngs, Louisiana
November, 1965
DEIRDRE

MY MOM was riding on a fire truck down Washington Street in the Fire Prevention Parade, directing the band that was marching behind. I wanted to die. There was no reason for her to be on the truck. She could just as easily have been marching with the band, which is where she should have been. Dr. Frye, the dentist and the volunteer fire chief, was driving the truck. He had a little black mustache and was sort of humped over the wheel. It was a big joke around town that if you were in the chair and had your mouth all propped open with shit sticking in it and a fire call came in he would run off and leave you there, sometimes sitting for hours while he and the other men put out the fire. It never happened to me, but I don't doubt it.

"I didn't know your mom had volunteered," Lydia said.

"Ha," I said. Maybe she had. I could just see my mom racing to a fire in her old Cadillac.

I don't know what it was between my mom and me. It was like we were on some kind of collision course, like we were at war or something. I know part of it, maybe most of it, was my dad. She made him leave. I know there was a lot of gossip about him, but none of it was true. My dad wouldn't do any of those things. He loved me too much, for one thing. It was all her fault, I just know it. She told me he just left to be by himself for awhile, to "find himself". Shit. Anyway, we were headed to a huge total collision. And soon. She doesn't want him to come home for Thanksgiving, and she won't leave it alone.

To be honest, she hasn't been the same since she had that fucking operation. It changed her. I know it changed me. I can't look at her without thinking about her body now. I got a good look at her chest one morning when she was getting out of the shower, and it was creepy. Just one boob, and flat on the other side with this raw looking scar that ran down and around under her arm. It scared the hell out of me. I was scared for Mom, and scared for me. I didn't know it could happen to my mom. I didn't know it could happen at all. I was a woman, too.

Lydia asked me one time if I had seen it. She wanted to know what it looked like, but I told her I hadn't. I didn't want to talk with her about it. I couldn't.

And my mom was freaking out about the rapist, who she thought was still in town and just looking for another victim. If there's not a real reason to restrict me, she'll make one up. I told her that Jane McKissick put out all over town, who would rape her? But she was touchy about me even going out of the house, especially at night. She carries on about it all the time. She feels guilty about it. It's driving me crazy.

When the truck got even with where we were standing Dr. Frye turned on the siren. Everybody jumped about two feet and cried out and put their hands over their ears. It was so loud it rattled the inside of your head. He saw me standing there, so he yanked the siren, or whatever you do to it. It was for my benefit. Everybody was looking at me. They looked at my mom and then they looked at me, and I thought *Oh my God!*

The truck sat there and the band behind it played *"America The Beautiful"*. Then the fire truck and the band moved on down the street, with just snare drums tapping. Behind the band were the volunteer firemen. Some just walked, others marched briskly to the beat, exaggerating their steps like Clydesdales. They thought they were funny. Max was one of the ones just strolling along, not looking left or right. It was his first year not to be a junior fireman. He had on his red jacket. He looked bored. He was trying to look that way, I knew.

Lester Underwood and Chris Carter went by. They were the junior firemen this year. They grinned at us.

Lydia and I had not talked about her kissing Lester. Maybe some things are just best left unsaid. Lester and I were progressing, I guess you could say. And I was pretty pleased with that. I didn't want things to get complicated again. I was anxious for me and Lester to take the next step, whatever that might be.

Old man Tucker Carpenter came by sputtering along in his Model T. The only time he ever drove it was in a parade. People laughed when he came by. I didn't see what was so funny about an old car.

Some Brownies went by, and some Girl Scouts. I was never in either one of those. Then came the 4-H Club, some farm kids. A yellow school bus with the football team jerked along, guys slouched in the seats shooting birds to their friends as they went by. The Harvest Queen, Lisa Bramblett, was riding in a Ford convertible. Lisa, the eleventh grade queen, would be crowned at the Harvest Festival, because the eleventh grade had made the most money with car washes and candy sales. I think Lisa went out with Max one time. Jane McKissick probably had, too, but I wasn't about to ask him about it.

Mr. Rayford Means's church, the Dogwood Baptist, always had a float, a pickup truck with streamers on it, and it came slowly down the street. Some kids were in the back holding up signs. One said W W J D? Another had flames painted on it and said GO TO CHURCH, THE DEVIL WILL GET YOU. Brother Means was driving the truck, beeping the horn, grinning. I hadn't seen him since that day he acted so strange to Lester and me. All you could see through the window of the truck were his gray flat top and his pale, vacant blue eyes. Lydia snorted when she saw him. Even sitting behind the wheel he looked like he was holding his breath, holding his stomach in.

"What make you wear your pants so tight?" I said. Lydia laughed. Brother Means saw her laughing.

"Come to church!" he called out cheerfully.

"In your dreams," Lydia said, and we both laughed some more. He had no idea what she said and he kept on smiling as he drove on.

A dump truck rumbled by. It was a sign the parade was over.

"Let's go to the D. Q." Lester Underwood said at my elbow.

He had on a jacket and was sweating. It was almost hot. Indian Summer. Chris Carter was with him. He was looking at Lydia. Chris had a crush on Lydia. Every boy in school had a crush on Lydia.

"I love a parade," Lydia said.

"Yeah," Chris said, and Lydia rolled her eyes and winked at me and laughed.

"You buyin'?" she asked.

"Yeah," Chris said.

We fell in step down the sidewalk, me walking with Lester, the two of them following. Little kids darted around all over the place. One little boy almost ran into Lydia. "Ooops," she said, and the little kid stared at her with this frightened look on his face. She was so pretty. He ran into the park.

We took our cones to the park. The crowded Dairy Queen must have been selling a lot of ice cream that day because it was runny, not completely set, and melted almost faster than we could get it to our mouths. Lester and Chris got theirs all over their shirts.

"We ought to get our money back," Chris said, but none of us moved to go and challenge them. We found a bench near the gold fish pond. We sat there licking our fingers. Amy Newhouser went by. She hung out with Willie sometime. I think she liked him. She was a cute girl.

I was highly suspicious that my mom was running around with Boyd Floyd, and I knew that if my dad knew about it he'd kill him. My dad told me in his letter that he loved my mom and was going to make everything up to her and to us when he came home. He said he was going to make us proud of him. Lydia was prattling on about something or other and I was sitting there with tears in my eyes. I don't know what I did to deserve all this. It was in that same letter that my dad said he'd be home Thanksgiving, and I believed him. He always kept his word.

"Okay, which one of you assholes raped old Jane?" Lydia asked.

"Don't say that," Lester said.

"I was just trying to be funny," Lydia said.

"Don't joke about something like that."

"Okay," she said.

I hated that what had happened made me look at people different, even Lester. Boys, I mean. I didn't seriously think Lester would do something like that, it just made me think about him more, maybe in a deeper way, which I guess is not altogether a bad thing.

We walked over to Lydia's house. Her folks were in New Orleans for the day. We sat out around their pool and Lydia got us cokes from the kitchen.

"The Bulldogs are gonna stomp Vidalia Friday night," Chris said.

"Shit," I said. "Who cares?"

"Your folks got any beer, Lydia?" Lester asked.

"They don't drink beer," Lydia said.

"Well, liquor then."

"They would kill me."

"How're they gonna know? Just put a little water in, they'll never know the difference," Lester said.

"Ha," Lydia said. "My mom would know when she walked in the door."

"Your mom is hot," Chris said.

"Pervert," Lydia said.

"No, really..."

"Shut the fuck up!" Lydia snapped. Her mom was as beautiful as she was. She had a perfect figure.

"Okay," Chris said. "I just..."

"Shut up about it, okay?" Lydia said.

"Mrs. Founier looked good on that firetruck," Lester said.

"Don't you start," I said.

"I only said she looked good. God, it was a compliment."

You could see right through boys. They were an open book.

"Why don't we change the subject?" Lydia said.

"Okay," Chris said. "The Bulldogs..."

"Fuck the Bulldogs," Lydia said.

"All right. You pick the subject, then."

Nobody said anything for a minute. You could hear the pump burbling the water in the pool. It was sparkly and clean in the afternoon sunlight. It made me thirsty. I took a good drink of my coke.

"It's hot as hell," Chris said. "And it's almost gettin' to be Thanksgiving!" He had his sweater draped over the back of his chair.

"Indian Summer," I said.

"Wooo, Wooo, Wooo," he said, popping his palm against his mouth.

"Why don't we have some, Lydia?" I said.

"What?"

"Some drinks."

"They would kill me," she said.

"Come on, Lydia," Lester said.

She went into the house and came back out with a half filled quart of Old Forrester Bourbon. She poured a little in each of our glasses. "Kill, as in dead," she said.

We tested the drinks. I could feel the nutty bite. It was the same stuff that Lester had had that Friday night. I liked it. It cut the sweetness of the coke.

"Nice," Chris said.

I felt wicked and prickly. Lester told this joke about a little boy named Little Johnny Fuckerfaster that didn't make any sense. It wasn't even funny. I tried to think of a joke but couldn't. I didn't know any, really. The whiskey made me feel laid back and relaxed. Warm in my head.

I don't know how many drinks we had, just sitting and talking about nothing. I didn't know I was getting drunk until I got up to go in to the bathroom. I wasn't drunk, just head-swimmy. When I got back out and sat down they all looked at me and then at my drink. I could see it was fuller than when I'd left. They'd topped it up. So I just sipped.

Lydia and Chris were arguing about something. I didn't make any effort to follow it. I was just thinking about my father, over there waiting to come home. And it seemed to me that nothing in the whole world was fair. My mom was insane. My dad was right to go and defend our country. That's why he left. I don't care what anybody said.

I don't know how much time passed. Lydia and Chris were kissing, and Lester moved over and sat on a glider with me. He kissed me. We kissed for a while, French kissing. The sun was beating down and it got hot on the patio. I was totally sweating, afraid I was starting to stink. Maybe that's what put the idea in my head. I whispered in his ear, "Let's go swimmin'."

"We don't have any swimsuits," he whispered back. He leaned back and looked at me. I didn't say anything. He just kept looking at me, his face puzzled. "I bet Lydia's got some that would fit you," he whispered. "And her old man's probably got a couple of 'em lying around." I just stared at him with what felt like a lop-sided smile. "Don't you think?" he asked. He was still whispering, and I still didn't say anything. I bet a whole minute went by, with us just frozen there, looking into each other's eyes. Finally, I could see it dawning on him. His eyes lit up and he broke into this wide grin. "You mean...?"

"Yeah," I said.

All of a sudden I was up announcing that I was going swimming.

"It's November!" Lydia said. "You'll freeze your ass off."

"It's hot," I said.

I peeled off my shirt and pushed my peddle-pushers down around my ankles and stepped out of them. I knew I had to do it fast or I wouldn't do it. And I wanted to. It was like it wasn't really happening, that it was just a dream. I was excited; my heart was racing around inside my chest. I stood there in my bra and panties. All of a sudden I thought, what if they think I'm ugly? I realized that if I kept on and did this, and Lydia followed suit, there she would be with her perfect body, and the boys would be looking at her and not at me. Their eyes were bugging out. They were looking at me plenty right then. I thought they were going to faint. I knew I looked great. I guess it was the liquor, but I didn't care if my hips were a little too fat and my boobs weren't as big as Lydia's. I thought what the hell.

"Damn," Lester said.

I calmly unsnapped my bra and rolled down my panties. The air felt cooler on my naked skin where my clothes had been. I strolled to the diving board and walked up on it. "Jesus Christ," Chris said. His mouth was hanging open. I paused there a minute, letting them get a good long look at me. Then I dove in.

The water was so shockingly cold it took my breath away. I came up and dog paddled over to a ladder and grabbed hold. I was gasping for breath. My teeth were chattering and my lips were trembling. I hoped they weren't blue. My hair was plastered all over my head. I hoped I didn't look too silly.

The three of them were just standing there looking.

"Chick, chick, chick," I clucked. "Y'all are chicken!"

Lester and Chris acted like their clothes were on fire, struggling so to get them off. They both wore white jockeys. Lester was the first to get to the diving board, and I noticed his dick was sticking straight out, a real boner. Chris's was littler, dangling. They dove in, one by one. They swam around, splashing water at each other and at me.

"Come on in, Lydia," Lester said.

She didn't move. I felt a little stab of self-consciousness, then. Abruptly, I felt bashful, shy. She was going to leave me in here with these boys. Shit. It would be just like her. Dammit. I started to urge her to join us. Then I just didn't say anything.

"Chicken," Lester said.

Lester just wanted to see her naked, I thought. I was thinking that I never should have started this.

Lydia stood up. We were all looking at her. It was like I was in some kind of zone. I could feel my pulse in my ears. Lester had swum over to me and was treading water right behind me. I thought of his dick, sticking out under the water. Lydia took off her shirt, then her slacks. Her bra. Her panties. She walked naked toward the diving board, sort of drifting along. Lydia had a knock-out figure, nice boobs already. She had a nice crop of black pubic hair, where mine was a kind of tannish blonde. She stood on the board for a minute, like she was posing. Then she dove in.

We swam around for a little while, splashing each other and laughing. The water seemed to get warmer. The boys tried to get us to have a water fight in the shallow end, but we wouldn't. We laughed. We knew they just wanted us to stand up so they could get a better look at our boobs.

The boys feasted their eyes on Lydia when she got out to go in and get some towels. She looked fantastic, the water slick on her butt. I decided I'd wait and be last to get out. The whiskey was still heating me. Fueling me. First Chris and then Lester dove down and swam around me and I knew they had their eyes open looking at me underwater. I didn't give a crap. I even started to kind of look forward to getting out and having the boys watch me, either from the deck or still in the pool. It didn't make any difference. I could give them a show. I would probably have goose bumps and my nipples would be stiff and hard, but I didn't care. The boys would see the water shiny on my butt, which was every bit as pretty as Lydia's. I didn't have to be told that. I knew that. I just didn't want to be getting out right next to her.

Lydia came back out with a stack of towels. She had on a white terry cloth robe.

"Hey, no fair," Lester said.

"I don't want to get you too excited, Lester," she said.

The three of us were treading water. "You first," Chris said to me.

"No, I'll wait on y'all," I said.

"Oh, come on, Dee," Lester said. Their lips were blue, shaking like a leaf in a breeze. I knew mine must be, too. I swam over to the ladder. I climbed up. I knew exactly how I looked from behind. I could feel the water, warm now in the colder air, sliding down and dripping from my body. Lydia held out a towel for me and I wrapped it around me. We sat down at the table. I gulped the last of my drink, rubbing my skin with the towel.

"Throw us a towel," Chris said.

"Come and get it," Lydia said.

"Awww, come on," he said.

"What's the matter?" I said. "You chicken?"

Lester laughed. "All right, you asked for it," he said.

They swam over to the ladder and climbed up, Lester first. He still had his boner. Chris followed and he, too, now had a hard on.

Lydia and I got a good look. They took towels and started to dry off. They didn't seem to want to look us in the eye. I thought that was a hell of a time to get shy. They seemed to be trying to hide their boners from us.

"Aren't you nice and modest," Lydia said.

They rubbed themselves vigorously. Then they pulled on their jockey shorts.

"Shit, it's cold now," Lester said. He was shivering all over. Their jockeys were pushed out in front.

We watched them put their clothes back on. Lydia looked at me and smiled and winked. She really was my best friend. It was like we were already women and we were, at that moment, miles ahead of the two of them. They sat there at the table, their hair matted to their heads, and I realized that mine must look like that, too. Lydia, with her new short haircut, looked great.

We let them watch us get dressed. Lydia kept bumping and grinding like a stripper. The boys couldn't take their eyes off Lydia. I mean, they looked at me, too, when my turn came.

"That was fun," Lester said, when we were all dried off and dressed.

"Yeah," I said. I had never seen a boner before, and I still hadn't touched one. With my hand. I could have, right then and there. If I'd been alone with Lester I might have. I might have anyway if I'd had just a little bit more to drink.

Then I had the weirdest feeling that somebody was watching us through the privacy fence. I didn't see anybody, I just knew. You know how you can sense something like that? I sat there wondering if I was drunk, or if my mom hadn't scared me so I was imagining perverts all over the place. But it was so real. It's really eerie how something like that rape–that maybe wasn't even a rape at all–can make you all jumpy.

"I think we had a peeper," I said.

"No way," Lester said. "Did you see him?"

"No. I just sensed him."

"You're just spooked. Anyway, he sure got a show," Lester said, and he and Chris laughed. Lydia didn't laugh. She just looked at me.

Then she took the bottle back inside and brought a bottle of Listerine out and we all washed our mouths out and spit in the shrubbery. The Listerine burned worse than the whiskey. We sat in the sun and let our hair dry. When Lydia's folks got home I could tell they knew we'd been in the pool and were pissed about it by the way they paused before they'd say something to us, like pause "Hey, kids," like there was something more they wanted to say. They knew we'd been up to something. It was like they didn't really want to know but thought they should want to know.

I was looking at Lydia's dad. He was very good looking. But so was Lydia's mom. She looked like a model. She had been on the tennis team at Tulane. They were the only people in town, besides my mother, who pronounced my name "De-er-dra." Everybody else said "Deedra."

"How was the parade?" Lydia's mom asked.

"Great," I said, too quick and too loud, and I realized that I could still feel the whiskey. Everybody was looking at me. "Well, you know," I said.

"I'm sure it was," Lydia's mom said.

Lydia's dad headed into the house. "You want a drink, honey?" he asked, and she said sure. We all sneaked quick looks at each other. She followed him inside.

"Did you water the bottle?" Lester whispered.

"I forgot," Lydia said.

We sat there all tensed up until we saw them crossing the living room to the den with their drinks in their hands.

"Parents are stupid," Lydia said. "They never notice anything."

"They knew we'd been in the pool," Lester said.

"Yeah," I said. "But they didn't want to know that they knew."

I heard an airplane droning like an insect overhead. It looked like Boyd Floyd's little plane. I watched it moving across the sky, headed south toward the municipal airport.

We are not having turkey. I am so furious I could die. And I've had a pretty good indication now that my mother is a whore. I went with her out to Fosque Park to pick up the barbecue, that the Rotary

Club was selling, and she told me that that pervert Mr. Pitts paid for it. As a "gift." My ass.

"He wanted to do something nice for our family," she said on the way home.

"Why?" I asked.

"Because he's a nice man," she said, meaning unlike my father that she hates.

"But I don't even hardly know him," I said.

We drove along in silence for awhile. "Is it charity?" I said, and she cut her eyes over at me.

"Of course not, Dee," she said. "He just wanted to give us something for Thanksgiving."

"I'll bet," I said.

"Why not?" she asked.

"Why not indeed?" I said, exactly like I'd heard this woman in a movie say it.

She didn't respond to that. I think she shrugged a little. "Mr. Pitts is probably the one who raped Jane McKissick," I said.

"Don't joke about that, Dee," she said.

"I'm not joking," I said.

She shrugged again. She had on very dark lipstick. I just watched her drive. "Have you heard anything further from your dad?" she asked. She asked it real casually, like she was asking me if I'd heard it was going to rain. Thanksgiving was coming up.

"No," I said. I hadn't, but I could tell she thought I was probably lying.

"Well..." she said, and sighed this big sigh.

"He'll be here, Mom," I said.

"Okay," she said. She was really focused on the road. I looked at the way her hair curled around her ear. She had thick hair, a deep mahogany brown. She had it cut sort of medium short. Lots of boys said she was hot. She had nice boobs. One of them was false, of course. Which was something I guess I would always have trouble getting used to.

"I've invited Mr. Pitts to have Thanksgiving barbecue with us," she said.

That shocked me totally out of my mind. How could she do that? "You can't, Mom," I said.

"I already have," she said.

"But...but Dad..." I sputtered. I was mad as hell.

"Mr. Pitts did a nice thing for us, Dee," she said. "It's as simple as that."

"Mom!" I said. "God!" I could feel the tears stinging my eyes. "You can't have that pervert over. You're married!"

"It's not like that. He's just a family friend. That's all."

"Daddy'll kill him when he gets home."

"No, he won't. There are just some things you don't understand, Dee."

"I understand that plenty!"

"Watch yourself!"

"You watch yourself!"

"That's enough. Just stop it!"

I thought she was going to wreck the car. So I sat there with my arms crossed over my chest and stared out at the road.

She took a deep breath. "At this point, Dee," she said slowly, "it is very unlikely that your dad will be coming home for Thanksgiving. I would know about it if he were. He's not coming home."

"Well, don't act so gleeful about it."

"I'm not gleeful," she said. "It's just a fact."

"You are gleeful! You hate him," I said.

"And what's this 'pervert' shit?" she said.

"He's a pervert to try to take another man's wife," I said.

"He's not trying to take me. Now listen to me. He's just a nice man we know who wants to do something nice for us. That's it. I don't want to hear any more."

"You're committing adultery," I said. And then I started crying.

"Oh, for God's sakes," she said.

" 'He's just my friend'," I said, mocking her voice. " 'He's just my friend that I fuck for barbecue!'."

"Goddamit, Deirdre, I'm warning you. You're gonna be so grounded you won't believe it."

We drove along for a while. I was sniffling.

Then she dropped the real bomb. "I've invited Boyd Floyd, too."

I know my mouth fell open. "Are you kidding?" I said. She was crazy. Plain fucking crazy. Our house at Thanksgiving full of perverts and rapists and adulterers! My dad was going to have to walk in on that? I wanted to cry. So I did. Hard.

"I wanted you to be prepared," she said, louder, over my sobbing. I let it go pretty good. "Because it'll be nice to have company at Thanksgiving. And your dad is very likely not coming home. You need to understand that, Dee."

I cried all the way home. Maybe I put it on a little heavy. I didn't want to push it too far. I knew I'd be grounded all to hell and back.

When we got home I put the heavy butt in the freezer in the basement. Why don't they come up with something besides "butt" for that piece of meat, that you're going to put in your mouth? Then I washed my face. Then I called Lydia.

"You won't believe what she's gone and done this time," I said.

"Got drunk and slept with Mr. McFarland?" Lydia asked. Mr. McFarland was the janitor at the school. He was about a hundred years old.

"She invited that pervert Mr. Pitts over for Thanksgiving dinner," I said.

"Who's he?" she asked.

"The banker. You know."

"That guy? With the hair?"

"Yeah. He bought us this big chunk of barbecued pork and she invited him over to help us eat it. And the other guy, too. The pilot. We're not even having a turkey."

"I hate turkey," Lydia said.

"You're not gonna be here. My dad loves the drumsticks."

"Your dad's really gonna be there?" she asked.

"Well, yes. Maybe. I don't know." I hadn't told her about it, had I? I didn't think I'd told anyone but Mom and Max. I hadn't even told Willie. I was afraid to tell anybody. Tears started up in my eyes and I didn't know why.

"Cool," Lydia said. I just hung up.

I went up to my room and cut on the radio. It was a little pink clock radio that my dad had given me when I was nine. It was tuned to a country station. Patsy Cline. *"It wasn't God who made honky tonk angels"*. Lydia and I sometimes called ourselves honky tonk angels.

I stretched out on the bed. I still had on my penny loafers and my mom would croak if she saw me on the bedspread with shoes. I didn't give a flying fuck. She could croak. It was my bedspread. I wanted to cry, but I didn't know exactly why. I couldn't figure out what one thing in all the shit I had to endure I should cry about. I heard my mom downstairs talking on the phone. I didn't know where my brothers were. I felt tucked away. I didn't have to move. Nobody could make me move.

My mother was a whore. Mr. Pitts was a doofus, but at least he was better than Boyd Floyd. He wasn't a total redneck. But that hair. Like a clown I saw in the circus one time.

I wished everything would just go away. Just fly off and leave me there lying on my bed. That was not going to happen. I imagined that I could feel myself moving with the earth. I think you could feel it moving if you just concentrated and made yourself more aware of it. Because it was moving, unless that was a lie, too.

I don't know how long I lay there. I might even have dozed off. Pretty soon I got up. I swiped an Archie comic book out of Willie's room and took it out on the back porch. It was chilly but sunny. It was a corny story about Veronica and Betty having some fuss over something. I would die if anybody saw me reading an Archie comic book.

Anybody but Willie. He was walking in the back gate. Just sauntering in, like his mind was a million miles away. He'd probably be pissed that I had his comic book. Let him. He walked up onto the porch. He had on baggy brown corduroy pants, that I think he wore every day. They probably stank. I didn't think he'd even noticed me sitting there.

"I like Mickey Mantle and Willie Mays, too," he said, as if he was still carrying on some conversation with someone else. "Both. You can like them both."

"So?" I said. Willie was a freak for baseball. During the season, he read the statistics every morning before anybody else got the paper. I'd bet he could tell you the batting average of every major league player.

"So nothing," he said. "Whatcha doin?"

"Reading."

"I can see that," he said. I waited for him to say something about my having his comic book, but he didn't. He just stood there, looking off out into the back yard. I looked back at the book: a whole page with Archie's face on it, big freckles. I had lost track of the thread of the silly story.

I looked at my brother. He was getting taller. He'd probably be as tall as Max, as tall as my dad. Thinking that made me start missing my dad all over again. I wanted to hit something, to take my fist and hit something. Maybe I wanted to hit my mom. I remembered being shocked and scared when the first thing I wanted to do when I was told about my mom's cancer was to hit her, just haul off and slap her. I am crazy, I know that. Willie was just gazing out into the back yard like his mind was ten million miles away. I wondered if he missed our dad. We never talked about it. Willie told me one day, right after Daddy got sent overseas, that he hated him. He had never mentioned him again to me.

I let the Archie comic drop to the floor next to my chair. Willie noticed it and then looked back away. He didn't comment on it. How could a little kid be so lost in thought? Willie was deep. I loved him. He stood there for a long time. Then he asked me, "Dee, do you ever get scared?"

"Of what?"

"You know, that guy. Whoever it was who attacked that girl."

"Don't be scared, Willie," I said, which was like something my mom would say. When somebody is scared, it doesn't do any good to tell them not to be. "He's probably in Cuba or somewhere by now."

"If Daddy was here, I wouldn't be so scared," he said. "He'd take care of us."

"He would, Willie. He's comin' home."

He pointed and said, "Look."

I looked where he was pointing. On a wilted sunflower that looked like it was just about finished for the winter, next to the back fence, sat a bright yellow butterfly. It was like it was poised there, looking back at us. It was probably the last butterfly we'd see that year.

"Nice," I said. I thought he might get his net and try to catch it, but he didn't. We watched the butterfly until it lifted off the dying flower and fluttered over the back fence.

"Okay," he said. He stood very still.

After a bit he started through the back door. He glanced at the comic book on the floor of the porch. "Don't let that get rained on," he said.

"I won't," I said to his back as he went on into the kitchen.

Chapter Thirteen

Near Chen Thien, South Vietnam
November, 1965

PATRICK TRUDGED across another flooded rice field. Haskins was moving across down to his right, leaving a muddy wake. It was early morning and Patrick was already thirsty; gnats prickled at his eyelids. He swatted mosquitos away from his face. He had been in Nam now so long he had lost track of time. He had not had a shower in days. His body stank and itched, his balls burned. Each early morning, when he jerked awake, he could not be sure if he had slept at all. His eyes would be scratchy and stuck together. He'd developed a painful hemorrhoid.

He kept going across the rice paddy, putting one foot deliberately in front of the other. The high sun was in his eyes. He thought he saw the glint of sunlight off metal down to his right, at the edge of the field, and then he saw movement. He froze. Two Viet Cong, hidden partially behind a stand of rubber trees. "Git down," he yelled, and he hit the grimy water face first and squirmed up behind a ridge, just as he heard the popping of their AK-47s. He hoped that Haskins had made it down. Their rounds zinged over his head. When the firing stopped he peered over the ridge, keeping behind the grass that grew there. He could see the Viet Cong clearly, one of them gesturing toward the field, toward where he was. I am a sitting duck, Patrick thought. This is it. What the hell am I going to do? He scrunched down behind the ridge. To jump up and run for the cover of the jungle would be suicide. Maybe there were only the two of them, which gave him a chance.

He peeked through the grass. The paddy stank so sharply of the animal and human shit that had been used to fertilize it that Patrick thought he might pass out. He had never smelled anything so terrible in his life. He gagged. As he was watching he heard Haskins's M-16 rat tat tat tat and the Cong hit the ground. He heard them chattering away in their moronic language. Who could understand such chickenshit gibberish? He hated them. They were like some crude animal shaped vaguely like a human being. He hoped to be able to put a round in each of their heads.

He got his rifle up on the ridge, hoping there was no fucking mine there right in front of his face, and sighted down the barrel. He could just barely make out one of their pith helmets, where they were crouched in the bushes. He squeezed off a round and the hat went flying. They were squawking like a bunch of startled turkeys. Motherfuckers. He fired again, and they returned fire, the bullets whacking into the ridge and raising spurts of water in front of him. He heard Haskins's firing. One of the Cong had stood up and was spraying the field with his rifle, and Patrick saw him go down. Haskins had gotten him!

The other Viet Cong, bareheaded now, tried to run, and Patrick got on one knee and aimed carefully, catching him in the middle of the back. He crashed face first into the rubber trees. Haskins fired one more time, and then there was quiet. There must have been just the two of them. Patrick stood up. So did Haskins. Both of them had slimy water and shit running down their fronts.

Patrick saw several other men in their squad come out of the jungle at the north edge of the rice field. One of them was Mac. He motioned for Patrick and Haskins to get low and move on toward where the dead Viet Cong were.

Patrick came up out of the field, stepping carefully. The fucking Viet Cong scattered mines everywhere. There was never any pattern to them. They could be anywhere. You could never stop being aware of them, or you'd be going home without legs or worse.

Patrick found a small bamboo bunker, overlooking the field. Two men had been there five minutes ago, alive, watchful. Now it was still and quiet, incredibly empty. Haskins eased up beside him. "Whew, man, you stink," Haskins said.

"You, too," Patrick said.

"What this that stink so bad?" Haskins asked.

"It's Gook shit, man, what you think it is?"

"Gook shit? Awww, naw." Haskins frowned and looked like he wanted to throw up.

"It's awful."

"You got that right."

The two men inspected the bunker, looking around. They found a captured US Thompson submachine gun. Jammed. "Look at this mother," Haskins said, holding it up.

"Don't pick that up, Haskins!" Mac said, coming up. Haskins quickly put it down.

"Goddam, you one lucky Spade that that thing wasn't booby trapped. Don't be pickin' up shit like that, okay?"

"Yes sir," Haskins said.

"Don't call me sir!" Mac said. The Sergeant looked around the small encampment, at the low bamboo wall and the fan palms used for shade and camouflage. "Go find the gooks, Founier," Mac said, "And make sure they're dead. And be careful. These fuckers booby trap their own selves."

Patrick pushed through the rubber trees. His blood pressure must have been returning to normal. He felt as though he were coming down from a high. But he hadn't run. He hadn't even thought about it. He'd just gone on instinct. Maybe that was the secret. He came upon the body of the dead Viet Cong, the bareheaded one he had shot. He lay sprawled face down in the grass, bandoliers crossed across his back. He wore a stained, blood-soaked T shirt and loose black cotton pants cut off raggedly at the knees. His hair was a shiny black buzz cut on his small head. With the toe of his soggy jungle boot Patrick turned him over. "Goddam," he muttered aloud. It was a boy. Not more than fourteen or fifteen years old. Patrick stood staring at the boy's peaceful face, his eyes closed, his face relaxed as though embraced in a placid, tranquil sleep.

Oh Jesus, Patrick thought. He was going to cry. Jesus. I'm not gonna cry over any dead fuckin' gook! No way, man. He stood there with hot tears flooding his eyes. The boy looked like Kim Ly, her delicate porcelain skin burned by the sun. The boy's mouth looked as soft and sweet as hers. He wanted to kiss it. I am losing my fucking mind, like Cue-ball, I am losing my fucking mind. He was astonished to realize he had an erection. He heard Haskins or someone approaching, so he held his rifle over his erection to hide it. As he stood there looking down at the face of the motionless boy, stilled for the rest of eternity, he saw Willie's face superimposed over it. Oh My God. He could not hide his tears from whoever was pushing up to him, so he didn't try.

"You okay, Founier?" Mac said.

"Yeah."

An ant crawled across the boy's cheek. Patrick watched it move slowly down toward the corner of his mouth. As Patrick watched, the ant disappeared into the crack between his lips. The boy didn't flinch. He didn't move. Of all the millions of people on the earth, Patrick had become connected in that moment only to this one, this strange boy – connected in death, at Patrick's hand – a random, chance encounter that altered both their lives forever. Maybe you shouldn't think about that; maybe you couldn't think about that.

"The bunker's secure," Mac said. "We'll take ten for a smoke."

"Okay," Patrick said, his voice shaky and tight. He had been holding his breath.

Patrick followed the Sergeant back through the tangle to the Viet Cong bunker. The squad was racked back, smoking, a couple of them eating bananas they'd picked.

"Y'all wasted those motherfuckers," Gerald Abbott said when Patrick sat down.

Abbott's words echoed hollowly in Patrick's ears, as if he were in some enormous empty church. "We did, didn't we?" Patrick said. He could barely hear his own words.

"We each got us one," Haskins said.

"I'm puttin' you both in for a fuckin' silver star," Mac said.

Everybody laughed and Patrick felt his tight anxiety begin to ease. He realized he'd been tensing his muscles; they were starting to ache.

"You fuckers smell like a privy," Marvin Whitehead said.

Patrick pulled off his soaked jungle boots and began to wipe them against palm fronds. He needed to occupy himself, do something mundane, anything. He would never get the boots clean. His legs were stinging. He pulled his pants legs up. There were four leeches on his right calf, three on the left. "Goddam!" he said. Henry had several on his legs, too.

"Shit, you can't even see 'em on that dark meat," Alvin Cosper said. He laughed.

"Git 'em on you, white boy, won't be so funny," Henry said.

"When it rains, it pours," Marvin Whitfield said, handing Patrick a packet of salt. Patrick sprinkled a liberal dose on each leech and handed the packet to Henry. The leeches started to fall away one by one, each making a little sucking sound before it dropped in the dirt. Patrick ground them under a rock. They left little puckered red spots on his skin that had already started to itch. Patrick lit a Lucky. His hands were shaking. He leaned back and tried to relax.

"Man, I hate it about Davidson," McChesney said.

"Shit. The fucker's goin home," Seelbach said.

"Goin' home? What the hell you talkin' about, Nazi?" Mac asked. "Section eight."

"Jesus," Mac said, laughing. "He's gonna be court marshaled for murder."

"All the same, he'll get outta this shit-hole."

"Yeah, great!" McChesney said. "Man, I envy him!"

"I'm just sayin'," Seelbach said.

"Yeah, you're just sayin'," Jason Morrison chimed in.

Patrick leaned back, smoking, with his eyes closed. He was hearing the men, not really listening. He tried to force the image of the dead boy from his consciousness. He heard Davidson's name. It shook him. He knew he might be next. There was just a thin, filmy veil between the familiar part of himself he had lived with all his life and some terrifyingly unknown equation that was threatening to emerge in his own brain. It was there, shadowy and elusive and as persistent as an enemy soldier.

That night, back at the compound, Patrick and Haskins sat smoking and talking quietly, leaning back against some sandbags.

"The one I killed, Henry, was a boy," Patrick said. "I don't think he was even as old as my oldest son."

"This is some shit," Haskins said. He stretched his legs out and sighed.

Patrick could not stop thinking about the boy. He couldn't get the stilled semblance of his innocent face out of his mind. Innocent, my ass. He was trying to put some hot lead in your gut. He wouldn't hesitate. Patrick couldn't allow himself to forget that. He wondered if the boy would have paused and looked at him if he'd been the one dead. Or just spit on him and walked on. The speculation intrigued Patrick; he'd never really thought about anything like that before. Actually picturing himself dead. That's what war made you do. It was more than just being scared. It was different. It was hard to force his mind onto it. He saw in his mind's eye the boy's face and he could see his own visage in it, his nose, his mouth, his eyes.

"Did you look at the one you killed?" he asked Henry.

"Hell no. I didn't want to see him."

"I wish I hadn't."

"I coulda told you that."

Asshole, why didn't you then? Patrick thought angrily. Who the hell was he mad at? Nobody. Himself. He thought again that he might be close to losing it. That's what this shit does to you: if it doesn't kill you it drives you insane.

"That's what we're here for, ain't it?" Patrick asked. "To kill other men, that we never even knew existed until they're dead?"

"You're thinkin' too much, Pappy. You can't think about it. You got to just do it." Patrick drew on his cigarette, the red coal on the end brightening the lower part of his face. "You think about it too much, it'll drive you nuts," Henry went on.

"Yeah. Well, you go nuts then you can section 8 out."

"Shit, man. Who needs it? You want to spend the rest of this goddam war in a fuckin' army mental hospital? No, thank you sir. Not me. I ain't thinkin' about it!"

"I don't know how you keep from it, Henry," Patrick said.

"Well, I can't tell you how, I can just say don't."

Patrick didn't sleep much that night. He lay awake, his eyes wide open, listening to the scurrying of the animals back in the banana trees and the buzzing of the insects. If he closed his eyes he saw the dead boy. He was troubled by the memory of the erection he'd gotten, baffled by it, dazed by his sudden surprising compulsion to kiss the dead lips. He feared that deep down inside he was some terrible pervert. He felt unmoored; he was the dead one, floating around in hell, and the beautiful Viet Cong soldier – he cringed with revulsion that his own mind called the boy beautiful – was alive and observing him as he lay there. I am losing it, he thought, I am losing it. Just like Davidson. But I didn't run. At least I didn't run.

Chapter Fourteen

Bay Springs, Louisiana
November, 1965
OLGA

THE WOMAN in charge of the AA meeting was named Theresa Hill. I didn't want to be there. The smell of stale cigarette smoke and scalded coffee was familiar and overwhelming. Patrick and I had both gone to AA a bunch of times in the past and it never lasted. I don't think either one of us ever really wanted to quit drinking, to tell you the truth. The meeting was in the basement of the Episcopal Church and Deirdre was in an Alateen meeting in a Sunday School room down the hall.

Deirdre was very concerned about my drinking. I had come to the meeting for her, because she kept after me. And I was worried about her. She was still convinced Patrick was coming home for Thanksgiving. I figured she was frightened about the rape and would feel better if her dad were home. Anyhow, going to a meeting together was a chance for the two of us to get out; I planned to have another talk with her after the meeting.

Theresa Hill was leading us in the AA pledge. She had her hand over her heart, as if it was the Pledge of Allegiance. To some of these people it was. I had promised Theresa I would speak tonight. She had begged me. The same people talked over and over again, the same stories, the same tired old cliches. It was not a big group, not nearly as big as the one in Breaux Bridge. I guess I needed a meeting from time to time, even though I found them tedious in the extreme. I really needed to cut back on the drinking, I knew that. The truth of the matter was I knew I needed to quit again, but I didn't want to. Not right then. Not with things like they were. God knows, I needed something. I knew how hard it was to quit. The idea of living the rest of my life without a drink was terrifying. It was inconceivable. I might as well be dead. It would be easier that way.

I had scribbled a few notes on the back of a power bill. I wanted to get on with it. I felt like I'd be meeting some kind of obligation, paying some dues, and then I could relax for awhile. The boys didn't seem to be bothered by how much I drank. But then they weren't bothered by much of anything. They seemed to be able to deal easily with everything that came along. Except it was hard to know what was in Willie's mind sometimes; he kept so much to himself. My coffee in the styrofoam cup was getting tepid. It was awful coffee. I hadn't had any really good coffee since we'd left Breaux Bridge.

I went up to the front of the room. I looked out over the scraggly crowd. They all knew who I was. There was little anonymity here for me. Everybody knew who the band director who jumped out of an airplane was.

"My name is Olga Founier," I said. "And I'm an alcoholic."

"Hello Olga," they murmured, not entirely in unison. About half of them were a little drunk. I knew that from experience. There were a couple of first timers with startled, frozen grins on their faces, scared and nervous to be in a room with a bunch of drunks.

"I want to stop drinking, but I can't," I said tentatively. They all looked at me expectantly. "I mean, I just don't think I've hit rock bottom yet."

"Don't bullshit yourself, lady," said a man in the back of the room. He had on overalls.

"Okay, mister, I don't want to stop drinking," I said. "You're right. Who am I kidding? I have no intention of quitting the booze. My husband's in Vietnam. I've got three teenagers. I'm a cancer survivor; I had a mastectomy and now I have only one boob. When we moved over here from Breaux Bridge, I wasn't anything but some nimby housewife, but somehow I had the good sense to go across the river to Bay Springs College and get me a degree in music education, so by the time my husband ran off to join the army, I had a pretty good job. I'm a band director. I get so weary of banging my head against the wall, dealing with parents who are not supportive, who won't pay the band fees. I wind up giving free reeds to kids, paying for them out of my own pocket. And I don't make much money and it's rough. My children don't understand why they can't have things. I drive a ten year old car."

"Get off the pity pot," the man said.

"I'm not on the pity pot," I said. "I'm not sitting around feeling sorry for myself, really I'm not. I don't have the luxury of that. I'm too busy trying to keep it all together. I'm just trying to be the best band director I can be and the best mother I can be. I don't know what else I can do."

"You could quit drinking," he said.

"I've done that before, sir," I said. "And things stayed just as fucked up as they'd ever been." I looked back to where he was sitting. Before I thought it through I said, "Who are you? For all I know you could be the rapist." I looked around the room. "Any of you could be the rapist! We sit in here talking about our goddam drinking and there's a dangerous criminal out there running loose!"

"They'll catch him," a woman said.

"Just a isolated incident," another said, which set off a wave of murmuring and protests.

"How you know it's a he?!" the man in the back shouted, and the clashing voices increased in volume.

"We're not here to discuss all that!" Theresa Hill's strident voice cut through the noise. She had been looking daggers at me.

"Just the same," the man in overalls said. Then there was silence.

"Okay," I said after a minute. "To get back on the subject. My husband is an alcoholic, too. We've tried together to stop drinking, and it didn't work, not for long. My husband and I we... we weren't getting along all that well before he left. He... he ran around on me. I guess that's no secret." Their faces seemed impassive. "But shit happens. I manage pretty well. In spite of the fact my husband is in

Vietnam and there's always a chance, God forbid, that he'll come home in a body bag." There were frowns on a lot of faces. I couldn't tell if they were sympathetic or judgmental. But I couldn't worry about that. "All families have problems, I guess," I said. What a crapped up speech. It was not at all what Theresa Hill wanted me to say. Or what I'd intended to say. I'd wanted to talk about the night terrors, when you wake up wide awake at three in the morning and lie there feeling the sedation leaching out of your veins, leaving you totally alone, as alone as you were when you were born or will be when you die. You don't share that, you can't. It's just you. And you've got to battle back somehow, and sometimes you might have the energy and the power to quit, to go turkey, and sometimes you just can't summon any shred of strength so you reach for the bottle, your medication, your source, your friend, who understands and doesn't judge and make you feel even less a human being, so you can at least focus your eyes and get up and walk the floor, hoping for more sleep but knowing it won't come, and you wait for that click when you'll get some semblance of normalcy again, you've risen up from the depths and needed two or three drinks to get you there. And you drink coffee, and calculate before taking half a shot just to keep that edge, that keel, and you struggle to maintain that balance, to keep yourself from sliding over into drunkenness again. You function. Your best friend drives the demons away, and you know just how many short nips it'll take to keep you going through the day, so you plan, and most everybody you see or talk to has no idea that you are running under the influence of a powerful drug. You pull it off. Again and again. One day at a time. And you meet your commitments, your responsibilities, and you do it well and good, a hell of a lot better than you could have done it without the alcohol that day, and as the day wanes the demons come back, the world is too much, and you need help again. Who have you hurt? Nobody. But maybe yourself.

Theresa, of course, was looking for another 'rock bottom' story, a canned story, one straight from the script: you pick yourself up off the nasty floor and make the fucking altar call. They all were; they liked going through the motions. Okay. I tried to get a little serious, to try to give Theresa a little of what she wanted. "I think it would help if my husband sobered up," I said. "But my sponsor down in Breaux Bridge once said to me, she said, 'You sober up a drunk horse thief, and all you've got is a sober horse thief. It takes more than just puttin' the stopper in the bottle.'." They just sat there looking at me; some of their expressions were puzzled. Theresa Hill was staring at me with venom in her eyes, a scowl on her face. She was a real estate agent with a tight permanent. Nobody said anything. They weren't sure if I'd finished or not. I went on. "I accept that it is a cunning and baffling disease, and that I am powerless against alcohol. And that I have to admit that I am an alcoholic and truly own up to it to gain the power to stop drinking. It's just that I don't want the power to stop, not just now."

A woman on the front row piped up. "Is your life unmanageable because of drinking?" she asked.

"Well," I said. "It's pretty unmanageable, but I don't know if it's all because of drinking. Life's been fucking me over for a long time."

"Bullshit," the man in the overalls said.

"What's bullshit about that?" I responded. "It was just an honest answer."

"You're bullshittin' yourself," he said. "That sponsor of yours was wrong. The only way out is to stop drinkin', period. That's the whole purpose of this." He waved his arm around the room.

"Okay," I said. "Look, I'm not being flippant. I know a lot of you are really trying to kick the booze, and I'm all for you. I've been through it before. I've quit I don't know how many times. But I want to be honest with you. Booze is my best friend. You can always depend on the booze, because you know what it's going to give you. It's always there. It doesn't let you down."

"It'll let you down in the end," Theresa Hill shrieked, her voice shrill and tense.

"Like a lot of other friends, I guess," I shot back. "Who the hell can you depend on? Maybe your kids, but a grown woman depending on her kids? I can't do that, because they depend on me. Who else loves you? Who else?"

"Lady, you're fucked up," the man in the overalls said.

"Tell me something I don't already know," I said.

I sat down. At least I didn't bore them. We all stood in a circle and held hands and Theresa Hill lead us in reciting the serenity prayer, and everybody squeezed hands and said, "Keep coming back." The alcoholic's amen. People started milling around the coffee machine. There was a tray of dry, hard chocolate chip cookies. Everybody seemed to forget all about me as soon as I was finished.

"Well, that was quite something," Theresa said at my elbow. She had a styrofoam cup with coffee the color of sand. "I thought it was just a terrible thing to do." She was furious. "I can understand, Olga, how women in your situation can become cynical," she said. She could barely control the tremor in her voice.

"My situation? What's my situation?" I snapped.

"A husband in Vietnam. A drinking problem that causes you to do... regrettable things."

"Okay," I said. "Is this where I fall down on my knees and beg forgiveness?"

Her mouth was a tight, disapproving line. Her lacquered hairdo wrapped around her head like a helmet. "You will know much more sorrow from liquor, Olga," she said, her voice trembling, her lips a straight, tight line.

"Yeah, well," I said. I didn't know what I was going to say, so I just shut up. There was nothing more to say, anyway.

I saw Deirdre in the hallway. She was talking to some boy in a sweater vest. I was always amazed to see my kids going on. Surviving. She was laughing at some joke. Her blonde hair shone in the light of the hallway. She looked great, in a khaki skirt, too short, but not much shorter than mine. We both had good legs. She was looking around for me. She met my eyes.

"How about some hot chocolate?" I asked when we were outside. The night was crisp. We had on light jackets.

"Sure," she said. "I don't care."

Never a simple yes or no. We got into the Caddy and I turned it out toward the highway. "The Cherokee okay?" I asked.

"Whatever," she said.

We got a booth. I wanted a drink but I ordered coffee and Deirdre ordered a coke. I cocked my eyebrows at her. "I don't like their hot chocolate here," she said. "it's got powdery shit floating on the top."

"Okay," I said. "How was your meeting?"

"Okay, I guess," she said. "How was your talk?"

"I think I did all right," I said. "You guess?"

"Well, you know." The waitress brought our order. Deirdre seemed absorbed by the bubbles in her coke. The coffee at the Cherokee was passable. Better than Sapfat's, and certainly better than the muddy water at the AA meeting. There was a bottle of hot sauce on the table and I was tempted to splash a little in my coffee. Deirdre would be horrified if somebody saw me do it.

"What did y'all talk about?" I asked.

"It's anonymous, Mom," she said. She rolled her eyes.

I honestly wasn't trying to pry into what they had talked about, but I thought maybe she wanted to talk about it. "Okay," I said.

She sipped her coke. She was looking around the restaurant. Looking for somebody she knew. Somebody other than her boring mom. "I hope you didn't leave any homework until we get home," I said.

"I don't have any homework, Mom," she said. I watched to see if she'd roll her eyes again, but she didn't. After a minute she said, "Max doesn't ever do any homework, and Willie hardly ever."

"I know," I said.

She shrugged.

"Well," I said, after a minute. "There's something I'd like to talk to you about." She shrugged again. She was still looking around the restaurant. "What did your dad say exactly in his letter about Thanksgiving?"

Her eyes flashed. "You mean you didn't read it?" she said.

"Of course not. I don't read your mail."

"Shit," she mumbled under her breath, "my ass."

"Well?" I said.

"He said he was going to come home. Like I told you. He can get a furlough or a leave or something. They let our guys do that, come home for a holiday. I didn't get all the details. Just that he'd be here for Thanksgiving."

"More coffee, hon?" the waitress asked. The waitresses at the Cherokee were all elderly women. I pushed my cup toward her and she filled it.

"You ever hear of putting hot sauce in coffee?" I asked her. Deirdre was scowling at me.

"Can't say as I have," the waitress said, shuffling off.

"Go ahead, put some in there," Deirdre said. Her jaw was set defiantly. "I dare you."

I tipped the bottle and shook a few drops in. I stirred. I sipped. Not bad at all. An improvement. "Ahhhh," I said.

"You're nuts, Mom," Deirdre said. Not unkindly.

I was wishing I had a drink. "It just seems to me, Dee Dee, that it is unlikely that they'll let him come home. He has almost a year left on his tour over there."

"What do you mean, 'unlikely'? He said so."

"All the same, you shouldn't get your hopes up."

"You don't want him to come home," she said. She was looking at me as if she hated me. Maybe she did. Maybe my own daughter hated me. Or maybe she was being a brat.

"Oh, for God's sakes, Deirdre," I said. I was trying not to be exasperated.

"He's my father." There were the beginnings of tears in her eyes.

"I know he is. He's my husband. And I know you love him. I love him, too, but he's the one who left, I didn't."

"You ran him away," she said.

I never should have started this conversation in the Cherokee. Other women seemed to have a much easier time than I did being a mother; I was forever launching into things before I'd even thought them through. "I didn't run him away," I said. "He..." I caught myself. "He joined the army, Dee. I didn't even know he was gonna do that."

"Why were you always fighting?" she asked.

"We... we just weren't getting along," I said.

"You're gonna get divorced, aren't you?" she asked. One tear leaked out of her eye and down her cheek. She didn't wipe it.

"No," I said. "Never! Not in a million years! We shouldn't be talking about this in here, we should wait till we get home," I said.

"You made him leave. You drove him away."

"Honey," I said, reaching for her hand on the table.

"You did. You ran him away." Oh how I wanted to tell her her dad was cheating on me, on us, on her, too, but I was not that bad a mother. I would never do that. Besides, I knew how much of it was my fault, too. Her lips were trembling, her face scrunched up in an expression so close to one she'd always had before a tantrum when she was little that I was choked with compassion for her. I could hardly bear to see her hurt so much. I wanted to throw my arms around her and weep with her. But I couldn't.

I swallowed. I sat up straight, cleared my throat. "No, that was all his big idea," I said.

She just sat there for a long time, staring at the table. I opened my purse and gave her a Kleenex and she wiped her eyes, then gently blew her nose. She took several deep breaths. Then she looked steadily at me.

"Are you going to quit drinking?" she asked. It was my turn to look around the restaurant. We were the only people in there, except for two old ladies who were watching us from a table near the front and trying to pretend they weren't.

"That's not for you to worry about right now, Dee," I said. "It's not something..."

"Are you?"

"...I need to decide right now. Finish your coke." It would have been so easy just to say 'yes, of course,' and end the conversation. But I couldn't bring myself to lie to her any more than I already was.

"You don't have any intention of gettin' sober, do you? You bitch."

"Deirdre!" I said. Her face was red from the crying, her eyes charged with torment and hurt. I loved her so much. I wasn't mad. I was proud of her for having the courage to call me that – I needed to be called that – but I was pissed off at the same time. I was afraid I was going to lose it and start crying myself. The two old ladies' ears were perked up. They were watching us. Deirdre's fists were clenched on the table. I covered them both with my hands. "Honey," I said. "Honey."

She sat very rigid, her breath sucking in hoarse, strident gasps. She looked tiny and defenseless. The tears still crawled across her cheeks. I got out some more Kleenex and got up and went around the table and slid into the booth beside her. I put my arms around her. The two old ladies were watching. She trembled against me. I pressed my face into her hair. She smelled of lilac shampoo and Ivory soap. She smelled like a child.

A few days later, on a rainy, ugly late afternoon, cold and almost dark, I was on my way home from band practice, not looking forward to another lonely evening, so I stopped in at Sapfat's for a drink. I sat at the bar and ordered a double Scotch on the rocks. Susan Willingham had told me she'd heard a rumor that I was going to get in trouble over my drinking, that some people in town had complained to the principal about it. I guessed I'd have to deal with that if it came up.

Another customer came in, a man, and Allie, the bartender, a tall thin blonde, went over to take his order. He looked vaguely familiar. He wore glasses and had his dark hair brushed straight back. He was wearing an old tweed jacket; his shoulders were bulky. The man started talking to Allie and I went back to staring into my drink.

"Olga!" I heard the guy say. He had a big grin on his face. I couldn't quite place him. "I guess you didn't expect to see me in here," he said.

"I'm sorry," I said. "Do we know each other?" I was also doubly cautious when a strange man approached me now.

"I'm Bo, from AA," he said.

"Oh." I remembered where I had seen him, at one of the meetings. "How's it goin', Bo?"

"So so," he said. He laughed. "I'm off the wagon. I guess you are, too."

"No," I said. "I haven't been on it." I laughed, too. "Recently," I added.

"Well," he said, holding up his glass, "cheers!"

"Cheers," I said, and nodded. He moved two stools down and sat next to me. "You mind?" he asked.

"Not at all."

"I was at the game when you parachuted down," he said. "Pretty cool."

"Really? My daughter wants to kill me."

"I'd think she'd be proud."

"You don't know my daughter," I said. He obviously didn't know adolescents in general. "She was mortified."

"Well, I thought it was pretty neat," he said and drank down the rest of his drink. "Can I buy you another?" he asked.

"Sure."

When the drinks came, he sipped his. "Well, here's to Bill!" he said. I drank, and he paused. "What you said that night in your talk about your husband being in Vietnam? If we're going to be friends, I think I should tell you that I'm very much against this war. I'm active in the anti-war movement."

"I'm not real fond of the goddam war either," I said.

"With me it's a commitment, though. I think we've got to get us out of there. It's immoral, what we're doing."

"You mean you get out and march? Protest? I've read about that in the paper," I said.

"It's growing," he said. "Gettin' bigger every day. I'm sort of taking a leadership role, with some of the kids over at the college. They can get really fired up. There are a lot of people who are against this war."

I thought of Patrick, over there doing whatever it was he was doing. I realized I had no clue what he was doing. I didn't like to think about it too much, because it upset me. I saw the reports on the network TV news, but I didn't follow it very well. Just a lot of strange, unfamiliar place names and shots of American soldiers walking along jungle roads or riding in troop carriers. Deirdre was always looking to see if she saw Patrick. She never had.

"Okay," I said. "I guess I'm against it, too."

"Good," he said.

I was curious about the anti-war stuff; what little I'd read had seemed alien and distant, the hippies. Bo obviously wasn't a hippy. But apparently there was some of that going on right here in Bay Springs.

Another customer came in then: a man. He stood at the end of the bar, just inside the door. It was dim in the bar and I had to squint. I was surprised to see it was that preacher, Rayford Means, who hung out with the football coaches. His daughter was in the band. He wasn't ordering something to drink, though, but was just standing there, looking directly at me. His face was sort of pig-like. I could feel his eyes on me. Staring. He seemed to suddenly become aware that I was looking back at him and he turned and put this stack of what looked like little pamphlets that he'd been holding onto the counter next to the cash register. He looked back at me again, a long stare. Then he quickly left, the door swishing to behind him.

I watched Allie walk over and pick up the stack of whatever they were and toss them into a waste can behind the bar.

"Listen, let me buy you a drink again sometime, okay?" Bo said,

"Sure," I said.

*****

The rain had slacked up and there wasn't as much water standing in the streets on the drive home. It was late afternoon, getting dark early with the heavy clouds. When I got home the house was dark. All three of them were out somewhere. Wandering around town in the rain with a sadistic rapist on the loose. Dee hadn't bothered to even leave a light on.

I turned the hall light on and went into the living room. I got some ice from the kitchen and made myself a drink. I sat in the dark.

I was on my second drink when Willie came in.

"Whatcha doin' in the dark, Mama?" Willie said from the hall.

"Come in. Sit down," I said.

He switched on the overhead light and I squinted. He was looking at me inquisitively. He was baffled by finding me in the dark, but, more so by the invitation to come in.

"What do you want?" he asked suspiciously.

"Nothing. Just to talk."

"About what?"

"Nothing."

He looked at me out of the corners of his eyes. He shrugged. He sat down on the sofa, perched on the very edge. "Okay."

"You have a good day?" I asked. He cut his eyes at me again, then away. He thought I was drunk. "I'm not drunk, Willie," I said.

"I didn't say you were," he said.

He looked so unlike his father he could have been someone else's son. As dark as Patrick was fair. He had on his dark brown corduroys, smudged at the knees. Maybe it was the accumulation of alcohol over the last few hours, but I sat there with tears in my eyes because my younger son was so vulnerable, so much in danger, too. "How many days this week have you worn those trousers?" I asked.

"I don't know Mama," he said. "God!"

"I was just wondering," I said. Why did I ask that then? Was I drunk? No, I had been pretty sober when I got home. This was just my second drink this go round. The glass was empty, just a couple of ice cubes. I held it out to him. "Go fill that up with ice, will you, sweetie?"

"The bowl is empty," he said.

"No," I said. "I just cracked a couple of trays a few minutes ago. There's ice."

He took the glass and trudged out of the room. The pants were still a little large on him. They hung on his butt like pajamas. He was the smartest one of all of us. He'd never made below an A in anything. Deirdre had to study hard; I drove her. Max was too much like his father; it was a losing battle. He was content with Cs. There had been a time when I'd tried, but I didn't worry about him any more. He'd do what he would do. But with Willie, it was different. I knew I didn't give him enough attention, but then he didn't need much. He was independent, content to be by himself, to entertain himself. He was my little man.

Willie came back in with the glass full of ice. I sloshed some Scotch in. He sat on the sofa, watching me.

"Do you not like for me to drink?" I asked.

"I don't care."

"You can say what you feel about it, Willie."

Willie shrugged. "Whatever. Can I watch TV?" he asked.

"What's on TV?"

"Somethin'," he said. "It doesn't matter."

"Okay," I said. I watched him get up and amble into the den. A minute later I heard the TV come on. It was Perry Como. It must be nine o'clock. I wanted the light out again but I didn't want to move. I stretched out my legs in front of me. My skirt was wrinkled and there was a small smudge on the hem.

I heard Deirdre coming in. "Hi, Mom," she said from the hallway.

"Dee," I said. "Come in." Too eagerly.

"I was just going to..."

"Where have you been?!" I asked more harshly than I intended.

"Not again. Mom!" she said.

"Where have you been?" I asked more softly.

"Out."

"With who?" Whom. I didn't correct myself.

"A boy," she said defiantly.

"What boy, Dee?"

"Lester Underwood, if it's any of your business."

"Have you been riding in his car?"

"Yes," she said, on the verge of crying. "It's his grandmother's car."

"That's a lot like a date," I said. I couldn't seem to stop myself. I was angry, but I was relieved she was home safe. I should be pleased she was with a boy, in a car, not out on the street. I tried to calm myself.

"It wasn't a date, Mom," she said.

"Okay," I said. "Okay. Come in a minute, okay? Talk to your old mother."

She sighed dramatically. She sat on the sofa where Willie had been sitting. Neither of us said anything for a moment. "So talk," she said. She was antsy to get to her room. She kept the phone tied up every night. She wouldn't quit it no matter how much I nagged her.

I took a deep breath. "How was your day?" I asked.

She rolled her eyes. She looked around the room. I knew there was no way she was going to tell me. She crossed her legs at the knee and kicked her foot a couple of times.

"Dee, honey, let me ask you something," I said.

She looked defensive. We really hadn't talked much since that night at the Cherokee, so she was wary of me. She also looked guilty. I wondered what she'd been up to. She chewed on her lower lip. "Sure," she said.

"Have you ever heard anybody gossiping about me getting drunk?" I blurted. "About my drinking?"

Her eyes snapped up. "It would be hard not to hear it, Mom," she said. She looked at the empty glass in my hand. "People talk." She looked away.

"I go to AA meetings," I said. Weak. Lame. "People see me going."

"Yeah," she said. "They do."

We sat there for awhile without saying anything. Finally she said, "Anything else, Mom?"

"No, I was just..." I said. She started to get up. "Did you get some dinner?"

"Couple of hot dogs."

"Ugh, those things'll kill you," I said, which was what she always said when I served them.

"If that were true, there would be nobody left in the United States still alive," she said, which was what I always said back to her.

Chapter Fifteen

Near Pleiku, SouthVietnam
November, 1965

PATRICK HAD another cold shower and sat naked in the sunshine to dry off. A couple of guys walking by whistled. It had been seven days, he had just taken three straight showers, he had washed every shred of clothing he had, and he could still smell the stink of the rice paddy on himself. It was lodged in the pores of his skin. He knew he'd have it for the rest of his life, like a new birthmark.

He'd had a letter from Deirdre. It was written in early September. She'd been excited about the football season. She went on and on about the Bay Springs Bulldogs. She told him that Max was no longer on the team. He'd been kicked off for violating training rules. Probably drinking beer, Patrick thought. Willie had mounted some more butterflies and taken them to school for his first science project of the new school year. He did that every year, and he always made an A. She asked him to send her a Viet Cong flag, that that would be way cool. She said she hoped he'd stay safe and be home soon. She said that she was studying very hard and she loved him very, very much. She did not mention her mother.

Patrick lit a cigarette. He lay back, feeling the sun's rays warm on his skin. The weather was balmy, very like early summer on the

Gulf Coast. He still didn't know exactly where they were and had stopped thinking about it. Odum had told him they were now much closer to the Cambodian Border than they had been, but that meant very little to Patrick. He had only the vaguest sense of the country.

They had come further out packed into Huey helicopters, a great swarm of them. They had been shot at from the ground a couple of times. Odum said he'd heard they would be moving out again in the choppers very soon. They were at a small temporary compound at the edge of a swamp. It reminded Patrick of Louisiana, except that the vegetation was more exotic and alien. Instead of cypress and live oaks, there were palms, bamboo and jack-fruit trees. But there was the same rank odor of decay and mold. And there were snakes and tiger leeches in the swamp.

Harry Hamilton, their medic, came by and gave Patrick a handful of quinine pills. He was making his rounds. "Who you think you are, Marilyn Monroe?" Hamilton asked him.

"You wish," Patrick said.

Hamilton gave him two new water-tight plastic cigarette boxes.

"Where the smokes?" Patrick asked, opening one and peering inside.

The medic ignored him and went on to the next man.

He felt drowsy and relaxed. He thought a lot about Kim Ly now. He tried to relive the night in Saigon in his mind, going over and over every detail. He woke up at least once every night with a hard-on, and lately he'd had a couple of wet dreams, the first he'd had since high school. He'd tried unsuccessfully to force the memory of the hard-on he'd gotten when he killed the soldier from his mind. At least he didn't dream about that when he had his wet dreams. He dreamed about Kim Ly and Olga and Joy, who used to love to give him blow jobs. Because underwear irritated his skin, he didn't wear any, so after he had one of the dreams he had a big wet spot on his pants in the morning. It dried quickly, thank goodness.

When the sun had dried him, he dressed and had a can of fruit cocktail for lunch. The syrup was sweet and cool. It was the same thing he'd had for breakfast, and would probably be the same thing he'd have for supper. He had the runs every day. Haskins heard him in the latrine and yelled, "You too old for this, Pappy!"

"Fuck you, Henry," Patrick called back.

A sameness, a new and dull routine had set in. They had been here three days and had never left the compound. As far as he knew there was no enemy activity in the area. After he finished his lunch, Patrick lay back, closed his eyes and tried to relax, only half listening to the men's chatter and laughter.

"This is your in-country R & R, enjoy it," Mac said.

"You full of shit. This ain't no in-country R & R!" Seelbach said.

"Yeah," Morrison said. "Where the girls?"

"Right over there," Mac said.

"Where?" Seelbach said.

"Right over there behind that bunch of ferns where you jack off." The men laughed.

"You a cruel motherfucker, McMillan," Gerald Abbott said.

"Yeah," Mac said. "And don't you forget it."

Patrick supposed that one of the things that so disturbed him about the boy he'd killed was that he looked so much like other teenage boys. Patrick thought about the boy's life before he was in the war, imagining him eating a candy bar, going to the movies. Watching television. Screwing a little teenage gook girl. The boy had had an entire life, a complete history, and Patrick had obliterated it with one pull of the trigger. He couldn't get the image of the dead boy's face out of his mind. He knew it would be lodged there forever. He felt an odd intimacy with the boy that he didn't fully understand, as if the bullet Patrick sent his way was his own arm reaching out, his hand touching him just as he'd do with one of his own sons, except he wanted it to be before the bullet found its mark, when the boy could still look back at him with vigor and spirit in his young eyes.

Patrick tried to doze in the warm sunlight. It was hard to be angry at the war, because it was a huge abstraction that was just there, that was now as natural a part of his existence as the air he breathed. And looking at the face of the young boy he'd killed had complicated his anger at the gooks. He hated them, but now they were people and not just shadowy scarecrow figures in funny hats.

Chapter Sixteen

Bay Springs, Louisiana
November, 1965
MAX

MY MOM calls it 'acting out', the way trouble seems to find me wherever I am. I'm always just blowing up and doing crazy shit that I don't know where it came from. The guidance councillor at the high school said I had a lot of 'anger issues' I 'needed to work through'. I knew I was mad that my mom had to have cancer, even though they said she was over it. I didn't know if you really ever got over cancer. And I was pissed off with my dad, for the way he treated mom, and for running away and abandoning us. I wasn't sure what the other 'issues' were, but I didn't doubt I had them. I was seeing her because I'd been kicked off the football team for getting caught drinking beer. I mean, I was with five other underage guys when we got caught, and I just happened to be the only one who was on the football team. Like coach says, 'win some, lose some'. When I got suspended for two days for fighting in school, it was because this other guy, Lucas Phillips, wouldn't let me alone so I finally conked him one. I should have walked away instead of hitting him, my mom said. My mom was in the principal's office in about two seconds flat, because she works at the school. She was royally pissed. She grounded me for a week.

Ever since my mom got sick, and specially after my dad left home, my mom gets easily pissed. I tried to stay out of her way. She and my dad had some mammoth fights, I mean some classics. Ever since I could remember they'd drink too much and wind up yelling at each other. I could understand, because my dad was fooling around. I heard things around town. And he was never interested in anything I was interested in. I just let him go his own way. He was hardly ever there when I was little, anyway. Always out at The Good Lady's drinking beer with his buddies. When I was in Dixie Youth League baseball, I told him one time that I wanted to play in the major leagues one day. He was about half drunk and he just laughed and changed the subject. I got the idea in a hurry: he didn't give a shit what I wanted to do. So I just quit trying to please him. I did okay playing ball. And I did all right in school, I guess. I just wasn't your National Honor Society type, that's for sure. My mom used to keep after me about improving my grades, but she doesn't do that much any more. My dad would get all pumped up and joyful about Dierdre's and Willie's grades, but he would never even look at mine. So I just said to myself: fuck him.

And I was worried that the police were going to question me about the rape. They had been talking to a lot of guys I knew around town, and I figured they'd get around to me. I mean, I didn't have anything to hide, but it made me nervous to think they might question me.

The girl I was with the night that I got into the ruckus out at M & L, Beverly Angstrom, was from a nice family. I was tired of dating skags. In fact, I had been out with Jane McKissick, the majorette who was raped, a couple of times. She was in my English class. I kind of liked her okay. She was from a poor family, poorer than mine. Beverly Angstrom's dad was the district manager of the power company. And she was good looking. I had got it in my head that what I needed was a good woman. I didn't need skags. They made me mad as hell with all their teasing and carrying on. The girl I really liked was this princess named Vicki Mason, a cheerleader. I had dated her a couple of times, but we hadn't seemed to get anywhere. I strongly suspected that her dad didn't want her dating me. He was the Ford dealer in town and he'd had to repossess a car one time that he'd sold my dad, and it got kind of ugly. My dad got way behind on the payments, and when Mr. Mason repossessed it he claimed that my dad had trashed it. I knew, though, that my dad hadn't done it to get back at Mr. Mason. My dad just drove it around that way, covered with dust and mud and full of paper cups and empty beer cans and shit.

So that night I had a fifth of vodka under the seat. I had some coffee beans I would chew later, because I knew my mom, if she was still up, would want to smell my breath when I got home. They claim vodka doesn't have any smell, but I don't trust that. Coffee beans will do the trick. I drink a lot of coffee. I was always out at the Cherokee Restaurant drinking coffee and eating coconut cream pie. So my mom would expect coffee. I don't know how the hell she could smell anything, anyway, as soused as she gets every night.

Beverly Angstrom pulled the bottle out and turned it up. I checked the bubbles; she was really drinking. Some girls will keep their lips closed and only pretend to drink. I drove along for a while. "You look like that actor James Dean," she said.

"Come on," I said. Other people had told me that. My dad told me one time they used to say the same thing about him. He told me to watch this movie Rebel Without A Cause. I saw it on TV one night. I liked it. I even had a red jacket like James Dean wore in that movie, but I didn't have it on tonight. I combed my hair like his. I drove like him. Not that I wanted to look like my dad, but James Dean, that was another thing.

"No, you do," she said.

"Okay."

I pulled into the crowded parking lot at the M & L Café out on the highway. When I killed the engine I could hear the juke box blaring from inside. The M & L had a dance hall in the rear and it was packed. I was looking forward to walking in with Beverly on my arm. I knew Vicki was probably there, and I wanted to make her jealous. Harold Tucker and Claude Autry were probably there. The place rocked all night on the weekends.

"Max! What's happenin', man?" I heard someone say. It was Dimwit Anderson, a tackle on the football team. He was with some other guy I couldn't recognize in the shadows.

"Hey, Dim, what's goin' on?" I said.

"Who's that you're with, Vicki?" he asked.

"Vicki?" Beverly said. "You go out with Vicki Mason?"

"You know Vicki?" I asked her.

"She's a cheerleader, right?"

"Yeah," I said, then, out the window: "Thanks a lot, Dim. This ain't Vicki."

"Oh," Dimwit said. The other boy laughed. I recognized the laugh: Jack Neely. He was a guard on the team, a boy with only one hand. He'd lost his left hand grinding hamburger out at his father's meat packing plant. He was a dirty player. I guess he was mad at the world about his hand.

"Y'all been inside?" I asked.

"Naw," Jack Neely said. He had this stiff hard plastic fake hand that looked like a mannequin's hand; I guessed girls didn't like to grab hold of that thing while they were dancing with him. He hardly ever had a date. And Dimwit Anderson made model airplanes and was a ham radio operator who spent most of his time at home and didn't have many friends. He weighed about two hundred pounds and told whack-off stories in the locker room.

The front room of the M & L Café had tables and booths, all full. It was loud. The juke box in the back room was making the place vibrate. We went on through to the dance hall. There were several couples dancing. There were a few people I knew from school – including Harold and Claude – at a big table in the corner, and we went that way. I set the vodka, in a brown paper sack, on the table. One of the girls at the table was Vicki. She looked at Beverly and me and looked quickly away. I felt real self-conscious all of a sudden, because I didn't want Vicki to think I was playing silly games. I really did like her a lot.

"Hi, Vicki," Beverly sang out in this phony voice. I could tell the vodka was already getting to her.

"Hey," Vicki said. She was much better looking than Beverly. She was wearing slacks and a little blouse that showed the tops of her tits. Harold and Claude had drinks in front of them. They were grinning, checking out Beverly. Harold Tucker pushed out a chair with his foot.

"Sit, girl," he said, like a dog command. Beverly giggled and sat down.

"Get us some glasses and ice, Max," she said.

"Hop to it, Max," Vicki said.

I felt like I was blushing. There was already a big bowl of ice and some extra glasses on the table. I grabbed two and made us a drink with some lemon-lime soda that was there. "Anybody mind?" I said. "I'll buy the next round." If I was blushing, nobody seemed to notice, except that Vicki had this little smile that I couldn't interpret. That made me feel even more self-conscious.

"Help yourself," Harold said.

I got busy with the drinks. I didn't look at Vicki. The other girl there was Sally Nelson, a junior. She was sitting up real close to Claude Autry. She looked drunk. The juke box was playing *"Stop, In The Name of Love"*, by The Supremes. Harold sang along with them, in this high, falsetto voice.

I sat there watching the people dance. I knew Beverly probably wanted to dance, but I really wanted to dance with Vicki. But even I knew that would be a bad move. Vicki seemed to be ignoring me. Beverly was pouring her second drink since we'd sat down. That must have been at least four. I didn't want to have to carry her or have her puking in my car, but that was one of the hazards of girls drinking.

Then Kirby Shaw and Curtis Benson walked over to our table. They had both graduated a couple of years ago and worked out at Gulf States Paper Company. They considered themselves badasses. They were both big guys.

"Hey, Founier," Kirby said. I could tell by his voice he was pretty drunk.

"What?" I answered.

"How's the Cajun motherfucker tonight?"

"I'm fine," I said. "How are you?"

"Dandy," he said. They stood there, looking around our table.

"Somethin' we can do for you?" Claude Autry said. He was a third string guard. Coach called him "Ironhead." He put him in on kickoffs and Claude would take the return man's head off.

"Ain't you gonna offer us a drink?" Curtis asked.

"You've got your own, don't you?" I said.

"Who's with her?" Kirby asked, looking at Beverly.

"She's my date," I said.

"Nice tits," Curtis said.

"Thanks," Beverly piped up. She was getting bombed. Vicki and Sally laughed.

"Hey, you ought to ditch this Cajun and go with me, angel tits," Curtis said. He still had on his khaki shirt with the green collar and "Gulf States Paper Co." stitched over the pocket. He was always talking about how he didn't take any crap from girls. I had heard him say one time that they needed to be knocked around from time to time. It crossed my mind that maybe he was the one who'd fucked old Jane McKissick and beat her up and left her in the woods. I wouldn't put it past him.

"I don't think so," Beverly said. She was smiling. She was enjoying the attention.

Kirby was looking at Harold. "I heard the Bulldogs have really been stinking up the joint lately," he said.

"You heard right," Harold said.

"Nothin' new about that," Kirby said. "We used to win some games."

"Back in the old days," Harold said.

"That's right, the old days. You got a problem with that?"

"A problem with the old days? Hell no," Harold said.

"Hey Cajun, your mom always jump out of airplanes?" Kirby said.

"Not always," I said.

"She's one crazy lady."

"She's hot," Curtis said.

"Hot to trot," Kirby said.

"Hey, that's my mom you're talkin' about," I said. It's a tough thing if your mom is hot and has had cancer. They had no right.

"Hey, you want to dance, angel tits?" Curtis asked Beverly.

Beverly looked at me. She looked around the table. "Go ahead if you want to," I said. She got up and let Curtis lead her out onto the dance floor. Couples were dancing all around them. She staggered a little.

"Girl's drunker'n Cooter Brown," Sally said. I looked over at Sally. Her mascara was running. Her hair was in her eyes. She played clarinet in the band. I snuck a look at Vicki, and she was watching Beverly and Curtis on the dance floor.

I just sat there. I would have liked to sneak off out the door with Vicki while Beverly was dancing with Curtis. And just kept on going. Going and going, far away from here. I could feel the vodka working in me, like hot pepper sauce in my veins. Maybe Beverly would hook up with Curtis. Then I could grab Vicki and we could run off, maybe get married. That would be okay. Get in my car and go and start our lives.

Curtis and Beverly came back to the table. "This girl can shake it," Curtis said.

"Cool," I said. I could tell he was looking for a fight, had been ever since they'd come over. He was trying to provoke me. I didn't want this to go on in front of Vicki.

"What do you hear from the Cajun-ass baby-killer?" Kirby asked me.

"He's over there makin' the world safe for assholes like you, Kirby," I said.

"Shit, he's over there killin' babies. Why don't he come home?"

I could feel a silver, mercury-like anger at the back of my throat and I tried to swallow it down. I figured they would get around to going on about the war. People were always doing that. They didn't know anything about it. They were just spouting off. I could see Vicki out of the corners of my eyes. I didn't say anything.

"What's he over there for again?" Curtis asked.

"He's takin' a vacation, savin' the world from the dirty commies," Kirby said. "That right, Cajun?"

"That's right," I said.

"Who's the Cajun-ass baby killer?" Beverly asked. She was pretty drunk.

"Max's sorry ass father," Kirby said. She looked like somebody'd thrown a cold drink in her face. "Fuckin' war mongerer."

"Hey, you better cool it, man," Harold said.

"Wooo hooo, I'm shakin' in my shoes," Kirby said.

"Why don't you go back to your table?" I said.

"I just asked about your daddy, boy," he said.

"Go back to your table, okay?" I said. I didn't want to fight. I didn't want Vicki to see me get bloodied. But I didn't want her to think I was a coward, either.

"You're such a damn bully, Kirby Shaw," Sally said.

Kirby laughed. "I guess we better take this thing outside," he said.

"What thing?" I asked.

"The thing where I kick your ass."

"I don't think there's any need to fight," Beverly said. She looked like she was about to cry. "Come on, Max, let's go," she said.

"In a minute," I said.

"Nobody ever solved anything by fighting," she said.

"Shut up, angel tits," Curtis said.

"Hey, go back to your own table," Ironhead said. "Before somebody gets hurt."

"And who's gonna do the hurtin'? You?"

"No," he said. "Max." He laughed. He was trying to defuse the tension, but it didn't work. Nobody else laughed.

Curtis and Kirby stood there looking around. I thought for a moment they were going to back down and I hoped they were.

"What are you waitin' on, Cajun?" Kirby said.

"This is crazy," I said.

"You scared shitless, ain't you?" he said.

He was a big guy. I was scared, but I didn't want Vicki to see I was. I wanted to be a bad-ass for Vicki, but something in my brain was telling me that she wouldn't like a bad-ass. She wouldn't like a coward, either. I wouldn't like myself very much if I didn't stand up for myself. I was sitting there trying to think my way through it when I heard my voice saying,

"Hell no, I ain't scared of you, asshole."

"All right," he said. "Come on."

I stood up. We were about the same height, but he outweighed me by about fifty pounds. I looked at Vicki. I couldn't read her eyes, what she was thinking, but there was something there. Concern for me. Or fear, maybe. But she wasn't indifferent. And she wasn't laughing.

I followed him through the dance hall and through the front room and out into the parking lot. I could hear people shuffling and crowding out behind us. "Hey, fight!" I heard some guy yell, and Claude said, "Shut the fuck up!"

The lot was well lit and I was hoping old Mr. Lancaster, the cop who moonlighted as security at M & L, had gone on home. A lot went on in this town that parents never knew about, and I was praying my mom wouldn't find out about this one. I could see Kirby's face. He looked scared. Nervous. Was he? Or was he just acting, to throw me off. The crowd made a kind of ragged circle around us.

He tried to take me by surprise before I was ready and lunged at me and I heard Beverly squeal in surprise or fear – I couldn't see her, I couldn't see any faces clearly – and Kirby let fly a vicious swing that went by my head whistling like a rifle bullet. Almost as a reflex I jabbed my fist into his mouth and he staggered back, blood on his lower lip. I could hear him breathing. He had barely missed me. But I had rocked him. I started to think that maybe I could get through this without too much damage. I circled around him. I could taste vodka and lime on my tongue.

He started back at me and I skipped away. He was big but awkward, and he was drunker than I was. I couldn't let one of those fists catch me solid. He landed a glancing blow on my ear that hurt like hell. I punched him in the stomach and jabbed him in the face again. I was so much quicker than he was that I was gaining confidence.

"Goddamit," he snorted.

He was shaking the hand that he'd hit me on the side of the head with. There was laughter and hoots around us. Everybody was enjoying the show. I wondered what Vicki was thinking. I jumped toward Kirby, my arms flailing. He looked startled, surprised. He backed up, got his fists up. I kicked him hard in the shin.

"Goddamit, no kickin'!" he said.

"Says who?" I said.

"The rules," he said.

"Fuck the rules," I said and kicked him again.

I tried to kick him in the balls but he let go a right that got me on the cheek. I tried to look like I hadn't even felt it as I circled him, bouncing on my feet. I wanted to feel my cheek with my fingers to see if I was bleeding, but from the dull way it was hurting I didn't think he'd broken the skin. I wouldn't let anybody – especially Kirby – see me checking it with my fingers, though.

The night was cool but I was sweating. He was shaking his hand even more now. I hoped he had fractured it. I jabbed him hard in the nose and I could tell it hurt him. Blood spurted and he looked startled. I had felt something give, so I thought maybe I'd broken his nose. His eyes were watering and his breathing was more ragged. I moved in quickly and hit him again in the mouth. He just stood there, his mouth hanging open, spit and blood oozing down in these long drools. I hit him again. He looked like he couldn't move his feet, like they were set in concrete. He bent over at the waist, leaning toward the ground, and I thought he was going to barf. I took a couple of steps and pushed him, hard, and he went down and just laid there.

I looked all around but I didn't see Vicki anywhere. Now that the excitement was over, everybody was just filing back inside, jabbering and laughing. My ear ached where he'd hit me and my hand, the one I'd busted his nose with, hurt like hell. I stood there gripping it and loosening it. It had a lot of Kirby's blood on it, so I couldn't use it to check my cheek. But I didn't feel any of my blood there.

There was none when I checked it in mirror in the men's room, but there was going to be a bruise. I was hoping it wasn't going to be a black eye. I hoped my mom would think it was a hickey when she saw me the next morning. I washed the blood off my hands and splashed my face with cold water.

When I came out of the men's room I saw that our table was empty. Everybody had gone home. I had left Beverly sitting out on the front steps of the place. She was liquored up. She was a sponge.

She sat right up next to me all the way back into town, practically sitting in my lap. She had brought our bottle, which we passed back and forth a couple of times. My ear hurt like hell where Kirby'd pounded it. I got the car up to eighty before I had to slow down for the speed zones. (Harold said the highway signs out there on U. S. Highway 80 were the speed limit.) It was late and there was no traffic at all.

When we got into town I turned toward where Beverly lived. I started taking the blocks really fast, trying to get her home before she was completely wasted.

"Here," I said, taking the bottle out of her hand. "Don't drink any more of that." I shoved it back under the seat.

I could tell she was sitting there pouting. But she was too far gone to argue. I screeched up in front of her house. I had to practically carry her up to the door and she planted this big sloppy kiss on me when we got there. She didn't want to go inside. I started to just leave her on the front porch, but I thought about Jane McKissick. I got the door open, shoved her inside and pulled the door to.

I drove on home. I sat in my car in the driveway for a long time, chewing some coffee beans. It was almost two o'clock and I didn't really need to, but you never knew. Everything was still and quiet. Sometimes, when I'm by myself in the middle of the night, I start thinking about what my dad might be doing right then. It's silly, because I don't even know what time it is way over there, halfway around the world.

I thought about Vicki. It drove me crazy that I didn't know whether she had watched the fight or not, whether she thought I was a crude Cajun redneck or a brave guy who could take care of himself. Or something else. I would know the next time I saw her, I guessed. I was really eager to see her and dreading it at the same time. The only lights still on were from my room upstairs at the back. And the porch light and one lamp in the downstairs hall that my mom had left on for me.

I sat there in the car thinking of my mom, the engine cooling and ticking. Thinking of her leaving the light on for me. It had been hard on us when she got sick and had to be in the hospital, and my dad wasn't any help. He went on one of his binges. Sometimes I resented him so badly I didn't know what to do, the way he hurt my mom.

I must have been more crocked than I'd thought, because just the thought of my mom facing cancer all by herself and being brave about it, and still switching the lamp on for me before she went up to bed, making sure I had light to see, made me get these big tears in my eyes. I knew I'd never get a woman as good as my mom was.

Chapter Seventeen

Near Tay Ninh, South Vietnam
November, 1965

IT WAS dawn. Orange and pink ropes of thin clouds stretched horizontally across the sunrise. It was a stunningly beautiful beginning of a new day. The men were bunched in units of ten, waiting to move out to the landing zone and board the helicopters. They were anxious and tense.

"What the hell are they waiting on?" Seelbach complained.

"What's the hurry?" McChesney said. "The Charlies'll wait on us."

The men were silent for a moment. They could hear the chopping of the Hueys up ahead. They were taking off in waves. Maybe it was the wait that was causing Patrick's anxiety to increase; he could feel his fear rising up in him in spurts echoing the sound of the choppers. He felt a sickening foreboding. He thought about being in the quiet and security of home and he would have given anything if he could have been magically transported back there instead of into the havoc of the conflict that awaited them in the jungle, the fray in which he knew he would lose all personal control. There would be nothing to do but lash out like a trapped animal savagely striking at whatever threatened him. Or run like the threatened animal for safety and to hell with any consequences. Patrick was almost certain that this would be the time he'd do that.

Run like the coward he secretly knew he was. His hands were trembling.

"My little girl started walking," Gerald Abbott said, his voice quivering. He looked scared, too, as though he might break down. "My wife said she..." He stopped. He swallowed. Patrick knew all the other men were feeling as petrified as he was. But they wouldn't run. They wouldn't flip out; he would be the one to do that.

"She'll be fuckin' before you know it," Odum said.

Nobody laughed. Odum's lame joke didn't dent the tension in the squad.

"Kiss my black ass, white boy," Abbott said.

"No. Really. Walkin', huh?" Odum said, trying to recover.

"Yeah."

"How old is she?"

Abbott looked at him as if he didn't know who he was. He shook his head. "I don't know," he said. "One?"

"How the hell do I know? She's your kid, ain't she?"

"One," said Abbott, as though he were reassuring himself.

"There you go," Odum said and chuckled feebly.

Nobody laughed. Patrick shook his head. He spit into the dust. The banter wasn't working. Everybody was scared shitless and they might as well admit it. Patrick was thinking about what it would feel like to be hit. He tried to really visualize it, to feel it. He had this private theory, that he wouldn't tell anyone else, that whatever you thought would happen wouldn't happen. Like when you were watching a baseball game, and your team was trailing by one run, and your team had two men in scoring position and one of your good hitters was up there, then you had to clear your mind and not think "gapper," because if you did he would never hit one. If you believed hard enough you were going to get shot, you wouldn't.

"Move it," Mac grunted, and the men moved off down the trail. Patrick's field pack was crooked on his back, uncomfortable. He felt oddly chilled inside his chest in the early morning. His coffee was acid in his stomach. Just then a formation of fighter jets roared overhead, headed in the direction they were trudging.

The jets disappeared over the treetops, their loud whoosh lingering. Patrick pictured them up ahead, spewing bombs and napalm.

They were soon packed into the helicopter, crowded together. Seelbach's rifle poked Patrick in the side. "Shoot me, why don'tcha?" Patrick growled, but his voice was drowned out by the shuddering pounding of the copter blades. The big Huey swayed upward, dipped, then shot ahead, and Patrick's stomach turned over. He closed his eyes and held onto the man in front of him. He didn't know who it was. When he peeked he saw the thick green jungle zipping by beneath them, and he closed his eyes again. He didn't know how long they'd been in the air when he heard the big 50 Cal machine gun mounted in the Huey start chattering. He smelled the caustic smoke from the gun mingling with the men's farts.

They touched down in an LZ that was just wider than the copter's blades. The blades kicked up a blinding cloud of dust and sticks and bits of grass that swirled around the men as they dropped down. Patrick hit the ground too hard and felt a jolt to his knees. Another ache, another pain. He gripped his rifle, crouched down and scampered to the brush lining the zone. When all the men were off, the Huey lifted up, dipped as though acknowledging them, then turned and headed back to where they had come from. Its racket diminished and melted into the sound of artillery pounding a hillside a half mile away. Patrick knelt in the tangle, his knee on the damp ground.

Then he began to push through the bamboo and fan palms. The growth opened up and became less dense. There were some scraggly looking pine trees. They were to meet at a small stream and regroup. He could hear the rattling and snapping of machine gun fire up ahead, discern the stuttering cracks of M-16s, the popping of Vietnamese AK-47s. There was a steady thundering of the artillery and the concussive drumfire of grenades. There was one hell of a firefight going on. Patrick considered dropping down in the heavy undergrowth and simply staying there. He could wait it out. Maybe this was his chance. He would not be the first ground pounder to do that, he knew. He wanted to get back to Saigon, he wanted to see Kim Ly again. He wanted to see his family again. But he kept moving, using his shoulder to push through the palm fronds. They slapped against his helmet. He was sweating now; he could feel the sweat running down the insides of his clothing, cooling his skin. He saw a little clear valley with a stream up ahead. He stopped and scanned the creek banks for movement. The noise of the battle was deafening. He was almost upon it.

There was a sudden burst of machine gun fire and Patrick went to the ground face first. The rounds raised sparkling little water spouts from the surface of the stream. He heard them ripping though the vegetation over his head. His heart was racing. He saw where the firing was coming from and he squeezed off several quick rounds of his own. The machine gun went silent. He did not move. He peered into the shadowy woods across the stream. Nothing moved.

He heard rapid rifle fire down to his right. Then more from his left. He thought he saw some movement. He sighted and fired, his automatic rounds tearing into a small, tight grove of banana trees. He saw Mac emerge at the edge of the stream. He was holding a BAR, pumping lead into the woods. Everything went quiet and Mac stood motionless for a long time, then signaled to cross the stream. Patrick saw other men in the squad, then, stealthily crossing the shallow creek. He followed.

Thirty yards in he came upon a dead North Vietnamese soldier, the first PAVN he'd ever seen. The body had been there awhile. Most of his face was blown away. He wore a dusty olive green uniform that seemed too tight for his body, and Patrick realized the corpse was already swelling. The enemy soldier had a Russian AK-47 gripped tightly in his hand. He had two fragmentation grenades attached to his belt. He smelled almost as bad as the rice paddy. Patrick was reaching for one of the grenades when he remembered Mac's admonition about booby traps and stopped himself. What the hell? What difference did it make? Who would miss him? He blinked a couple of times, swallowed, then snatched the grenade. Nothing happened. I'll just be damned. He had a souvenir. He worked it carefully into his field pack next to his plastic cigarette box. Willie will love that. He'll shit in his pants!

He moved on away from the dead gook. The fighting sounded more distant now. He stopped to smoke. He sat down with his back against a tree trunk and lit up. While he was resting he saw a butterfly. A black and gold one. It fluttered in a shaft of sunlight and came to rest on a white wild orchid blossom. The orchid made him think of Olga. She loved orchids. She always wanted an orchid if she was getting a corsage. She would miss him. Of course she would miss him. She loved him, even though she tried to say he'd killed her love for him.

He watched the smoke curl up into the leaves overhead. And Willie would miss him. The butterfly, poised there on the orchid blossom, made him think again of Willie. He drew on the cigarette, watched the smoke drift upward and disappear into the green growth overhead. Patrick's boyhood had been sterile and deprived, and he had wanted his boys to enjoy growing up. Max was interested in nothing but sports, and since Patrick had never played ball and couldn't throw very well, or do anything else on a field or court, Max had grown impatient with him, soon preferring his own friends. Patrick had been determined to do a better job with his second chance. He tried to get Willie interested in hobbies they could share. Willie hated hunting and he grew bored with fishing. Finally, after several failed tries with other things, he hit on butterfly collecting, and Willie had taken to it. So the two of them had spent hours romping in the fields and woods around Bay Springs, capturing and mounting butterflies.

They amassed quite a collection. They were mounted all over the walls of Willie's room, and Olga had put one or two boards in the living room downstairs, like paintings. They had some prime specimens: they had blue morphos, cloudless sulfurs, common birdwings, glasswings, Grecian shoemakers, mocker swallowtails, tawny owls and a prized zebra longwing. What Patrick prized the most was the bond he grew to share with his younger son. He had never been able to relate to Max at all; he could relate to Willie through the butterflies. But only through the butterflies, he thought sadly. For the most part, his children were strangers to him. He knew that, like his own old man, he had been a poor father, but he didn't know how to be any better. Over the years, the task of trying had been so daunting to him that he preferred being away, drinking with his buddies, doing his own thing. He had avoided facing up to it.

He and Willie lost themselves in the pursuit and in the sometime tedious process of drying them and mounting them with dressmaker's pins. Side by side they worked. It was the only prolonged thing Patrick had ever done with anybody else, outside work, and he loved it.

One day, when Willie had been eight or nine, they had been sitting on a bench, resting after a long afternoon of collecting, when they looked up and saw a huge, bright yellow and red Monarch lighting on a flower about ten feet away. It was incredibly beautiful, and about the largest one either of them had ever seen. Patrick had taken the net and started to get up when Willie stopped him with his hand on his arm.

"Wait," he'd whispered. The butterfly perched there, perfectly still, as though watching them. "Let's don't catch that one. We'll let him go, but he'll still be ours. He'll be our secret butterfly, okay?"

"Okay," Patrick had said.

The butterfly sat there for a long time, then finally fluttered into the air and over to another bush and then away, through patches of alternating shadow and sunlight. They watched it out of sight.

"Now," Willie'd said. "We'll see him again, and whenever you see him or I see him we'll know he's our secret butterfly, okay?"

"Okay," Patrick had said.

"And we'll know he'll always keep us safe from harm," his young son had said, using a phrase that Patrick didn't have in his vocabulary, that he knew Willie must have picked up from his reading.

"Okay," Patrick had said again.

He was remembering all that as he watched the butterfly lift off the orchid and flutter upward and away. He had thought at the time that the kid was just chattering some childish superstition, but now he wondered if Willie had known something profound about their relationship that Patrick hadn't known. He realized he had felt closer to his youngest child when he'd seen the butterfly, if only just for a moment, and maybe he'd felt safer, too. The boy was smart, and sensitive.

Patrick stood up and ground the butt into the ground with the heel of his boot. He moved off through the jungle, stepping carefully. Patrick was confident in that moment that he would survive the war and go home and Olga would welcome him back and everything would be fine. They would be happy. For those fleeting seconds he knew that as clearly as he had ever known anything in his life.

He saw Seelbach up ahead, Alvin Cosper about fifty feet further on. They were now in a ragged single file, moving down a shallow ravine lined with mangrove trees. He held his rifle at the ready, his finger on the trigger, his thumb on the safety. He saw Cosper drop to his knee and fire, scattering into the mangroves at the end of the ravine. Seelbach got down. Cosper continued to fire and Patrick lumbered up to where Seelbach was. There were quick pop, pop, pops from AK-47s and rounds thunked into the bank of the ravine. Patrick and Seelbach fired toward where the rifle fire was coming from. They could now see the forms of olive-brown clad Vietnamese regulars bunched back in the trees. They crawled up to the edge of the ravine and leveled on them. Cosper was peppering them with his rifle. Patrick saw Mac further down the ravine heave a hand frag. He heard it explode, felt it vibrate in his chest, saw the smoke. The enemy fire kept coming. He grabbed one of his own fragmentation grenades, pulled the pin, and hurled it high into the jungle. There was a satisfying, thunky concussion.

He was startled by a deafening, ear-splitting whistling roar as two Thunderchief bomber jets went over very low and Patrick could see their bombs spinning toward the ground. The explosions were thunderous and the ground shook. Debris – clods of mud and splinters of wood and leaf – rained down on Patrick and Seelbach. "That ought to settle the gook bastards down," Seelbach said. Another formation followed the first, three jets this time, and a huge explosion went off behind Patrick and Seelbach. The two men looked at each other.

"Jesus," Seelbach said. "The fuckers'r bombin' us. They don't know we're here!"

The air was full of flying debris. The two men huddled tightly against the ridge of the ravine. Patrick's heart was rattling so in his chest he was afraid it would burst out. He expected the next split second to be it. He tensed for it. At least it would be over quick.

One blast followed another, all around them. He could see Mac and a couple more of the men clustered together in the ravine, pressing close to the dirt. He closed his eyes and curled himself into the tightest ball he could manage. He thought about praying, but he had no idea how.

"Mac?!" he heard Cosper yell. "Mac?!" He could see Mac motioning frantically for them to keep down. The air was so hot and thick with dust it was as though the sun had disappeared forever into a heavy cloud. The bombardment continued, incessantly, an intense ear-piercing deafening clamor. There was no end to it and they were in the middle of it. It seemed to be coming from every direction. They hugged the ground.

Patrick didn't know how long it had gone on. His body was so rigid and tense it started to ache. All of a sudden he felt a searing pain in his leg; his first thought was that someone had jabbed him on the outside of his thigh with a hot poker. He had been hit but he couldn't see any blood. The fabric of his pants looked singed in one spot; he thought he actually saw a wisp of gray smoke rising from it. The pain was so acute and consuming that he felt sick. He thought he was going to puke. Then he passed out.

They were in the ravine. It was finally quiet. Most of the rest of the squad was there. Patrick was leaning back against a rise, his leg stretched out. The pain was searing. Hamilton, the medic, had cut Patrick's pants open with a pair of scissors. Patrick had been hit in the leg with a small piece of shrapnel or wood. Maybe a rock. It was a glancing blow and had barely broken the skin, but the burn was fairly severe. Hamilton rubbed burn ointment into the skin and taped a two-inch gauze pad over the wound. "It's a million dollar wound," Patrick said to the medic. "Ain't it a million dollar wound?"

"Shit," Hamilton said. "Maybe thirty bucks at the most."

"What? Come on."

"You ain't really hit, Founier," the medic said.

"I can't walk!" Patrick said.

"The fuck you can't."

"Don't be such a goldbrick, Pappy," Mac said.

"You ought to have a piece of hot shrapnel up your ass!" Patrick said angrily. "Goddamit to hell. This is a million dollar wound and I'm goin' home. Get used to it, Sarge."

McMillan laughed. "Dream on, boy," he said.

"Garrett's got the million dollar wound," Seelbach said, and nobody said anything. Everybody looked down at the ground. Trussel Garrett had had his right arm blown off at the elbow and had lost a lot of blood. He had already been carried out on a litter back to the LZ. Sylvester McChesney had been killed. He had taken bomb shrapnel in the chest. His body was still there, at the end of the ravine, covered with a ground cloth, awaiting transport.

Patrick found it hard to believe that Syl was dead. It did not seem possible. He was still in a state of utter disbelief. Nothing seemed remotely certain. It was as if God had secretly changed Patrick's old reality, substituting a twisted and misshapen materiality that was whimsical and bizarre. Terror turned to deliverance and back to dismay as quickly as a snake's strike. God was a trickster who made nightmare worlds real and left you stupefied and disconcerted and floating in a smothering hot cloud of the most inscrutable mystery.

Chapter Eighteen

Bay Springs, Louisiana
Thanksgiving, 1965
WILLIE

BOYD FLOYD and Mr. Pitts and this new guy were in the living room, drinking whiskey. They had all come for Thanksgiving dinner. Dee and Mama were in the kitchen pulling meat off this huge chunk of pork butt that Mama said Mr. Pitts had bought for us. They were mad at each other, probably over my dad. He hadn't come home, but Dee was still insisting he would, at the last minute. Maybe he will come popping in. Everything was like some loony soap opera. I could see that this was going to be a Thanksgiving Day to remember. I could hardly wait to see all the freaky stuff that would transpire. I just hoped my mom wouldn't get too drunk. She'd already been in the booze for a while.

My mom said she invited the three men because you needed company on Thanksgiving, and they didn't have any family to eat with so we were sharing ours. She sometimes had weird ideas. I was sitting in the living room with the three men. My mom had told me to "entertain" them while she and Dee got the dinner ready. I was just sitting there watching the three of them put away the liquor. I had started to really pay attention to men who were about my father's age, but it was hard; I wanted to understand my father.

Maybe observing them would help. Somehow I doubted it. Boyd Floyd told me he'd take me up in his plane. I won't hold my breath. His big bushy mustache hangs over his mouth sort of like a loose curtain. I don't know how he eats. It looked like he was straining his whiskey through it when he drank .

"So what grade are you in, Willie?" Mr. Pitts asked me. It sounded like it would if he was asking me how old I was and expecting me to hold up some fingers.

"Seventh," I said.

"Middle School," he said.

"They call it Junior high school," Boyd Floyd said. "I think."

"Is that right? I didn't know that," Mr. Pitts said. "Junior high school."

We all sat there for a minute not saying anything. Max was still asleep upstairs. I could hear Dee's and Mama's voices in the kitchen. It sounded like they were still arguing about something. Dee was mad as hell that mom didn't believe our dad was coming home for Thanksgiving. From Vietnam! I hadn't really believed he would. Only a girl would believe that. I was staying out of her way.

"What instrument do you play, Willie?" Mr. Pitts said.

"I don't," I said.

"You're not in the band?"

"No sir," I said. I thought he was going to ask me why. But he didn't. He was staring at his ice cubes in his glass. "Would you like another drink?" I asked, polite as hell.

"Well..." he said. He cleared his throat. "You are allowed to pour drinks?" he asked.

"I don't see why not," I said. I got up and took his glass. Boyd Floyd held his up and so did Mr. Bobo, so I did the same for them. What kind of name was Bo Bobo? I went into the kitchen and fixed their drinks. I don't think my mom and Dee even noticed me in there. They were still talking away over the barbecue. I went back holding all three glasses in a triangle with both hands and held them out.

"Which one is mine?" Mr. Pitts asked.

"Oh," I said. I had no idea which was which, so I just shoved the glasses toward Mr. Bobo like I did know and he took the first one and I looked at the other two like I was making sure I had the right one for each of them. They took them and I sat back down.

"What the hell's takin' em so long," Boyd Floyd said.

"Well, you know women," Mr. Pitts said and chuckled.

"No, I don't know women," Boyd Floyd said. He didn't seem very happy that the other two men were there, was my take on it. And Mr. Pitts seemed confused. Like he didn't know what to make of it. The three men had just met each other a few minutes ago. I knew Dee didn't much like that they were here. Maybe that's what they were arguing about back there.

Mr. Bobo had on a coat and tie. Mr. Pitts had on a neat pressed flannel shirt and khaki pants and wingtip shoes. Boyd Floyd had on a ratty old denim work shirt and blue jeans tucked into his scruffy cowboy boots. Boyd Floyd and Mr. Pitts were smoking cigarettes. I started to ask them for one, but I thought that might be pushing it. Boyd Floyd had this leather band on his wrist, like a watchband without a watch on it. Mr. Bobo was just leaning back in his chair, sipping his drink, smiling. Like he was on the front porch in the sunshine.

"So you're crop dusting?" Mr. Pitts asked.

"Yeah," Boyd Floyd said. "Soybean and rice fields over in Wilcox Parish."

"You enjoy your work, I suppose," Mr. Pitts said.

"Wouldn't do it if I didn't," Boyd Floyd said.

"I mean, it must be fun, up there in the air, looking down on everything."

"Yeah," Boyd Floyd said. "What do you do?"

"I'm first vice president and trust officer at Bay Springs Commercial Bank."

"You enjoy your work?"

"Oh, yes. I do. It's... well... fascinating, really. It..." He started to say something and then stopped. I thought he was fixing to tell us what was so fascinating about it and then thought better of it. He probably thought his job was boring compared to Boyd Floyd's. I did.

"And what do you do, Mr. uhhhh...?"

"Bobo. Bo Bobo." Boyd Floyd snorted. "I sell time," he said. Boyd Floyd snorted again.

155

"Time?" Mr. Pitts asked.

"Radio time. WGOX, in New Orleans." My ears perked up.

"Oh yes," Mr. Pitts said. There was a long silence. Mr. Bobo didn't say anything more about selling radio time, and I wasn't about to ask.

Mama had the house too warm and Mr. Pitts was sweating in his flannel shirt. I had on a sweatshirt and I was a little hot, too. It was a gray, damp day outside. It looked cold as hell but it wasn't. I was sitting there wondering what Amy was doing right then. Their grandparents were there. Donly and Amy said their grandfather had such bad breath you could hardly stay in the same room with him. I was wishing I was that cushion in whatever chair Amy was sitting on. I could feel myself getting a semi just thinking about her. I thought about excusing myself and going upstairs and jacking off.

Deirdre came in then with a tall glass of tea. In the other hand she had a platter of crackers and about fifty different kinds of cheese. She set it on the coffee table in front of the men. She came across the room to where I was and sat down in a rocking chair. She looked like she'd been crying. She had her glass crammed full of ice. Mama was always after her not to use so much ice, so she used as much as she could.

"And you're in high school, aren't you?" Mr. Pitts asked.

Dee looked at me like she didn't know which one of us he was asking about. Then she looked at Mr. Pitts. "Yeah," she said. "Whoopee."

He coughed again and looked at his drink. It was like he didn't know what to do with the information and had no clue why she had added what she did.

My mother came in then. She had a glass of liquor in her hand. She looked around. She had on her green tent dress. She looked beautiful. "Well..." she said. "Happy Thanksgiving, everybody."

"Whoopee," Dee said again.

My mother cut her a look. The kind of look I never liked to get. She sat down in another rocker, her dress draping all around her. She had on some clanky bracelets. She sipped her drink and smiled. "Did everybody have some cheese? There's a good brie, some pepper jack, some Gouda, some others," she said.

"Yes, excellent," said Mr. Pitts.

Deirdre mumbled something about perverts or something that sounded like that.

"What?!" my mom said.

"Never mind," Deirdre said. She looked like she was going to cry. Her face was pink and she was holding her breath. My mom looked disturbed, too. She looked sad and angry. She slugged back her drink.

"Maybe these men would like to watch the football game on TV," Deirdre said. She almost had a snarl on her face.

"No," my mom said, and even though Boyd Floyd looked like he was about to say something, like maybe he wanted to watch it, she went on, "They don't want to." He just looked blank. He was a pretty stupid guy, in my opinion.

I was trying to think of something nice to say, just to help my mom out. Boyd Floyd had been in the Korean war; I didn't know if Mr. Pitts had. I doubted it. Mr. Bobo looked just old enough to be over there in Vietnam with my dad. I wondered why he wasn't. He was younger then my dad. He looked like he might have come to see Dee.

"Mr. Pitts, were you in the Korean War?" I asked. I didn't really give a shit. I was just thinking they would expect a boy my age, with a dad in Vietnam, to be interested in war and it would give them something to talk about.

"Why no," he said.

"I flew thirty two missions off a carrier in the Gulf of Siam," Boyd Floyd said.

"How'd we get on that?" my mom said.

"Your son..." Boyd Floyd began.

"My son has a name," my mom snapped.

"Willie. Willie, he just asked..."

"I heard him ask Knox," she said.

Uh oh. Some adult shit was going on. I started to ask if I could be excused, but I knew what the answer would be. I didn't want to get hit when the shit started slinging. Deirdre was sitting there looking like she could barely keep a straight face. One minute she was crying, the next she was about to bust out laughing. I wasn't curious about whatever the adult shit was. I didn't want to know what was going on. I just wanted them to let me alone.

"Thanksgiving was always my favorite holiday," Mr. Pitts said.

"Mine too," my mom said.

"Maybe I ought to go," Boyd Floyd said.

"But we haven't even had dinner yet," my mom said.

"We don't have a turkey," Deirdre said.

I was surprised she didn't say "fuckin' turkey". That morning, when I got up, I stopped at her room to tell her good morning. She was just sitting there on the edge of her bed looking out the window. "Mornin'," I'd said. She'd just kept on staring outside. "Dad's comin' home and we don't even have a fuckin' turkey," she'd said.

"That's okay," Mr. Bobo said. The other two men looked at him.

"Dee, fix these guys some more drinks, will you? They're all drinking bourbon."

My sister frowned and got up and slouched over and got their glasses and went into the kitchen to get some more ice. She moved like her legs were stiff.

"Bring me a root beer," I called out.

"Fuck you," she said under her breath, but it was loud enough for everybody to hear.

"Deirdre, I'm going to have to ask that you have some manners," my mom said.

"Yes mam," Deirdre's voice said from the kitchen. She came back in with their drinks on a tray and gave them to the men. The drinks looked almost clear, like they were mostly water.

"Where's my root beer?" I asked.

Deirdre ignored me and sat down. She began to rock. She had on her loafers with some of Max's red and yellow argyle sox. She looked again like she was about to cry and I was sorry I had asked her for the root beer. I was just about sick of adult shit. They could just leave me alone. I wanted to run away with Amy and never come back. All of a sudden I felt like I was going to cry. I felt lonely or something, I don't know.

I didn't ask to be excused, I just walked out. I braced my ears and the back of my head, but my mom didn't say anything. I went into the downstairs bathroom and closed the door. I sat on the john and had a good cry. I let myself blubber like a baby, trying to be quiet so nobody would hear me. I don't know how long I sat in there. I just couldn't make myself get up and go back. When I finally came out they were all going into the dining room to eat. I followed them in and sat at the table. There was a big platter of barbecue meat, a plate of buns, and a bowl of pork and beans.

"Beans, beans, the musical fruit," Boyd Floyd said.

"Gross," my sister said.

"Help yourself," my mom said, passing the platter of meat.

It was pretty good barbecue, just a little dried out. The whole room smelled like barbecue sauce. Everybody was making eating noises. Making small talk. I tuned them out. I thought about Amy, about how her ass would look if her slacks and her panties came off. I was getting a semi-hard. I fantasize a lot. The house was still hot, almost stifling. I could hear and feel myself chewing in my ears. I was thinking: this is a pretty good Thanksgiving dinner. It was probably a good thing my dad wasn't there, because he would have been mad that there wasn't a turkey. His favorite thing was to eat turkey breast sandwiches for supper and again the next day, on white bread with plenty of mayonnaise and black pepper. One time he made a dressing sandwich, some dressing between two slices of bread, and my mom laughed at him and told him he was eating a "cornbread sandwich" and it made him mad. My dad got mad a lot. He and Mama used to get very drunk and there was no telling what he might do. One morning I found him asleep on the front lawn. I guess he'd been out there all night. His clothes were wet from the dew.

My sister said. "I may have gotten it wrong. He's coming Christmas."

"Dee," my mother said, in this warning tone. I could tell my sister was angry. She looked about to burst.

"Maybe he will," I said. Everybody at the table looked at me like I'd farted or something. I guess it was the first thing I'd said in a long time. My voice felt kind of rusty.

"Is this your father?" Mr. Pitts asked. "He's getting to come home?"

"Well," my mother said. "We'd hoped that he might be able to come home during the holidays. It's a disappointment for us all that he can't."

Deirdre shrugged and grunted. She just sat there chewing on her lower lip. She hadn't eaten the first bite of the barbecue and she'd let the bowl of beans bypass her plate. Nobody at the table but me – not even my mother – knew how furious she was. She was going to pop.

Maybe for her sake I wished my father would come home. And for my sake, too. I mean, I worried about him all the time, worried that he'd get killed. I really missed him. I didn't want to even think about it. I couldn't begin to understand what all went on with my mom and dad. All I knew was that I loved them both and I worried about them both. It was too freaking complicated for my brain.

My mom started to talk a blue streak. I heard nothing but the sound of her voice. Sometimes, in certain situations, Mom would just take off and talk. She'd had enough to drink to go on and on. Mr. Pitts looked interested; Boyd Floyd looked like he was nodding off. Mr. Bobo's eyes were glazed over. Deirdre interrupted her.

"I hear somebody at the door," she said and pushed her chair back and started to get up.

"Deirdre, sit down!" my mom said.

"But..."

"There's nobody at the door," my mom said. "What was I saying?"

"I heard somebody knock," Dee said. Her lip was poking out about a foot.

"Who wants more wine? Boyd? Knox? Bo?" The men held their glasses out and my mom filled them from the bottle.

"You want me to go check?" I asked.

"No, I don't. Sit down, Willie," she said, though I was still sitting.

Deirdre started in then to really cry. Her shoulders slumped and she began to sob. Her eyes were closed real tight and she wailed. Mom got up and went over and put her arm around Dee's shoulders and knelt beside her chair. She put her forehead against Dee's cheek and just held on. Boyd Floyd and Mr. Pitts and Mr. Bobo looked like they wanted to run for the hills. I didn't know what to do. Dee just continued to sob and sniff, and Mom just held her. Then I heard somebody say, "What's goin' on?" and I looked up and Max was standing in the doorway with his hair all sleep-mussed and his eyes sticky, in a T shirt and his pajama bottoms.

"What's wrong?" he asked.

"Max!" I said, glad as hell to see him.

He came on in and knelt down on the other side of Dee's chair, where I realized I should have been, but I felt like my ass was glued to the dining room chair. I thought I was going to start to cry again, too, and I sure as hell didn't want to in front of those men. My eyes were stinging. Max and Mom just held on to Dee while her sobs gradually started to die down. My mom looked around the table, at me and then at the two men still seated.

"Y'all will just have to excuse us," she said, and they all started muttering "Of course," and "That's all right," and stuff like that.

I wanted so much to make things okay for Dee, but I couldn't. I couldn't make them let my dad come home. I couldn't do much of anything. The barbecue was burning my stomach and I felt like I might barf. I swallowed. I dipped my fingertips in my water glass and put cold drops on my forehead, and that helped.

"Is there something I can do, Olga?" Mr. Pitts asked then.

"Yeah," Boyd Floyd said.

My mom stood up then. She still had her hand on Dee's shoulder. "It's just... just a family matter," my mom said.

The three men at the table were nodding, making these sympathetic sounds. I could sense all three of them getting ready to get up, to make their excuses and say their thank yous and get the hell out of there. Max stood up then. He looked kind of stunned or startled, like somebody waking up from a dream and not knowing where he was.

"If there's anything I can do, well, you just..." Mr. Bobo said. He didn't finish. He just let it trail off. Boyd Floyd stood up, scraping his chair on the floor.

"It was nice of you to have me," he said, like a little boy minding his manners.

"Thank you for coming," Max said. It was the first time he'd acknowledged their presence. I wasn't sure he even was aware they were there. They mumbled and my mom walked with them, through the living room to the front door. We could hear them talking. My mom laughed, this shrill cackle.

I was still stuck to the chair, looking at Max and Dee. Dee's face looked blank and chapped. Her cheeks were red and her lips looked pale and dry. Her hair was kind of messed up, too, just like Max's, and she was running her fingers through it. I would have given most anything for my family to be all together again. I loved them all so much it felt like some bowling ball was sitting on my chest. I felt like I needed to move, to get up, but I'd forgotten how. My muscles just wouldn't work. Like I was paralyzed or something. My mom came back in and sat back down at the table. I could see she had tears in her eyes. It was just the three of us then.

"Well..." my mom said.

"Don't start," Dee said.

"I'm not, darling," she said. "I don't know what to do any more, but I'm not gonna start in on you."

"I embarrassed you in front of your boyfriends," Dee said.

My mom snorted. She laughed. "No, you didn't," she said.

Dee sniffed. Max sat down and started to make himself a barbecue sandwich. "Menfriends," he said. "Not boyfriends."

"They're not anything," my mom said. "Just friends."

I was glad they were gone. We all just sat there. It was like I was listening for some music that was supposed to start up, somewhere outside. I didn't know what it was supposed to be, or even if there really was something out there, but it was like my ears were cocked for it. I burped. The barbecue was repeating on me. I think my stomach was like a tightly pulled knot. I didn't feel nauseated any more, just all of a sudden kind of bloated. I hadn't eaten that much. It wasn't the food.

Max was chomping into the sandwich. He chewed. We watched him like he was playing on the guitar or something. He ate the sandwich in about three bites.

I got out of that house as fast as I could after dinner. I remembered from when I read Huckleberry Finn where Mark Twain said that Huck's sense of relief about something was "like church lettin' out."

My mom had hauled us to church a few times and I knew what he meant, and that's the way I felt when I emerged from that Thanksgiving dinner. I didn't plan it, but I found myself walking toward Amy and Donly's house. The afternoon was almost muggy, not like November at all.

There were several cars parked in the circular driveway in front of their big house. There was no sign of Amy or Donly, or anybody. They were probably all still around the table, or in the den watching football. It was surely a more normal family gathering than what we'd had at my house. I stood out there looking at the house, thinking maybe one of them would see me and come out, but they didn't. There was a little curl of smoke coming out of the chimney. I thought what a hell of a thing to have a fire in the fireplace on a day like this, and then I realized it was probably Amy's idea. I was almost sure it was. That's the way girls are. They would want to have a fire on Thanksgiving, even if you didn't need it.

I kept on just ambling down the street. I passed the statue, with the red hat. Nobody seemed to give much of a crap that it was red. There was a lot of reaction at first, but then it died down. The city didn't even scrub the paint off. I guess they were waiting for it to just wear off. This girl at school, Martha Gaines, told me she knew for a fact who had done it, that it was some boys from New Orleans who'd come up here and swiped the Parish High School bass drum and done the painting and all. I just nodded and said, "Uh-huh." I wanted to tell her I'd done it, but I didn't.

I sat on a bench down near the marina and looked out over the river, the same bench I'd been sitting on the day that crazy Mr. Means had talked to me and acted so bonkers. Downright deranged. There was hardly anybody out, it was so overcast and gray. A couple of joggers with head bands on went by in the park across the street. I started thinking about my dad. I didn't understand all that grown-up shit. For example, I suspected that one reason my dad left was because of my mother's operation, and that didn't make much sense to me. But I wasn't sure why he left us. I figured he must have had his reasons. It's not like he would have told me what they were. I didn't know why he and my mom couldn't work all that out about my dad's running around. Adult shit, like I said. And they both drank an awful lot. Deirdre said that our mom was an alcoholic. I don't know about that. But maybe she is.

I had that one letter from my dad right after he got over there, the one where he said he was going to find us a Vietnamese butterfly. I knew he didn't have time to sit around writing letters, so that was okay. I did kind of worry about him, though. I was mad at him one day and I told Deirdre I hated him. She said if I ever said anything like that again she would slap me winding. Sometimes I did hate him, though; I was angry at him for leaving us. I don't know if I had a right to be mad, but I was. It was all just so freaking complicated.

Chapter Nineteen

Near Tay Ninh, South Vietnam
November, 1965

PATRICK HAD his shirt off, a red bandana tied around his head. He was eating his C-rations. A cold can of beans and wieners. Everybody called them beans and dicks. There was a little packet of powdered cocoa, but he didn't want to waste his water making it. Anyway, his stick of C-4 was gone, so he had no way to heat it. Two sticks of Spearmint chewing gum that he put in his pocket for later. And a little package of four cigarettes, filter tip Winstons. He preferred his own, but he lit one up.

It had been raining off and on all day. Everything was wet. He and Haskins had made a lean-to with his ground cloth, against a huge rock, and tried to stay dry under there. Haskins had been wounded, too, a bullet through the fleshy part of his arm. He'd thought, like Patrick, that he had a million dollar wound. He was flown out in one of the choppers. But then they patched him up and sent him right back out. He was still sulking about it.

"Motherfucker hurts," he kept saying.

He told the rest of the platoon about his confrontation with the medical officer back at a field hospital. "I tell him I don't want to go back out. He say, 'Soldier, don't you want to fight for your country?' I say 'What country you talkin bout?' 'The U S of A,' he say. I say, 'I don't owe the fuckin' U S of A a goddam thing.' He swell up. He say, 'Son, you could be court marshal.' I say 'Court marshal my black ass, then. And I ain't your son.' He say, 'Well, you can just get your black ass right on back out there to Gook land. And Merry Christmas to you, too'."

"How come you didn't lay him out?" Seelbach asked.

"Shit. The motherfucker was a Captain, that's why."

He had a bandage around his upper right arm. He had fashioned himself a sling out of an old towel and was walking around with it when Mac said, "Git that goddam thing off, Haskins, or I'll put a round through your other arm."

A huge blister had come up on Patrick's thigh and Hamilton had lanced it, slathered on antibiotic salve and put another large bandage on it. It stung like hell but it didn't hinder his movement at all, no matter how much he at first had wanted to pretend it did. He was given a couple of days off so he lay around the LZ and slept. He thought a lot about Syl McChesney, so vital and present and then abruptly just gone. Sylvester's absence, his blank space in the platoon, was palpable. Patrick found himself wondering who would be next. He thought, over and over, It's going to be me. I know it is.

One morning Mac had kicked his good leg and said, "Okay, goldbrick, up and at 'em. Vacation over."

Patrick's platoon went out on search and destroy. The North Vietnamese Army seemed to have withdrawn, but there were still Viet Cong in the area. They came upon bunkers dug into the ground, covered with bamboo and small logs, and some of them had dead gooks in them, their bodies black and swollen and rotting. Some of the bodies were charred, like burned barbecue meat. The smell was overwhelming. They moved around the bunkers carefully. Patrick saw Jason Morrison, ahead of him, stumble and step on a corpse. His boot pulled the skin apart at the shoulder and a tangle of maggots boiled out. Patrick puked into the bushes. There is more death in this world than life, Patrick thought. He could not get used to seeing what he had to see, every day.

They came upon a broad, cleared area and knelt at the edge of the jungle. There was a village in the distance. Mac surveyed the area with his binoculars. Everything seemed quiet. Mac motioned for them to sit down and smoke. While he was resting, Patrick heard a dull metallic clanking, faint at first, then drawing closer. All the men heard it and sat up, alert, grabbing their M-16s. They watched, listening, as the sound drew closer. Patrick switched the safety off on his rifle. Then they saw some movement. "Hold it!" Mac said. Then, "Fuck!" It was a scrawny cow, with a bell. A little gook girl about five years old was walking beside it with a stick in her hand. She wore a stained, loose cotton white dress. The men watched the cow and the girl go by and disappear down the way.

"You wouldn't get no steaks off that bag of bones," Cosper said.

"I wouldn't mind tryin', though," Morrison said.

"Looked like that girl would be some pretty good pussy," Nazi said. "I wouldn't mind dippin' my dick into that."

"Shut your fuckin' mouth, white devil," Abbott said.

"Jesus. I was makin' a joke," Nazi said.

"Ha. Ha. Ha."

They observed the village for awhile from the cover of the woods. Then Mac moved them out. Mac was a huge man, muscular; he carried a BAR slung over his shoulder. The weapon was so heavy most men couldn't carry it, but Mac prided himself on being able to. They formed a line and began walking across the field. "Mines!" Mac warned, and every man looked at his feet. Patrick inspected the ground in front of him as he walked. As they approached the village it looked deserted. There were several thatched roof houses and some sheds with tin roofs. There were a number of empty pens with bamboo fences. There was no one around. Surely the little girl was not the only one living there. Patrick kept his rifle at ready. He moved down a path between two shanties.

He heard a sudden burst of fire from Mac's BAR. Patrick dropped down behind what looked like an empty hog pen. About twenty quick rounds and then silence. He waited. He peered over the bamboo fence. He could see no movement, no activity, in the village. He watched two of the men walk casually down between another two shacks. He waited another couple of minutes, then followed. The squad had gathered in front of a thatched roof house with a tattered cloth for a door. As Patrick walked up he saw an old man and an old woman on the ground, covered in blood. Their bodies were twisted into such an awkward stillness that he knew immediately they were dead.

"Fuckin' gooks," he heard Seelbach say when he walked up.

The men just stood there, not saying anything. They looked at each other. They looked away. Patrick felt a terrible sinking in his chest as he looked at the old couple. Then Gerald Abbott said, "They didn't even have any weapons. They just..."

"Shut the fuck up!" Mac interrupted him.

"A gook is a gook," Seelbach said.

Patrick felt vulnerable and guilty for thinking of the old gooks as somebody's parents or grandparents. This was their house, their village. Maybe they'd lived here all their lives. Maybe they were even the grandparents of the boy he'd killed or the little girl with the cow. His eyes were watering; he couldn't help himself. He was a fucking fool for thinking and feeling that way. You couldn't feel. Before he realized it he said, "Goddamit, Mac!"

Mac stared at him, his eyes narrowed. "What's your problem, Founier?" he said.

Patrick couldn't stop himself. "What'd you waste em for, Mac, the fun of it?" he said.

"There ain't no fun out here, Founier, ain't you learned anything yet?"

"You didn't have to..."

"I said shut the fuck up!" He stood looking around at the men. Nobody said anything. Then, he spat on the bodies. "Zippo the fuckin' place," he said.

The men hesitated, then began to move. Patrick had trouble budging himself from the spot. He just stood staring down at the bodies of the old Vietnamese people. He knew he couldn't allow himself to really feel the immense commiseration that rose up in him. The empathy. These people. He had never seen such suffering, such misery. He didn't understand how people could bring this down upon themselves, whatever was going on in this fucking country that was way beyond his comprehension. He swallowed. He forced himself to move away.

He took out his lighter and set fire to the roof of a house. The dry thatch began to crackle and flame up. All the men were doing the same thing and pretty soon the whole village was burning. Black smoke belched up and rolled over the treetops at the edge of the woods. The men began to laugh and cheer.

Patrick made himself forget the old couple. All too soon he found himself swept up in the excitement. "Burn, you motherfucker!" Patrick shouted as a small hut he'd ignited went up.

"Anybody got any fuckin' marshmallows?!" somebody else yelled. There were whoops and shrieks. As Patrick joined in the gleeful merriment he felt some of the rigid tension that had locked him in begin to ease. He even giddily wished that he'd been the one who'd wasted the gooks. He hoped that very soon he'd have the opportunity to blast another one of the slimy bastards. He hated them with a passion that constantly gnawed at him and helped to keep him exhausted. He had to hate them. There was no other way to survive.

Back at the LZ they spent two days resting and guarding the perimeter. They were issued fresh jungle fatigues and supplies. It was the first change of clothes Patrick had had in over a month. They got four cases of Long Range Reconnaissance Patrol rations, freeze dried portions of chilli con carne, spaghetti, and chicken and rice, which was all delicious. They were issued new sticks of C-4, which they could break and roll into balls and light to heat water for the meals. They could have hot coffee. Patrick got six packages of Lucky Strikes. And every man got four cans of Falstaff Beer.

"Shit, that ain't enough to even feel," Morrison said.

"Give me yours, then," Seelbach said.

"Up your gigi, Nazi," Morrison said.

"All we need is a TV so we could watch 'The Fugitive'," Cosper said.

"Man, what I wouldn't give for a TV," Haskins said.

"I can get you one for a sawbuck, Henry," Abbott said.

"What the fuck is a sawbuck?"

"Shit, this is like Christmas!" Bob Odum said.

All the men fell silent. Christmas was coming up, and they didn't want to think about it. None of them were sure of just how far away it was. They had been out on a search and destroy on Thanksgiving day, and Patrick had been unaware of what day it was until that night. Ted Walker, a new boot who'd been sent out to replace McChesney, was reading a little book called "Day by Day," and he'd looked up and said to Patrick, "Hey, did you know today was Thanksgiving?" Patrick had said, "Yeah, I been feelin' thankful all day."

At the LZ Patrick slept soundly for the first time in weeks. His leg was healing and he could get more comfortable. He felt rested and refreshed. It made him feel good just to have clean clothes. He had two new pairs of socks. He spent the afternoons sitting in the sun with his shirt off. He did his couple of hours of guard duty at night. And then he slept.

They were also re-supplied with ammunition and several new weapons. Patrick's platoon got a new Thompson submachine gun and it was assigned to Patrick's squad. Mac gave it to Patrick, so he turned in his M-16. The platoon got two new mortars as well. The new equipment was good to have, but it was telling them, reminding them, that they would be back in the fight all too soon.

Of the new replacement grunts sent out, Patrick's squad had two, Ted Walker and a very young black kid named Steve Nance. Steve was from Batavia, New York, and he was skinny as a pool cue. Ted was from Fort Meyers, Florida. Both men had been in the army less than ten weeks.

From where Patrick was crouched down he could see the four Viet Cong moving stealthily down a ridge into a mangrove swamp. They carried AK-47s and a machine gun with a swivel. One of them had on a dark green PAVN uniform shirt and black pants cut off at the knees. He was the only one who had a helmet. They all had bandoliers draped around them. Patrick gripped the Thompson. Okay. Bring it on.

He whistled sharply, twice. He could see Mac down to his left. He held up four fingers and waved toward the swamp. Mac waved his arm and the other men began to move up through the banana trees. Patrick had a clear view down an incline to the row of mangroves where the Viet Cong had disappeared. He knew they were right there. He knew they had heard him whistle. He envisioned them setting up the machine gun on its swivel. He could see them in his mind's eye kneeling, cowering behind the gun, readying their rifles. He could see their squinched gook faces, their eyes slits, their greasy lips fat and pink. Rather than the dread and horror, this time he felt, for some reason he could not fathom, a sense of anticipation. Almost elation. He felt energetic and invulnerable. He was going to have fun.

The Viet Cong's machine gun suddenly racheted as they sprayed up the hill. They must have seen some movement from the squad. Patrick heard several rifle pops. He heard Mac's BAR spitting, kicking up dirt in front of the row of trees. He pulled the Thompson up and leveled it and fired two quick bursts into the trees. He saw leaves and bits of wood flying. The gook machine gun kept sputtering. Their rounds were going high, whining over Patrick's head. He could see their forms now, in the undergrowth, and he cracked down on them. The Thompson jumped and burped in his hands. It grew hot. The Viet Cong gun kept chattering. The little cluster in the mangroves was drawing automatic rifle fire now from all along the top of the ridge, Patrick's Thompson and Mac's BAR pumping a steady stream of lead into them. Someone heaved a grenade. It bounced into the edge of the woods and exploded in a small ball of fire then white smoke and dust. The machine gun went silent.

There was quiet then for almost a minute, then someone yelled, "All right!"

A couple of more spurts from an automatic rifle. "For good measure," Seelbach shouted.

They waited. There was no movement from the machine gun nest. Wisps of dirty smoke rose into the air, and broken branches hung crookedly. Mac moved off down the incline, motioning for everyone to stay back. He held the BAR in front of him. He crept up carefully. He stood looking into the nest, then fired three quick bursts. Then he motioned for the men to come on down.

The four Viet Cong were tangled together and bloody, their limbs splayed about in aberrant, freakish poses. One's face was

171

turned upward to the sky, his mouth open wide, the sun glinting off gold teeth. "I want those," Seelbach said, and smashed the dead gook's face with his rifle butt. He began to pick at his mouth with his field knife.

"Goddam. Nasty," Cosper said. "How can you put your hands in that shit?"

"It's gold man!"

"Yeah, gold in gook shit."

Seelbach was working his bloody knife around in the gook's gaping mouth. Patrick stood looking at the bodies. He knew he had killed every one of them. He felt a comfortable satisfaction settling in his chest. He felt gratifyingly removed from the act of killing. He wanted to stand there and gaze at them, admiring his work. There was none of the nagging unease that had followed his killing of the Vietnamese boy.

"Come on," Mac said. "Move it."

"Wait a min..." Seelbach said, working on the dead gook's bloody mouth.

"Stow it, Nazi," Mac growled.

He pulled them back into the clearing. He counted. "Who's missin'?" he said, and everybody looked around. "Walker," he said.

They went back up the incline. They found Walker lying on his back. He had caught a round right between the eyes. His helmet was askew, his face bloody. "Shit," Mac said.

"Damn, he never even saw a fuckin' Viet Cong and he's already dead," Cosper said.

"Still a fuckin' boot," Morrison said, shaking his head.

"He probably never even got to fire his rifle," Marvin Whitfield said.

"Po shithead..." Haskins said.

"You assholes cut it out," Mac said. "You act like this is a fuckin' wake."

"Jesus, Mac," Gerald Abbott said. "Have a heart."

"I ain't got any fuckin' heart, spade. Fall in."

"Don't call me spade."

"I'll call you any goddam thing I want to call you. Now fall in."

"What you think this is, a parade ground?" Patrick said. "Fall in?"

"Don't give me any lip, Founier," Mac said. He glowered. The men stood quietly, looking at him. He stood there looking around, like he'd momentarily forgotten where he was. Then he said, "Git a litter. We'll haul this motherfucker back to the LZ."

Chapter Twenty

THE GOOD LADY'S had fresh oysters, and I'd already eaten two dozen of them right off the shell, with horse radish, holding the shells up to drain the brine into my mouth. The best taste in the world is fresh oyster brine. Vicki Mason was with me. She wouldn't eat oysters. She was having catfish filets. She was toying with her baked potato with a fork.

I looked at her across the booth from me. She had had her hair cut real short and she looked terrific. She was really a good looking girl, perfect mouth, full lips and shiny teeth. Her eyes were bright and animated, not dull like so many girls' were. She was quick. I'd never said anything that confused her, and she didn't feel the need to pretend. She always got it. You didn't have to explain everything to her. She was just about perfect, which made me worry that whoever raped Jane McKissick would go after Vicki in a minute if he ran into her. I wanted to protect her.

I've really been thinking a lot about Vicki, about Vicki and me. I'm not getting anywhere in my life. I don't care about school. I'm pretty bored. I'm bothered as hell by my home situation, the way my mom is acting. Sometimes I feel like cutting loose and drifting, like there's nothing solid I can hold on to anymore. Like when you're in a seat at the top of a Ferris wheel and it starts swaying back and forth and you grab hold of the bar in front of you and it's swaying back and forth, too, and the pit of your stomach drops out. I want something fixed, something rooted in my life.

I want to run away with Vicki and get married. That's what I need. I know what's best for me, and that's it. And her, too. I want her next to me.

"Let's get married," I said to her, just blurted it out.

"What?" she said. She just looked at me. "You're nuts," she said. She didn't smile or anything. What kind of a dunce was I?

"I don't mean really," I said. "Let's just tell everybody we got married."

She laughed. "Oh brother," she said. "I've heard a lot of lines tryin' to get in my panties, but that one takes the cake."

"Okay," I said. I didn't know what else to say.

She took a dainty bite of catfish. She chewed. She put her fork down. "Are you serious?" she asked.

"No," I said. "It was just a thought."

"Why ever would you want to do something like that?"

"I don't know. It'd be fun, I guess," I said.

"My mother would have a cow," she said.

"Do her good," I said. Her mother was a country club lady. She played golf every day.

"Probably would," she said.

I ate another oyster. "We could get married for real," I said.

"You are nuts," she said.

"Why not?" I asked.

She laughed again. "We're not old enough to get married, Max. It's not legal or something."

"Who gives a shit about legal?"

"Stop it," she said.

"No, really. Give me one other good reason why not?"

"Like we needed another one. Okay. Because we're not in love," she said.

"What do you mean? I love you."

"I said stop it."

"Why?"

"Because this is bullshit, and you're not laughing," she said.

"No, it's not," I said. "I'm serious."

"You're not serious, Max, and I'm about to get pissed."

"Okay," I said. "I'll shut up about it." Neither of us said anything for a minute or two. "But I still want to marry you," I said.

"Maybe you ought to take me home," she said.

"Okay, I'll stop." Right at that moment I wanted to marry her more than anything. I wanted her warmth and her smell all around me. All the time. Her limbs were smooth and perfect. Her skin was something you just wanted to lick. Her lips were soft and her tongue was strong. I wanted to run away with her, to California or Europe or somewhere far away from this stinking town.

"Let's talk about something else," she said.

I had to pause and swallow and get my bearings. I took a deep breath. "Okay, what do you want to talk about?" I asked.

She narrowed her eyes at me. "You're in a mood," she said.

"Yeah," I said.

Her voice got gentle. "What is it?" she asked, "your dad?"

"All of it," I said, and damned if my eyes didn't fill up with tears. I didn't know what the hell was happening to me. She reached out and twined her fingers into mine. Her hand was hot and silky. I felt like my head was swelling up, hollow and airy, and I was going to drift straight up through the roof. Her hand was holding me to the table. She patted my hand.

"He's gonna be okay, Max. He'll come home okay."

"Maybe," I said. "Maybe not."

She held my hand and squeezed it. "Oh, Max," she said. "Is it your mother? Is she..." Her eyes were full of tears then.

"No," I said, but I realized it was her, too. "She's fine. If you can trust the doctors."

"You have to," Vicki said.

"I guess so," I said. "All I know is I love you."

"I love you, too, Max," she said. I raised my eyebrows. "Not like that," she said quickly.

"Like a brother, I guess," I said. My head was deflating. I pulled my hand out from under hers. I wiped the back of my hand across my eyes.

"No, not like a brother. Just not getting married kind of love."

"Okay," I said. I took several deep breaths. We sat there looking at each other. Goddam, she was gorgeous. I felt better just looking at her. She started eating her salad. She always ate her salad after she ate her meal. She said that's the way they did it in Italy.

"Did you have a nice Thanksgiving?" she asked, looking at me over her fork with those eyes that were jabbing holes right through me.

"Shit," I said.

"I guess not."

I shrugged my shoulders. "You know. Lame."

"Me, too," she said. "My folks are shitty. They drive me crazy."

I had finished my oysters and I pushed the metal platter away. She was just looking at me. Her eyes were olive brown, not blue like a lot of blondes. She reached out and touched my hand again. "Max," she said. "I'm sorry I tried to talk to you about your dad. And asked about your mom. I shouldn't bring that up."

"That's okay," I said, not looking at her.

"No, really, I mean, I had no right. I mean, I'm not..." She stopped. "Not really your girlfriend or anything," she said.

"It's okay, Vicki," I said. Maybe she wasn't my girlfriend, yet, but she was the closest thing to it I had. "I do miss him," I said. "I mean I miss him being around the house. My little sister Deirdre? She's all bent out of shape about it. She thought he was coming home for Thanksgiving, just gonna pop in and surprise us. All the way from Vietnam. Can you believe that? She says he told her he was. I wouldn't put it past him. He's got me so I don't trust him much. Why would he tell her something like that?"

"I don't know."

"It's really weird," I said. "Sometimes, when I think about him, I can't even really visualize what he looks like. I mean, I know, but I can't really put it into a picture in my mind. My own father! I'm losing my fucking mind."

"No," she said.

"I am. I'm failin' two subjects. I may get tossed out of school. And then maybe I'll get drafted and sent over there with him. You can just get them to throw me in the looney bin."

"I thought you couldn't even register for the draft until you were eighteen," Vicki said. "You've got almost a year yet, Max." I didn't say anything. "You'll do enough to get by. You always do," she went on.

I gave her a Winston out of my pack and I lit them both with my Zippo that my dad had sent me right before he went overseas. It had U.S. ARMY engraved on it. She sucked the smoke really deep into her lungs and closed her eyes and sighed with pleasure. She blew the smoke toward the ceiling. She smiled at me. I asked her if she wanted any dessert and she shook her head. With her blonde hair she reminded me of Deirdre. Deirdre now thinks the old man is coming home for Christmas. I didn't have the heart to tell her no way. I worry about her. She probably loves him too much. I should tell her to grow up.

"Penny for your thoughts," Vicki said.

"It would take more'n that," I said.

"Okay, a dime."

"You don't want to know," I said.

"Yes I do. Please," she said. I wanted to tell her all about it. About how I knew my dad was running around on my mom and I could hear my mom crying at night when he wouldn't come home until dawn. About how she was careful not to cry in front of us when she learned about the cancer, but I heard her. About how all that sometimes made me want to cry, too. I wanted to tell her how much I loved Deirdre and how concerned I was about Willie, who was still a kid and had cried like a baby when my mom got sick, and he always just wanted to be by himself. And seeing my mom drink the way she did and get bleary eyed and sad. I couldn't tell a girl all that. It would make me sound like some kind of pussy.

"It's nothing, really," I said, and I'll be goddamed if I didn't start to get tears in my eyes again. I didn't know what the hell was wrong with me. She was just looking at me. She reached out and put her hand over mine again. I think that's when I really knew I loved her. And that made me feel sad, too. Because I knew she would never love me back.

"Damn, you're in a funk," she said. "Is anything wrong?"

Everything's wrong. "No, nothing big. I flunked that algebra test this mornin'. Gets me down." I wasn't going to burden her with all my troubles. Her mom didn't have cancer and drink too much and jump out of airplanes. Not that I cared if my mom jumped out of airplanes, I actually thought it was kind of cool.

"Ha!" she said. She didn't believe me, but she let it drop. She knew I didn't care about any algebra test.

It was raining when we came out of The Good Lady's and walked down the steps to the parking lot. It was one of those early winter rains that sort of hang in the air. It was turning colder, and we both turned the collars of our jackets up. I had on my red one. I was James Dean and she was Natalie Wood. She was better looking than Natalie Wood. Not so bug-eyed. And she wasn't skinny.

Up on the highway I turned the Chevy toward the old river bridge and town. The windshield wipers were slapping back and forth. Vicki turned on the radio. It was The McCoy's, *"Hang On Sloopy"*. I didn't want to go home. I never wanted to go home. I wasn't really listening to the song, and I knew she wasn't either, because if she had been she'd have been singing along with it. I wanted to keep driving and take her to never never land.

The draw bridge was up and we had to wait. The song changed and it was The Temptations, *"My Girl"*.

"They know we're here," Vicki said.

"What you mean by that?" I asked.

"They're playing it because they know we're sittin' here and you would sing it to me."

I thought she might be having me. But she was smiling at me, not laughing. "You mean because you're my girl?" I asked.

"Well," she said. "Maybe. Maybe not."

Okay. Not that I needed it, but that kind of answer reminded me that she was a girl. Parsimonious. It was a word Willie'd found in one of his books. He told me one time that he thought girls were parsimonious. Whatever the hell that means, but it sure sounds right. We could see just the lights of the tug and barges down on the river, headed for New Orleans. The bridge went down and I drove on over into town. "What do you want to do?" I asked.

"I don't know," she said. "You?" Why did that not surprise me?

Dr. Zhivago was showing at the movie theater down on Washington Street. I'd seen it in New Orleans when it first came out. I wouldn't have minded seeing it again. But I couldn't make myself suggest it. I just kept driving. We passed the theater and she didn't suggest it either. Maybe we could just drive around all night. Maybe we could drive around forever. Around and around the world. Stopping off from time to time to get some oysters. And some catfish.

We made a date for Friday night. I dropped Vicki off at her house and drove out to the Cherokee. There was nobody at the Cherokee. I was driving back down Main Street when I saw Willie walking along under the street lights. He sort of skipped when he walked.

I stopped and rolled the window down. "Hey, faggot!" I called out.

He jumped like I'd hit him with a pebble. "What?" he said.

"Want a ride?" He was already walking around the car, climbing in. "Where you goin'?" I asked.

"Home," he said.

He had mud on the knees of his corduroy pants. When we had first moved up here from Breaux Bridge my mom made me wear these corduroy knickers that came down to my knees. She saw them in some magazine. She let Willie wear regular pants. There's something to be said for being the third kid. By then they've gotten tired of dressing you up so they just leave you alone.

"You been playin' football?" I asked. He looked over at me and I pointed to his knees.

"Oh," he said. "Yeah." I could tell by the way he answered that he hadn't been. I knew Willie didn't care about football, either watching it or playing it. I think the boys who got out there screaming and yelling and knocking each other down in the mud just bored the living shit out of Willie. He probably fell down chasing a butterfly and didn't want to tell me. Not because he was embarrassed about chasing a butterfly, but because it wasn't any of my fucking business.

"You better pick that mud offa there before Mom sees it," I said. "But wait till you get out of my car."

"Okay," he said. He shrugged. He sniffed. "Smells like bubble gum in here."

"I'll tell Vicki Mason you said her perfume smelled like bubble gum," I said and chuckled. Had she had on perfume? Or maybe she had just been chewing bubble gum. Girls smell great, whatever. "Don't you like it?" I asked him.

"Yeah," he said. He wouldn't look at me. He was looking out the window, his eyes trained on the sidewalk. We were getting close to the house.

"Willie, you ought not to be out walkin' after dark," I said.

"Why not?" he asked.

"Now that Bay Springs has become the rape capital of Louisiana," I said. We both laughed.

"Bay Springs is the capital of weirdos – not just of Louisiana – but of the whole United States," he chuckled. But he didn't look at me. He just kept peering out the side window, like he was looking for something, like he expected to see the rapist or something out there on the sidewalk.

I parked in the driveway behind my mom's Caddy, where I'd have to move it if she was going out anywhere. I hoped she wasn't. She was probably on her second drink by then. We walked up the walk and into the house without saying anything else. I could sense and feel his aloneness, almost as if he was putting out heat. I didn't know what else to say. I wished I hadn't brought up about that rape. But everybody in town was talking about it.

Deirdre was standing in the kitchen when we got in. She was drinking a glass of tea. Willie stomped off to his room.

"What's goin' on, Princess?" I asked.

"Nothin'," she said. "Nothin's ever goin on in this town."

"We had a lot of excitement the other week."

"What?"

"Jane McKissick."

"Shit," she said. "Mom's so bent out of shape over that she's got me nervous about it."

"You ought to be nervous. Careful."

"You think she was really raped, Max?"

"Somebody beat her up pretty bad. I don't know how they could tell she was raped, putting out the way she does," I said.

She looked thoughtful. "Maybe rape does somethin' to your...you know," she said.

"Yeah, maybe," I said. "When you were little I used to call it your 'mouse's ear'."

"You looked at me?!"

"Hell, Dee, I used to change your diapers when I wasn't much older than you. Somebody had to do it."

"I don't remember that," she said.

"Course you don't remember it. You were little."

She thought about that for a minute, staring at her glass of tea. My sister had turned into a beautiful young woman.

"But you and your friends really ought to be careful," I went on, "the police don't have a clue who did it."

"He's probably half way to Timbuktu right now," she said.

"I wouldn't count on it. Where's Mom?"

"Out."

"Her car's in the driveway," I said. I could hear the radio playing up in Dee's room. I sat down at the table, listening. It was The Righteous Brothers, *"You've Got That Lovin' Feeling"*.

"I think she said she was goin' somewhere with Miz Willingham, probably out tossin' down a few." She held her glass up. "You want some?" she asked, "I made a pitcher."

"Yeah," I said. I watched her get a glass and get ice from a bowl in the refrigerator. We never had enough ice. Deirdre was the only one who always filled up the trays, and when she cracked one she always put the extra cubes in a bowl. If everybody did that, we'd have ice for our tea at suppertime and Mom would always have rocks for her drinks.

Deirdre was inspecting her fingernails. They were painted a kind of rose pink. She was looking at them closely, frowning. When had she turned into a woman? I was probably going to have to whip some ass. She was so sweet it almost made me cry, unless I was so mad at her I wanted to kill her. I thought about her maddening side so I wouldn't cry. I was turning into some kind of weeping shithead.

I watched Deirdre looking at her fingernails. I was thinking about how much I really loved her, but in a different way from the way I loved Vicki. I felt very close to my sister, like we were two stray kittens in a thunderstorm. I wanted to protect her, too. I guess I wanted to make it up to her for the way our dad had hurt us. But she didn't even admit that he had hurt us. She adored him. Blindly.

"He's not comin' home Christmas, Dee," I said.

"Fuck you," she said. She stood up and turned toward the stairs.

"I only want you not to get yourself all worked up again," I said. "I don't want to see you disappointed and crying when he doesn't show up."

She stopped and turned to me. "What do you know," she said. "You don't even like him."

"Of course I like him," I said. "I love him, he's my dad."

"You don't," she said "You and Mama both hate him."

"We don't, Dee," I said. Her eyes were getting filled up with water and I knew she was going to start to cry. I was praying that she wouldn't, because I was afraid I'd break down, too. "It's just, well, it's so complicated."

"Yeah, like I'm just a little kid and I don't understand. Well, I understand plenty."

"Okay," I said. "But he's not comin' home."

She sat back down. She did start to cry then, boo-hooing, and it ripped my heart out. I was just trying to help her and I'd fucked it up. I was wishing I had talked to Vicki, gotten some girl advice, because I sure as hell didn't seem to be able to say the right thing. I just sat and watched her cry for a minute, then I reached out and put my hand on hers, the way Vicki had done for me. She jerked it away. Something turned over in my chest. I took a deep breath. Then she moved her hand back and put it on top of mine. And then I did lose it. I wasn't sobbing like her; I was just sitting there letting tears leak down my cheeks. We cried together for a long time.

Finally she stopped sobbing and gradually calmed down. She picked up a paper napkin from the table and blew her nose. She was sniffling. "Maybe I know something you don't," she said.

"I just don't want to see my little sister with her heart broken," I said, and my voice cracked on the "broken."

She looked up at me then. She wiped her eyes with the sleeve of her sweater. She looked so much like she had as a little girl. God, she was beautiful. Even with her eyes red and her cheeks looking raw. "Mind your own business," she said. Then she smiled a quick little smile.

"Okay," I said.

She moved her glass back and forth, watching the moisture that gathered under it. The house was quiet. There'd not been a peep from Willie's room. She looked at me out of the corners of her eyes, a sneaky look.

"I love you, Max," she said, just barely above a whisper.

"I love you, too, Princess," I said.

Chapter Twenty-One

Tay Ninh, South Vietnam
December, 1965

PATRICK WAS on his way back from the latrine at the compound when he spotted the bayonet. It was lying on a ground cloth next to a tent. It was polished and shiny, the sun glinting off the long blade. He picked it up and inspected it. He could see gook letters stamped along the ridge of the heavy steel handle. It was a Vietnamese bayonet that someone had found, a souvenir. Patrick immediately coveted it. He wanted to take it home to Willie or Max. Willie would love it. He could take it to school for show and tell. He would be proud of his father. Out here, Patrick figured it was just as much his as anybody else's. He tucked it alongside his arm and started to walk away.

"Hey, grunt, that ain't yours," he heard a voice say. This was another platoon, but Patrick thought the guy's name was Williston. He was leaning back against a sandbag in the shade, smoking.

"It is now," Patrick said.

"It belongs to Bean," Williston said. "He ain't gonna be any too happy you took it, Founier."

So the guy knew who he was. "Finder's keepers," Patrick said. He walked away.

When he got back to where he and Haskins were bivouacked, he tucked the bayonet into his field pack. He was getting quite a collection. Odum had told him it was hard to get stuff like that out, but there were ways. You couldn't carry it out, but you could take it back to the base camp with you and ship it home or somewhere and then retrieve it when you got home.

Patrick went over and sat with Odum and Steve Nance, who were smoking weed. Odum was using a short black pipe. Steve was shirtless and wore a soft boonie hat. He was so skinny you could count every rib and his skin was hairless and shone like well-browned freshly baked bread.

"I heard 'fore I come out that some guys used shotgun barrels," Nance said. He sucked on his joint and passed it to Patrick.

"Yeah," Odum said. "I heard that, too. I bought this pipe in Saigon for four cents."

"Shit, Nance," Patrick said. "You nigger-lipped it."

"Watch your mouth, Cajun."

"Sorry."

"I honky-lipped it," Nance said. He had a peculiar upper New York accent that Patrick had never heard before.

"Whatever the hell you did, stop doin' it," Patrick said. "Your spit tastes like cat piss."

"You ought to know," Nance said.

"How old did you say you were, Nance?" Odum asked.

"Eighteen."

"Shit. You lied. You couldn't be over twelve."

"Yeah, I lied. I'm actually fifty seven."

"This is some good shit," Patrick said.

"I could get fifty dollars a lid for this shit back home," Nance said.

A formation of six or seven helicopters went racketing over them, heading northwest. "Where those fuckers goin'?" Nance asked.

"Where you think?" Odum said.

"What the hell we doin' out here?" Nance asked.

"What you mean?"

"I mean, we don't do nothin' but go out and tromp through the shit and come back here and smoke some dope and then go back out again. So what we doin'?"

"Just what you said, Nance," Odum said.

"But what the purpose for it?"

"How the hell should I know?"

"You been to college, ain't you?"

Odum laughed. "Shit," he said. He drew on the pipe, sat for a minute, then blew the smoke toward the cloudless sky. "I reckon some shitheads somewhere know what the hell we're doin'. You'd think that, wouldn't you?"

"Six months ago I never even heard of South Vietnam," Nance said.

"You livin' under a rock?" Patrick asked.

"I might'uv heard somebody mention it, but I didn't know what they's talkin' about," Nance said.

"Well, you do now," Odum said.

Richard Bean, a corporal from another platoon, came strolling up. Everybody called him L L. He, too, was shirtless; he had a little cartoon skunk tattooed on his upper chest, with "Lil Stinky" written under it. He stopped and stood there, his hands on his hips.

"What can we do you for, L L?" Odum asked.

Bean looked narrow-eyed at Patrick. "This Cajun son-of-a-bitch can return my gook bayonet," he said.

"I found it," Patrick said. "You lost it and I found it."

"I didn't lose it, motherfucker! It was on my ground cloth. You took it and I want it back."

"I didn't see your name on it."

Bean looked at Odum. "I'm gonna kick this bastard's teeth in," he said.

"No skin off my ass," Odum said. He was high. He started to giggle.

"Give me the bayonet, Founier," Bean said. He was standing with his legs spread, his fists jammed onto his hips. His pants were drooping in front almost to his pubic hair.

"No, goddamit, it's mine," Patrick said.

"You stole it, asshole," Bean said. "Give it here."

"I ain't got it. I sent it home to my son," Patrick said.

"You lyin', man. How the fuck you gonna send somethin' home from out here? You lyin' like a cross tie."

Patrick stood up. He couldn't back down. He didn't want to disappoint Willie. He wiped his hands on his pants. "You gonna have to take it," he said.

Bean grunted and swung. His fist caught Patrick on the tip of his chin and spun him around. The blow startled Patrick. Heat surged behind his eyes. A swelling of energy and strength came with his sudden anger. He counterpunched quickly and his fist smashed into Bean's nose. Patrick felt the cartilage give, felt hot blood spurt onto the back of his hand. He punched again, then again. Bean stood there helpless, his arms hanging, his eyes glazed, and Patrick kicked him as hard as he could in the balls. Bean went down and Patrick was on top of him. He grabbed him by the throat with both hands, squeezing. He was panting and wheezing. He kept on choking him.

"Goddam, Cajun," Odum was yelling, pulling at his shoulder. Nance was yanking back on the other one. "Stop, man! Don't kill the sonofabitch!" Odum said.

Bean was moaning. Patrick jumped up. He was shaking all over. He didn't know what had overtaken him. Maybe he was trying to kill Bean. He had acted without even thinking about it. Bean sat up, dusty, blood pouring from his nose. "You better watch your fuckin' back, Cajun," he said, struggling up, then staggering off toward his bivouac.

"Jesus!" Odum said after a minute.

"This man a total bad ass," Nance said, looking at Patrick with admiration.

"You coulda killed the motherfucker, Patrick," Odum said. "What got into you?"

"He called me a liar," Patrick said. He wiped his bloody hands on his pants.

"Remind me not to ever do that," Odum said.

Haskins came strolling up, followed by some of the other men. They had passed L L Bean on the path. "What happened to Bean? He looked like he'd been drug through a barbed wire fence backwards," Haskins said.

"You'd look like that, too, you done been attacked by a grizzly bear," Nance said. He laughed.

"What's goin' on?" Haskins asked.

"Pappy done kicked some ass," Nance said.

"Jesus," Odum said. "This sonofabitch was gonna kill the man over a fuckin' knife." He was shaking his head.

"Me," Nance said, grinning, "I wants to be standin' next to this mean motherfucker when the fuckin' Viet Cong come."

Chapter Twenty-Two

Bay Springs, Louisiana
December, 1965
OLGA

I WAS AT my desk in the band room, listening to Jeannie Thompson practicing her French horn in the practice room next door. Jeannie was determined to try out for Honor Band, and, even though she wasn't very good, I was encouraging her. It was always nice to have students who were eager to excel. I had some excellent musicians, like Clyde Smith, the first trumpet, and some others, who always made Honor Band without half trying. They were all very into marching band, which, to be frank, I was pretty bored with. I was excited that football season was over and we could concentrate on symphonic band. The All-State Band Contest was coming up in February, and that was fast approaching.

I was trying to make out an expanded rehearsal schedule for the concert season. One of the most annoying things about my job was trying to juggle all the extra-curricular crap. For example, I had three boys–some of my most talented–who were also on the basketball team, and practice for them had started even before football season was over. I needed them for the concert band. We were doing *Marche Slav* by Tchaikovsky, and *Fiddler On The Roof Medley*, songs from a show that had opened last year in New York, new music the band had never played before. I loved both pieces but they were very difficult, especially for the younger students. Though my band was officially classified by the state board as a Class C band, the music I'd chosen was Class AA. My goal was to motivate the students, to make them better. I drove them hard. They didn't complain a lot about the long practice hours–at least to me–but their parents did. I demanded a lot of discipline from them, more than I demanded from my own kids. My motto was "Early is on time, on time is late." I knew I was probably a better band director than I was a parent.

I looked up and Winston Larkin, the principal, was standing there. Because of the loud flat blasts that were coming from the French horn, I hadn't heard him come in.

"My God," he said. "You got a dying animal in there?"

"I wish," I said. "At least it would get quiet when it died."

He laughed. "You got a minute? I need to talk to you."

"Okay," I said. I went to the door of the practice room. "Jeannie," I called out, "your practice session is over."

Blessed quiet rolled over us. "Mam?" she said.

"I said, that's enough for today. Don't you have a class?"

"Not for another fifteen minutes," Jeannie said.

"Well, take a break, then," I said. Jeannie came out into the band room and found her case and started to pack away her horn.

"Hi, Mr. Larkin," she said, very flirtily. She was an attractive girl, a senior. Larkin was in his late forties, an ex-football coach. He enjoyed the attention from the pretty girls, a joke among the women teachers who were my friends.

"Hello, Jeannie," Larkin said. He had sat down in the first row, in the first trumpet chair. We watched the girl put away her instrument, leaning over to put the case in the rack. I could see him taking her in, as though it was some show just for him. It probably was. She grabbed her jacket.

"Bye," she said as she went out the door, her pleated skirt swaying. Larkin stared after her, then looked at me.

"What's on your mind?" I asked, sitting back down behind my desk. I had shattered his pleasant reverie. He blinked.

"Do you know this guy Rayford Means? The preacher?"

"I know of him. Isn't he the chaplain of the football team? I don't know him. Why?" I abruptly recalled vividly seeing him in the bar at Sapfat's that afternoon, his eyes, the way he looked at me.

"Well, he doesn't think you're morally fit to be a teacher. He wants you fired."

I was startled. Speechless for a moment. Then, "Not morally fit?"

"Yes."

"What gives him the right to make that judgement?"

"Jesus," Larkin said. I thought at first he had cursed. "He had all sorts of claims; he'd heard you came to school drunk one day. That you were drunk that night after the football game, when you parachuted. He said people in town were talking about you being drunk in public, being out with other men..."

"Whoa," I said. "Whoa."

"Did you come to school drunk?" he asked.

I hesitated. Did I? No. Maybe after a snort or two, but never drunk. "No, of course not, Winston," I said. "And I have friends. Not lovers."

"He said that God wanted you to be punished. He said you were a harlot." The word "harlot" made a tiny little light go on in my head, but I couldn't recall why. I was beginning to get angry.

"Drinking is not a sin, in my view," I said.

"It is in his," Larkin said.

"Friends," I said again. How dare this pious preacher question my morals?! And go to my boss about it? "I'm allowed to have friends, aren't I?" I was mad now.

"Come on, Olga," Larkin said. He just stared at me.

"What?" I asked.

"It's not exactly a secret that you drink too much occasionally. Means says he saw you going to an AA meeting."

"Is that a sin, too?" I snapped. "I have never been drunk in front of my students!" I said adamantly. It bothered the hell out of me that this bastard was watching me, spying on me. That's what he'd been doing that afternoon in the bar.

"I told him as much," he said. "Calm down."

"I can't afford to lose this job, Winston," I said tightly.

"A man like that can make trouble, Olga," Larkin said.

I took a deep breath. We sat in silence for a moment. "His daughter's in the band," I said. "I've never talked to him, just seen him around. He drives a pickup truck. I've seen him when he picks her up after practice. Three different times this fall he's been late, and I've had to sit with the girl and wait on him. She seems like a troubled girl. I've been teaching her to play chess."

"Chess?"

"Yes," I said. I realized I'd been rattling on nervously. "I'm afraid her flute playing is beyond redemption." I didn't mention that I'd seen Means observing me when I was sitting drinking with a man who was not my husband. I wanted to, wanted to shout it defiantly. I was thoroughly pissed off. If that old son of a bitch thought he had any control over my life, he had another thing coming!

Larkin leaned back in the chair and crossed his legs. His collar was unbuttoned, the tie loosened. I wondered why he wore one if he was going to look so half-assed in the middle of the day. My throat felt dry and hot, like I was catching a cold. This was almost too much.

"Olga, I'm talking to you as your friend as well as as your principal," he said. "I know I have no right to tell you who you can have for 'men friends'." He stopped. I just looked at him. "Don't think this is easy for me," he said. "But I don't think it's a good idea for you to be seen with a guy – a boy really – who hangs out with the anti-war crowd over at the college. One who leads marches against the war. Okay?"

After a long silence, I said, "Okay. I see what you mean."

"And you with a husband over there in Vietnam," he said.

"I said okay, Winston! Is this the thing that has that ass-hole preacher all riled-up? Because..."

"No, not that specifically," he said quickly, "that was more... well, more my observation."

"Oh," I said. "Really?"

"Not that I..." He paused. "Look, Olga, it's your own business what you do with your life. But things have consequences, that's all I'm saying."

"What am I supposed to do, go into a convent or something?" I asked bitterly.

"No, no, you know that's not what I'm saying. I just mean you need to be more... discreet, I guess."

"I've really got to get on this," I said sharply, indicating my desk. I struggled for control.

"Okay," he said. "Now you know, at least."

"Yeah," I said. "Now I know." I watched him walk out.

I looked at the schedules. They were a confusing hodge-podge of scratchings. I couldn't afford to lose this job. But I wasn't going to let that nosy preacher tell me what to do. I needed to calm down. Put this out of my mind. I took a couple of deep breaths. I picked up my pen.

I stopped by Susan Willingham's classroom after I left the band room. When I looked in the door she was getting up from behind her desk. I didn't know how much I'd tell her. Susan sometimes took things too seriously or not seriously enough at all.

"Let's go to the teacher's lounge," she said before I could say anything, "I'm dying for a cigarette."

We walked down the hallway. The maintenance women had been cleaning the floors and the air smelled like pine. The school was almost pleasant in the afternoons after all the students were gone. It was intensely quiet after all the babble and prattle of shrill adolescent voices all day. There was one other teacher in the lounge, Cameron Herman, a biology teacher who looked young enough to be one of the students. He looked up at us and then back at his book without speaking. He was drinking a cup of coffee. He was so young he treated us like the students did, like we were semi-visible.

We found some chairs across the room.

"How's it goin'?" Susan said, lighting up her cigarette. On impulse, I bummed one from her. That's the way it always happened. With drinking, too. In the past, when I would get all pumped up and feeling saintly and resolve to quit drinking, I'd go sometimes for several months without a drink and then have a relapse. The first couple of drinks were down the hatch before I really even realized I was doing it. And right at that moment I really needed a cigarette.

"Are you sure?" she asked.

"What?"

"I mean... you know." She drew on her cigarette. "I don't know if I believe all that stuff I read in the papers about it causing cancer, but still..."

"Nobody takes all that very seriously, Susan." She watched me draw on my cigarette. "Reverend Means is trying to make trouble," I said. "He says I'm 'immoral'. The Lark just came by and told me."

"Shit," Susan said. "Your drinking? What's he gonna do about it?"

"I don't know," I said. "At least he didn't fire me on the spot."

"Shit, you've got your rights, Olga. He can't fire you because of what some kook says."

The second I'd inhaled I'd known I was hooked again. The smoke was harsh in my throat but soothing and quieting. It tingled in my brain. It lit me up. I loved smoking almost as much as I loved drinking, but I had quit to try to set an example for Deirdre and Willie. A cigarette was a portable high. Just smoking it made me anxious to get home and have a drink.

"It would be nice to have a bottle of Scotch in the lounge," I said.

"Make mine vodka," Susan said. "We can dream, I guess."

"That guy sees sin behind every tree. He is truly messed up." My unease bubbled within me, like water coming to a boil.

Susan waved her hand in front of her face, as though waving Means away like a gnat or a wisp of smoke. "He's not worth worrying about," she said.

I knew, of course, it was not just because of what Means said, but because there was some basis in fact that I couldn't deny about his charges. But drinking too much was a weakness you had to struggle with, not a moral failing. "Maybe not. But he could make trouble." I savored the cigarette. It calmed me. We sat there smoking for a minute or two; I knew Susan was waiting for me to go on. Susan's husband was a policeman, so I said, "Hey, I heard they arrested that Crumpton fellow, works out at the paper mill. Maybe he was the one that raped the girl. Huh?"

"Naaaah," she said. "Ottis Crumpton. They didn't arrest him. They hauled him in for questionin'. Steve said no way he did it."

"How do they know that? I mean, why'd they bring him in?"

"Somebody tipped them they saw him hangin' around out behind the gym after the game that night. But Steve said there was nothin' to link him to the rape."

"How'd they know? He's a slimy looking bastard."

"I don't know, Olga. They have ways I guess."

"Maybe they gave him a lie detector test."

"Maybe so. But Steve said he didn't do it. I mean, they were satisfied."

"Huh," I said. "I was hopin' they had him. I worry all the time. I feel like shit lettin' Willie and Dee walk all over town by themselves. I feel like a lousy – lousier I should say – lousier mother for letting them do that. Most of the parents of the band kids drive up here to get them after practice. Everybody in town is shook up."

"Yeah. Well..."

"And now I guess everybody in town is yakking up about what a rummy and a slut I am."

"Oh, come on, Olga," she said. "A slut? Come on."

"Do they? Talk about me, I mean?"

"Nobody says anything to me. I guess they know I'm your friend." I just looked at her. "I mean, shit, somebody's always gossiping about something."

She just sat there, then, not saying anything. "Do you think I'm a lousy mother?" I asked her.

"No. You don't drink any more than anybody else. And you're taking care of your kids."

"I guess," I said.

"Pays to be careful," she said. "No. I don't think you're a bad mother, Olga. And the guy is probably in California or somewhere by now. So quit worrying about it."

"You don't have children," I said.

"No," she said. "I don't."

I called Bo and arranged to meet him for a drink. I thought, by damn, that's my perfect right. I wanted to tell him about Means, about how the man had spied on us that day at Sapfat's. I met him at The Good Lady's across the river. Bo and I were innocent of any wrongdoing. We'd only had a couple of drinks together, and though I knew that we each found the other attractive, nothing had passed between us, not even any real flirting. We were just friends, not even friends, really, just acquaintances. I knew that, and that was enough for me. I might see somebody I knew at The Good Lady's, but I was feeling just rebellious enough not to care. To hell with Reverend Means.

Bo had been at the college all day helping to organize a march against the war. He had two students with him when he arrived, a boy and a girl. The girl had long, straight blonde hair parted in the middle. She wore jeans and a loose, too-large gray sweatshirt with a peace sign and the words FUCK FOR PEACE on the front. The boy wore jeans and a faded denim jacket. The two of them slid into the booth across from Bo and me. Bo introduced them. The boy's name was Bernard, the girl's Sam. "For Samantha," she said.

Bo was excited. They were chummy, obviously sharing something that I was not a part of. They had been planning an anti-war march for the next day. I found myself feeling self-consciously matronly. I could have been their mother! Bo was flushed, more animated than I'd seen him. "It should be great," he said. "You'll have to come see it. I'd love for you to march with us."

"I don't know about that," I said. I thought about Means. I smiled to myself. That would push him over the top. And Deirdre would crawl through the floor.

"I don't see why not," Bo said.

"I'm not much on marching," I said.

"I'm gonna burn my draft card," Bernard said. He had zits on his cheeks. He looked about twelve years old.

"You're not old enough to be registered," I said and he laughed.

"I wish," he said. "I'm eighteen."

"In front of the courthouse," Bo said. "We'll probably have about fifty or sixty folks there. Bernie's gonna burn his, and a couple of other guys."

"What about you?" I asked. "You gonna burn yours?"

"I'm 4-F," he said, rather proudly, I thought.

"You are?"

"Yeah. Bad back."

I was surprised. I hadn't noticed any "bad back." He seemed completely healthy to me. His satisfaction in being classified 4-F annoyed the hell out of me.

"I wish I had a draft card so I could burn it," Sam said.

"Why don't you burn your bra?" I asked her.

"I would, but I don't wear one," she said, completely missing my sarcasm. She was in college, but she seemed less mature than even Deirdre.

I was wondering what I was doing in this crowd. Bo and I had whiskey, Bernard a beer, and Sam had a coke. She ordered a platter of French fries. In the middle of the afternoon. Exactly what Deirdre and her friends would have done. But the three of them were serious about what they were doing, and I was certainly in sympathy with their cause. I was "against" the war in Vietnam, but then I was against war, period. What they were doing about it seemed remote from my own experiences, just as the war – and Patrick over there in it – seemed distant and alien, abstract and illusory. "Protest" was something that was not a part of my normal sphere of involvement.

What the hell did I think I was doing? I didn't belong here. I felt as lonely with them as I did without them, lonelier. They seemed so focused in on their cause, but I couldn't join them, wouldn't have if I could. I didn't fit. I felt like a teacher supervising a kindergarten class. I didn't know if I fit anywhere, except as a mother to my children. I would be as ferocious as a sow bear if anyone tried to harm any one of them, I knew that. I was confident I'd be focused on that.

"I want another drink," I said.

Bo signaled for the waitress.

"Listen," Bernard said. "Sam and I better get back." They both stood.

"Okay," Bo said. "Have everybody together at that little park at two sharp. And Bernie, try to keep those other two guys from going chickenshit and gettin' cold feet, okay?"

"They won't do that, Bo," Bernard said.

They gathered their coats and left.

"She's a cute girl," I said, when our drinks came.

"Who?" he said.

From the way he said that one word, "who", I knew he was sleeping with her. And why not? Even though he was probably fifteen years older than she was. They were part of a world from which I was alienated. It made me feel grizzled and hoary, tired. Out of it. They were probably very casual about it, the way I supposed Patrick was with his little sluts. I was completely different, old fashioned, unhip and geriatric, someone who came of age in the fifties. And it made me feel ludicrous just being with him. Self-conscious. I shifted in my seat. I took out a package of Pall Malls that I'd bought from a machine in the lobby of The Good Lady's. He looked surprised, cocking his eyebrows. "When'd you start?" he asked.

I shook out a cigarette and tapped it against my thumbnail to pack it. I stuck it between my lips. He picked up a folder of paper matches that had come taped to the Pall Malls and struck one and lit my cigarette. He put the matches on the table. I took a deep, full draw, feeling the smoke flood my lungs. I sat reading the little matchbook. Be an artist, it said, Learn to draw. Take our free test inside.

"I wanted to tell you," I said. "That there's this preacher in town who's trying to get me fired from my job."

"Really?" he asked. He didn't say anything else for a minute. Then he said, "Want me to kick his ass for you?" I sighed. It was exactly the kind of thing Max would have said. Or even Patrick.

"No," I said. "I don't want you to kick his ass for me."

"Why does he want you fired?" he asked.

"Because I have a drink or two. Ha Ha," I chuckled. "And he saw us together one day at Sapfat's bar, and he doesn't think that's appropriate."

"The bastard," Bo said.

"Well, maybe he has a point."

He looked at me peculiarly. He shook his head. He looked away, then back at me. "Olga," he said. "Let's go back."

"What?" His quick shift confused me.

"To A A."

I took a sip of my drink. "Go ahead," I said.

"I want you to come with me," he said. He was looking at me with an earnest, almost mournful expression. It was a look of compassion that I'd liked about him before, but now it struck me as patronizing. He was talking to the sweet old lady. The sweet little old lady drunk.

"I don't want to go to AA," I snarled. "AA is a crock of shit."

"Yeah, it is. But we both ought to go."

"Why 'ought' we go to a crock of shit?"

"Come on, Olga."

"I'm not going to let it fuck me over, Bo," I said.

"What? What are you talkin' about?"

"Everything that's trying to fuck me over. This goddam war. That moron the reverend Means. My no-good husband, whom I foolishly love, idiot that I am. You get all excited over your little draft card burnings, but what excites me is beating this fucking system, all of it. Not letting it beat me down. The booze, all that. I'm not powerless over it, Bo. I'm going to win."

"You're gonna do it on your own? Cold turkey?"

"I don't know."

He just looked at me, that same searching look. "How will you know when you've won?" he asked.

"I'll know," I said. "I'll just know. If I keep plugging away, keep on surviving, don't give up, one day I'll look around and say, 'hey, I've won'! All the love will come back, uncomplicated and pure."

"I don't think I follow you," he said.

"You're too fucking young," I said.

"You mean prevail over that preacher?"

"Fuck the preacher," I said.

"What kind of burr has got under your saddle?" He looked genuinely perplexed.

"I've got to pull back. Circle my wagons. That love I was talking about? I'm alone there, buddy. Except for my three kids. I'm a total nut-case, but I'm all I've got."

"You're not a nut-case."

"Look, if I say I'm a nut-case, I'm a nut-case. You don't know me. You don't know what I am. Means doesn't either. Nobody does. Knox Pitts doesn't."

"That guy? Who was at..."

"Yeah, that guy. I don't know why I said that. Forget that. I don't know where that came from."

"You're upset."

I drained my drink and held my glass up. One of the elderly waitresses came shuffling over, one of my sisters. She took both our glasses back to the bar. "No, I wouldn't say 'upset'," I said. "I'm not upset. I've just got the black-ass. But I'm not on any pity pot. I won't allow myself to get on any pity pot. Everybody can just go fuck themselves. The only person I can control is me, and they can't hurt me unless I let them."

I took out another cigarette. I lit it and leaned back. I let my eyes stray around the room, half expecting to see the good reverend, spying on me. There were only two other tables of people, but I could tell they had been watching us, trying to listen.

Bo leaned back and peered at me. He said, "I'd like to help you, Olga."

I didn't want help from any clueless man. But there was no need to tell him that. "I don't want to go to any useless fucking meeting," I said. "That's not what I need right now." What I needed was for Patrick to come home safe. Clean and sober. I drained my drink and signaled for another. Maybe he'll survive. Maybe he'll change. God knows I couldn't ever change him. I had tried. I smiled to myself.

"Okay," he said finally, still regarding me with that openly questioning look, "Okay, you're the boss."

"You're goddam right," I said.

Chapter Twenty-Three

On Thahn, Vietnam
December, 1965

THEY WENT out in six helicopters to a landing zone on the edge of a large tract of woods covering patches of jungle and rolling, stunted scrub hills. The woods were tall mahogany trees and saplings and high grass, with tangles of ferns and briers. They covered about ten square miles. Patrick's platoon was part of Alpha Company, and the entire unit was going out on this mission. One hundred thirty four men.

"It's gonna be rough," Chad Simpson said to them. He was a new First Lieutenant. His camouflage jungle fatigues were clean and crisp. He had colored over his bars with a black magic marker.

"Where we goin', sir?" Steve Nance asked.

"It's gonna be rough," the lieutenant repeated. He was tall and blonde, with wide eyes and plump cheeks. He went on down the row of men who were slumped along a narrow road cut into the forest.

"Shithead don't know where we goin', no more'n I do," Seelbach said.

"He looks like the fuckin' Pillsbury dough boy," Nance said.

What the lieutenant was saying frightened Patrick anew. It was like being on a roller coaster, up and down, being relieved that you survived and then plunging down into anxiety and trepidation again. Patrick recalled the pain of the shrapnel burn, and he forced himself to imagine how it would feel when steel coated bullets ripped into his body; he compelled himself to keep the sense of foreboding in the forefront of his mind. He wanted it there. He did not want to deny it. He wanted the sensation of terror. After each fire-fight he'd been in he'd told himself that he was not a coward, he hadn't failed, but it didn't work because there was the next one and then the next one; it was never-ending, totally without mercy; nothing in the universe gave a shit about his pathetic little life. He was as dispensable as a piece of used tissue. Knowing that, how could he turn his face into it and keep going and not fall down in a whimpering heap? How could he keep on when nobody seemed to really care whether he lived or died, whether he charged or not, stood his ground or not? There was always the choice. He knew how thin the membrane between courage and cowardice, between pride and shame, was, how easily it could be broken.

An M48 Patton tank came grinding down the road. The men squeezed back against the undergrowth to let it pass. A machine gunner on the turret, in a canvas field hat, said to them, "Any of you ugly boonierats want a ride?"

"Fuck you," Seelbach said.

As they waited, two more tanks came by. There were a couple of grunts riding on the back of each one. Patrick stood up and looked after the second tank. Mac shouted, "Sit down, Pappy, keep your britches on."

Patrick decided he would get on the next one that came along. Why should he walk when there were rides? But before another tank came they moved out down the road, walking in a ragged single file. Branches fanned out over the roadway. The road's surface was a sticky mustardy shallow layer of mud. The men's fatigue pants had clots of the mud on them that had been thrown up by the tanks' treads.

They walked for miles down the winding road.

"There better be somethin' at the end of this thing," Jason Morrison said.

"It's the fuckin' yellow brick road," Gerald Abbott said.

"Dorothy, Dorothy, suck my cock," Marvin Whitfield said.

"Hup two three four, hup two three four," Haskins said.

"Shut the fuck up, Haskins," Mac said.

"I can't talk? How come? Cause I black?" Haskins said.

"Fuck you," Mac said.

"Cause you a nigger, yeah, you can't say nothin'," Seelbach said.

"You gone get your balls sliced off, cracker," Steve Nance said. "Don't be niggerin' me."

"I ain't niggerin' you, I'm niggerin' Henry," Seelbach said.

"I'm gonna feed you your little white pecker, Nazi, ain't no bigger than a Vi-enner sausage."

"You know right what it looks like, don't you, Nance?" Seelbach said.

"I looked for it. I couldn't find it," Nance said.

"Y'all shut that shit up," Mac said. His voice was edgy. When Mac got skittish, something was up.

They trudged along in silence for a while.

"What you reckon this mission is?" Patrick asked Henry.

"Whole damn company. Somethin' big, maybe," Haskins said. Patrick could tell that Henry was jumpy, too.

"The entire fuckin' gook army could be in these woods," Patrick said nervously.

"Probably are," Haskins said.

They assembled along a straight stretch of the road. The woods were sparser, mostly bushes and saplings. The three tanks were positioned along the road, facing into the woods, facing north. They were spaced about a hundred and fifty feet apart. The men fell in behind the tanks as they began to move slowly through the woods, bending and cracking the saplings, grinding the undergrowth underneath the treads. The big 90 MM cannons on the tanks swung back and forth and the machine gunners sitting up in the turrets scanned the forest ahead.

Patrick and Haskins picked their way through the tangle left by the tank. They walked through ditches and over ridges. There was a sudden burst of machine gun fire, and return fire, and all the men hit the dirt. Patrick could see the gunner atop the tank firing. The big gun turned slowly in that direction. Boom, boom. Silence. The tank began to move again and Patrick saw Mac motioning for the men to follow. They came to a large bunker that had been reinforced with logs and sandbags. Patrick passed close to the low opening. He could see the jumbled entanglement of bodies and body parts that had been live gooks only minutes before.

Patrick had no idea how far they had come from the road. They encountered several more bunkers of various sizes and some small groups of Viet Cong. There was firing from the tanks and men on both sides of Patrick, spasmodic barrages that erupted and then were over. Patrick and Henry took cover behind a pile of stumps and fired at a machine gun nest until the tank's 90 MM wiped it out.

"This is fun, seein' that big mother wastin' them slants," Henry said.

They kept going. They were back in the taller trees. The going was tougher for the tanks, the trees more difficult to deal with. Once the tank looked like it was going to climb right up a tall banyan that it pushed to a forty five degree angle.

"Look at that mother!" Henry said.

"I wish I was ridin' on that thing," Patrick said.

"Get on it," Henry said. "You chicken?"

"Hell, no," Patrick said. He kept low and loped up behind the tank. It was going very slow. Patrick climbed up on the back. He held on. The Thompson seemed heavier sitting up there. The gunner, who had a helmet on now, turned around and looked at him.

"That'll be fifty cents, plus tip," he yelled over the noise of the grinding engine.

"Deal," Patrick called back.

"Watch yourself," the gunner shouted.

Patrick held on tightly. Leafy branches slapped at him, almost knocking his helmet off, almost blinding him. But he felt insanely happy to be on the tank, to be riding instead of walking.

The tank ground on through the woods. Patrick saw Haskins behind them, a big grin on his face. He gave Patrick a thumbs up. All of a sudden, without warning, there was a spurt of automatic rifle fire that tinged into the side of tank, very near where Patrick was, the rounds ricocheting with high whines around him. He saw the machine gunner spin around. The gun erupted, spitting toward the woods. Patrick was clumsy; he couldn't get the Thompson into position to fire. Haskins and some other men were crouched down, firing where the shots had come from. The firing ceased as abruptly as it had begun.

The tank was stopped. Haskins and Gerald Abbott stumbled up behind it. Haskins wet his finger in his mouth and made an invisible mark in the air. "One more dead gook," he said. He and Abbott were grinning. Their teeth were extremely white in their dark faces.

Patrick laughed. What the fuck are we so happy about? he thought. We're giddy. He started to climb down. We're as ditsy as puppies, he thought. Something very very bad is going to happen. His jungle boots hit the ground and he hefted the Thompson. He heard Lieutenant Simpson tell them all to take ten.

He squatted and lit up a Lucky. His odor drifted up from his crotch. He hadn't had a shower in over a week. He had a two week growth of beard that was coming in sprinkled with gray and he'd decided that he might as well go ahead and grow it out. His scalp itched and he kept gouging up crusts with his fingernails, which were getting too long, too. He tried not to think very often of home. It made him sick to think that Max and Willie might have to get in this shit.

After the break the company moved deeper into the tangled jungle. It was darker under the trees as the day waned. Patrick could feel the night coming; he felt as if he were being slowly enmeshed in some impenetrable, unfathomable green, a verdant and immense inscrutability. He was afraid that at any moment he might be sucked into it and disappear. It was slow going for the tanks. And for the men as well, as the growth got thicker. The trees towered overhead. The slight breeze up high shook the leaves and made rotating shafts of late slanting sunlight dance on the men on the forest floor. The trees were so big and thick the tanks could go no further, but the men kept moving. They went on for several miles as the afternoon wore on. It was hot and sticky. They encountered nothing. The steaming rain forest was quiet, empty.

Patrick and Haskins were passing through a ditch where there was a small spring, when Patrick heard a loud clicking noise. It seemed to come from all around him, mostly from up in the trees. Some fucking monster gook cricket, Patrick was thinking, just as the firing started. It was a thunderous outburst of fire from all sides. Patrick and Haskins wedged themselves against the overhanging lip of the ditch. Haskins had his M16 switched to automatic and he peppered the woods around them. Patrick heaved the Thompson up and steadied it. He could see nothing but smoke and bushes and bits of leaves flying, but he fired several prolonged bursts. The noise was deafening. The smoke was so thick Patrick could barely breathe, but he kept firing.

"Motherfucker!" Haskins yelled.

"What?"

"I'm hit, goddam, I'm hit." He whimpered.

Patrick pulled him down lower in the ditch. He didn't know what good that would do. Bullets were slamming into the ground on all sides of them. Patrick could see Cosper further along the ditch. He was firing. While Patrick was looking at him Cosper jerked back and flopped to the ground. Part of his shoulder was gone and there was a gaping, bloody hole in his chest. His face was turned toward Patrick. He looked at Patrick, panic in his eyes. He didn't seem able to move. Patrick thought he was trying to say something.

He rolled Haskins over. "Where you hit, Henry?" he said.

"I don't know, shit, I don't know," Henry said.

Patrick looked down. "Jesus," he muttered. Haskin's gut was chopped up. He must have taken some rounds in his lower back and they'd exited the front. There was blood everywhere. He could see some of Henry's intestines poking out. The smell was sickening. "Jesus, Henry," he said. Henry had grabbed hold of Patrick's hand and was gripping it, squeezing it. His body was trembling.

"Band-Aid!" Patrick yelled as loud as he could, "Band-Aid!" He knew the chances of being heard in that chaos were not good and getting a medic were no better. The whole company must have been getting chewed up. The intensity of the firing had not let up.

Mac came diving into the ditch, a natural shallow foxhole, followed by Whitfield and Seelbach. Patrick was glad to see Mac, relieved. He was still holding Haskins' hand, though his friend's grip had relaxed. "Haskins got hit," he said to Mac. The two men looked at Henry. He was motionless, his face frozen, his eyes open and glazed.

"Goddam," Mac said. Another burst of fire made him duck his head.

Patrick shook Haskins. "Wake up, asshole," he said.

"He ain't gonna never wake up, Founier," Mac said. "Watch your head." The men cowered in the ditch. Machine gun fire rattled on. Patrick peered down the ditch to where Cosper was. His mouth was locked open. Patrick wondered if he had actually seen Cosper trying to say something or just imagined it. He was not sure of anything right then. The machine gun fire continued to spray over them and around them; he could smell it, charred gunpowder, caustic. He could not fathom being pinned down in this dismal place, abandoned by every remnant of certitude he'd ever managed to absorb. He huddled against the fetid smell of the mud, shaking, his arms over his face.

The men were bumping against each other, shoving, trying to get lower. The only one returning fire was Mac with his BAR. He was trying to protect himself, crouching, holding the big rifle up high to fire over the lip of the ditch. The enemy rounds were interminable, unrelenting. It went on for so long that Patrick lost all perspective of time; he had only the sensation of the rapid ripping of the seconds, each one surely to be the last.

"We're fucked," Mac cried out in the clamor.

Patrick opened his eyes. His mouth was so dry he couldn't swallow. He couldn't see anything but Mac's muddy battle fatigues, four inches from his face. His limbs were clinched stock-still, cramped; he couldn't move. The tumultuous roar was so constant that he was no longer listening to it; it existed only as a long, bawling rumble at the back of his mind which would take a mighty effort of will to turn his first attention to. It was as though it had always been there, a part of him, something he'd carried with him forever. He could no longer imagine any existence without it.

Then they heard the jets, coming in low. The first bombs sounded like they were about a hundred meters away. "Thank God," Mac grunted next to Patrick, "it's the fuckin' air support!" A jet came right over their heads and the next bombs were so close they were staggered. They would have been knocked off their feet if they'd been standing.

"Goddamit, do they know where we are?" Mac screamed. "Hell no!" he answered himself.

The ground shuddered with the bombing; they could feel it in fluttering waves up through their bodies. They were showered with clots of mud and rocks, chunks of wood and branches from the exploded trees. Fragments of shrapnel whined crisply over their heads. The darkening sky flickered white with the napalm up ahead of them. It seemed that all the wrath and fury of the universe was being funneled into that narrow ditch, directly over their heads. The bombing might have lasted ten minutes, but it seemed to Patrick like an aeon, a millennium.

Suddenly something knocked him backwards and sideways in the ditch. He thought at first that Mac had turned and slugged him, then the most blinding, the most searing, pain he'd ever felt jolted him. The back of his head hit the muddy bottom of the spring and his helmet went flying. His eyes, aimed toward the smoky darkening sky, went into and out of focus. He tasted blood in his mouth. Then there was only silence and murky darkness.

He bolted back into awareness. Something was tugging at his face, twisting his head. He blinked his eyes. His head throbbed with scorching pain, as though his brain were so swollen it was about to burst through his skull. He didn't know what he was looking at. Then he realized it was Mac's face in the darkness.

"You decided to wake up, huh?" Mac said. He was wrapping something around Patrick's head.

"Whu...whu...?" Patrick mumbled. His lips felt puffy, numb.

"Looks like you got hit with a piece of shrapnel," Mac said. "Up side the ear." He was pulling the bandage tight, knotting it. "You gonna have one fine cauliflower, Founier," he said.

"Whu...?"

"Shhhhh," Mack said. "Here." He held a canteen to Patrick's mouth. Patrick could only dimly feel it, but his mouth and body were soaking it up thirstily. His body seemed not a part of him at all but was something else, some strange thing lying there in this remote place that was incompatible with his accumulation of experience, that could not possibly be him. He did not know where he was, and then he did.

"I wish I had some morphine," Mac said. "Then we could both get to feelin' better." His voice rang with an echo, as though he were speaking from down inside a well. Then Patrick slid again into the blackness.

It was first light, the sun not yet up. But the brightness hurt Patrick's eyes and he closed them. His head ached dully with his pulsing heartbeat. Mac was slouched against the side of the ditch, snoring softly. Patrick could hear nothing else. No animal noises, nothing. The silence had its own power, as though yesterday's cacophony, in its withdrawing, had left a vast white void that sang with its own hush.

The back of Patrick's head was icy cold from the spring. He struggled to lift his head and jagged bolts of pain shot through him. There was a ghastly taste of spoiled meat in his mouth. Slowly he managed to pull himself upright from the waist and turn enough to sit back against the side of the ditch. The side of his head–his ear, he remembered Mac saying something about his ear–burned like a red-hot poker was stuck in it. He could see part of the bandage sticking out beside his face; it looked like khaki colored cotton cloth, blood stained. Patrick realized Mac had bandaged his head with what must have been several army-issue handkerchiefs tied together. Mac was still sleeping, jammed close to Patrick. Seelbach and Whitfield were sprawled at the bottom of the ditch, twisted together on top of Haskins' body in what looked like a freakish and ludicrous lovers' embrace. Patrick did not look at their faces; he knew they were dead by their awful stillness.

The ground fog of the morning, mixed with the battle's smoke, was lifting in graceful slow curls and he could see the jungle around them again, the remaining taller trees and the thicket tangled together in a twisted devastation. Mac's breathing, his gentle snores, were the only sounds in the empty morning. Patrick wanted to wake him, then thought no, let him sleep if he can. Though it hurt to twist his neck, Patrick looked around; everything was unfamiliar then instantaneously recognizable in the same second, like the fleetingness of a recalled dream.

It was only when something caused Patrick to jerk awake that he realized he'd fallen back asleep. His eyes were scratchy, the sunlight bright. It was Mac's movements that had roused him. Mac was going over the bodies of their dead comrades, pulling out fragmentation grenades and their side arms, their canteens.

"Shit, Mac," Patrick said. His voice sounded to him like someone else's. He didn't know what he had started to say. He didn't know if there was anything to say.

Mac glanced at him. He grunted. "You ain't dead," he said. "Good."

The Sergeant continued his rummaging. Patrick took a mouthful of water and rinsed his mouth. When he spat, it was pale red. He drank.

"Just so you know," Mac said. "You ain't got much ear left up there. You got one left, though. That's what they call a 'consolation', ain't it?"

Patrick's head felt swollen to twice its size. He was not in the mood for sarcasm. "Fuck you," he said.

Mac leaned back against the side of the ditch and sighed. His face was so covered in mud and soot he was almost unrecognizable, and his battle fatigues were caked with it. Just about all Patrick could see clearly were his eyes, and for the first time Patrick noticed they were a livid blue. Mac got out a squashed and wrinkled package of Chesterfields and gave Patrick one. They lit up.

"Where're the gooks?" Patrick asked. He looked around.

"Fried, I guess. Most of 'em, anyway."

"I mean..." Patrick began.

"How the hell do I know, Founier? Gone bye bye, I guess. Would you stick around in all that shit?"

Patrick's head was beginning to clear. He kept looking around, searching the scorched jungle. He saw a G.I. helmet hanging in a tree. "Where's everybody else?" he asked.

Mac just pointed at the three bodies on the bottom of the ditch.

The severe silence hanging around them was bleak and somber, even in the bright sunlight and the persistent green of the jungle. Nothing moved anywhere. There was no breeze. The foggy smoke had lifted completely away; all that remained was the smell.

"Maybe we were too far forward," Mac said. "Shit. I don't know."

"We just kept goin', like we were supposed to," Patrick said.

"Yeah." Mac rested his head back against the lip of the ditch. He inhaled deeply, then blew the smoke upward. "Fuck it," he said. He stomped his boot. "Goddam fire ants, you can't kill those motherfuckers." Patrick was looking at the neat row of grenades that Mac had gathered. "I loaded the Colts, including yours." He pointed to a pistol on the ground. "Put that one in your belt," he said. "It was Haskins'."

Patrick glanced at Henry's body, half concealed under Seelbach and Whitfield. It was still frozen in the same awkward posture. Patrick swallowed and looked away, back at Mac. He noticed that Mac's helmet had a large dented crease in the top. The canvas cover was ripped off and hanging by his face. "What happened to your helmet?" Patrick asked.

"Probably the same kind of shrapnel that nipped your ear," Mac said. He grinned, his teeth startlingly white in his grimy face. "I've got a harder head than you." He stood up and stood with his hands on his hips, looking around at the jungle. "Probably got a harder dick, too, but that might not matter a whole hell of a lot anymore." He gave Patrick a hand and hoisted him up. He adjusted Patrick's bandage. "Put your helmet on," he said.

"What does it look like, Mac?" Patrick asked.

"What? Your ear?"

"Yeah."

"Ain't much left of it, but it musta been a glancin' blow, maybe just sliced it right off. It was hard to tell with all the bleedin'. You was lucky you didn't get it dead center, or you'd be layin' down there with them fuckers."

Patrick stared at the twisted bodies. "They were our friends, Mac," he said.

"Yeah," Mac said. "But there'll be plenty of time to cry about it when we get out of this fuckin' place. If we get out."

"The rest of the company...everybody...?" Patrick asked.

"I don't know what the fuck happened to 'em."

They stood there looking around. The jungle was contorted. It was infested, haunted with a beguiling quiet.

"We ain't in Kansas anymore," Mac said.

"You from Kansas, Mac?"

"Fuck no," Mac said. "Jesus, Cajun, are you for real?"

"I know where that came from. I just..." He didn't go on. He just shrugged.

Mac pulled a compass out of his field pack. He pointed. "We came from that direction. I don't know how far it is back to that fuckin' road, but I'm ready."

They started out. Pushing their way through the undergrowth. It would thin out and they could go faster, until they came to another thicket. It was hot. Patrick's body was raw and sweaty under his fatigues; when he'd taken a piss earlier he'd seen that he was seriously chapped between his thighs and around his balls. Walking was painful. They were weighted down with the extra grenades and ammo. And his head rumbled dully with every step he took.

"Goddam, Mac, my head hurts," Patrick said.

"Tell me somethin' I don't know," Mac said.

"I mean...shit!" Mac kept walking. Patrick struggled to keep up.

"You've probably got a concussion," Mac said.

"I ain't ever felt anything like this in my life. I didn't know your head could hurt so goddam much."

"Well, Cajun, you got a choice. You can keep going with me or you can lay down and wait for the gooks to come bring you some aspirin."

Patrick kept plowing ahead. He couldn't not think about his head, no matter how hard he tried. He just kept putting one foot in front of the other. He didn't even feel the branches and palm leaves that smashed against him.

They crashed through the morass. The dense undergrowth was wet; it stank of ground rot and burnt powder. Patrick's breath was getting short. The Thompson was heavy, and the straps of his field pack were blistering his shoulders. They pushed on through the fan palms and bushes. He focused on Mac's back, on the floppy piece of canvas still attached to his helmet that trailed after him.

Mac stopped abruptly. He crouched and motioned for Patrick to do the same. They had come up behind a low bunker. It was no more than thirty feet in front of them. "Shit," Mac whispered. It was a big bunker, facing away from them; it looked like one that was dug into the ground. It had a bamboo roof covered with fronds and branches.

"Do you think they're in there?" Patrick whispered, so faintly that he couldn't hear it, but Mac did.

"Maybe," Mac whispered, and Patrick read his lips.

Mac motioned. "You that way," he whispered. "I'm gonna try to get close enough to toss a grenade in."

"Okay," Patrick nodded.

The two men crept stealthily through the thickness. Patrick watched Mac going around to the other side of the bunker. He moved up closer. Nothing was moving. For the first time since before the ambush he heard a bird chirping. As he was listening to it there was a loud muffled thud and the bunker rattled, then dust and smoke rose over the top. He heard the BAR then, three bursts. "Come on," Mac shouted.

The front of the bunker was open. A machine gun that had been mounted in the opening was lying outside in the mud. Mac was sliding through the low door. Patrick slid in behind him. It was close and dank inside, smelling of piss. Light came in from the front opening, where the empty machine gun mount was, belts of rounds stacked near it. The bunker was deep enough for a tall man to stand. It was wide, dug back underground for ten feet or so.

Patrick saw a form against the back dirt wall and recoiled. "Shit!" he shouted, and fired off several rounds from his Thompson. Gradually they could make out the outlines of a man. They crept closer. The dead Vietnamese was sitting with his back against the wall in such a relaxed position it was almost comical. Even his feet were crossed. Patrick flicked his lighter in front of the soldier's face; the eyes were wide open. There was a hideous, mirthless, grin on his face.

"What's so funny, motherfucker?" Mac said. The soldier looked as though he'd been dead for several days. "Well, you ain't laughin' now, are you?"

"Wouldn't you shit if he answered you?" Patrick said.

They climbed back out of the bunker. Mac looked at the compass. Patrick fell in behind him and they went along in silence for a while, the only sounds the rustling and scraping of the bushes as they pushed them aside. Patrick's legs were so achy he had to walk stiffly. Mac slowed to let him catch up. They were passing through an area where the undergrowth was not as thick, bright sunlight beaming through the trees.

Just at that moment a burst of machine gun fire rang out and Mac stumbled and went to the ground. Patrick hunkered down beside him. "Shit, shit, shit, shit," Mac said. He groaned. Patrick peered around, the Thompson ready. There was little cover. He thought the rounds had come from over near some thick banana trees. But he couldn't see anyone. "My leg. My knee. Goddamit," Mac said.

Patrick could see that Mac's lower leg was protruding at an odd angle. The leg was covered in blood and slime. Mac's knee had been shattered by a direct hit. The machine gun, which sounded fairly close by, rattled again, the rounds puncturing the foliage over his head. Patrick saw them then, two RAVNs–a gunner and a loader– with a Light machine gun, helmets covered with leafy branches. They were dug in inside the stand of trees. He didn't pause to think. He jumped up, firing the Thompson as he did. He could see for a split second the Vietnamese soldiers' faces, then saw them disappear as his rounds sliced into them.

"You get him?" Mac grunted.

"Yeah, I think so," Patrick said.

"Better make sure. But be careful. Don't touch him or his weapons, you hear me?"

"I hear you, sir."

"Don't fuckin' 'sir' me!"

Patrick made his way carefully toward the banana trees. He fired again at where he knew the two men had been. He found them sprawled on the muddy ground, their chests ripped by his Thompson. A Russian design Light machine gun lay between them, similar to the one that had been in the bunker. Patrick thought of Seelbach. He would never get his Chicom machine gun. "They're all over the fucking place, Nazi," he said aloud. He trudged back to where Mac was.

He got his web belt off and wrapped it around Mac's thigh. He twisted it as tight as he could with a stick he found, and Mac flinched from the pain.

"Shit! Go on and cut it off, why don'tcha?" Mac grunted.

"Sorry," Patrick said. "You've lost a lot of blood."

"We got to move," Mac said. "There must be others around. Like fuckin' cockroaches."

Patrick got to his feet and helped Mac to stand, his wounded leg dangling below his knee, his foot dragging in the dirt. It felt like lifting a bale of cotton. "Goddam, how much do you weigh, Mac?"

"Two hundred and fuckin' sixty," Mac said thinly between clinched teeth. "But you forget that. You got to carry me."

Patrick stripped off Mac's field pack and strapped his Thompson and Mac's BAR around his own shoulders. They were heavy and pulled him downward. But they had no choice. They had to have the weapons. They started out, making slow progress. Patrick could barely get one foot in front of the other, and the more Mac tried to help with his good leg the worse it got. Mac moaned with the pain of moving. Patrick was winded almost immediately; they were passing through a range that had been bombed; the air was smoky and dusty and reeked of explosives. He kept coughing and spitting. Patrick was relieved they were out of the thickest jungle growth, but that left them more exposed.

One step at a time, Patrick kept telling himself, one step at a time. He couldn't let himself think of how far they had to go; he was afraid if he did he would just lie down and prepare to die. Mac grunted with every agonizing step, gritting his teeth. Patrick's back began to ache, a sharp pulsating just above his hip. He bent forward with his load. The afternoon wore on. Patrick could catch glimpses of the beginning colors of the sunset in the sky.

Patrick labored. It was torture. They seemed to be inching along. Mac began to groan louder. Patrick almost dropped him. Patrick thought he could feel blood running down his neck from his ear. His head throbbed.

Then they stopped to rest. Patrick consulted the compass. "You think we're goin' in the right direction?" Patrick asked. He propped Mac against a tree, holding him upright. The Sergeant's grimy face was contorted in agony. His breath came in convulsive gasps. The muscles in Patrick's thighs and calves were cramping; he knew he needed to keep moving. But they needed to recharge.

They both heard it at the same time: shrill voices, laughter. Gook talk. Close by. Mac's eyes grew wide. Patrick cupped his hand loosely over Mac's lower face to muffle the harsh intakes of air. The sound of the chatter grew nearer. It sounded like five or six Vietnamese soldiers.

The two men kept as still as they could behind the tree. Patrick saw them then, six RAVN infantrymen, branches of leaves camouflaging their helmets, carrying their AK-47s and one machine gun with a dangling swivel. They were walking casually, leisurely, yapping away. They were completely unaware of Mac and Patrick's presence. The men passed within ten feet of them, so close that Patrick could smell their sour rice-sweat, their stale tobacco. They moved on another twenty meters and stopped in a small clearing. The chatter increased in volume. Shit! They were taking a break.

Patrick's legs were growing numb; they were trembling. There was no way they could move without being seen. The Vietnamese soldiers were smoking, passing around a canteen. Mac motioned toward them with his eyes. Patrick, as slowly and quietly as he could manage, slid his Thompson from its sling around his shoulders. With all the energy he could muster, Patrick vaulted away from the tree, opening fire as he saw the startled expressions on their faces. Their astonishment was so great they were only reaching for their weapons when the Thompson's rounds chopped into them, rocketing them back, flinging them to the ground. Patrick stood very still in the silence that followed. Then he made his way over to the men. There were six of them, sprawled with their arms and legs akimbo. One of them was still alive; he whimpered. Patrick fired a quick blast. The soldier's body jerked and then lay still.

Patrick walked among them, holding his Thompson at ready. They had canteens, cloth bags of cooked rice. He gathered some together and went back to Mac. Mac had slid down the tree and sat with his back to it, his eyes closed. It was getting dark. "We stay right here," Patrick said. He got down next to Mac, close. The two men ate the rice and drank from the canteens. One of them had rice wine in it. They passed it back and forth. They tried to rest.

"One of us ought to be awake," Mac said.

"Okay," Patrick said.

They huddled together, passing the night, sleeping fitfully now and then, taking turn about, listening to the jungle sounds. It was sleep and not sleep; they were never unaware of where they were, their hearing always alert for more voices, more chatter, the noise of something moving.

At first light Patrick stirred. His entire body ached. He took some water, spit it out. He drank, slaking his parched throat. He tried to stretch. He didn't see how it was possible to go on. He could not will himself to stand. He wanted to weep, to surrender. He suddenly became aware that Mac was awake, watching him. The two men looked at each other.

"I can't make it, Founier," Mac said.

Patrick didn't reply. He looked away, then back at Mac.

"You got to..." Mac began.

"No," Patrick said. "No way."

"You dumb, fuckin' Cajun. Can't you see..."

"No, so just shut the fuck up about it," Patrick said. "I ain't leavin' you."

Mac just stared at him, his pale blue eyes narrowed. He winced with pain. Then he grinned. "Well, okay then, Cajun," he said. "I didn't think you..." He stopped. He winced again and closed his eyes.

After about a minute Patrick said, "You were gonna say you didn't think I had it in me."

Mac opened his eyes. He took several deep breaths. He shook his head.

"No," he said. His eyes were level on Patrick's. Their faces were inches apart. "No, I wasn't gonna say that," he said.

Patrick had to battle his body, striving to get upright. When he was standing he was so lightheaded he thought he might pass out. He held onto the tree. He and Mac worked together to get him up, Mac gasping in pain. "Shit," Mac said. "Shit."

Patrick studied the compass. He pulled Mac's arm around his shoulders. They started out again. Mac was getting heavier. Patrick knew he could not support him much longer before he, himself, fell in an exhausted heap. Every step was arduous; the cramps in his legs were excruciating. Their progress was slow. Mac grunted and moaned. One step, Patrick kept repeating to himself, one step at a time. His sweat dripped into his eyes and stung them. He wanted more than anything to drop to the soft ground and curl up and rest, but he kept putting one foot in front of the other.

Patrick lost any sense of how far they'd come, how far they had to go to reach the road, if the fucking road was even up there. How long had it taken them to get in there where they were ambushed? And suppose they did get to the road and there was nothing fucking there? They would still have a long way to go.

They were moving automatically. They were long beyond their capacity for endurance, yet they still kept going, dragging, creeping. Patrick was delirious. He found himself looking for butterflies. He would find Willie a butterfly. He was losing his fucking mind. What the fuck good was a mind? What did it matter, if he just kept grinding?

It got dark on them again and they stopped for another night. They didn't know how long it had been since they'd been at the LZ. How many days. The next day Patrick had to work even harder to get his legs working. They were swollen, stiff. His shoulder was a mass of cramps where Mac's arm was slung as they moved along.

But they kept going. There were periods when Patrick thought Mac had passed out on his feet, when he became almost dead weight. Patrick didn't know where the strength to propel himself and the bigger man forward came from. He no longer thought about their effort ending; he just listened to the scraping of their feet through the undergrowth. There was just the moment, just the moving of the legs, the straining onward, their stressed breathing.

They came out into a clearer area. Patrick recognized it as where the tanks had employed. Then he saw the road, the yellow, sticky mud. When he got to the edge of the road he slumped down, letting Mac down hard, almost falling face first into the ditch. He lay back in the stiff, scratchy grass. Mac moaned. The sun was high, warm. Patrick didn't know if they'd gotten anywhere significant or not, but they were back at the road. His eyelids drooped down of their own accord.

He was startled awake by the sound of a truck's grinding gears. He was disoriented, not knowing immediately where he was. He had no idea how long he'd been sleeping. He lay listening to the approaching engine. He could not move his arms or his legs. He saw the truck, then. It was a deuce and a half; he could see the white star on the passenger door. The truck stopped. A young private in the passenger seat was looking at him, and his eyes grew wide when Patrick lifted a hand and motioned.

He did surrender then. He could hear them talking, but they were just voices, as they put him and Mac on litters and lifted them into the back of the truck. The truck started. He was aware they were moving. He let himself be rocked gently by the roll and sway. He was awakened by the chopping of an approaching helicopter. He and Mac were lying side by side on the ground, both with IVs. The rhythmic whirring of the Huey grew louder and louder. He closed his eyes again.

Chapter Twenty-Four

Bay Springs, Louisiana
December, 1965
WILLIE

SO THERE I was, with about a hundred questions and nobody to ask about them. I needed advice; for one thing: about Amy. It had been almost two months since I'd had that little bit of tongue, and mostly she'd acted like nothing had ever happened. Sometimes you would have thought she still thought of us as sort of brother-sister, but after that business with her tongue I didn't see how that was possible. It was just about a total mystery to me.

My mom was drinking a lot. She had started smoking again, which was okay by me since she brought home a carton of Pall Malls and I could sneak a pack. I kept it in my room and I could take some out to share with Donly and Amy. I still didn't know what was up with that business on Thanksgiving. I asked Deirdre. She said, "Mom is a whacko." I already knew that. There's no point in my asking Deirdre anything.

When my mom was home, she always had a cigarette and a drink in her hand. Once I was in my room and I saw her go into Dee's room, and after a minute I heard her say, "Where the hell are you, you fuckin' son-of-a-bitch," and I knew she was talking to the picture of my dad that Dee kept in there on her chest of drawers. I could tell from her voice she wasn't angry, she was crying, and it ripped my heart out. I closed my door real quietly and had a good cry myself. I didn't know if I was crying for me or my mom. My mom has been really sad ever since she got cancer and had to be in the hospital and all. Or my dad. Or Max and Dee. I guess I was crying for all of us.

I was leaving the school building to wait for Max to pick me up. I stopped by the front door. There was a girl standing there. I stood there beside her. She was about as tall me. She was skinny and she wore glasses, these big wire-rimmed things that made her eyes look like a wasp's eyes.

"Hey," I said.

"Hey," she said.

Her eyeballs looked like blue golf balls behind the glasses. She just stared at me. She looked pale and washed out. She had a flute case in her hands. Her book satchel was propped against the wall. She was poised to make a dash away from there. She was probably waiting for somebody to pick her up, too.

"Whatcha doin?" I asked, which was stupid.

"Waitin'," she said. When I didn't say anything more, she said, "On my daddy to pick me up."

"Well," I said.

"Uh huh," she said.

She had on a light green sweater that was about two sizes too big for her, and her skirt came down to her ankles. I tried to get a look at her cupcakes, but if she had any you couldn't see them under that tent of a sweater. She was about as sexy as a Chihuahua. I get isolated with a girl and she looks like road kill.

I just kept looking at her, and she started to squirm. Then I recognized who she was. It was Melissa Means, that crazy preacher's daughter. I could see him in her eyes. "What you doin'?" Melissa asked.

"I don't know. I was just headed home."

"Yeah," she said. "Me too."

I looked at her flute case. "You're in the band?" I asked.

"You know I'm in the band," she said.

"Yeah," I said. I didn't, but I guess she thought I did because my mom was the band director. I mean, I had noticed her flute case.

"Why aren't you in the band?" she asked me.

"I don't know. Just haven't gotten around to it, I guess." I had thought about it. My mom never put any pressure on us about it. I knew Max and Deirdre wouldn't have been in the band if you threatened to shoot them, simply because it was my mom's thing. They'd both told me that. But that didn't bother me. I didn't think it was corny. I had been thinking maybe I'd take up an instrument that interested me. Maybe a bassoon or something, one that nobody else played.

I was just looking Melissa Means over then. She was looking back at me out of those thick glasses. I was wondering what it was like to have a dad like Mr. Means. About a minute went by. She said, "I know who you are."

"Yeah," I said.

"My daddy says Mrs. Founier is a harlot," she said.

"Your daddy is crazy as hell," I said.

"I know it," she said. She just kept staring at me through those glasses. "I'm scared of him," she added.

"Well, join the club," I said. "Has your dad ever hit you?"

"Now you're the one crazyer'n heck," she said. "He don't ever hit me. He cries a lot."

"Cries?"

"Yeah. He drinks whiskey and he gets all sad and cries. You know what I mean?"

I did know what she meant, of course. My mom cried all the time, too. "Yeah," I said.

"I feel sorry for him," she said.

And the funny thing is I felt sorry for him, too. The idea of Mr. Means crying was pretty depressing. I guess he was a pretty sad guy. And I felt sorry for Melissa as well.

I peered into her eyes. "I'm not supposed to talk to boys," she said.

"I guess not," I said. She just kept staring at me. It began to give me the creeps. We started playing chicken with our eyes. I wasn't going to look away first. The rims of my eyes started stinging. I didn't want to blink.

"Hey, you want to do the nasty?" I asked. I had heard Max call doing it "doing the nasty."

"The what?"

"You know. The nasty. Fuck." I whispered the "fuck."

"I'm not supposed to talk to boys," she repeated, like it was something she had memorized. Our eyes were still locked.

"Tough shit," I said.

"Don't curse at me," she said.

She chickened out first and looked off out at the street. She was looking for whoever was picking her up. Probably her crazy father in his sad pickup truck. She shuffled her feet and hugged her flute against her bony chest.

"You don't know what you're missin'," I said. She wouldn't look at me then. She kept searching the street. I followed her eyes and saw Max's Chevy coming down the street. He pulled over to the curb. He waved out the window for me to come on.

"Here's my ride," I said. She didn't respond at all. "So...," I said. Nothing. "Okay then, see you around," I said and hoisted my book bag and strode down the sidewalk. She was as weird as her dad. I opened the door of the Chevy and slung my bag into the back seat.

"All right!" Max said. "Getttin' you some pussy, huh?"

He got a wheel. You could hear the tires screeching like a banshee. I looked back and saw her still standing there.

"Who's your girlfriend?" Max asked. He had a cigarette in the corner of his mouth. He was concentrating on the street in front of us, squinting through the smoke that curled up in front of his face.

"That was Melissa Means," I said.

"Who?"

"Just some girl."

"You fuckin' her?"

"I might be," I said.

"Hey, okay."

"I was just talkin' to her," I said.

"No kiddin'? What were you talkin' about?"

"Nothin'." We rode along in silence for awhile. After a few minutes, I said, "Max? Listen. Do you think Reverend Means might be the one that raped that girl."

"Who?" he asked.

"You know, Reverend Means."

"That old preacher? No way," he said.

"Why not?"

He squinted over at me and shook his head. "He's old, Willie," he said. "He probably can't even get a hard on."

"He can't? Why?"

"Cause he's old. Ain't you listenin' to me?"

I was all of a sudden getting tongue-tied. He pulled into the Dairy Dee and bought me a butterscotch dip. Then he just kept driving around. I liked riding around with Max in his car. I was hoping Amy would see us. Not that she'd be impressed or anything. Maybe I was just hoping I would see Amy. Just thinking about Amy made my balls squinch up. Cruising in Max's car always made me horny. One time, right after he got it, I heard him tell Dimwit it was his "pussy wagon."

Max had his hand draped over the steering wheel, real cool. I'm going to get me a red jacket like that. I sniffed then to see if I could smell Max's girlfriend's perfume. All I could smell was cigarette smoke.

"Buy me some of that perfume your girlfriend wears, okay?" I asked.

"Buy you some?"

"I don't mean for me, Max. Get serious. I want to give it to somebody." I wanted to give it to Amy.

"Oh," he said. "Okay." After a minute he said, "That Means girl?"

"Oh, hell no. Somebody else I'm fuckin'." Now why in the hell did I say that?

"Oh," he said. "Okay."

I knew he would buy some for me. And he wouldn't ask me again who I was going to give it to. He was a cool guy. I loved him. He was a great big brother. "Max?" I said.

"Yeah?"

"I want to talk to you about something. About some things."

"So talk," he said.

I realized then that I didn't know exactly what I was going to ask him. After a couple of minutes, I said, "Max, did you ever feel angry at Daddy?"

"Sure," he said. "I got pissed off at him over the way he was mistreating Mom. He acted like an asshole. He..." He paused. "He didn't have the balls to stick around and work it out."

"Work what out?" I knew, of course. I just wanted to hear what Max said about it.

"Well..." He glanced over at me. He threw his cigarette out the window. "How much do you know, buddy?" he asked.

"Plenty," I said. I just blurted that out before I thought. If I knew "plenty," why was I asking him? I thought surely he was going to ask me that same question. All I had was a pretty good idea that I was pretty sure was accurate, but then I really didn't know.

"You know, work out married people stuff," he said. Adult shit.

"What kind of stuff?"

"I thought you said you knew," he said.

"I know Daddy was fucking another woman," I said. "Having an affair."

He looked over at me. He squinted. "Yeah, somethin' like that," he said.

"What do you mean, 'somethin' '?"

"I mean, yeah, you got it." He got out another cigarette and lit it with this lighter Daddy gave him. I thought he was going to say something else, but he just kept driving along, blowing the smoke out the window.

"Do you ever hate Mom?" I asked.

"Mom? Why would I hate Mom?"

"I don't know. Maybe not hate. But I was confused when she got sick. I was mad at her. I thought she was going to leave us, too."

"Jesus, Willie, don't talk that way! Mom is fine, she's okay." He glanced over at me. "She's well. They got it all," he said.

"I know they got it all," I said.

We rode along in silence for awhile. I didn't tell Max, but I was still scared my mom was going to die. I was scared when she jumped out of that airplane; she got through that okay. But it seemed like every night before I could get to sleep I thought about some squid-like piece of chum eating away at her insides. Pulling her away from us. I mean, I knew she was going to die, eventually, everybody did. Even your mom. She was a tough mom. She was brave, and I felt warm and safe just knowing she was there. Where the hell would I get that feeling if she was gone? I wanted to quit thinking about that.

"Do you miss Dad?" I asked.

"Sure," he said.

"Do you ever cry about it?"

"Sure I cry. Everybody cries, Willie. Nothin' wrong with cryin'."

"It's not sissy?"

"Hell no," he said. "Don't sweat it."

"Why do you cry?"

"Whattaya mean, why do I cry? I cry because I'm sad."

"Sad about what?"

"Jesus, Willie. When Mom got sick. Things. You know." He was staring ahead through the windshield, concentrating on his driving. He didn't say anything more. I could tell by his tone he didn't want me to ask "what other things?"

He drove across the bridge and headed north. We passed The Good Lady's, a place I went to once with Max. I ate pickled eggs while he drank a couple of beers. It was a neat place. We passed the college and Max kept going. He drove for about five or ten miles and turned off into the parking lot of a joint called Rooster's Place. There were several pickups parked out front. He got out. "Be right back," he said. "You want a Dr. Pepper?"

"Root beer," I said. At least it was beer. Or they called it that, anyway.

I don't know how long I sat out there. I rolled the window down; it was cool and pleasant. I watched the occasional car go tearing by on the highway. They sounded like they were ripping the air.

When Max came back out he had a brown paper sack that I knew had a six-pack in it. He had come all the way out to Rooster's to buy something he could have bought at The Good Lady's. He had a cold can of root beer in his other hand that he handed me when he slid in.

"Sorry," he said. "I lost track of time. I had a couple of beers with Nap Beasley. You know Nap Beasley?"

"No."

"Well, he's..." he said. "He's this guy." He shrugged then. He took a Pabst Blue Ribbon out of the sack and cracked it. He threw the tab out the window. "We got to talkin' about football. Nap played ball over at Scooba Junior College. Must have been about a hundred years ago."

He cranked the car and headed out onto the highway. He turned north instead of heading back toward town. He had his beer between his legs. He lit a cigarette; the flame of the Zippo was bent sideways and sputtered in the wind from the open window. He sucked the smoke in deep and then blew it out the window. I watched him drive. I was looking forward to the day when I could have my own car, just like his, and drive around just like him.

"You can't let all this shit get to you, Willie," he said. "I know you worry about Mom. Drinkin' like she does."

"You drink," I said.

"Yeah," he said.

He drove along not saying anything, sipping his beer. We crossed another bridge and he slowed down. He handed me his empty. "Crack me another one, will you?" he said.

Finally he turned around and we headed back south toward Bay Springs. Then all of a sudden he hit his fist on the steering wheel. "Shit!" he said.

"What's the matter?" I thought we might have hit something in the road or something. We came to a side road and he pulled off and stopped and just sat there. "What is it, Max?" I asked. He kind of scared me. I was afraid he'd gotten drunk or something. I didn't know what the hell. He just sat there staring at this clump of willows across the ditch. "What the fuck, Max?" I said, loud. I was starting to get kind of mad.

He didn't answer me. After a few minutes he hit his fist again. "Goddam," he said. Then he turned his face away from me and was looking out the driver's side window. I let about two whole minutes go by.

"Max?" I said. It dawned on me suddenly that he might be thinking about my dad, and maybe my mom and her cancer. Maybe he was crying. He wasn't sobbing, shaking his shoulders, or anything. He was just so very silent. It was eerie. I waited. I didn't want to interrupt him again. Maybe he was even praying, but I doubted it. None of us are very big on praying.

Finally he turned around and looked at me. His eyes looked moist. He had been crying. I just instinctively felt myself tuning up, too, and I swallowed hard. I couldn't just bust out in front of him. "Hey, Willie," he said. "You like to go fast, don't you?"

"Sure," I said, confused, like where'd that come from? But I didn't like to go fast. It scared me to go fast, but I wouldn't let on. He backed the car around and shot out onto the highway, the tires screeching. He started speeding up. There was no traffic. I gripped the seat on both sides of my knees. I trusted him, but it still frightened me. Earthbound. That's what I was. I ran across that word in a book and looked it up. I was earthbound. Going fast was no fun for me. No thrill like I guess it was for him.

He was floor-boarding it. We were flying down the highway. I snuck a look at the Speedometer: 80. It crept up to 85. I was starting to sweat a little bit under my windbreaker. I wanted this to be over. He was still driving with one arm, stiff, his hand draped over the steering wheel. I was just getting ready to say, "Max! Slow down!" when I heard the siren and he looked in the rearview mirror and said, "Shit!"

I scrambled to put the beer and the empties on the floorboard, and he said, "Get 'em all back in the sack, Willie. Shit, shit, shit."

We coasted to a stop beside the highway and the state trooper's car eased in behind us. The cop just sat back there. We waited. Max kept sneaking looks at him in the rear view mirror. We waited some more. "What's he doin' back there?" I said.

"Callin' in my tag number," Max said. "I'm fucked."

"What's takin' him so long?"

"Checkin' to see if I've been arrested before. Or if this is a stolen car, I guess. Some such shit as that."

"You were goin' eighty five miles an hour, Max."

"Once I got it up to ninety, Willie, old buddy," Max said. He didn't seem to want to look at me.

"You're under age, drinkin' and speedin'," I said. "We're in trouble."

"I know," he said.

I was nervous as shit. Scared nearly to death, to tell you the truth. Mom was going to be majorly mad. The cop walked slowly up to the driver's side of the car. He had on one of those Smokey the Bear hats cocked on his head.

"How old are you, son?" the cop asked in this bored sounding voice.

"Six...sixteen," Max said. "I have a license."

"License and registration," he said. Donly had told me cops always had some smart-ass remark. But this one didn't. Max passed the license and the slip of paper over. The cop examined them. He looked at Max, then across the car at me. I knew my hands were shaking so I kept them gripped together in my lap. I saw him notice the sack on floorboard. I started to push it further under the dash with my foot but I was afraid that would get us in more trouble. "Mr. Founier," he said. "I clocked you at eighty six miles an hour. The speed limit along here is fifty."

"Yes sir," Max said. I could see he was pretty terrified, too.

"You're a little young to be drinkin' beer, too. Where'd you buy it?"

"I didn't buy it," Max said. "It's my uncle's. He gave it to me."

"Uh-huh. What's your uncle's name?"

"Uh, Floyd," Max said.

"Floyd what?"

Max hesitated. "I don't know. I mean, I forgot," he said.

"You don't know your uncle's last name?"

"I forgot."

"I'm going to have to ask you to get out of the car," he said. He opened the door and Max started to slide out. I opened my door. "You stay right where you are, buddy," he said, quickly. He didn't sound too friendly. I closed the door and sat very still. I watched them through the windshield. He seemed to be asking Max all kinds of questions. He made Max walk the white line along the side of the road. I thought he did pretty well. They talked again for a while. I couldn't hear anything they were saying. Then Max came back to the car and looked in. "Hand me the beer," he said. "He's confiscatin' it," and he winked at me. He handed the beer to the cop and then reached in and got the key out of the ignition. He gave that to the cop. I wondered if I was getting busted, too. I shuddered. Damn Max. He ought to know better!

After a minute the trooper went back to his cruiser and Max got back in behind the wheel. He just sat there. "What's he doin' now?" I asked.

"Callin for backup," Max said.

"Backup?!" I was really scared then. I liked to jumped out of the car.

"No, no, not like that," Max said. "Somebody to come out and drive you into town. I've got to go in and take a breathalyzer test."

"Shit. No," I said. "He's arrestin' you?!"

"I can't drive, I've been drinkin'," he said. "That's the way they do it." He looked at me. "Willie, I might have to spend tonight in jail. But don't you worry."

"I'm not worried," I said. I doubted he would have to. I had a lot of feelings right then, but worry wasn't one of them. To tell you the truth, I was relieved I was going home.

"You just take care of Dee and Mom."

I laughed nervously. I thought that was a little melodramatic. Sometimes I thought I was smarter than everybody else in my family put together.

"We don't have any Uncle Floyd," I said. "You weren't talkin' about Boyd Floyd, were you?"

"I don't know. Who knows? Take it easy, Willie."

"I am takin' it easy," I said.

So we sat and waited. After about ten minutes he said, "I'd play us some music, but I can't cut the ignition on."

"That's okay."

Not only was my father in the war in Vietnam, but now my big brother had been busted for speeding and underage drinking. And some cop was going to drive me home and I guessed I'd have to tell Mom and she'd cry. I could hardly bear that, seeing her cry. Again. Talk about lonely. Talk about being out there by yourself. Like out in the Gulf without a paddle. I wished I had Amy there to talk to.

"What about your car?" I asked. My voice was shaking a little. I was pissed off at him for adding this new complication to our lives, but I didn't want them to take him away from me. I was scared for him and angry at the same time.

"They'll keep it in the lot," he said.

There didn't seem to be much else to say, so we just sat there. The sun was setting over the swamps. It was beginning to get dark. First dark, they call it. I could hear the bullfrogs in the bar pits along the highway start up; they would go all winter. Another police cruiser came up behind the first. The cop came back and told Max to get out, then he took him and put him in the back of his car. A young cop who looked no older than Max slid into the car. He didn't have on a hat. He told me to give him directions and started driving me home in Max's car.

I started thinking about my butterflies. When I was a little kid, I thought butterflies were magic. I thought they somehow kept evil away. I really believed they had some special power. I didn't tell anybody but my dad about that. It was weird, I know. Maybe some people thought my butterfly collection was nutty. But I loved them. I still did, even though I no longer believed in all that magic business. They were just butterflies. But that was enough, if you really thought about it.

The light was queer and unnatural, a kind of greenish blue tinted orange from the remains of the day. The cop didn't talk to me except one time when he asked me if my dad wasn't in Vietnam. When I told him yes, he said, "I'm gonna enlist and get in that fore it's over."

I didn't know how to respond, so I just said, "Okay."

I told him where to turn. He pulled up in front of the house. The lights were on in the living room. All of a sudden I felt those tears starting to well up behind my eyes. It was a hell of a time to start crying. I was home. It was dark in the car and I don't think the cop saw me crying. I couldn't stop the tears. It was almost too much for me. My mind was swollen with it. It was all just so goddam sad.

He told me to take it easy and I told him good night. He sat there and watched me until I was inside.

Chapter Twenty-Five

Tan Son Nhut Base Camp, Vietnam
December, 1965

PATRICK WAS flown out by helicopter to the army field hospital at Tan Son Nhut. His right ear was split open and required surgical reshaping and twenty six stitches. He had no hearing in that ear. He had suffered a severe concussion. He was in surgery for an hour. The cut was jagged, and he would have the scar for the rest of his life. He was wheeled out of the surgery tent and down a row of large tents to a recovery area. He had a startlingly white bandage covering half his face, with a hole cut out for his eye. They gave him enough drugs to keep him relaxed and tranquil. That first night, in the recovery tent, as he lay reposed on the clean white sheets, all he thought about was going home.

It was the first time in his life he'd been in the hospital. As the hours passed slowly he had plenty of time to think things through, to think about Olga and the kids and all he'd put them through. The smells of grain alcohol and disinfectant in the tent and the presence of the nurses caused him to flash back to the time Olga had been in the hospital, to how uneasy and anxious he'd felt, how it had frightened him; and how it had shamed him at the same time because it was her in the hospital, not him, her with the cancer, and what right did he have being scared? He had been so confused he'd just gone off and gotten drunk, gone on a bender, and he winced with guilt when he remembered it all. He had been a shit.

After about a week, Patrick was beginning to feel close to normal again. He had had awful headaches from the concussion for a few days, but they'd dissipated. An army nurse named Susan Conklin, who was from St. Louis, would stop by to sit on a low stool by his bed and talk with him and bring him cigarettes. Susan Conklin liked to talk; she'd rattle on about just about anything. She was full of all the gossip and rumors that went around the hospital and the base camp. She told Patrick that Mac was in the next recovery tent over, doing better. He'd had an acute infection and had almost died in surgery. They had been afraid they were going to have to amputate his leg, but they hadn't. They thought they had the infection under control. He might still lose the leg, though, after he got back stateside.

"How the hell you know all that?" Patrick asked.

"Trust me," Susan Conklin said, grinning. "I know everything." She was tall, very slim, with blond, feathery hair down to her shoulders, and she was fair, a reverse negative of Olga. She wore a white uniform dress, short sleeved and buttoned up the front, and a little white nurse's cap perched on the top of her head like a bird. Susan was one of several nurses who would occasionally come through the ward and talk with the wounded men. She would sit and smoke with Patrick, and Patrick would enjoy looking at her legs.

She told Patrick about the rec area near the nurses' barracks. There were always parties there, music and dancing and plenty of drinks. "I go there every chance I get," she said, smiling.

"Party girl, huh?" Patrick asked.

"You need something to relieve the tension and stress," she said. "I work hard." She waved her hand around, taking in the whole room. The tent Patrick was in had ten beds, each one occupied. "I'm working now." She smiled.

"This is all there is to a nurse's work?" he asked. "Sittin' around smoking and talkin'?"

"Oh, God, no," she said. "That's not my main work. Just a small part of it." She drew on the cigarette and smiled again. "I like to chat up the guys in my free time, make them feel better. Don't you feel better?"

"Yeah," he said. "I do."

Her attention confused him. When she'd first started stopping by he'd thought she was on the make. But she seemed sincere, not interested in him in that way. She just seemed to want to be his friend. He'd never had a woman friend before without the strain of sexual tension, and he doubted it was possible. He surprised himself by not making any kind of move on her himself; he had no idea why that impulse – which had been second nature to him all his life – seemed to have disappeared after his wounding. "When you get discharged from recovery, you gotta come over there with me. Have a few drinks and dance with me."

He started to make a joke, laugh and ask her if she was hitting on him, but he didn't. He was comfortable with her. He wondered if maybe she just wasn't his type. But women as attractive as she was – even though she was awfully skinny – had always been his type. He was relaxed with her; he didn't feel he needed to impress her. He didn't have to be anybody but who he really was.

"I can't dance," Patrick said.

"Anybody can dance, Patrick," she said.

Some nights he had trouble going to sleep, so they talked late in low, soft voices. He told her all about his kids, about Olga. About her surgery, her mastectomy, and how difficult it had been for him to cope with it.

"I mean, it was happening to her, and I was the one that freaked out," he said.

"It was happening to you both," Susan said. "Not an excuse, but give yourself a break."

One night he found himself telling her about that day when Haskins was killed. He tried to recall everything in an orderly fashion, so as not to leave anything out. He told her about riding on the tank, about the strange clicking in the trees, about Mac and the agonizing journey out. How fucking heavy Mac was and how he struggled to carry him. He talked on and on, with her not saying anything, her face only vaguely visible in the darkened room, brightened occasionally by the bright orange-red of her cigarette tip.

On another night she told him her story. She was a widow. Her husband had been killed at Bien Hoa, six years before, in July of 1959. "Jim was one of the first American soldiers killed in Vietnam," she said. "He was sent over here as part of a Military Assistance Advisory Group. There was a surprise attack on a MAAG compound at Bien Hoa. He was regular army, a major; he wanted to make the army his career. Five months after our wedding, they sent him over here. An adviser. I didn't know what was going on, and suddenly my husband was killed. It hit me like a bolt out of the blue. I'd never heard of the Viet Cong. Guerillas, the newspapers said, when they finally got around to reporting his death. I wasn't informed about it until almost a month after it happened. Can you imagine what it's like to be told the person you love more than anyone or anything else in the whole world has already been dead a month, before you find out about it? You've been waking up, going to work, checking the mail every day, going about your business, and all that time he's been dead, gone. I wasn't even worried when I didn't hear from him, because the mission he was on was so hush-hush."

She paused to light a cigarette. The lights were still on in the ward and Patrick could see her face. It was drawn. She wore very little make-up. She blew the smoke toward the canvas ceiling. "I cried for about a year," she said, "Before I started to piece myself back together again. The most painful thing about it was that I wasn't with him when he died. I didn't know if anybody was with him. I couldn't bear to think of him dying alone. A year went by and I went around like a zombie. I was working as a surgery nurse at a hospital in St. Louis, just living day to day, smoking too much, drinking too much. I read that the army was sending more and more nurses and medical personnel to Nam, so I volunteered. I joined up. I guess I wanted to be where he'd been. See what he'd seen."

She stopped talking. She took a long drag off the cigarette. He could detect a thin film of moisture in her eyes. She sighed.

"And you wanted to be here for somebody else," he said.

She looked at him. "Yes," she said.

He was still sore all over but getting better every day. Susan Conklin had found out for him that of the one hundred thirty four men in Alpha company, there had been eighty eight casualties and twenty one wounded. Patrick had a lot of time to lie around thinking about that. One hundred and nine men that he knew personally, some his friends, eighty eight of them dead. Haskins dead, and Seelbach and Whitfield. Cosper. Sometimes it seemed like a terrible dream that could not possibly have happened; he would wake up in the night and it would be so real he would think he was back out there. He could smell the bitter smoke and the mud. He would wake up sweating, crying out, and some nurse or medic would be there calming him down. Some of the other men would yell at him to shut the fuck up. Sometimes they had to give him a shot to quiet him.

A surgeon named Simmons, a captain who was younger than Patrick, had done the work on his ear. He was a slight, wiry man, brusque and business-like. "It's like patching a punctured tire," he told Patrick. "A get-by, temporary move. You'll want to have reconstructive surgery when you get back stateside. You'll be going straight to Walter Reed, where you'll be evaluated." He wore a torn white smock over battle fatigues.

"When?" Patrick asked.

"You're on the list. Only so much room on a plane, and we've got a lot of men who are more crucial than you are, but soon."

"Plastic surgery?" Patrick asked.

"Yeah," he said. "Boxer's ear."

"Huh?"

"Ever look at an old boxer's ears? That's what yours is going to look like, even with reconstructive surgery. You won't ever regain the hearing in that ear. The ear drum is too severely damaged."

"I can live with that," Patrick said.

"You'll have to," Simmons said.

Patrick was able to get up and walk some around the camp. Sometimes he walked with Susan Conklin, and sometimes with Steve Nance, who had come by to see him. Steve told him that neither he nor Jason Morrison had gotten a scratch.

"We was down aways from y'all," he said. "I just kept pumpin' them gooks with my M3 Grease. That baby slings some lead!" He paused, shaking his head. "Then some shit-head lieutenant come up from behind and told us to pull back. I didn't argue with him."

"The Pillsbury Dough Boy?"

"Naw. It was somebody else. I couldn't see his face too good with all that mud and shit."

"We're some lucky bastards."

"Yeah. The way that shit was flyin', man! They was all up in the trees, man. I didn't know where all that shit was comin' from. You wasn't all that lucky; you got your ear tore up."

"I don't give a shit about that, Nance. I'm fuckin' alive."

The two men sat in the sun and smoked together and talked. Nance told Patrick he was bothered by this urge to apologize to somebody just for being alive. Patrick said that he felt guilty for being able to sit there in the sunshine and fresh air of the base camp in clean fatigues. He was there, and the others who were with them that day were not, and something was badly off-kilter about that. Their friends were just gone, vanished, evaporated into invisibility. Patrick said that when he thought about them, he thought maybe they were only imaginary and had never really existed at all.

Nance told him that he and Morrison were in a barracks tent on the other side of the compound. He told Patrick they'd been to a party over at the nurses' barracks. "Nice," he said. "Plenty of booze and music and women. I'm gonna get me some of that white pussy before they send our asses back out."

One day Patrick was summoned to the headquarters tent. He was puzzled as to what it could be about. Susan Conklin told him he was going to be on TV. "CBS News. They're here, and they want to interview somebody who was in the firefight at On Thahn. Major Pierce picked you and two other guys. I'll put you on a nice, clean bandage."

Patrick peered at her quizzically. "Do you run this goddam hospital?" he asked.

"You got it, bud," she said.

She walked him over. Nance and Morrison were waiting for them outside. It was a big wall tent with a camouflage net over it. Sandbags were piled behind it. Nance whistled when they walked up. "Woohoo, Pappy done got himself a girl friend," he said. "He can still get it up."

Susan laughed. Patrick introduced her to Steve and Jason.

Susan left and they waited half an hour before they were ushered into the tent. An officer was there, behind a desk, and he stood and came around and held out his hand. The men saluted him and then shook his hand. He was Major Pierce, baldheaded and thick-necked, about forty. He smiled at them. He waved them to folding chairs.

He commended them on their courage and bravery under fire. He told them they were to be interviewed by CBS News about the Battle of On Thahn. He told them to simply hold their comments to what happened to them personally. He was emphatic in telling them, several times, that they were not to use the word "ambush" in any circumstance. Then he dismissed them.

Outside the tent, Nance said, "Whoowee."

"Keep your voice down, Steve," Morrison said.

"If that wasn't no ambush, I'll kiss your ass," Nance said. "Even he said somebody fucked up. Shit. Them motherfuckers ain't puttin' me on no television."

Susan walked up then.

"Here yo girlfriend," Nance said.

"She ain't my girlfriend, Nance," Patrick said. For some reason he wanted Nance to understand that.

They told Jason and Steve goodbye and began to walk back over. The idea of answering questions about On Tahn, of reliving it, filled him with anxiety and dread. He didn't want to talk about it with any television reporter. He felt the horror growing in him again; he could almost smell the smoke. His arms and legs began to ache anew. "I don't know, I don't know," he said aloud.

"What?" Susan asked.

"He doesn't want us to say 'ambush'," he said.

They walked along. Susan didn't look at him. "Are you surprised at that?" she asked.

The bright sun washed out everything; the tents were pale olive, the plank walkways faded, the wet mud in the street reflecting silver. "No," he said.

Patrick walked over to the tent where Mac was laid up. The big Sergeant was propped up on pillows, covered from the waist down with a white sheet. He had on one of those cotton hospital gowns, the kind that tied up the back and still left your ass exposed. Black chest hair was poking out over the top. He was smoking, a plastic ashtray sitting on his stomach. The ward he was in was only about half full. Patrick pulled a chair up next to the bed.

"How you been, Founier?" Mac asked.

"Okay," Patrick said. He looked at the younger man, his upper arms like hams under the short sleeves of the gown. He could not quite believe he had half-carried this huge man all that way. He could still smell the jungle, their bodies, the scorched air. He recalled it all like a vigorous daydream, brilliantly clear yet fragile, as if it might instantly dissipate, be dispersed in the air, be lost if it slipped from his mind. "How're you doin'?"

Mac grunted. "Hurtin'," he said. He took a drag off his cigarette. "But, hey, hell, they saved my leg. For now, anyway."

"Yeah," Patrick said.

"What about you? You didn't get any of that shrapnel in your pea brain, did you?"

Patrick laughed. "Naw," he said. "Just left an ear out there. Lost my watch and my ear. Don't know which one I miss the most."

"You look like shit," Mac said. Patrick wondered if his eyes were as hollowed out as Mac's, his skin as pasty. Neither man said anything for a few moments. They looked at each other, then away. Patrick could hear low murmuring a few beds over; a nurse in camouflage fatigues walked by the foot of Mac's bed. She nodded to Patrick as she passed. After a silence, Mac said, "Ain't we some beat up lookin' sons a bitches?"

Patrick laughed again. He shook his head and sighed. "Nance and Morrison made it out," he said. "And you and me, that's it for the squad."

"Shit," Mac said. "We didn't stand a chance."

"But it wasn't an ambush," Patrick said.

"Says who?"

"The brass. Orders. I'm gonna be interviewed on the teevee, and I've been ordered not to even use the word 'ambush'."

"The television? You? You fulla shit!"

"No, really," Patrick said.

"They ain't puttin' no ugly old Cajun on the teevee," Mac said. He shook his head.

"You just watch," Patrick said.

Mac lay there in silence as though lost in thought, his eyes focused on nothing. After a long pause he shook his head again. "No ambush, huh?" he said. "What the fuck was it, a Sunday school picnic?"

"I guess they don't want to admit we were ambushed," Patrick said.

"No shit. Admit to who?" Mac strained and sat upward. His blue eyes flashed with anger. He let his head fall back on the pillow. He blew smoke toward the slanted canvas overhead. "Well, anyway," Mac said. "We're goin' home, Pappy. You and me, we're gettin' out of this shit hole."

"Yeah," Patrick said. He stood up. When he did he felt woozy; he grabbed the frame of Mac's bed to steady himself.

"You okay?" Mac asked.

"Yeah. Just still a little..." He swallowed and shook his head. "I'm okay."

"Listen, Founier," Mac said. "I just want to say..."

"You don't have to say anything, Mac," Patrick said.

The Sergeant fixed him with his steady, blue gaze. "Okay," he said. After a silence, he said, "I know I don't have to say anything, Cajun. I just want to say thanks."

Patrick opened his mouth to make a joke, to brush it away, but he found he couldn't speak. A year ago, Mac had been a stranger, someone whose life was faraway, whose essence – whose heart – had not yet touched his own. Now they were bound, sealed almost as one. He was the one who should be grateful; he was the one who should be giving thanks to Mac. But he couldn't find the words. He felt beholden, felt obliged. He knew in his heart that feeling it was enough.

He and Morrison went before the camera one sunny afternoon. They had it set up outside, with a sandbag wall as a backdrop. The reporter was young and looked like another grunt, except that his camouflage fatigues were new and crisp. When he told Patrick his name it sounded familiar to him, but he had never been one to watch much of the television news. The interview was going on before Patrick even realized it. He was finding it hard to concentrate, with all the medication he was taking. It was difficult to follow the reporter, who was speaking too fast. He said some long introduction. Patrick heard the words "On Thahn" and "U. S. Infantry," something about The New York Times, he heard his and Morrison's and Mac's names. The reporter turned first to Morrison. He asked him to describe what it had been like. Morrison said Jesus had been with him, God had spared his life, there was a bigger plan for him. He said it was terrible, he had been scared, but Jesus had come to him right there on the battlefield and held his hand and told him he was blessed. "I'd just like to give a shout out to the folks in Oak Park, and a big hello to the guys at The Crow's Nest," Morrison said.

Patrick was listening to Morrison droning on, his mind wondering, when he realized the reporter was talking about him.

"... Over three days, himself with a head wound, carried his severely wounded comrade through hostile enemy territory back to safety," the reporter said. He was looking at Patrick, waiting for him to speak. "Tell us about it?"

"Well..." Patrick said. He didn't know how to respond. He could think of nothing to say. But he had to say something. "I..." he began, "I don't know what, you know, what was happening," he said. He was damning the medications. He was wondering if he had a more severe head wound than he'd been told.

The reporter was smiling sympathetically. "Just tell us in your own words what happened out there," he prodded.

"What happened?"

"Yes."

"Well, I can't describe it. I don't have the words to describe it." His mind was cloudy, foggy. He began to say whatever came into his head. "My son Willie could describe it. He has the words, he reads a lot of books. He has this butterfly collection, all these butterflies..." He paused. He thought of Haskins, and he gulped to keep from sobbing. "Anyway, you don't think out there. You just do, you know what I mean? I mean, if you think then you won't. You know?" He felt as though he were talking utter nonsense, making a fool of himself. He couldn't make himself be understood. Olga was right; he was ignorant. And he was demonstrating it, right here on national television. Olga and Deirdre and Willie and Max were sitting there looking at him. He hadn't really thought about that before then, how his face, his head with the white bandage, was right there in the den at home. In some odd way, that made them together. "Is this live?" he asked the reporter.

"What?"

"You know..."

"No, we're taping it, Private Founier."

"Okay, well.... Look, I'm sorry I interrupted you about that."

"Don't worry, we'll edit it." He kept smiling encouragingly.

"Anyway," Patrick said. "We were out there, pinned down, and my buddy Haskins got killed and..." He choked up then. He couldn't go on. The reporter patted him on the shoulder. Patrick swallowed. He was embarrassed. He had forgotten what he was going to try to say. "It was...it was...lonely out there," he said. "We were...we were friends."

"You and your buddy Haskins? You and Sergeant McMillan?"

"I mean, we all were." He couldn't see the reporter through the mist in his eyes. He felt like a total pussy, crying like that on television. He was thinking Haskins is going to give me hell for this, he won't let me forget it, then he was sinking, no he won't, he can't, and that made him cry harder. Turn that fucking thing off. Did I say that out loud?

"According to the New York Times," the reporter was saying,"the battle of On Thahn was a major turning point in the conflict. The North Vietnamese army is now on the run, retreating toward Hanoi." He continued talking. Patrick was relieved the reporter was wrapping up, that the interview was over. He had completely blown it. They would know he had totally lost his mind.

*****

When Susan came by his bed that evening she said, "Hey, so how's the hero?"

"Don't fuckin' kid me about that," Patrick said harshly. "Don't laugh at me."

She stood there looking at him. She didn't say anything for a minute. "I'm not laughing at you, Patrick," she said. "I'm not, you dunce." She smiled and shook her head. "Listen, I don't want you to misunderstand this, okay? But I love you, Patrick Founier," she said.

Chapter Twenty-Six

Bay Springs, Louisiana
December, 1965
MAX

MY MOM asked me if I wanted to have a drink with her. I was floored. You just never knew with my mom; she was totally unpredictable. Out of the blue, she offered me a drink of her Scotch. I'd never drunk in front of her before. We were sitting around in the living room. I was home a lot because my license was suspended; I had to catch a ride wherever I wanted to go. She was smoking cigarettes one after the other; I hadn't seen her smoke like that since before my old man had left. They used to puff away together.

"Go ahead, pour you one," she said. "I'd rather see you drinking at home than out on the road, gettin' arrested again or killin' somebody. I know you're gonna do it. But for God's sakes, Max, be a little more careful." The Scotch was kind of lame. She used to buy Chives Regal; now she bought Usher's. I wished I'd put a little water in mine, but I didn't get back up.

"How was your day?" she asked.

"Okay," I said. "Yours?"

"Fine," she said.

I could tell she wanted to talk to me about something. It was already dark outside and had turned off cold. That's the way it would do in this part of the world, get real cold for a couple of days and then warm up and the days would be almost spring-like. Dee and Willie had spent the afternoon decorating the Christmas tree, and it stood in the corner. It was covered with the ornaments we'd collected over the years, many of them hand-made by me or Dee, or Willie, when we were little kids. Several of them were little frames holding some of Willie's butterflies. It was going to be the first Christmas without our dad being there, and I figured that was what was on my mom's mind. Willie and Dee were in the den watching television, so that left the two of us alone.

"Max," she said. "You're the oldest."

"Yeah, I'm the oldest," I said.

"Smartass," she said. She smiled.

My mother was a beautiful woman. She was classy and smart, a lot smarter than my dad was, and I think that had been part of the problem. My dad went to work as soon as he got out of high school. He had a bunch of jobs. The longest, he said, was in a crawfish packing plant, and he hated it. It made him want to leave Breaux Bridge and never come back. He was working there when he met my mom at a Cajun restaurant outside Lafayette. They told us that she was up dancing to this zydeco band and he was drunk and jumped in and started dancing with her. She told him he couldn't dance. They had a big laugh.

"Okay, so I'm the oldest," I said. "Yes, mam?"

"This hasn't been an easy time for any of us," she said. "Your dad and I... Well, we've screwed up a lot of things. But maybe that's all in the past. I don't know what the hell is going to happen with that war, or with the two of us, but we all love each other, and we'll make it through because of that. Your dad loves us. I don't doubt that. He just can't seem to get it together." A sad, conspiratorial smile. "You and I, as the ancient ones, have got to help Dee and Willie deal with all that, with the uncertainty and the pain. Okay?"

"Yes mam," I said.

I just sat there looking at her. She was my mother. I was smart enough to know how courageous and brave she'd been about the cancer and that awful operation, how she'd never let us see her cry through all that, but I'd heard her, at night, behind her closed door. I felt this dropping sensation all of a sudden, and something warm swelled up in my chest, just like it had that night I'd come home drunk and seen how she'd so carefully left the light on for me, and I thought, Oh shit, I'm not going to fucking cry again! Maybe it was me who ought not to drink.

I drank the whiskey down. I wanted another. I started to ask, then I just got up and made it. I didn't want to be the oldest one; I didn't want to be mature. Maybe I was still more a kid than I thought I was. Maybe I was almost as scared of the situation as Willie. I tried to think about something else. I was hoping Vicki would come by. She was going to try to get her father's car for the evening. Her father had not been too happy when he heard about the DUI. I sat back down.

"There's something else, Max," she said. I turned to her. I could tell by her voice that she was nervous. "That Reverend Means is trying to make trouble for me. You're going to hear some things about it."

"Rayford Means? What trouble?"

"Seems he's decided I'm not a fit person to be a teacher. He went to Mr. Larkin and complained about my drinking. And some other things." She was trying to be real casual, but I could tell she was pretty up-tight about it. "He's been spying on me, has seen me having a drink with a guy. A friend. He's jumped to all kinds of conclusions."

"One of the guys from Thanksgiving?" I asked.

"Yeah," she said. "It was all innocent, but..."

"Wait," I said. "You don't have to tell me that. I know that."

She just looked at me. Her eyes were dead serious, but then she smiled. "Thanks, Max," she said. "I knew I could count on you."

"What a jerk," I said.

"Yeah. He makes me feel attacked. Violated. But I'm strong. I have you and Deirdre and Willie, and that makes me strong. But you have to help me make sure they understand. Help me take care of them. They need... Well, you're the man of the family right now. Until Dad comes home."

"Sure," I said. I almost choked on the word.

"Mama, Mama!" we heard Deirdre yell from the den. "Mama!" Willie chimed in. "Come quick, Daddy's on television!" Deirdre screamed.

"I don't believe it," my mom said. We got up and my mom was wiping her eyes with the backs of her hands and I knew she'd been crying. We hurried into the den. Willie was sprawled out on the floor and Deirdre was on the sofa. Sure enough, I saw my dad's face on the television, half of it covered with a white bandage. He didn't look much like himself. He had a straggly beard. He had lost a lot of weight and was hollow eyed. And that bandage.

He reminded me of those pictures of people from the concentration camps in Europe after the world war. Or drummer boys on posters with a white bandage around their heads. And he looked lost and sad.

"What–?" my mom began.

"He's been wounded!" Deirdre said. She was crying.

"Shh, shh," my mom said.

Dee turned the volume up. We all got as quiet as we could and listened. The reporter, a young guy with a crewcut in an army uniform was talking. The camera shifted to my father's face while he was talking, "He was one of only four survivors in his platoon, and after the battle he, over three days, himself with a head wound, carried his severely wounded buddy through hostile enemy territory to safety. Private Patrick Founier, from Bay Springs, Louisiana."

"A hero! He's a hero!" Deirdre screamed.

"Shhh, shhh," my mom said sharply.

"I don't know what all...you know...," he said. "I mean..." He stopped speaking. The camera stayed on his face. He was twisting his face around in this way he had when he was trying to think of something, to figure something out. The reporter's voice said, "Tell us what happened out there."

"Well, I can't describe it. I don't have the words to describe it. My son Willie could describe it. He has the words, he reads a lot of books. He has this butterfly collection, all these butterflies..." He stopped again. He looked like he wanted to cry. My dad, crying! He had that same straining expression again. He was groping, trying to pull himself together. "Anyway, you don't think out there. You just do, you know what I mean?"

"My butterflies!" Willie exclaimed. "He mentioned my butterflies."

"Shut up, shut up," Deirdre said, but we'd missed something.

Willie was crying then, too. "What's he saying?" my mother asked over the blubbering.

"Listen," Deirdre cried. "Listen to what he's sayin'."

"Anyway, we were out there, pinned down, and my buddy Haskins got killed and..." And then my dad started crying for real, just blubbering. It tore me up royally. I had forgotten how much I loved him. The camera focused tightly on his eyes, one of them peeping out from behind the bandage. "It was...it was...lonely out there," he was saying. "All of us were friends."

"You and your buddy Haskins?" the reporter asked. "You and Sergeant McMillan?"

"I mean, we all were." He started then to sort of sob.

"He's cryin'," Deirdre said. And then we all were. Deirdre was sort of crying and laughing at the same time, like a crazy person. Willie was kind of making this uhh, uhh, uhh noise. I looked at my mom. She was trying to hold it in, but I could tell she was about to lose it. She looked like she was in a state of shock. But inside that, in some way, she looked happy, for the first time in a long time.

The reporter went on talking about The People's Army of Vietnam and the National Front for the Liberation of Vietnam, using all this military jargon that I was unfamiliar with. He mentioned the Viet Cong several times. I couldn't follow it very well. They kept showing little snippets of my father's face.

The reporter was holding a microphone, squatting on one knee in front of a pile of sandbags. He kept talking about On Thahn. He talked about Alpha Company of some infantry division that I didn't catch. He said that an aggressive advance by the Vietnamese army out of Cambodia had been thwarted and turned back, and that a pentagon spokesman said this was a major turning point of the conflict. Then, while the announcer droned on, they showed about ten seconds or so of my father, just sitting there, like he was unaware the camera was even on him, and I couldn't take my eyes off the bandage, the wound, and it stunned me because he was my father and I could almost feel the pain myself, in the same way–when she had been sick–I experienced my mother's suffering, her loss. Both wounds became all our common, shared ache and anguish. I guess that's what being a family means. I had never loved either one of them more than I did at that moment.

The newscast went to some other item. Then Speedy Alka Seltzer was dancing on the screen.

"What did he say, Dee, before we got in here?" my mom asked. Her voice had this weird, dreamy quality to it.

"Nothin'," Dee said. Her voice was quivering.

"What?" my mom said. " 'Nothin'?' That was it?"

"Some other guy was talkin' about Jesus," Dee said. "And we heard Daddy's name and then there he was."

"He said," Willie said from the floor, "that he was lonely when he was fighting."

"They heard him say that, dumb-ass," Deirdre snapped. Then she burst into tears again.

"Deirdre, I'm going to have to ask you to be nice to your little brother," my mom said. Her voice was shrill and tight.

"Fuck you," Deirdre said.

"Maybe he'll get a medal," Willie said.

"I bet he will," I said.

My mom and I looked at each other. I could tell by the kindness in her eyes that she wasn't going to rip into Dee for saying what she did. It was rougher on Dee and Willie. We hadn't heard a word from my father in months, and we were finding out he'd been wounded by seeing him on television. And that he, my dad, had done something really brave. Willie was lying flat on the floor, his arms stretched out to the sides, his face buried in the carpet. He wasn't crying anymore, though. He was just dead silent.

Nobody said anything for a minute. The little tinny song kept playing on the television.

"That's all?" my mom asked. "That's all they're gonna show?"

Deirdre spoke up. Her voice was stronger now. She seemed to have begun getting herself together. "If he's wounded, he may be coming home," she said. "You know he's coming home if he's wounded."

"How bad was his injury? Did they say?" my mom asked.

"No, but he's alive," Dee said. "My dad's alive!"

"He is," my mom said. "At least we know that."

"Why haven't they told us," Deirdre wailed. She was off again.

"Surely they will soon," I said. "We'll hear soon."

"Probably just some screw-up!" Dee said.

Just as she said that the telephone rang. It was one of my mom's friends who'd seen the newscast. We listened to her end of the conversation. "We didn't know, Susan," she said. "Or I would have told you." She listened to her friend. "A surprise to us, too," she said. The phone rang a couple of more times. I answered it once and damned if it wasn't Vicki. "I'm on my way over," she said and hung up before I could reply.

My mom went back into the living room. I sat there and watched the rest of the news with Dee, but there was nothing more about the war. Willie was still on the floor, so still I would have been frightened if I hadn't seen him breathing. "You okay, buddy?" I asked him.

He didn't answer for a minute. Then he said, "Yeah."

The doorbell rang and I knew it had to be Vicki. I jumped up and ran down the hall. Vicki was on the porch, under the light. She had on a heavy coat.

"Hi," she said when I opened the door. She looked great. Her face was all full of color from the cold. She hustled in. "Brrrrr," she said. The chill and the smell of winter drifted in with her.

I grabbed her and put my arms around her. Her coat was cold. I kissed her and her nose was cold. We broke apart and she giggled.

We walked the few steps down the hallway and into the living room. Vicki said, "My God. Your dad!"

"Yeah," I said.

"He looked great," she said. "Except for that bandage, but it must not be... Hi, Mrs. Founier."

"Hello, Vicki," my mom said. She was up getting herself another drink. "Would you...I don't know if your folks let you drink or not. Could I get you something? Water? A coke?"

"Whatever you're having," Vicki said. She glanced at me and smiled. "What did you think? About your dad bein' on television and all?"

"Your folks are okay with that?" My mom asked her. "With you drinking?"

"Yes mam," Vicki said and sat down next to me. I didn't think they were, but I didn't say anything. My mom had to go out to the kitchen to get some more ice.

When she was out of the room Vicki leaned over and kissed me again. She ran her tongue around my ear. Mom came back in and poured Vicki a Scotch on the rocks. She gave it to her and sat back down with her own fresh one. Vicki took a long drink.

Just then Dee came into the room. Vicki jumped up and ran and hugged Dee. I didn't even know they knew each other. Of course they knew each other. Dee was a couple of grades behind us, but we went to the same school, and they were girls.

"Dee!" Vicki said. "How 'bout that? On television!"

Dee was jumping up and down in Vicki's arms. Both of them were jumping up and down. "Yes, yes, yes, yes," they said together.

Dee was so happy, and that made me feel happy, too. Vicki coming over was good for her, too. I looked at my mom. I don't know how to describe the look on her face. I should've paid more attention in English composition class. I guess, like my dad said, I should get the words from Willie. She was happy but still worried about my dad. The best I could do was just to say the expression on her face was one of grief all mixed up with joy. I hadn't known before that moment that that was even possible. But it was. It was possible to feel all that at one and the same time. My mother was okay. She was going to be okay.

Both girls were squealing and crying. Vicki was crying. She hardly even knew my dad, but she was crying as much as Deirdre was. My mom sat down and drained her drink. Willie came in then and stood there watching them. I was relieved to see him up; he had this huge grin on his face. I sat there and watched them dance around. For some crazy reason they started doing Bulldog yells. I was sitting there thinking: Girls are wonderful. I don't know the first goddam thing about them, but I can tell you this: they are goddam wonderful.

Chapter Twenty-Seven

Tan Son Nhut Base Camp, Vietnam
December, 1965

IN TWO days, Patrick would be leaving Vietnam and going back home. He would fly first to the Phillipines, then on to Washington to Walter Reed Army Medical Center. He was no longer having headaches. His dizzy spells, his sudden sensations of disorientation, occurred less frequently and were milder. Captain Simmons was still cautious, but he told him he could do most anything he wanted to do, "short of playing football."

Patrick had been to one party with Susan, but she wouldn't let him have a drink. "Dr. Simmons said with the half-life of all the painkillers you've been on, you could OD," she said.

He had pouted. "Okay, I won't dance, then. I can't dance without booze." He was glad to have an excuse. He wasn't really sure how to dance, and it embarrassed him. He'd always had to be half drunk before he would dance.

"Okay," she had said. "But if Dr. Simmons gives you the go-ahead before you leave, I'm bringing you back, and you're gonna dance with me."

"No, I'm not," he had said. She had just stared at him, her eyes narrowed. "I can't. I might hurt my head," he had added.

"What are you, Founier, a pussy?" she had asked. "You're gonna dance with me!"

"No shit I'm not!" he'd said.

Patrick still had trouble sleeping. The nurses had put up a small Christmas tree in the ward, and he would lie there looking at it, thinking about Olga and the kids back home. He knew he wouldn't be in Bay Springs for Christmas, but he would be out of Nam. He was going to see them again, he knew that now. A couple of weeks earlier, he would have thought it was a sucker's bet that he'd ever get home. When he was lying awake he would try to focus on Olga, the way she'd looked when he used to watch her sleeping – she was well, she wasn't going to die any time soon – and Deirdre, growing up and her boyfriends and all; Max, no telling what he was up to, and Willie, Willie and his butterflies. He was trying to keep his mind from jumping, of its own accord, to that day at On Thahn and the agony of his and Mac's journey out, when his mind would be bombarded with the terrible images and sounds: Cosper's face as he died, the horrible lifelessness of Haskins' body, the endless ear-splitting chatter of machine guns, the strident thunder of bombs, the terrifying babbling of the Viet Cong soldiers that day, the torturous pain he and Mac had suffered.

On the night before he was to leave, he went with Susan and Steve Nance to the recreation room at the nurses' barracks. Patrick intended to get very drunk, then maybe dance. Simmons had cleared him to drink. ("One or two, Founier," he'd said and laughed, shaking his head. "No more than that.") The nurses lived in two long concrete block buildings; on the end of one of the barracks was a large rec room with ping-pong tables and shuffleboard courts painted on the floor. The nurses had pushed back the tables and made a bar; there were couches and chairs and small tables, and a cleared area for a dance floor. There was a portable stereo on one of the tables, where they played an eclectic collection of records, some of them scratchy, that had been donated by people back home. There were some wreaths and strings of colored lights on the walls, and behind where the bar was set up was a large, plastic Santa Claus lit from behind.

They sat at one of the card tables grouped around the little make-shift dance floor. Nance and Susan had long necked bottles of cold beer, Patrick had a Scotch on the rocks. He looked at it eagerly when Susan set in on the table in front of him. He sipped it tentatively. It tasted tinny, stannic. He put it down, disappointed that he didn't want to drink it. He wanted it, and then he didn't want it. It scared him. It was like the time when he was a little boy and he'd swiped some of his father's rot-gut whiskey and taken it into the swamp to drink it. He had craved its enigmatical, magical power and was terrified of what it might do to him.

Nance turned to Susan. "You sure you old enough to be drinkin' that horse piss?" he asked her.

"You kiddin'?" She laughed.

"I'm flatterin' you," he said, grinning. "Ain't that the way to get in a white girl's britches?"

"It's one way," she chuckled.

"Ol Pappy might be goin' back stateside, but I'm gonna be here," Nance said. "At least till they send my black ass back out to the jungle. I've heard that all my life, 'send em back to the jungle', but I never knew they were talking about the Viet Cong jungle. Shit."

The music playing was the Stones, *"I can't get no satisfaction"*. There were about twenty people in the rec room, mostly nurses, some in fatigues, some in white uniforms.

Patrick was enjoying watching some of the nurses dancing with other grunts. He kept glancing at his drink, moisture beads collecting on the sides. It was the first Scotch he'd seen and smelled since his In country R & R in Saigon, and it made him think of Kim Ly. He felt sad that he'd never see her again. Not that he wanted to see her again, just that it was sad he wouldn't. He picked the drink up and looked at the cool amber liquid. It was enticing; he could taste it on his tongue. The song now was Bob Dylan, *"Like a Rolling Stone"*.

Susan came back to the table with two fresh beers for her and Nance.

"You're not drinking," she said to Patrick. She smiled. "You think you're gonna get out of dancing. It's not gonna work."

"I'm not gonna dance," he said. "I told you I don't know how."

"You don't have to 'know how,' soldier boy," she said.

"I don't see how white folks can dance to that shit," Nance said.

Patrick and Susan laughed, looking at each other, smiling.

"Uh oh," Nance said. "This a good time for me to go shake the dew off the lily." He got up and headed for the men's room.

"He's sure we're havin' an affair, no matter what I say," Patrick said.

Susan laughed again. They sat for a few seconds, the music blaring. Finally, Susan looked at Patrick and smiled again. "He's young," she said.

When Nance got back, the music was The Supremes, "Back In My Arms". "That's more like it," he said. He went to the bar and came back with a girl. She was a cute little blonde nurse with glittering, spirited eyes. Patrick was surprised that a white girl was going to dance with Nance. But he reflected that maybe war changed everything. The war turned everything upside down. The girl told them her name was Betty and she was from Carlisle, Pennsylvania. She had a purple streak dyed in her hair. She and Nance started to dance.

The music battered at Patrick's head. He was longing to savor the whiskey, to feel it casing through his blood. He didn't know why he couldn't drink it. The confusion was getting to him. Maybe he was going batty. He was just sitting there, looking around. He saw Henry Haskins standing at the ping-pong table serving as a bar. He stood up and headed over there. He felt a little dazed and light-headed and staggered a little bit dodging the dancers. The man was facing away from him. He put his hand on his shoulder. "Henry!" he said.

The black man turned and looked at him. "I ain't no Henry," he said.

"Scuse me," Patrick said.

He walked slowly and carefully back to their table and sank into his chair. "What was that all about?" Susan asked him.

"I thought...I thought..." He didn't finish. He felt fragile. He was fighting the urge to cry. He was teetering on the edge. He swallowed, feeling the tears spring at the backs of his eyes. He didn't know if they were tears of grief and sadness or tears of relief and gratitude. He blinked and looked at Susan. He breathed deeply.

She reached out and gripped his hand. "It's okay, Patrick," she said, "It's okay." They sat like that for a while.

The party was taking off. It was getting noisy, rowdy. A recording of Chubby Checker's *"Let's Twist Again"* came on and it seemed that everybody in the room was up dancing.

Susan stood up. "Come on, 'Pappy'," she said, saying his nickname just like Nance said it.

"No," he protested. She pulled at his arm but he resisted.

She began to twist then, expertly, like he'd seen Deirdre doing. Her eyes were fixed on his face and the smile never left hers. She kept dancing. "Like this, Pappy," she said. "Like you're dryin' off your ass with a towel."

Patrick stood up. He began to move. He tried to catch on. He tried to copy Susan. Everybody was having a ball. There were hoots and laughter. Patrick danced, then, not caring that he didn't know how, just letting himself go. "Look at old Pappy," he heard Nance say. They all danced with a hysterical frenzy that was almost desperate. They were in high spirits, blissfully intoxicated with booze and with being alive.

The song ended and they all flopped down at their table, laughing, panting for breath. Someone put on another record. The song began. It was Pete Seeger's *"Where Have All The Flowers Gone?"*.

"Can't nobody dance to that," Nance complained.

Pete Seeger's voice rasped through the room.

"Man, that honky can't sing," Nance said.

But everybody was listening. There were brief spurts of laughter, talking, the sound of people shushing others. Then the whole room fell silent. Seeger sang about the young girls: where had they gone? Patrick swallowed. He gripped his glass. The song went on. The young men had gone, too. Seeger's voice drifted out over them and around them. It was harsh, crude. Graveyards. They've gone to graveyards. Jesus! Patrick felt the tears coming again, and this time he couldn't, wouldn't stop them.

The song ended and everyone just sat there. For a moment Patrick couldn't move. Tears kept sliding down his cheeks. Patrick looked at Nance, at his little blonde friend Betty. They were motionless, hushed. He knew they were feeling it; he saw tears there, too. He swallowed again.

"Why'd they have to put that on?" Betty whispered, her voice barely audible.

Susan was clasping Patrick's hand. Young men... He thought of Max, of Willie. He thought of Cosper, of Haskins, of Mac. All the rest. And of himself, all of them together, all of them strung out in a long, straggling line down a perilous and lonely jungle road.

Chapter Twenty-Eight

Bay Springs, Louisiana
December, 1965
WILLIE

I WAS WALKING home from school when I heard her voice calling to me. "Hey, Willeeeee!" She was practically singing it out. I stopped and looked behind me. She waved this short little flag of a wave. I waited on her to catch up. She looked awesome. A gray tweed skirt and a green sweater. Tight. I had seen her earlier in class, but I'd not really had a chance to absolutely study her the way I liked to do. I watched her walk toward me. They told me I have a slight heart murmur from the rheumatic fever, and when I'm looking at Amy, I can feel it. Like a little ripple that goes through me.

She was holding her geography book over her chest with both arms. When she stopped I reached for it. "Why Willie," she said. "You're a gentleman."

"Yeah," I said, taking the book. Not knowing if she was laughing at me or not.

"That's sweet," she said. "Carrying my book."

"Well..." I said. I was all of a sudden tongue-tied.

We started to walk together. When it was the three of us I could chatter away like a magpie, but when it was just Amy and me it was harder. We walked a block without saying a word. There was a nip in the air. Christmas was coming. It smelled like Christmas. Like winter, and the colder weather we usually got for a month or two.

We just sort of ambled along, not saying much.

"What are you getting for Christmas?" she asked.

"Are you kidding?" I said. "Socks and a shirt or two. Practical shit."

"Yeah," she said. "I asked for a watch."

"Maybe they'll get you one."

"Maybe."

We were following the same route we'd taken that night with the drum. We turned up Washington Street. All the store windows were decorated for Christmas, with trees and stars and fake snow and stuff. Which is ironic, since it hasn't snowed in Bay Springs in about a hundred years probably. We took a short cut, down an alley behind Bailey's. We came out on Capitol Street and we could see the statue of the soldier a couple of blocks over. His hat was still red.

"That was my finest hour," I said.

"Yeah," she said. "Our finest hour."

"Sure, our's," I said.

"I was actually referring to the hour after the one when we painted the statue."

"Oh," I said. I looked at her. She was smiling. Surely she meant the kiss. That would have to be what she meant. I didn't say anything.

All of a sudden she punched me on the arm, hard. "You're too much, Willie," she said, and laughed.

We resumed our walking. We cut down another alley and came out on a quiet street that curved off down toward the river. I felt Amy's hand–first her fingers, then her whole hand–grip mine, and we strolled along like that, holding hands. I couldn't think of anything else but those two hands locked together. I worried that I was maybe clutching her hand too tight, or too loose. I had seen other couples walking hand in hand, of course, but I never looked to see how they did it. I tried to relax and just let it be natural. And it was. It was the most natural thing in the world. I was hoping the road to Amy's house would keep getting longer and longer, would elongate like Pinocchio's nose. I tried to walk slower, to make it last.

The street we were on ran between a few houses set back among some trees on one side and the back side of Merchants Grocery Company's huge old red brick warehouse on the other. The warehouse took up a whole block and cast shadows from the lowering sun. We crossed over to the sidewalk away from the warehouse, where it was still sunny and not so chilly.

A pickup truck eased to the curb beside us. I'd heard it's motor back behind us down the street. I had sort of been waiting for it to pass us, headed on down toward the river, but it pulled over. I saw immediately that it was Reverend Means's truck, and I could see him sliding across the seat, rolling down the passenger side window.

"Hello, Children of God," he said. He had this slappy grin on his face, that I think must have been his way of showing his immense compassion and love and all, but instead just looked fixed and lifeless like the expression of a wax dummy. I yanked Amy's arm.

"Keep walkin'," I said.

She sort of held back. She looked at me with this questioning look. "What...?" she asked.

"Just keep walkin'," I said. "Don't talk to him."

"But it's Mr. Means," she said. "He's the chaplain of the football team."

"Max says he doesn't do anything but pray before the games for God to let the Bulldogs win."

The pickup inched along with us.

"Where are you children going?" Mr. Means asked.

I pulled on Amy's arm and tried to keep walking.

"Don't be rude," she said. "We're just walking home from school, Mr. Means," she said.

The truck moved ahead of us a little bit then stopped abruptly, its tires making a little squeak. I could see him moving to get out. Then he was coming around the front of the truck toward the sidewalk.

"Crap, we're in for it now," I said.

"What?" Amy asked.

"He's crazy, that's what," I said. He was now blocking the way ahead of us. "He's gonna try to get us to pray with him or something."

"Pray with him?" Amy said.

"Yeah. Keep walking." I figured we'd just go around him. I certainly didn't want to get in another conversation with him. He had on a white shirt buttoned up to the collar and wrinkled khaki pants. And, I noticed, he was wearing cowboy boots, like Boyd Floyd.

He just stood there in the middle of the sidewalk, still with that wonky grin on his face. "Why are you children in such a hurry to get where you're goin' in this life?" he asked. He used the long "I", like "liiiife."

"We're just goin' home," I said.

"We're all goin' home," he said. "Eventually."

I knew what he meant. Like that mother in the comic book he showed me that day. I don't think Amy had a clue about what he was talking about. He didn't make a lot of sense. When we got closer to him I could smell the whiskey on him. He reeked with it. There was no mistaking that stink. I think I had lived with it since before I even knew what it was. It scared me. He was not only crazy, he was drunk. I felt that familiar trembling sense of imbalance, like I was standing on marbles, that I used to feel when I was a little kid and the adults in my life were not in control.

We stopped. He stood there, weaving a little. "You better let us alone, Mr. Means," I said.

"I only want what's best for you," he said, and I thought, whew, I've heard that one before. "Some people don't know the vengeance of the Lord is harsh," he went on. "You young children are up to no good. Where you goin', to the bushes?"

Amy knew what that one meant. She moved closer to me and pressed her arm against mine. "I don't think it's any of your business, sir," I said.

Mr. Means was acting weirder and weirder. He was weaving around and snorting through his nose, like he was having trouble getting his breath. His eyes were glinting with moisture and I was startled to realize he was crying. At least he looked like he was crying.

"Mr. Means, we've got to get home. Our parents…" I said, and he interrupted me.

"Terrible things," he said. "The Lord makes me do terrible things. I am a prophet. Like John."

I didn't know who John was, and I didn't care. I was about to bust out and run, but Amy said, "John? Like the disciple in the Bible?" She and Donly went to the Presbyterian Church with their parents.

"The divine one!" he snorted, like Amy had asked a dumb question. "Seven golden candlesticks and feet like fine brass," he said.

"What's he talkin' about?" I asked.

"I don't know," she said.

"Vengeance is mine, sayeth the Lord!" he shouted. Real loud, and we both jumped back away from him. I could hear his voice bouncing off the brick wall of the warehouse. "Ye that go down to the ground like serpents!" he yelled. I was really scared then, and I knew Amy was, too. She was squeezing my hand and huddling against me. Means moved closer to us. The alcohol was overwhelming, like he'd been drinking kerosene. I could smell his old man sweat, too. Then he dropped to his knees, right there on the concrete sidewalk. His head was tilted back, his face to the sky; his eyelids were squinched shut, and I could see tears leaking out the sides and down his cheeks. "Lord!" he screamed, loud, and we both jumped again and held onto each other. "Make of me thy servant!"

Suddenly he leaned forward and grabbed Amy around both legs. She screamed, and I could hear her voice ricocheting off the bricks, and I thought surely someone was going to hear us and come to help us. "Help!" I yelled as loud as I could. "Help us!"

He knelt there, still and rigid, holding her tight with both arms, his face pressed right into her crotch. Amy looked completely panicked. "Turn her loose, Mr. Means," I said. "What do you think you're doin'?" I pounded him on the shoulder a couple of times with my fist. It was hard as a brick. I could see his pink scalp under his thin white hair. He was still grunting. It sounded like he was sobbing.

I don't know how long that went on, me hitting him and bellowing at him. Amy crying louder now, pushing at his head.

Then, "What's goin' on?" I heard a voice say. I looked up and it was Mr. Kinzer, the night watchman at the warehouse. He must have been just arriving for his shift because he had a black lunch box in his hand. He was an old man, stooped over, wearing overalls; he was a welcome sight even if he did look like he'd be no match for Mr. Means. "What's he doin'?" he asked, indicating Mr. Means. He looked puzzled, then angry.

"I think he's gone crazy, Mr. Kinzer," I said. "He's drunk, too." I was crying now, too.

"Get up from there," Mr. Kinzer said to Mr. Means. "Leave that little girl alone!" He whacked Mr. Means across the back of his shoulders with his lunch box. Mr. Means didn't budge. "You're drunk, get up!" Mr. Means just squeezed Amy's legs tighter. "You ought to be ashamed of yourself," Mr. Kinzer said. He thunked the lunch box against the back of Mr. Means' head a couple of times, swinging really hard. Mr. Means didn't move.

Finally Mr. Kinzer reached in his pocket and handed me his keys. "Here, go around front to the office and call the police," he said. "I'll stay here with the girl."

I ran. I was still holding Amy's geography book. I called the police station and told them that Mr. Means was drunk on the street and causing trouble. When I got back Mr. Means had released Amy and was sitting back against the tire of his truck. He had vomited down the front of his shirt, and it smelled awful. He had his eyes closed and was breathing heavily. He looked pitiful. He looked helpless and lost now. There were tear tracks down his reddened cheeks. I remembered what Melissa had told me that day about him crying. And even if I was scared of him, I felt sorry for him. I couldn't help it.

In a few minutes a police cruiser pulled up. There were two cops, one of them the young one who'd driven me home that afternoon when Max had gotten stopped for speeding and drinking. If he recognized me he didn't show it. They got Mr. Means into the back of the cruiser. They took our names and who our parents were and all. Then they drove off with him.

I was still trembling. We thanked Mr. Kinzer, then started on for home, holding hands. Mr. Means's truck was still sitting there at the curb.

"That was pretty amazing," Amy said. It was not the word I would have used, but I knew what she meant.

We heard later that Mr. Means got real loud and belligerent at the police station. He ranted and raved that God had told him to punish the harlot Jane McKissick. Boy, was he ever a maniac. He got arrested for her rape. Everybody all over town buzzed about it for awhile and they kept asking me and Amy about that afternoon, what happened and all. To tell you the truth, neither one of us wanted to talk about it that much.

A couple of days before Christmas, Donly and Amy's parents had a big party and Donly talked them into hiring us to help with it, passing platters of finger food and trays of wine. It was a big deal every year. Even my mom was there. I was thrilled to be working the party with Amy, and hoping like hell that it would finally, somehow, give me the opportunity to be alone with her.

My mom had finally gotten a telegram from the army telling her that my dad had been wounded in action and was going to some hospital in Washington, D. C. He was going to be okay and I was relieved out of my mind. I was hoping maybe I would get up there to see him and see the monuments and all. But I knew I probably wouldn't.

So we were working the party. Back in the kitchen, Amy stuffed this thing – I think it was a fig wrapped in bacon – in my mouth. It looked like a dead roach. "Eat this," she said. It was good.

"I bet he wants to eat somethin' else," Donly said.

"Shut up," Amy said.

She looked terrific. She had on a dark green dress-up dress. I never got to see her in a dress-up dress, and she looked great in this one.

They had this big bowl of warm punch that Donly said had rum in it. We kept sneaking shots of it when nobody was looking. When one of us came back to the kitchen with a tray of used wine glasses, most of them usually still had some wine in the bottom of them, so we were drinking it, too. Amy started giggling. God, she was pretty. Her mom had let her put on some makeup, and it was driving me bananas.

We knew we were starting to get a little high, so we started draining the wine into an empty bottle to put back and save for later. We mixed up red wine and white wine.

It was a little later, when Amy and I were carrying trays of dirty wine glasses to this woman I didn't know who was washing dishes, that we got to talking.

"Boy, you were really right about that Mr. Means," she said. "You really had that guy's number." It was about the twentieth time she'd said it since that afternoon, and I liked hearing it every time, especially since it was coming from her.

"Yeah," I said.

"So your daddy's comin' home," Amy said. "I was real worried about him."

"You were?" I was surprised. I didn't even know she knew my dad. I guess because she was a girl. I knew from watching my mom and Deirdre that girls worried. "He said it was lonely over there."

"Yeah, I heard him say that on television. That was really somethin', wasn't it, seeing your dad on television?"

"Yeah."

"He talked about you and your butterfly collection," she said.

"Yeah," I said.

"I mean, was that cool, or what?"

"Cool," I said.

Why couldn't I think of anything better to say than that? I wanted to be cool. Here I was with the girl of my dreams, and I wanted to be cool. I wanted to ask her if she wanted to come see my butterfly collection. If I could just get her in my room! They were my "etchings." I'd read about that in some book. Some guy with his "etchings," trying to get women to come see them so he could be alone with them. But it was like my tongue was glued to the bottom of my mouth. I think I was starting to get a boner just thinking about Amy coming to my room. "Oh, Willie, what lovely butterflies!" "Thank you, my dear." "Do you have a favorite?" People who saw the collection were always asking me if I had a favorite butterfly. I wanted to say, "I do, but I can't show it to you."

Amy's face was slightly flushed. A couple of wisps of her hair had fallen down. She had this big, silly grin plastered on her face. She was the most beautiful creature on the face of the earth. I probably got that out of some book, but I meant every word of it. She was perfection. She was even more radiant and lovely with her hair falling down.

When the party was over, Donly and Amy's parents made us work hard, clearing everything back into the kitchen. Finally they let us go, and we went out back with the bottle of wine we'd saved. Their house was on this canal that ran down to the river. The back yard sloped off down toward the canal. We went down to where there was this big stand of willows and Cherokee roses and flopped down on the grass. It was already good dark and getting cold as hell, but we had our jackets and Amy had brought out an old quilt.

We had some Dixie cups, so we poured us all some wine. There was a full moon, and it seemed to hover over the woods on the other side of the canal. It looked so close you could reach out and touch it. The three of us stretched out, leaning back on our elbows, and just looked at it for awhile.

"They say we're gonna put a man up there in a couple of years," Donly said.

"I want to go," Amy said.

I didn't think I wanted to. But if Amy went, I would. In a minute. Earthbound or no. I leaned my head back and looked up at the stars scattered all over the sky. The array was almost bullying. I felt like I was shrinking, getting further and further away from the stars and sinking into the earth. It was a weird feeling. I gripped Amy's hand. She slid up close to me. Maybe she was feeling the same way.

All of a sudden Amy and I were smooching. I didn't know who started it and I didn't care. I was aware that Donly was over there somewhere in the darkness, but he didn't seem to be paying us any mind. If he was watching us, I didn't care about that, either. Her tongue sent bolts of shock all the way through me. She had the softest, fullest lips I'd ever felt, just exactly like I had imagined. I felt her cupcakes, satiny and firm, yielding, rubbing on my chest. We rolled around like that until I thought I was going to pop. And then I did pop. All in my pants. I don't know if she knew it or not.

If she did, she didn't care. We kept kissing for a while, then we sat up to talk.

I looked around. "Where's Donly?" I asked.

"Who cares?" she said. She pecked me on the lips.

I was a happy man. We kept on drinking the wine and kissing and talking, all night long. I don't know everything we talked about. We just talked. We talked about my dad, over there in Vietnam, and Amy said she would pray that he'd come home safe. We talked about old man Means, how we still felt all churned up about him and yet were beginning to feel sorry for him, too, and about how bad we felt for Melissa, having a dad like that. Sometime in the middle of the night, when everything was still and it seemed like we were the only two people awake in the universe, I told her about my and my dad's secret butterfly, about how when I was a little kid I thought I was seeing the same butterfly whenever I saw one like it. I told her that now I knew, though, they were all different butterflies.

We lay there on the quilt, our bodies close, looking up at this awesome display of stars across the sky, splashed like tiny drops of silver paint flung from some stupendous brush. Sometime in the chill before dawn we must have fallen asleep. We woke up with the early first light.

"Oh, man," Amy said. "I'm gonna be in big trouble."

She tried to smooth the wrinkles out of her dress. She kissed me. Then she headed off back up the lawn to her house. I watched her go. I sat there for awhile, looking at the sunrise. I wasn't worried about getting in trouble. There was no way my mom was up this early. I still had plenty of time.

The sun was like this colossal burst of brilliant, incandescent orange, with wispy clouds picking up its color. I stayed there for a long time. I wished Amy was still out there with me. I wished Deirdre and Max were there to see it. My mom and my dad, too. I even wished old Reverend Means was there – maybe this time he could pray for something important, like for the cancer not to come back to my mom. Anyhow, when you see something like that – a sunrise or a nice butterfly – you want someone there to see it with you.

Acknowledgements

Very special thanks to:

Sena Naslund, Norman McMillan, Phil Beidler, Bill White, Lee Smith, Cassandra King, Brad Watson, Don Noble, Jennifer Horne, Pat Conroy, Joan McMillan, Sid and Barbara Vance, Ann and Jack Hamilton, Sam Brasfield, Kathy Weese Adams.

And to my family: Loretta, of course, and Meredith Smith, Sara Beth Smith and Jonathan Smith.

OTHER SIXFINGER TITLES BY WILLIAM COBB

Short Stories available on Kindle from
www.sixfingerpublishing.com

The Stone Soldier
A Very Proper Resting Place
The Hunted
"Suffer Little Children..."
Glad My Eyes
Birmingham: Mothers' Day, 1961
An Encounter With a Friend
Somewhere in All This Green
The Night of the Yellow Butterflies
Old Wars and New Sorrows
Passin' Side/Suicide
Walk the Fertile Fields
The Flowers of Her Summer Garden
Walking Strawberry
The Queen of the Silver Dollar
Brother Bobby's Eye
The Best of It

Anthology of short stories available from Amazon and all
good bookstores:

Sweet Home: Stories of Alabama